Ian Watts lives in Leicestershire with his life partner, Kim. Between them, they have five lovely children and two beautiful small ones. He loves all forms of music and has played guitar in many rock bands. Also a big rugby fan and of most sports, and enjoys a regular round of golf.

He has always had a love for writing, and over the past ten years has honed his craft with novels and screenplays. He loves writing very early in the morning when it's quiet and everyone is asleep for the most inspiration. More stories from I.P.D. Watts are in progress.

This is for my late father, Ian Watts, who always instilled in me and my brothers from a very early age, "You can do what you want to do and be what you want to be in life, and everyone has at least one book in them." This is for you, Dad.

For my grandchildren; Jude, Saffron, James and Willow. "A child who reads will become an adult who thinks." (Gail Hennessey)

I.P.D. Watts

A MATTER OF TIME

The Future Is Not Set

AUSTIN MACAULEY PUBLISHERS™

LONDON • CAMBRIDGE • NEW YORK • SHARJAH

A CIP catalogue record for this title is available from the British Library.

ISBN 9781528994651 (Paperback)
ISBN 9781528915304 (Hardback)
ISBN 9781528994668 (ePub e-book)

www.austinmacauley.com

First Published (2020)
Austin Macauley Publishers Ltd
25 Canada Square
Canary Wharf
London
E14 5LQ

Foreword

"What greater thing is there for two human souls, than to feel that they are joined for life to strengthen each other in all labour, to rest on each other in all sorrow, to minister to each other in all pain, to be one with each other in silent unspeakable memories at the moment of the last parting."

– George Eliot.

Prologue

Peter Collins disappeared on Wednesday, September 5, 2001, six days before Nine-Eleven. When he left the office, he was on his way to meet his ex-Marine buddies he had served with, in the Gulf War. His new Mercedes was still parked in the underground garage beneath his offices. The CCTV footage from the garage clearly showed that Peter never actually made it to his car, and in the blink of an eye, he was gone, disappearing into thin air. The CCTV tape was kept under wraps by the FBI, and the tape used in the report instead was deemed inconclusive as it was riddled with interference. Sheila Greenway, his PA had seen the original footage and was forced never to reveal what was in the original. His company was called Edwards and Collins Worldwide Security. The business at that time was a major player in the security sector, and he had recently secured major contracts at the Whitehouse. There was a suspicion that his disappearance was somehow linked to it.

Peter Collins was forty-two years old, at the top of his game, and left behind a thriving business and a family who loved him. The World Trade Center disaster that happened a week later took precedent, but still, the NYPD and FBI put in over a thousand hours, investigating his disappearance, and followed many lines of inquiry with no conclusions or theories as to what had happened to him, it was a complete mystery.

After years of hoping and praying he was still alive and would return one day. Peter Collins was finally declared legally dead in 2011 by his wife, Marie, and with the absence of a body, a plaque of remembrance for him was placed at Young's Cemetery in his picturesque hometown of Oyster Bay, where Theodore Roosevelt was also buried.

But no one actually disappears into thin air with no explanation and no evidence, do they? The FBI likened it to a Bermuda Triangle scenario, only to put a tag on it so that they could file it away under unexplained phenomena.

This is the story of Peter Collins.

Chapter 1

Peter was sitting in his colonial-style kitchen, at number 1 Steamboat Landing Road, Oyster Bay. He was balancing precariously on the back legs of his chair, pushing himself back and forth, while studying the *New York Times* crossword on his lap. Eleven down, first letter, 'A.' Nine letters. The clue: '*Reparation.*' He stared out of the large bay window over at Oyster Bay in the distance. The answer was on the tip of his tongue, lurking deep within his subconscious begging to come out, but he couldn't quite connect the neurons. He clenched his pen tightly between his teeth, flipping it up and down in his mouth like an over-active, '*Groucho Marx*' cigar. It wasn't coming at all.

He had already been up for two hours, had run his usual ten-mile route around the beautiful Oyster Bay, then a thirty-minute high-intensity workout in his gym, all to keep his physique toned to perfection. He had washed, changed, and was ready for the day ahead. Routine meant everything to him, it was a hangover from his days in Iraq as a marine. Awake at first light and be on your guard, ready for action, it was one of the many rules by which he lived his life.

Today though, he had dressed neatly in his new golfing gear, his 'Bayside Park Golf Club' polo shirt and trousers that Marie had bought him for Christmas 2000, and it was the first time he was wearing them. So, the day would consist of a quick meeting at the office, get the important stuff out of the way, and then he would be off for an enjoyable afternoon's golf with his mates from the squad, and a few beers at the nineteenth hole regaling stories about their time together as marines. After the Gulf War, they had all kept in touch and saw each other often. Theirs was a bond they could never break, a closed shop, born from putting their lives in each other's hands and coming through. After they all came home, some started small businesses, some stayed in the military. Peter, on the other hand, went into business in a big way.

He founded Edwards and Collins Worldwide Security with a good friend of his, Lawrence Edwards, in 1995. Now at forty-two, Peter was a successful businessman with offices in Manhattan, employing over a thousand people worldwide. Lawrence was the brains and the seed money behind the venture, and Peter brought his enthusiasm and expertise, which was all that was needed, and he had heaps of it. Peter turned out to be an expert in covert security, and everyone wanted his services, including the government.

His business grew over those five years into a hundred-million-dollar-turnover Company, and that meant he could afford all the trappings of wealth. Peter didn't get injured in Iraq, he was one of the lucky ones, but so many of his comrades did. Some were wounded and survived, but others never made it back home at all. He felt blessed he'd made it back in one piece, and as soon as his plane landed at Andrews Air Force Base, Maryland. He kissed the ground of the United States of America and asked Marie to marry him, and much to his pleasure, she said yes.

"Have you done that yet?" Marie said, smiling, looking over his shoulder.

"Not yet, darling, a bit stuck."

"No surprise there then," she laughed.

"Hey, Cheeky," he laughed as well.

The *Times* crossword was a mental challenge he undertook most days of the week to keep his mind sharp and alert, but he only ever completed it once a week if he was lucky, and it was always on a Wednesday. 'Something to do with the person who sets it,' Marie had once said jokingly.

Marie was funny, sarcastically funny, intelligently funny and would have everyone in stitches at dinner parties with her quick wit and stories about her work in the field. She worked part-time as a health visitor around the New York Huntington area, looking after very sick and vulnerable children with a limited life expectancy, giving the family respite care for a few hours at a time. It gave her time for the family and an excellent work-life balance. Her forty-one years belied a much younger woman, with vitality, beauty, and a strong will.

As it was a Wednesday, she was busy making eggs for everyone's breakfast while hum-singing 'Run to you' by Whitney, and destroying it by singing off pitch. It probably sounded great to her, but to Peter, who had to listen to it, every other note was either flat or sharp. He tried his hardest to concentrate with his fingers in his ears. She then quite characteristically walked briskly across the kitchen and yelled upstairs.

"Come on you kids! You'll be late if you don't hurry up, it's eight o'clock!"

All hell was about to break loose as the peacefulness and tranquillity came to an abrupt end. Peter looked up tutting to Marie, who was smiling to herself having broken his concentration. It was a yell he'd heard many times before, she had a loving way of yelling, a loud rasp that could cut through walls and make windows shake. She said it with force, and she meant it.

Peter grabbed Marie's hand as she walked back over to the Aga, the kids would be trying to sleep a little bit longer than they should.

Peter said, "Listen to them, darling? They will now be scurrying around like little soldier ants. Why do they leave it until the very last possible moment to drag themselves out of bed? It can't be good for them. All kids are like that these days apparently, you know. All my friend's kids are like that too, it's endemic, it's too much technology and not enough outdoors."

"You will have to have a word with them, Peter. They are staying up too late playing on those 'GameBoy' machines you bought them for their birthday. I've told you before, they switch them on after lights out, I've heard them do it," she said, placing the blame firmly at his door.

Peter raised his voice slightly, "They're always late for everything, Marie. It's not my fault, it's how they are, no discipline. We never had games like that to play at their age, we were always outside in the fresh air playing football or soccer." His pen was attached to his bottom lip through natural adhesion and flipped up and down as he spoke. "And another thing." The pen then fell to the floor creating an intended comedy moment. "Didn't 'we' buy the GameBoy for the twins? I mean, you know. Together?" He picked it up.

Marie laughed at him, "You clown."

Marie loved the family life they had built around them, the children, Tom and Jake, '*the terrible twos,*' and Ashley, a beautiful, inspiring young girl, soon to be a beautiful young woman with a beautiful mind. Peter saw a lot of Marie in Ashley, her vibrancy, her tenacity, these traits had passed down a generation, and she had them in abundance. Marie rushed around after them, making breakfast, dinner, clearing up, washing, and ironing their clothes. Family life was for her, and she always had a smile on her face while doing it. She yelled again with a *that's the last time* tone to her voice.

"Look, if you don't come down soon, your eggs will be spoiled. I say, did you hear—!"

"I'm here, Mum, I heard you," Tom interrupted as he ran downstairs into the kitchen at breakneck speed, and straight to his seat opposite to Peter who was still trying desperately to stay in crossword mode.

"Hi Dad, what are you up to?" he said, out of breath but bounding energy coming out of every pore, his hair unkempt and his school shirt buttoned up out of sequence.

"Morning Son, you're looking fresh and ready for school, I see you've dressed yourself nicely. I'm doing the crossword Tom, would you believe. But I don't seem to be able to concentrate all of a sudden, do I?" Peter smiled at him, amused by his demeanour.

Tom had a look about him like he had a hundred and one things going on in his head at once. Marie was still trying to sing a Whitney tune and destroying it again. She set a plate for Tom and put his boiled eggs and toast soldiers down in front of him.

"Really? Awesome, Dad? Give us a clue, then?" Tom said, looking eagerly at his dad like an expectant canine about to get some food.

"Okay Son, if you must. Get those finely tuned neurons rushing around your head, why don't you eh! Here goes, are you listening, Tom?" Peter paused for a second and looked at him until he'd got his full attention. Tom listened with a toast soldier sticking out of his mouth. "Nine letters, beginning with the letter, 'A.' *Reparation* is the clue." Peter sat back in his seat, looking intently at Tom for a moment while he thought, his eyes pointing upward then back at his dad smiling as though he had almost got it, "Have you got it?" Peter asked, willing a single intelligent thought out of his toast encrusted mouth.

"Boring! What does that mean?" Tom said, shrugging his little shoulders and picking up another piece of toast.

"Precisely! Precisely! Eat your eggs before your mum blows a gasket," he said, shaking his head and smiling at him.

Marie let out a little snigger in the background. Peter was always challenging the kids whenever he could. 'Keep them on their toes, it is good for them' he used to say, 'mind and body, body and mind. Fit body, fit mind.'

Tom, at ten years old, was the thinker of the twins. He would always think before he spoke and would make everyone at school laugh at his misfortunate events, very self-deprecating as well, that made all the kids laugh with him, not at him. Jake, on the other hand, was the more boisterous of the duo and stronger than Tom physically, which worked out well. So when any kids picked on them at school, he would stand his ground for both of them. They had had a few scrapes early on in their first year and had come through the awkward stage when every child was trying to be a top dog. These days, they couldn't wait to get to school, they had a great time there and had made some good friends.

"Arms off the table Tom," Marie said.

"Oh sorry," he said as he hacked the top off his egg. "Mum, we need that money for the field trip today, remember?" he announced.

Peter commented, "What field trip is this then? And why am I always the last to know?"

"It's on a need to know basis, Dad, ha!" Tom said smirking, with the egg running down his chin.

"Yeah! And I don't need to know, do I? I'll just pay for it then, shall I?"

Marie explained, "His class is going on a field trip to the World Trade Center on the Eleventh, Tuesday next week. They are going with a few other schools in the area as well so some children they know from around here will be going. Should be an exciting day for them, shouldn't it Tom?" she said stroking and grooming Tom's hair while standing behind him.

"We didn't do anything like that at school when we were your age," Peter said, directing the comment to Tom, who wasn't listening anyway. "Your uncle Mike works on the eighty-second floor in the World Trade Center, did you know that Tom? That will be a fun trip, won't it?"

"Suppose so," Tom said, looking disinterested.

"A field trip! Into the big city! Where dad works! That's going to be great, what are you talking about Tom? I suppose so? Ca! If only we had the opportunities you kids get these days, well."

"Dad, I'm looking forward to it, really, okay!" Tom said, pretending to be enthusiastic.

Jake came down soon after and looked equally unkempt, 'The terrible twos' was a nickname Marie used a lot in jest but loved the fact that they both stuck together like glue. She used to dress them the same when they were younger, but now they had distinctly different characters and hair to go with it. Tom's short and neatly parted. Jake's long, straggly, and uncombed that drove Marie mad, they were not identical twins, but a lot of their features, eyes, nose, and forehead looked similar.

Ashley rushed into the kitchen soon after Jake. At thirteen years old, she seemed way ahead in years and intelligence for girls her age, gaining top marks in all exams throughout her schooling so far. She loved sports as well, especially running, which she did with her dad whenever she could, at the weekends.

"Here I am mother dear, no need to panic. Keep one's hair on," she orated in a very posh English actress's voice.

"Less of the dear, thank you, eggs for you too?"

"Fine, Aha! That hurts!" Ashley said as her mum started wiping her face with the corner of a tea towel.

"Toothpaste on your cheek!" she tutted. "Ever looked in the mirror, eh?" Marie said, looking her up and down as she did all the children before they left for school.

"What! And seen beauty mother? Well yes, just a moment ago in fact," she answered still in a posh accent.

Jake let out a laugh and gestured with his fingers down his throat. Peter laughed at the banter between them all, while barely concentrating on his crossword clue.

Ashley looked menacingly at Jake. "Well, tell me why you can't get a girlfriend again? Is it that you are a little dorky, dorky face?" she said, hoping to wound him verbally.

Jake followed it up by sticking his tongue out, "Don't want one." It didn't bother him, it was like water off a duck's back.

Peter, listening to the melee going on around him, looked up from his paper to tell a little joke to everyone.

"Hey, kids, did you see that tidbit in the newspaper about a dog with no nose?"

"Okay, Dad, how does it smell?" Ashley asked, knowingly.

"Bloody awful, Ha!" He lifted his hands in the air.

"Can't believe you didn't know that one," Jake said to Ashley, Tom laughed.

"I did, I was just humouring him?" Ashley retorted. Peter glared at her.

Jake said, "You're weird."

"Darling, my jokes aren't that bad, are they?" Peter asked.

"You do need some new ones," Marie said, "Don't you think kids?" A resounding 'yes' was the collective answer.

Breakfast at the Collin's household was always frantic and rushed, but never dull. The kids were still eating their eggs and toast as the time approached to go to school. They all got up together in unison, grabbed their bags and lunch boxes, and started to head out of the door, to catch the school bus at the end of the road. Theodore Roosevelt Elementary was only about one and a half miles away from their house and catered for eight to thirteen-year-olds. It had a good reputation, considering it was a state school. Comparing it to other private schools in the area, it had an excellent record.

Tom then said mischievously, "Ash before you go, dad needs a hand with his crossword, don't you Dad?" Peter looked up.

"What word is it, Dad? Is it an easy one?" Ashley asked, eagerly.

"I don't know, Chicken. If you must, the beginning letter is 'A,' nine letters in total. *Reparation* is the clue." Peter sat back and smiled, as the twins shuffled out of the door sniggering. "So, what do you think, darling?"

"Atonement. Yes, atonement," she said confidently. "Must rush, love you, Dad, love you, Mum," and walked out of the door.

As they left, Peter said, "Hey kids, before you all rush off, let's all go to Beano's steakhouse tonight, what do you think? A work celebration?"

"Sounds great Dad, we love that place," Ashley said. "Bye Dad," she said, giving him a little wave.

"Great, bye Dad," Tom and Jake shouted as they ran off down the driveway.

The kitchen was suddenly a peaceful quiet place, and Peter could get back to his crossword.

"Atonement, eh," Peter said as he studied it for a second. "Yeah, she's right, well bloody hell. Atonement." He sat back, a bit deflated that he hadn't got it and his thirteen-year-old daughter knew it right off the bat. He wrote it in.

"She is certainly a clever one," Marie said as she watched them go down the driveway and disappear around the corner. "We have a great family, don't we, Peter?"

"We sure do," he said as he grabbed her arm and pulled her down to sit on his knee.

"What do you want?" she said, smirking and giggling. "You had enough last night lover boy."

"Well, you can't blame me for trying. Give us a kiss then while you're down here."

"You better go to work before you get in trouble," she said as she kissed him, then got up and started clearing the pots. "The boss will tell you off if you're late," she said with a tinge of sarcasm.

"I love you."

"I know you do me too. You look like you've got an easy day ahead of you anyway," she said, "I've got to look after a sick child today that might not make it till the weekend, you know, a real day's work."

"Yeah, that's sad. It makes you realise how lucky we are," Peter said. "I've got a quick meeting at the office, then I'm meeting Jim and the lads."

"Lucky you, nice shirt by the way, suits you," she said, kissing him on the cheek.

"I'll be home early darling, after golf, and we can all have a lovely family evening at Beano's. I'll ask Larry and Jen, they would like that if he's well enough."

"Okay, don't have too much to drink at the club, you know the nineteenth hole."

"Never."

"Never? Remember the last time? I had to pick you up," Marie said, smiling.

"That was a special occasion, though."

"I'll let you off. Shouldn't you be going to work?" Marie said. "If that's what you call work."

"Asked and answered darling. Ha!" Peter laughed.

Peter smiled, kissed her again, then left for the office in downtown Manhattan.

Chapter 2

The Manhattan skyline looked magnificently dark, silhouetted by the morning sun as Peter drove into the office on the Two-Seven-Eight. It was a beautiful sight, and an iconic view featured on many postcards around the globe.

Driving his new car for the first time into work felt great, a brand-new Mercedes SL 55, bought as a present to himself after one of the best revenue years since he and Lawrence had started the business. Life was good, the family was good, and he felt on top of the world, Bruce Springsteen's Atlantic City sounded fantastic through the built-in state-of-the-art CD player as well, it was crystal clear.

Going over the Williamsburg Bridge was less attractive, but a necessary evil and it seemed less congested than usual, and the journey had only taken him forty-five minutes totally, so he was happy to be getting to work on time. A freshness had permeated the air as a light morning breeze from the North Atlantic, had taken away all of the smog from the previous day, and it looked like it was going to be a beautiful and sunny day ahead. It felt good to be in New York.

Just then, the music suddenly stopped, and his Carphone rang. Jim was calling him. "Hey, Jim, how's it going mate?" Peter said.

"Hey, Pete, yes, good thanks. Up for golf later then?"

"Yes, Jim, always."

"Awesome. When you get into your office, look at the front page of the *Post*?"

"Why, what's up?"

"Remember Jerry?"

"Yeah, course, I do."

"He's been involved in some international incident working for the CIA in Angola. They name him as Jerry Martin, an assassin, a mercenary. He's been caught trying to take out José Eduardo Dos Santos, you know, the president, he missed him and got his second in command."

"Bloody hell! I had to save his ass a few times in Iraq, remember? He's in a world of hurt there, then."

"Yes, I do. The *Post* is saying it's bad enough that he could be facing a firing squad."

"That sounds like it could turn into an international incident?"

"For sure, the slippery bastard will probably get away with it though, check it out. I'll let you go and see you at the club later."

As soon as he was gone, Atlantic City cranked back up again to normal volume for the rest of his journey. He wondered what could have gotten Jerry into that line of work. An assassin for the CIA, Nasty stuff. He would be hung out to dry, they would disown him, say that he never worked for them, Peter thought. He was glad he had taken a different route after Iraq, and it was a much happier one.

Jim Watts was a lifelong friend from his army days and always up for a game of golf. He was all but retired, he'd had a massive pay out from the government when he took one in the leg in Baghdad on the first wave of the invasion. Peter had to drag him to safety while under fire. He never forgot that Peter had saved his life and liked to bring it up regularly in conversations.

At his offices on Essex Street, he drove into the underground garage and parked in his designated spot. The time was 9:30 a.m. The garage was almost full as most of his staff started at nine o'clock, and everyone was already there.

He got out of his car, took his case out of the rear passenger seat, and then closed the door. He had to stand still for a moment because he heard a weird noise, it was quiet but audible, he could hear chatter, coming from somewhere in front of him around six feet away within the garage. He could hear the usual muffled sounds coming from the offices above, but this was different. He couldn't see anyone, there was no one there, but the chatter was there, people were talking. He walked over to the stairs, and as he did so, the chatter moved behind him, it was as though he had walked through it. He looked back to where it was coming from, and then it stopped all of a sudden. He shook his head, when unexplainable things happen, it's hard to make sense of it, and that was one of them.

Peter strolled into his office as always with an enthusiastic demeanour and a broad smile on his face and was warmly greeted by the girls on reception, most of whom were busily booking in visitors.

"Morning, Mr Collins, lovely day, isn't it? Sheila has the papers," Rachael said with a gushing smile.

"Hello, Rachael! Yes, isn't it?" he said smiling back at her, it was the usual mundane banter that had to happen in the office environment for it to work, a bit theatrical, but it kept the good feeling going around the office.

Behind Rachael, there was the new aluminium company sign. Edwards and Collins Worldwide Security Inc., and it looked very inspiring if a little overpowering. The new look of the reception oozed success, designed by a good friend of his. Marble floors, a circular oak reception desk and plush brown leather seats for visitors, a few Andy Warhol prints on the walls, everything looked great. Peter also enjoyed the walk down to his office from the reception area because it took him past all the signs of the famous 'big named' clients, it gave him a sort of inner warmth knowing they dealt with such good corporations. There was Lockheed, General Motors, ExxonMobil and Apple, even at the Whitehouse, he now had people and felt quite proud and humble when all he had known before was uniforms, orders, missions, fighting, and killing. He'd come a long way from those dark days.

And there she was, the lovely Sheila, a subtle mixture of beauty and brains. His trusted hard-working Sheila, sitting there, looking fabulous at her desk outside his office, in a two-piece cream suit, black patent shoes, black shirt and a perfectly groomed highlighted bob, efficiently working through the daily schedule, keeping the company on track. She looked expensive, too expensive to be just a PA, but she enjoyed what she did.

In a previous life, Sheila Greenway had been a PA to the vice president Al Gore in 1995. She knew what it took to run an office as she had done it for ten years in the corridors of power at the Whitehouse, and knew what she was doing, and she practically ran the business for him and Lawrence. Sheila knew everyone's business, and every client looked forward to seeing her. She was an invaluable asset to the company's success.

"Good morning Peter and what a lovely morning it is isn't it," Sheila said in her usual efficient way. "Did you have a good trip in?"

"Yes thanks, can't believe how many fire and police sirens go off all around you when you are driving, I couldn't hear myself think, couldn't even hear my music."

"Let me guess, Bruce Springsteen?" she said, smirking.

"Wow! In one for that woman!" he said, pointing the finger at her as if to say, well done, you were paying attention. "You can't beat a bit of Atlantic city to start the day."

"Well I wouldn't go that far, I have disco feet. Your coffee's on, shall I pour?"

"Great thanks. You are too good to me, aren't you?"

"Well, give me a raise then?" A wry smile flashed across her face.

"Ca! You never miss a trick, do you?"

"You wouldn't have me any other way, men need to be told often, women are undervalued in the workplace," she said and left the statement out there hanging. She was good at getting a response.

"Well, I value you, don't I?"

"Yes, I suppose you do. It doesn't hurt to ask now and then, though."

There was a sparkle of attraction, Peter couldn't deny it, but it had been kept well under wraps on both sides, she was too professional to get involved, and he was too much in love with Marie to enter into an office affair, they would have the banter but keep it professional.

"A strange thing happened in the garage earlier."

"What?"

"I could hear voices."

"Really, what voices?"

"Just voices I couldn't make them out or anything," he gave Sheila a curious look. "You've never heard them, then?"

"No, no, I haven't."

"We must have ghosts then, ha!"

He took his coffee from Sheila, walked in and sat down in his comfortable green leather director's chair, behind his antique oak desk, which he'd picked both up at an auction of antiquities a few months earlier. It didn't match the office for style at all and looked entirely out of place, but he loved it and thought, forget all the designers, what do they know? Beauty was in the eye of the beholder.

While drinking his coffee, he scanned the front page of the *Post* and the piece on Jerry. It even mentioned the tours of Iraq he did, someone had done their homework. There was one piece of information from those days in Iraq though, that would never be written about because it was too sensitive and too damning ever to be revealed. They all had a pact, never to mention it ever.

On his desk, Sheila had placed an important-looking letter from the NSA. It had the official stamp from the Pentagon and was unopened. He knew it was coming, but he had been putting it off in his mind for ages, most of the tenants in the building had moved out over the past two years as the NSA slowly took over every office in the building.

Sheila came in. "Yes, I thought that was important, and I can only imagine what's in it," she said, smiling at him.

"Bloody NSA, they think they can ride roughshod over everyone, and they probably can," he said flippantly.

He had been digging his heels in refusing to talk to them when they called, just being unavailable to them, but as other companies in the building slowly succumbed to the inevitability of government intervention, he had very much resigned himself to the fact, they had to go.

"They will say it's a national security thing, and you'll have to go eventually," Sheila said. She knew about how government bureaucracy worked, and still had friends at the Whitehouse. They had confirmed to her that the building would be taken over. "The only saving grace is the compensation you are getting to move, $500,000 goes a long way, you know?"

"It's not the money, although the money is great, it's the upheaval. We have built something special here. Who knows if it will work elsewhere?" He wondered what would happen if the bubble burst, and he had to go back to working tours of duty in foreign places he didn't know or even care about. He was very insecure about it, pinching himself every day, and feeling that at any moment this beautiful life he had built up around Marie and the family could come to an abrupt end.

"We will be fine," Sheila said reassuringly. "You have just got to get your skates on and get that offer in on the new place you like. You and Larry have seen it, you and Larry like it, so what are you and Larry hanging about for, seems simple to me?"

She was right, of course. Men were much worse procrastinators than women, it was a fact. "Pushy or what," he said, turning the conversation into something humorous, "we have plans to do it when he comes back off sick leave."

When that would be, was anyone's guess, it could be very soon, or it could be way down the line he thought.

Sheila handed him some papers to read, "oh, and don't forget to go over them tonight for the lawyers tomorrow at ten o'clock."

"Yes, Mother." He laughed.

"I'm only doing my job," Sheila said playfully.

"Yes, you are, and thank you for your efficiency."

"Now you are taking the P…" She laughed.

Getting the right people in the right positions was a big part of the company's strategy, and it worked like a dream. Clients were climbing over themselves to get the best in security, and now the web was taking off, the services his company offered were needed even more.

Peter could see the TV that was on just outside his office near where Sheila sat. It was a CBS report on the news channel, about Osama bin Laden, and that the country was on the highest alert for an imminent attack, since the bombings in Tanzania and Kenya in 1998.

Sheila commented, "Looks like something big is going to happen? We should have gotten rid of him long ago. We know where they all are, you know. That Saddam Hussein as well, we should have fixed that *'son of a bitch'* when we had the chance."

"They will get what's coming to them, you mark my words," Peter said thoughtfully.

He looked at the letter in his hand, it read, *'Final Moving Date of Friday, December 21, 2001,'* right before the Christmas holidays. That would give him just over two months to get everything sorted for the move.

He was about to ring Lawrence to tell him about the letter when his phone rang, it was Lawrence. This sort of thing seemed to happen to him all the time, but mainly with Marie.

"Hi, Larry, I was just thinking of calling you too, that's spooky isn't it, how's it hanging?" Peter said, anticipating some bad news.

"Hi Pete, not too bad to be perfectly honest," Lawrence replied much to Peter's surprise. "Doctors have said I'll be okay to come back next month. The stitches have healed inside and out, so they are just monitoring me now."

"That's great news, mate, we've missed you."

"Sorry to leave everything with you, but couldn't be helped, eh?"

Peter knew it was more serious than Lawrence had made out, because, the heart attack, when it happened at work, it was as serious as it gets. His first aid experience from Iraq took over as an automatic pilot. He pumped and massaged Larry's chest until the paramedics arrived. Degenerative Heart disease the paramedic called it at the time and didn't give him much of a chance. A triple bypass followed where he had another heart attack while undergoing surgery. Peter never expected him to return to work at all and was anticipating his retirement. Lawrence was a lot older than him, he was hilarious in conversation and had a story for just about anything, and Peter looked upon him as a father figure, if there were ever any issues within the company or personal, Larry could sort them out, he had a natural way of doing things, and it worked.

Peter said, "Listen, mate, you take your time. There is no rush to come back to work. This place runs itself like a dream," he said, glancing a look at Sheila, who was lingering in the room eavesdropping. "We can handle everything here. Is Jen, okay?"

"Yes, she's fine. Rock of Gibraltar that one," he said proudly. "I don't know what I would have done without her to be honest, Pete."

"Goodman! Say why don't you come for dinner later the kids would love to see you and Jen. I'll pay? I don't want you having another heart attack when you see the bill, ha!"

"Yes, funny, that would be good to see you both. I'll let you know later, Pete."

Peter never did mention the moving letter, he could worry about that when he was fit enough, he thought.

Peter looked at his watch and didn't realise where the time had gone, two hours had slipped by in what felt like a few minutes, and he would be late for golf. So, he did the important stuff quickly and left the rest for another day.

He had the feeling that he had achieved something and left everyone to get on with it and didn't feel guilty at all about sliding off to play golf. He said his goodbyes to Sheila and rushed down the stairs to the garage to retrieve his Mercedes.

As he walked over, he pointed the key fob and clicked, the headlights flashed momentarily. Then he was bumped into by a man who came out of nowhere, directly in front of him.

"Jesus, pal! Where did you come from," Peter shouted as he jumped back out of the way.

The man was wearing Islamic type clothing and sunglasses and seemed to be in a big rush.

"Sorry, excuse me," the man said as he rushed past him breathing heavy, and ran up the stairs, his heavy feet echoed around the garage.

"Who the bloody hell was that?" he shouted to himself.

He turned back towards the Mercedes, then the whole garage disappeared in front of his eyes, and he suddenly felt like he was slipping through a thin wall of cold water. There was wetness, but he wasn't wet, and as he moved forward, the feeling went from the tip of his nose to the back of his head. It felt like someone had walked over his grave, and it gave him a shiver down the back of his neck, travelling right down to his feet. He thought he was hallucinating momentarily, an out of body experience. Either was plausible.

Peter couldn't assimilate what he had just experienced, but he was now standing in what looked like a laboratory of some kind. The geometry of it seemed to be more or less like the garage, only now with brilliant white walls, and no cars to be seen anywhere. His heart was pounding out of his chest, his breath was heavy, and he had a high-pitched ringing sound in his ears as if he had been listening to loud music that had just stopped all of a sudden. He glanced back towards the stairwell where he had just come from, and directly in front of him was now a circular hole of shimmering water, about eight feet in diameter, with lasers firing light all around it creating a void. It was like peering into an aquarium, and he could see the staircase. Sheila had come to the bottom and was looking around, shouting his name as if she couldn't see him at all. The sound she made sounded very distant. He shouted back to her, she seemed to hear him, but couldn't see him. He quickly put his hand up to attract Sheila's attention and ran towards her, but before he got there, it disappeared. The lasers went out. Sheila was gone.

He stood there motionless for a moment, looking at the stairs that now looked entirely different, modern and silver, instead of concrete. He had worked out that he was in a test facility of some kind. He saw people in the next room in white coats laughing and shouting, doing high fives, and congratulating themselves as if something had happened that required celebration. Some of them were in full-body overalls with headphones around their necks, and some looked like scientists or doctors. Lights were flashing and beeping on a console to the side of him. Everywhere signs read 'Authorised Personnel Only' with lights flashing red. He started to feel very uncomfortable, like he was in the wrong place and needed to get out of there, so he quickly walked back up the stairs to his office and to see if Sheila could shed some light on what had just happened.

Chapter 3

Peter stopped for a moment on the stairs in a state of shock, confused at what he had just witnessed. He looked down at his Blackberry, in the top left-hand corner of the screen it flashed, no service, he tried to call Marie anyway, there was no answer, then he tried nine-one-one, there was no answer from that either. Peter thought that was stranger than anything, as the emergency services would always have answered. "Just when you need them, they're not there," he said out loud shaking his head with the frustration getting the better of him. He would now be very late for golf, and they would have to start without him, he thought.

He walked back into his office and was about to speak to Sheila when he stopped in his tracks and stared in disbelief.

"What the fu…" he said open-mouthed.

There was no Edwards and Collins sign anymore, and there was no Sheila or Rachael either. He walked up to the front desk while scanning the whole office and getting his bearings. The office had a government look about it, and was completely different from when he left a few moments before. The sign now behind the desk was a circular NSA sign, 'The National Security Agency of the United States of America.' His glass-walled offices had gone, replaced by solid walls and in a different configuration. The pictures adorning the walls were generic ones of the White House, the Lincoln Memorial, and what looked like high-ranking officials with a person called Barack Obama as President. The office felt about the same square footage, but how could this happen so quickly? He thought. They weren't supposed to take over for at least two months, so how did this happen? A woman in a government uniform behind the desk asked him a question.

"Can I help you, sir, you look a bit lost if you don't mind me saying?" she said politely.

"No, that's okay," he paused a moment to get his words out correctly. "What is this? You know, all this, I mean, doing here?" Peter said, gesturing with both hands, looking bemused, and sounding even worse.

"What is what, where, sir?" she said, pointedly sounding just as confused at the question, and looking somewhat annoyed at his demeanour.

"Well, let me put it another way, this wasn't here this morning, in fact, ten minutes ago all this wasn't here, what is going on?" Peter said, waving his arms about, fighting to get his words out, and now sweating profusely from every pore on his body like he was about to have a heart attack.

"Well sir, I'm sorry, but you are not making any sense at all," she said impatiently. "I'll call someone for you who can help. Please take a seat, sir."

The woman pointed in the direction of a set of grey plastic chairs for him to sit down on, as she picked up the phone and made the call. He looked out of the window over at Seward Park, it all seemed wrong, the buildings, the trees, he couldn't put his finger on it, but everything had changed, he was very disconcerted and nonplussed about everything. Within less than a minute, a massive security guard named Errol was standing menacingly over him. He was about three hundred pounds and looked beefy like he worked out, dark skin, black uniform with his name badge neatly placed above his left shirt pocket, and he had a thick black belt with a baton, CS gas and a firearm. It was obvious Errol took pride in wearing the uniform, as he had worked hard to get to that position, and it showed. He held the handle of the baton as he spoke down to Peter.

"Can I help you, sir," Errol said as if there would be no messing about on his watch.

"As I was explaining to the lady, all this wasn't here before." Again, Peter wasn't making any sense. "It's ridiculous, none of this was here at all, it's all changed," he said. Flummoxed, and now laughing at the ridiculousness of the situation, and waving his arms in the air like some Shakespearean actor.

"Sir, can I ask, have you been drinking?"

"No, definitely not. Not even a drop, I was going to play golf for God's sake."

"Golf, eh! Thou shall not take the lord's name in vain, especially with me. Would you be on any medication at all, sir?" Errol said, rapping his knuckles verbally then calmly going through a statutory set of questions, he had been given at his induction.

"God no, it's just that the office, my office that is, was here a short time ago and now all this is here, and I can't understand why. I'm not explaining myself well, am I?" he said, waving his arms about again.

"There you go again, blaspheming. Well, sir, I've heard enough, I must ask you to leave," Errol said firmly. "Please follow me, sir," feeling the immediate pressure from Errol, and not wanting to create a national incident, Peter followed him down in the elevator to the ground floor. He didn't recognise anything of the building that he had walked into only two hours before. "If you want to come back in, you will need a security pass, okay?" Errol said as he walked.

"Fine and thank you, Errol. You have been very helpful," Peter said, smiling a cheesy sarcastic smile.

On the ground floor, the reception area for the building was completely different. The concourse was bustling, with people rushing in every direction. A fully manned reception desk stretched all the way across the concourse, and there was now a smoked glass ceiling a hundred feet high, that partially let the light through. An even bigger circular NSA sign gleamed powerfully behind the desk, possibly twenty feet in diameter, and under the sign was a large clock, digitally ticking away the time. 11:42 a.m., with the date, Wednesday, September 5, 2016. Peter had looked at it for a split second, but he hadn't registered the year, he was too busy dodging everyone on the concourse going the opposite way to him, and he was following close behind Errol who was making his way to the front door with Peter in his slipstream. Peter left the building through a large automatic revolving door and now stood outside in the street with the sun bearing down on him. He gave a small wave back to Errol, who was eyeing his every move from inside the glass as if to say you are not coming back through that door.

Standing outside in the street for a moment, the surroundings seemed so familiar to him, but he didn't know what to do. He felt he was in a sort of limbo, he couldn't go back to his office or get his car, because it wasn't there. He walked one way, stopped, thought for a moment, then turned around and walked the other way, as people pushed into him on the pavement walking in both directions. One kind-spirited person called him an 'Idiot,' another called him an 'imbecile.' He walked over to the crossing at the end of the block, as he could see the familiar Seward Park on the other side of the road. He could have a rest for a while there, call Marie, and get his thoughts together.

He entered the park and sat down on the first bench that was free, which was close to the entrance. He was trying to get his mind around everything that had just taken place. What had happened to his office? Where had it gone? What happened to his car? All he had was questions and no answers. He looked at his phone again, he still had 'no service,' and It was the only form of communication he had in the world, and it didn't work. Although futile, he called Marie anyway if only to confirm the continuous tone again. Why was his phone cut off? Had someone in the office not paid the bill? But then he had seen different people in his office, his office had ceased to exist.

"Why won't you answer Marie?" Peter said, visually talking to himself and tapping his phone with frustration. Then as he stared down at his phone, a small white Westie rubbed up against his legs. He looked up with the sunlight blinding his eyes, and to his surprise, attached to the lead was the most gorgeous looking woman standing there in front of him, and she was smiling directly at him.

"You okay there?" she said.

The morning sun was shining through her blond hair and making it glisten. Time seemed to go very slow all of a sudden. Peter smiled up at her while patting the Westie, who had taken a fancy to his legs and was coiled around them as if to say you are not going anywhere. Peter was happy for the interaction and to speak to someone.

"Yeah, I think so, just having a bad day," Peter said, making light of his predicament while stroking the Westie.

"It looks like it, nice Blackberry though," she said as he clutched his phone as though his life depended on it.

"I don't seem to be getting any signal at all," Peter said.

"Not surprised, I haven't seen one like that for ages," she said, "They used to be all the rage."

"Ha! All the rage. What are you talking about? I've only had this one a week, and I'm still learning how to work it properly, ha! Like everyone, I never read the instruction manuals." Peter laughed and looked at her curiously.

She stood there shaking her head and smiling at him, "where have you been pal? I had one of those, what is it? The PDA 5810 model must be back in O two," she said, giggling, and as she said it, she made a gurgling sound in her throat that made it even funnier than it was.

"O' two, do you mean 2002?" Peter said, with a curious look on his face.

"Yes, 2002," she repeated. "Sorry, have I said something wrong?"

Peter had kept the same curious confused look on his face. "What is the date today?"

"The fifth of September."

"What year?"

"2016," she said.

"Really?" Peter went all quiet. His shoulders sank, and he put his head in his hands.

Then she said, "yes, really. You are having a weird day, pal, not a bad one."

"You can say that again," Peter said and began running his fingers through his hair, and scratching his head as though something was itching intensely. "It cannot be happening, this only happens in movies, it just does not happen!" he said, louder than usual, and people walked by looking at the pair of them wondering what was going on.

She looked puzzled by Peter's demeanour. "Sorry, I don't follow? What doesn't, happ—?"

"Could I ask a favour?" he interrupted. "Would you call my wife for me, please? I would appreciate it?"

"Sure, I can do that. You have a cute face," she said while cocking her head to one side and giving him a sympathetic smile. "Milo likes you, what's the number?"

The Westie now had a name, and Milo had nestled himself around Peter's ankles and sat there quite content. Peter looked at his contacts on his Blackberry and dictated the number. She tapped it in, but it was cut off, a continuous tone, she stood there for a few moments trying it a few times.

"Sorry, it sounds cut off. Do you have another number you want me to try?" she said, being as helpful as possible.

"You could try this one," he said, dictating Sheila's phone number, but that went to an answering service. "She might have had it turned off," he said. "She usually does."

"At least you know that one works. Did you want to try someone else? I don't mind, honestly," she said helpfully.

"No, it's okay. I can't seem to even think straight at the moment anyway?" he said, sounding sad and defeated. "I'll have to go and hire a car and get home that way, probably the best thing for me to do?"

She had done all she could for him and could leave with a clear conscience, she didn't want to leave, it just felt like it was appropriate. "Anyway, I've got to go. Nice to meet you. I hope your day gets better," she said. Then bent down to pat Milo and gently untangle him from Peters' ankles. "Come on, Milo."

"Nice to meet you too and thank you," Peter said, smiling.

In an instant, she was gone. He had a feeling of panic rearing up through his stomach watching her walk away through the park, her long blond hair flowing back in the gentle breeze. Peter studied her for a split second, then lept into action. He needed to know her, and who she was, realising, at that moment, she was the only person that could help him, and there she was, walking away. He pushed past a slow-moving couple walking in the park for a romantic stroll, caught up with her and gently tapped her on the shoulder.

"Excuse me! Sorry, but I don't even know your name?" he said, sounding slightly out of breath and desperate.

Her blond hair flowed over both shoulders simultaneously as she turned around, with the sunlight shining onto her hair and facial features, he caught a smile that melted him instantly. The last time he felt like that, was when he first met Marie, and an instant flash of guilt nestled itself in the corner of his subconscious.

"Well, hello again, it's Heather, please to meet you," she said, holding out a delicately manicured hand. "What's yours?"

"Peter. It's Pa-Peter," he said, stuttering like an adolescent schoolboy. "I suddenly realised back there, you were only trying to help, it sounds funny, but you are the only person I know here in 2016."

She thought for a moment looking at him with a puzzled look on her face and said. "Look, this isn't one of those creepy pickup scenarios, is it? Because I'm all burned out on those," she said, still holding his hand, and with the other holding the lead to Milo, who was rubbing himself around Peter's shins again.

"No, really, you are the only person in 2016. I have met, apart from a large security guard called Errol, who was in our building," he said, trying to convince her he was genuine, but still sounding ridiculous.

"Where's that, then?" she said.

"Just over there," he said and pointed across the road to his building.

"Why don't you go there? It must be a good start?" Heather said, trying to be helpful.

"I have, it is now a government building occupied by the NSA."

Peter slumped down onto a park bench lost in the moment, and not knowing what to do or say. Heather sat down with him partly to console him, but also partly because there was an attraction.

"You are not going to believe this, but when I woke up earlier today, I went out for a run and had breakfast with my family, it was September 5, 2001, and now I find myself sitting here talking to you, and it's now September 5, 2016. Do you know how crazy that must sound? It's bizarre, isn't it?" Peter asked, questioning himself in the process.

"Sounds a bit 'trippy,' if you ask me," she said, sniggering a bit at the thought, which made the funny gurgling sound in her throat again, as the air went back and forth, Milo thought it sounded funny too and yapped along with her.

"Well, yes, 'trippy' is an excellent word to describe it," Peter said, as he regained a bit of his humour back and sniggered along with her. "It must be something to do with that NSA building, my office and business are in there somewhere. I've just got to find it."

"What's it called then, your business?" Heather asked inquisitively.

"Edwards and Collins. We are in security worldwide."

"Your' shittin' me. I used to work there as a temp in the nineties."

"Really? Well, it is a small world. What did you do for us?" he said, happy that they had something in common at least.

"I looked after the booking of field visits, houses, and government buildings, that sort of thing," she said.

"Well, we do a lot of those."

"There was this woman I remember, she was nice. Sheila, that was her name," Heather smiled.

"That was her number you just rang for me."

"Wow, this is a coincidence."

Peter smiled back at the familiarity. "Yes, she is nice, she does or should I say, did a good job for me," he said, catching himself reminiscing. "Do you fancy coffee?" Peter said, changing the subject.

"Yeah, why not, it's not every day you get to help out someone from the past," she gurgled again. They both smiled at each other.

"Luigi's is just up here," Peter pointed.

"Yes, I go there, a lot."

"Great, we can walk there."

They both laughed, and walked in the direction of Luigi's coffee bar at the corner of Delancey and Allen Street, with Milo leading the way, it was a few blocks up from the park. As they walked, Peter recognised trees that had grown out of all proportion, businesses, and shops he regularly walked by or visited had changed their frontage. Cars going by had a different look about them, a more streamlined shape. New York had moved on in a big way, buildings seemed taller and more modern. Everything seemed more futuristic to him, and he was still in his Bayside Golfing Club polo shirt and feeling a bit out of place. He also became a little self-conscious while walking, as though people were looking at him with such a beautiful woman by his side. Jim must be waiting for him to arrive at the club. What would be going through his mind when he doesn't turn up? Peter thought. He switched his Blackberry off and put it in his pocket out of the way, it was useless to him now. No one would be calling him, and there was no point in calling anyone either, it was as simple as that. He was now with this beautiful woman in a place he didn't recognise.

Chapter 4

One Hour earlier...

If ever there was a person you would want on your side if you were in trouble, it would be Special agent Doug McClean. Six feet two inches tall, two hundred and fifty pounds, dark brown hair, well-defined muscles, impeccably groomed with a white starched shirt, and a black NSA emblem tie. An imposing human being by anyone's standards, who commanded respect from everyone. Many agents had fallen by the wayside on Doug McClean's watch. To be considered at all, candidates would have to endure long hours of intense scrutiny and concentration and have to be made of the right stuff to have any chance of being on his team. He had been in charge of many departments at the Pentagon over the years, but the NSA had been his calling in life, and now he had a reputation there for getting the job done, the *'go-to'* guy to get results and no matter what the cost.

Years of planning had gone into the next five minutes that were about to happen, and McClean sat at Centre point, orchestrating the proceedings like a conductor with the Philharmonic Orchestra at the Lincoln Center.

Agent Jed Ryman had spent the last five years at the Fort Washington Facility, training to become an NSA special agent. He relished his new position on the team and would be the first to carry out this special mission which he had been training for specifically over the past few months. Originally from Denver, Colorado, an Arabic looking young man with an olive complexion. Twenty-six years old, slightly scruffy, with long black scraggly hair and a stubble beard, which was deliberate for blending in purposes, and dressed accordingly for the mission. He was considered the best candidate for the job, because he spoke fluent Arabic, having studied it at university, then spending a lot of time in Arabic speaking countries, so he was fluent in many dialects. McClean had hand-picked him out of over one hundred possible candidates, some who had better qualifications. Although a little rough around the edges, that naivete would help him to get into the places McClean wanted him to go. The last thing he would want to happen would be for him to get exposed as an undercover agent working for the NSA. His life would be in grave danger with the shoulders he was about to rub. The Islamic Society in mid-Manhattan would be his first call.

Ryman's mission was to infiltrate the Islamic terrorist group Al-Qaeda, or get close to people who were involved in the Nine-Eleven attacks and find out how they communicated with each other through the chain of command. Al-Qaeda at that time was run by Osama bin Laden, Khalid Sheikh Mohammed, and Mohammed Atef, and they were the ones who plotted the attacks after meeting together in 1999. It is also believed Khalid Sheikh Mohammed was the one who planned the attacks and that Atef was the one who organised the hijackers. The facts about who was behind the attacks had been written and documented for fifteen years, it was the other bits of intel McClean wanted to know, and with all the heightened tensions around Nine-Eleven it should be easy for Ryman to befriend someone in authority.

"Edwards, can I get a check on the time?" McClean said through his headpiece.

"We are five minutes out, sir. We placed the marker two hours ago, and we have checked out the landing area that was here fifteen years ago, so there will be no obstacles," he replied efficiently.

"What was it back then?"

"Just an underground garage, so there is an open space."

"Okay, let's warm her up," McClean said.

Edwards then pressed the button to start the countdown on the console in front of him. The clock started ticking down from five minutes.

The Mag-Tron sprang into action, at eight feet in diameter, it was big enough for a six-foot-tall person to walk through with ease. Lasers would be spinning light at ten thousand revolutions per second to create a powerful magnetic field, strong enough to bridge the gap. It would take more power than a small city and would spike at maximum power for just a few seconds at its peak.

Twenty agents sat at consoles looking at their screens, each console handling a different aspect of the mission, it was very reminiscent of a NASA rocket launch at Cape Canaveral, and they all had ringside seats to watch agent Ryman as he steps through the portal's vortex, and back to the year 2001. They told him it should be like stepping from one room to another, but no human being had ever done it before, he was going to be the first, the first time-traveller, and all eyes would be on him. There was a slim chance it wouldn't work, and he would be fried, or stuck in limbo between one world and the next, but that didn't worry him as he would be making history he told himself. McClean came on the loudspeaker.

"Are you ready Ryman?" McClean asked, "We will be ready to go in four minutes?"

"Ready as I'll ever be, sir," he answered positively and gave the thumbs up. There was, however, nervous tension to his voice.

"Remember what we told you in the briefing and you'll be fine. Ryman all you have to do is step through when we give you the signal and make sure you are back here at this same spot in exactly seven days for us to bring you home," McClean said. "That will be Thursday, September 13, 2001, at eleven-thirty, that's nine days from now if you miss that slot, we will set again twenty-four hours after that, and then on September 20, at the same time. If you are not back by then, we will see you in fifteen years. But I don't expect it to come to that."

"No, I'll be here."

"Right okay, all set?"

"All okay here, sir," Ryman said.

He went to his mark to make the three steps forward through the eye of the machine. Everything went through his mind at that moment. What if he bumped into himself or someone he knew, it would be strange, and how would he explain it away. He decided it was a moment to make history and be part of something, he would go through and see how the cards fell for him, take a chance he thought, you only live one life and this was his.

"Edwards, what time do we have?" McClean asked again.

"One-minute, sir, starting the field now," Edwards said.

McClean gave the final order. "Okay, take your positions."

The Mag-Tron lasers went into overdrive, creating the vortex and made a high-pitched tone rather like a tuning fork. A circular hole appeared within the laser beams, eight feet in diameter, it looked like a shimmering wall of water, on this side 2016, on the other, 2001. Through the vortex, Ryman could see a staircase, that would be his exit he thought. Ryman got ready for the signal. In the control room, the tension was mounting, and the anxiety etched itself into McClean's facial expression. The digital readouts started counting back in years, 2010, 2009, 2008, and in a few more seconds, 2004, 2003, 2002, when it had reached 2001, McClean gave agent Ryman the all-clear.

Everyone in the control room watched in disbelief, as agent Ryman walked through the vortex and disappeared in front of their eyes. They all sat there for a moment, transfixed on the video feed from the Mag-Tron. "Great job guys and gals, we've done it," McClean shouted. The delight in his voice was evident to everyone, and they all breathed a sigh of relief.

The control room erupted with laughter, high fives, and clapping, they all knew that they were part of something special, and they had reached a milestone with this technology. Sending someone back in time was only dreamt of as the subject of sci-fi films and television series, but like all dreams, it takes someone with extreme foresight and tenacity to make things happen and change the world in which we live.

Peter Wong had invented the Mag-Tron technology in 2010. He began by sending small rodents back in time for a few seconds. He explained, it was like folding time over on itself, to bring two moments in time side by side. It took 10,000 GHz of electromagnetic energy from the lasers and a vast amount of computer programming to achieve it. Using lasers at that speed created a void of antimatter within the magnetic field, like a black hole so that matter could pass through unhindered. While he was carrying out his tests, and getting near to the discovery, the NSA was already eavesdropping on his communications between his team of experts that he was collaborating with around the world. As soon as there was a successful outcome, the federal government swooped in and seised it. They deemed the technology too important to fall into the wrong hands, so they made a compulsory purchase of it, feeling that it was in the interests of national security that they should own it lock stock and barrel. He reluctantly dismantled the smaller Mag-Tron at his facility in Kissimmee, South Florida, under the utmost secrecy. He then set about building a much bigger machine for a human being to pass through inside the secure NSA facility. Wong had initially been a designer for Microsoft, who had made billions of dollars personally from the programs he had designed that were now part of everyone's daily life. He also was given an undisclosed sum to provide full rights of the technology to the government.

On the other side, Jed Ryman bumped into someone who appeared straight in front of him, just after he came through the vortex. He was startled by the man at first and then apologised to him. He paused for a moment quickly looking around while he gained his bearings. He was now in a large garage area, precisely like Edwards had told him it would be, and he would have to remember the exact spot so he could come back here in nine days to get back home. He then made his way up the stairs to some offices and out through the main doors, he was now back in the year 2001.

Chapter 5

Luigi's café was always open, with tables and chairs sprawling onto the sidewalk. It was the ultimate place in café society that Lower Manhattan had to offer, open for business twenty-four hours a day, at the corner of Delancey and Allen Street. Luigi's served an array of speciality foods from Italy to satisfy most diners' tastes. They sat outside under a canopy, out of the midday sun so Milo could get a welcome drink of water in the eighty-degree heat.

Peter noticed the staff and the design of the café had changed out of all recognition from what he remembered. A distinct Italian feel still but more authentic. The staff uniforms were all black with white aprons, 1950's style and smart, white table cloths, and white napkins. They also had something called WiFi, was that a new kind of coffee? Peter thought. He'd visited Luigi's with a colleague only last week, and it felt strange to see such a difference. But then thinking about it, it was fifteen years ago, so trying to get his head around that was even more bizarre. When the coffee arrived, he asked the waitress if old man Luigi was still about, but sadly he'd passed away in June that year, she said, and it was his son Alessandro that had now taken over the business. Alessandro came out a short time later to say hello, and Peter couldn't believe it. Last week when he saw him, he was only thirteen years old, and in his Brooklyn International High School uniform. Now standing in front of him was a twenty-eight-year-old man with a chef's outfit on, full beard, a portly three hundred pounds bursting over a large black leather belt, and a friendly smile that he couldn't mistake.

"Good to see you, Mr Collins," he said warmly, instantly recognising him from before, he had an Italian-American accent Peter remembered, as all the family spoke in the same way.

"Likewise, Alessandro," he said, standing up to shake his hand, and give him a traditional hug. "This is Heather, she is a friend of mine," Peter said, Heather smiled and shook his hand as well.

"Nice to meet with you, Heather." He then gave Peter a curious look, squinting his eyes. "I haven't seen you around for a long, long time, Mr Collins, how have you been?"

"I'm great thanks, Alessandro, I've been away on business, I was sorry to hear about your dad, the waitress was saying. Your father was a good man."

Heather watched and studied Peter as he spoke to Alessandro, every thought went rushing through her head. Why had this lovely man suddenly come into her life? She asked herself. Would it ever get to be a permanent thing, or was that rushing things? As she now had a secret crush on him but wasn't going to cross the line, well not yet anyway.

Alessandro got a little emotional all of a sudden. "Yes, me too Mr Collins. The cancer got him in the end, you know, too many cigarettes," he said sadly. "But anyway, we survive, he is here with us in spirit, watching over us all and telling me when I have put too much Parmesan in the Bolognese, know what I mean?" He laughed sadly.

"Anyway, you have my condolences," Peter said.

"Thank you so much. See you again, I leave you now." Alessandro bowed as he left and went back to the kitchen.

"Bye." Heather waved.

While studying Peter, she noticed a small tattoo on his arm, protruding from under his Polo shirt, it read USMC, and a dagger pushed through a ghost-like skull.

"So, when were you in the army?" Heather asked.

"Oh that," he said, pulling it up a little further to show her. "The marines actually, in the early nineties, the gulf war, we were part of 'desert storm,' one of the first units to go into Kuwait, it was pretty hairy stuff I can tell you. I was lucky to get back in one piece, a few scary moments with my unit, though. My only regret is that we got Saddam out of Kuwait, but we didn't get Saddam himself, the bastard survived."

Heather smiled and said, "oh yes, you wouldn't know, would you? He was tried in court by his own people, found guilty, and convicted of crimes against humanity. They hanged him in 2006, it was all over the internet, pretty gruesome stuff."

"Really? Well that makes me feel a whole lot better, they got justice, and he got what was coming to him," Peter said, smiling. He then looked at her and Milo for a moment. "So Heather, a very nice name by the way."

"Thanks."

"What is it that you do now?"

"I work at the Elite model agency. I book the models out for different photoshoots around the city, and only work part-time, but it suits me."

Peter looked at her and smiled again. "Sounds great, are you sure you aren't a model yourself?"

"Thanks, but no, definitely not," Heather said, noticing Peter smiling at her. "What is it?" She smiled back.

"We were going to call my daughter Ashley, Heather, me and Marie I mean, but settled on Ashley."

"That's a nice name too, how old is she?" she asked.

"Thirteen," he said, then he had to pause for a moment and think again, "No, she'd be twenty-eight now. Bloody hell twenty-eight and Tom and Jake would be what? Twenty-six, Jesus, they will all be adults now."

"Sounds like you've got a lovely family Peter," she said unselfishly.

"Yeah, they are great. I only saw them all at breakfast this morning, but they would not have seen me now for fifteen years, that's weird when you think about it. I wonder what that has done to us as a family?" Peter said retrospectively, and mulling it over in his mind. He put himself in their shoes for a second, and it didn't feel good, it didn't feel very good at all and made his mood very downbeat and pessimistic.

"They will be fine, you wait and see," Heather said optimistically.

There was a newspaper rack on the wall outside the front door of Luigi's behind Heather, and Peter noticed the New York Times, he leaned over and picked it out as the headline caught his attention. "What's this, nine-eleven commemorations of the terror attack, when was this?" he asked inquisitively.

As he opened out the front page, Heather smiled at him, "I suppose lots of things have happened in fifteen years that you wouldn't know about, would you? I'll have to bring you up to speed with everything," Heather said, getting close and looking at the paper with him. "The World Trade Center, both towers came down after planes flew into them, there were over three thousand people killed that day. The worst thing I have ever seen in my life, everyone remembers where they were on that day, a bit like the day they shot Kennedy," Heather said.

Peter stared at the iconic picture of the North Tower collapsing and didn't say anything, not a word. He hadn't heard what Heather was saying either, it ended up being just a muffled sound in his head as the date hit him like a bullet straight between the eyes. He held his hands over his mouth and gulped for air to catch his breath, his eyes moistened. "Oh my God, no."

"What? What's wrong, Peter? You look like you've seen a ghost," Heather said, worriedly.

He held his head in his hands for a moment, "my boys, God no!" Peter struggled to form his words, "Tom and Jake, our twins, they were going there on a school field trip. On that very day. Oh my." Tears forced themselves to the surface, and he couldn't help himself.

"Tuesday, the eleventh? Patriots day?" she asked.

"Yeah, Tuesday the eleventh, a school field trip with loads of other schools, eight-thirty in the morning. They would have been there, Tom, Jake." He wiped his eyes with a serviette, reading the details and looking for anything and everything as he devoured the content of the article, the towers, the time, Osama Bin Laden. It was all there in a concise synopsis on the front page of the New York Times as to what happened on that day. He sat back hesitating to speak, not being able to get his words out. The pain and trauma were etched on his face as he thought about his boys.

"I've got to go," he said abruptly. "I've got to go and be with them. I'm sorry, I've really got to go Heather."

"I know you have Peter? I do really," Heather said as she placed her hand on his arm to offer support.

"I've got to go and find Marie, find my family, Tom, Jake, Ashley, I need to be with them. I have to know they are all okay," he said, getting himself into a bit of a panic. He put a ten-dollar note on the table for the coffees. "Where can I get a phone? A car. I need to drive over there. I have to see them, be with them. Is there a place I can buy a phone and rent a car around here?" he asked again, anxiously looking at Heather.

"Yes, there is, just around the corner. There's a Vodafone shop and car hire place near there as well," she said, trying to be as helpful as possible.

She wanted to say use my phone, use my car, but she didn't, she held back for some reason, not wanting to get involved, a personal survival mechanism kicking in where men with families are concerned. Families would always come first, she knew that, and she couldn't compete, she didn't want to compete, there was no point.

Peter held Heather's hand and looked into her eyes intently as he spoke. "Look, Heather." That was a bad start, she thought. "It's been wonderful meeting you, but I've got to go and see them, I hope you understand?"

"Of course, Peter, lovely to meet you as well?" she said as she stood there, awkwardly. "Hope it all goes well and everything's okay, I'm sure they will be okay."

"I hope so and thanks for everything, Heather. Before I go, would it be okay if I took your number?" he tentatively asked. "Just in case. Is that okay?"

"Yes, no problem, Peter," she jotted it down on a serviette quickly and handed it to him.

He gave her a quick kiss on her cheek, smiled at her, patted Milo and hurriedly walked away down the street in search of the Vodafone shop. Heather watched his every step as he disappeared into the distance, then sat down again to finish her coffee.

She stroked Milo thoughtfully on her knee. "They never stay long, do they, Milo? It's always just you and me, isn't it, my little friend?" Milo purred like a cat. "Why is that, is there something wrong with me? Do I put them off in some way, do you think? What do you know you're just a loving little dog, and I do love you so much," she said, grabbing the hair on his little face.

Self-doubt had reared its ugly head again. After a failed marriage to a philanderer that lasted only two years in her thirties, and then a string of affairs with high profile business-types and celebrities, she was now too old to have children and single. The last twenty years seemed to have gone so fast, and she realised at the age of forty-two that that was possibly it. Was she too pretty? Or too single, or probably too stuck in her ways to let anyone into her life, it must intimidate them, she thought? She was going to carry on the way she had been. She enjoyed her life, so men could all sod off until the right one came along, she told herself. She was just afraid that the right one had just walked off to find his family. She didn't blame him if it was meant to be, so be it.

Chapter 6

Jason Green saw a red warning light flashing on his console, he couldn't understand what was causing it at first, it must have been due to a surge in electromagnetic power he thought, and was probably a minor malfunction. Then he had a look at the timeline of events. He discovered that something had happened a few seconds after agent Ryman had gone through the vortex. He brought up the video footage onto his screen to investigate further. His suspicions were confirmed, moments after Agent Ryman disappeared through the vortex he saw a man appear in the same place, and he was standing there when the vortex shut down. It looked like a man in his thirties or forties, Green thought. Everyone had missed seeing him as they all were too busy celebrating, Green broke the news to Agent Edwards.

Edwards was in the middle of thanking everyone for their efforts, "what is it Green?" he said.

"We've had a breach, sir."

"A breach Green! What are you talking about?" Edwards said as it aroused everyone's attention in the room. The celebrations and the happy mood suddenly turned sour.

"Someone, a man, came through the vortex just after agent Ryman went through, it's all here on video," he said.

"Put it on the main screen, Green. A breach is all we need," Edwards said, sounding a little irked.

The video stream from six different angles came onto the one main screen, while Agent Edwards and everyone gathered around and watched Agent Ryman disappear again.

"There is no protocol for this Edwards," McClean said as he watched.

Edwards backtracked. "It's a one in a million chance that this could have happened at the same time the vortex was open, I mean it was only two seconds."

"It looks more like ten seconds to me Edwards, and yes, a one in a million chance and we won, didn't we? We now have a bloody fugitive from 2001 running around here with us in 2016, don't we? We had better get on it quickly and find him before he wreaks bloody havoc. That shouldn't be too difficult these days, should it Edwards?" McClean said pointedly with a sarcastically cutting tone.

"Piece of cake, sir, we will have him under wraps within the hour," Edwards said confidently. "We will get everyone on it, sir."

"I'll hold you to that, Edwards," McClean said. "It's who he comes in contact with I'm more worried about. We need to send him back with as little knowledge of 2016 as possible, call it a karma thing. We don't want him upsetting the balance of everything."

"Yes, sir. He's probably still in the building, I'll give reception a call."

"You have level five clearance on this Edwards, do what you have to do, don't let me down and keep me informed," McClean said and walked off to his office.

Doug McClean had worked with Agent Michael Edwards for over twenty years, and he had always been his boss as they both moved up the ranks together within the NSA. It was a relationship that worked well, he was his right-hand man, and he relied on him to carry out his wishes.

The NSA reception confirmed a man fitting the description had been in there for only a few minutes, but they ejected him out of security concerns. Edwards came off the phone looking a little annoyed, directing his thoughts to Agents Lewis and Green, who were watching him make the phone call.

"Well, it looks like we let him go," said Edwards. "Because he was a security risk, a bloody security risk, you couldn't make this stuff up? On drugs and disorientated, she said." Edwards turned to the other agents in the room. "So he's now in the wind, where is he going? If I were him, where would I go? I would want to reconnect, wouldn't I? So who is the family? Where are they living? We need to get eyes on them as soon as possible. He is bound to make contact with them at some point, don't forget they haven't seen him for fifteen years."

Agent Lewis commented. "Who is he though, sir? Tracking him down through usual methods could be difficult, as he has no immediate past in 2016 at all, no current mobile to track, or credit cards, or anything for that matter. He would be anonymous to everyone, I don't think it's going to be as easy as you think, sir."

They all looked at each other, nodding their heads in agreement with Lewis.

"We have his face that's all, can we track him with just that? You know, facial recognition?" Green said, he always was the one to come up with better ideas.

"The CIA has the best system for that," Lewis confirmed.

"He cannot be far away. I mean, how far can you go in twenty minutes for God's sake?" Edwards said, shaking his head and rubbing his temples, "Lewis, are you still in contact with that friend of yours in the CIA? You know the one I mean, the one you trained with?" Edwards asked.

"Yes, Jack, you mean, don't you," Edwards nodded. "I've not spoken with him for a while, but I'll give him a call. I'm sure he would help us out if he can." Lewis scrolled through his phone for Jack's number.

Jack Graham was now head of a dedicated surveillance unit for the CIA, at their headquarters located at Langley, Virginia. They could, in theory, find anyone anywhere in the world through secure satellite technology and pinpoint someone within minutes, no country had a better system. He and Lewis had trained together at Fort Washington after leaving university and had become good friends. Although taking distinctly different career paths, Jack was deeply involved with the war in Afghanistan, while Lewis was now a crucial part of

McClean's Mag-Tron Team. Jack had carried out many Drone attacks to support the troops on the ground, but working remotely from Langley. The technology now was so smart and accurate they could take out insurgents with little or no civilian casualties, and had the full backing of President Obama.

"Jack, hi, it's Mike Lewis here buddy, how's it going?"

"Very well thanks Mike, yes, all is good, long time no speak?" Jack said.

"I hear you've moved up in the world? Congrats on that. What you up to over there at Langley?"

"We are working on some interesting stuff, a lot is happening in the world at this moment, and we seem to be in the thick of it. We should catch up soon, Mike. We aren't getting any younger that's for sure. What's up?" he said, getting straight to the point.

"Yes, we should mate. The reason for the call is we need to find someone and fast. We have a small bit of video footage but nothing else," Lewis said hopefully. "We thought your facial recognition system could help? You have level five clearance on this Jack if you can help us out, we need a result fast, is that okay?"

"Who is he?"

"That's it, you see, we don't have a name."

Jack said. "Okay, I'll run it through the database, see if we can put a name to a face. Send it over. I'll get onto it myself. Shouldn't take long."

"Thanks, Jack, we appreciate it," Lewis said.

"Anything for the NSA Mike," he joked.

The reality was, the CIA didn't share hardly any information with the NSA unless they were told to, which was very rare. After half an hour, Jack came back and said he had nothing on him, he had gone through all databases, and it seemed as if he was a ghost, not on any record anywhere.

"Sorry mate, if he were alive, we would have found him," he said. "There is no record anywhere, is he a spy or something like that, working off the grid? Do you have anything else you can tell me about him?"

"Only that this is a person of interest from just before nine-eleven, and hasn't been seen since, so maybe if you look there that might help," Lewis shared as much as he could without actually telling him about how he ended up here in 2016.

"Oh okay, that's interesting," he said. "You should have said, these bits of information can make all the difference, even with systems like this you still have to know where to look." He typed something into his computer.

The CIA had every bit of hi-tech kit going. There were eight people on Jack's team, and fifteen other teams doing the same thing, seeking people out, tracking their movements, sifting through their lives. He sat in front of a bank of screens with his people busy on their workstations. The monitors showed real-time events from all around the world happening at that very moment. Their primary function as a department of the CIA was to seek out potential threats from wherever it may happen. Threats from foreign powers, insurgents in Afghanistan or Iraq, and a big focus at that moment was on the Middle East as a whole, as the

United States had 25,000 troops actively stationed there, and it was up to them to get the intel needed for them to fight off the enemy successfully.

Jack found something on file. "Mike, I think I've got something for you," he said as he was comparing pictures on the screen.

"That's good."

"I used the time-period you gave me and searched around that time with facial rec'."

"That sounds promising," Lewis said optimistically.

"There was a missing person report filed at the Manhattan Police headquarters at eleven o'clock on September 6, 2001, by a Marie Collins. Husband Peter, forty-two years old, missing just vanished, no reason given and never found. I'm sending you a picture over, looks like your guy," Jack said, with a triumphant tone to his voice.

"Yes, just got it," it flashed instantly onto Lewis's screen. "So, it's a Peter Collins," he said, looking at the two pictures side by side on the screen. "That's great mate," Lewis said, feeling somewhat relieved.

"I've already put a trace out on him, so if he steps in front of one of our networked CCTV cameras, it will flag up on our system. I'll let you know, if or when we get anything."

Jack signed off, and Lewis broke the good news to Agent Edwards.

Chapter 7

Peter stepped onto the pavement outside the Vodafone shop and looked down at his brand-new Samsung 'Pay as You Go' mobile phone, and tapped the screen hesitantly. The phone was terrific he thought, a video phone, voice recognition, even the internet flashed up in a millisecond if he touched the screen in a certain place. The midday sun caught the perfectly flat tempered glass and blinded him for a second. He could not believe how technology had changed in fifteen years, and this was just a phone.

It reminded him of back to the future two, and the DeLorean car that took Marti to 2015 where he came face to face with himself, it was like he was living in the movie, and the new technology he held in the palm of his hand was light years ahead. The girl in the shop ran him through what an 'Application' was, it would take time to understand the technology, but the worse thing was, it had taken one hundred and thirty dollars of the last two hundred he had in the world. A feeling of insecurity came over him, and he felt alone in a world he didn't recognise. He wondered what to do next and was anxious to see Tom and Jake. The feeling that they could have perished on that day made him feel empty inside, and he was almost in a state of mourning already. He tapped Marie's number into the Samsung and pressed the call, she was the only person in the world at that moment he wanted to speak to, he knew that Heather had tried twice for him, but he tried it anyway. There was a continuous tone again, it was disconnected.

Peter sat down on a bench a short way along from the Vodafone shop to study his new phone for a moment. He then scanned through some phone numbers on his old Blackberry to see who he could call. Larry's phone number came up, surely, his business partner would be there? He had spoken to him only a few hours ago. But then realising it again, it was fifteen years since they last spoke. Peter wondered how he would react to the news that he was still alive and well.

"Hello," she said. It sounded to Peter like the voice of a very old lady.

"Oh, hello there, who's that?" He inquired.

"This is Jennifer Edwards speaking, how can I help you?" she said very politely, and a little croaky, it was nothing like he remembered her voice to be like, but he could tell it was her, by the rich midwest accent under the croaking, slow and mellow.

"Oh, thank God Jen, it's Peter," he said and let out a sigh of relief.

"Peter, who?" she asked, a little confused by his familiarity.

He thought that she hadn't heard him right the first time, and maybe she was hard of hearing now. "Peter Collins Jen, it's me, Peter Collins," he repeated, speaking louder into the Samsung, slower and more enunciated.

"Peter?" she said, sounding bewildered. Suddenly there was a deafening silence, and he could hear her thinking on the other end, probably confused by what he had just said: "Is that really you Peter?" she asked.

"Yes, Jen it is me would you believe it, it's a long story but it is me," Peter said, "Look, Jen, I can't go into it right now but could you put Larry on please, I need to speak to him urgently?" There seemed to be an even longer silence this time. "Jen are you still there?"

"Yes, I'm still here, Peter," finally breaking the awkward disjointed silence.

"Jen, can you put Larry on for me please, I need to talk to him, is he there Jen?" he asked, slightly louder again. There was a hint of desperation creeping into his voice as he didn't seem to be getting through to her.

"No, Peter, Larry isn't here," Jen said abruptly. "Where have you been all these years?" A pointed but very pertinent question he thought. He felt there was a little anger in her voice, but he hadn't got time to explain over the phone.

"Jen, I'll come around and see you both soon, I promise, and we will catch up properly as we used to as it is something that needs explaining, is Larry going to be back later Jen?" he asked.

"No, he won't be back later either Peter."

Peter had the feeling he had said something wrong, "is Larry okay, Jen?"

"No, he's not okay, Peter. He passed away eleven years ago. Where have you been?"

He could hear all the emotions of her loss coming straight back at him through the phone. She sniffed, then a quiet sobbing and breathed inward.

"Oh Jen, I'm so sorry, I didn't realise," he said as the sucker punch came out of nowhere and hit him tightening his gut. "I'm sorry Jen, I didn't know, I'm so sorry I wasn't there for him and you, you must feel dreadful?"

He could hear Jen fading away and become more distant as he spoke to her. People walked by, some without a care in the world, ignorant to the plight that now faced him. He rued the loss of his mentor and the loss of a great man, a formidable businessman that had been his rock and his shoulder to lean on for so very long, and the person that helped him through the ups and downs of their business together. Her sobbing at the end of the phone he felt responsible for, and thought that it must have been hell for Larry and her when he didn't come back, disappearing with no explanation. He needed to ask more questions but wanted to keep things as brief as possible. "Jen, I'm sorry, can I ask, have you seen Marie at all?"

"No, Peter I've not seen or heard from Marie since it all happened," she said somberly, and still sniffing. He could hear her wipe her nose.

"Oh, dear, is she alright?" he interjected.

"What, with you going missing, we tried to help her Peter, we really did, but I think she was lost in her own grief, and with everything happening so fast, nine-eleven and everything."

"Nine-eleven Jen, what do you mean nine-eleven and everything," Peter said anxiously.

"I've got to go Peter. I'm so exhausted," Jen said, sounding very frail.

He could tell that it was a shock hearing his voice again and that he was still alive, it would have made Larry's death all the more vivid in her mind. "Okay, Jen, sorry, I'll call you again soon. I promise okay, and we will catch up?"

Before he could say goodbye, the line went dead. He had wanted to ask about Tom and Jake and if they had survived the towers collapsing, or hopefully never went there in the first place. He couldn't grieve for them yet because he didn't know, he was hoping for the best, putting a positive spin on it in his mind. But now he had Larry to mourn for, this was going to be a regular occurrence Peter thought, as a lot had happened in fifteen years and he would be surprised and saddened in equal measure as that was how life was, and things had moved on without him.

His thoughts turned towards transport. The anxious feeling that he needed to get a car of some kind hadn't subsided. He desperately needed to go over to his house in Oyster Bay and see Marie and the kids. It had become a matter of urgency.

Gary's Car Hire was just a few yards down the road from the Vodafone shop. It seemed the best choice to try as it looked like a business that would do some sort of a deal, not your usual big named branded car hire place, this was a one-man-band. He looked in his wallet, all he had was five out of date credit cards, and seventy-two dollars to his name. No one in their right mind would lend him anything, even the girl behind the counter who thought he was cute as well, couldn't do anything for him. He tried putting his Omega Seamaster down as collateral, but they wouldn't take it, and you couldn't blame them. Peter walked out of the shop thinking about getting a taxi, but that would cost three hundred dollars from where he was in Manhattan, he had done it before, but that was in 2001, in 2016 it might now cost as much as five hundred. He hadn't got a clue what bus to take either or how many buses would be needed.

He took out the neatly folded serviette from Luigi's and looked at the number for a moment. Using his new Samsung, he tapped it in and pressed the call. It rang only once.

"Hello?"

"Hello, Heather?"

"Hi, Peter, I had a sneaky suspicion you would be calling me?" she said with a very welcoming tone to her voice. She hoped he would call, she had missed him already, and it came over in waves. "How are you? It's been all of thirty minutes?" She gurgled. "You can't live without me, can you?"

Peter laughed, "Ha! Yes, I know Heather, I couldn't stay away?" he conceded, he was pleased that she seemed so lovely about it, and secretly he had missed her too.

"I see you sorted out a phone that works, Ha!"

"Yes." He laughed. "They're amazing these phones, I've got this Samsung thing. I thought they only made televisions."

"Yeah, it's a good make. They make lots of different things these days."

"Heather, I was wondering if you could help me out. I'm in a bit of a jam?" he said tentatively.

"Of course, Peter," she said without hesitation.

"I have tried to rent a car, but my credit cards are out of date, and I need to get over to my house in Oyster Bay to see Marie and the kids, I know it's a—?"

"No problem I'll take you," she said in a flash. He felt like a weight had lifted off his shoulders.

"Oh, would you?" he said. "You're a star, Heather."

"I know I am? Where are you? I'll come and get you?"

"I am near the Vodafone shop you sent me to on east thirty-fourth Street," he said. "I'm sitting on a bench next to it."

"Sure, I'll be there in twenty."

He could now get over to Oyster Bay, but he couldn't help the feeling of anxiety that was still there. He thought about Marie and the kids, they would be young adults, and how would Marie be with him? How would she take it? Seeing him again after fifteen years?

He would have to wait and find out. Anyway, he had the most beautiful driver to keep him company for the next hour.

Chapter 8

Peter was messing about with his new phone again when a silver Mercedes S-Class Sport appeared alongside him with the roof down, and a welcome face behind the wheel. Long blond flowing hair, sunglasses, it was as though the sun had lit the scene perfectly, she could have been a movie star.

"Going my way, honey?" Heather said with an exaggerated Marilyn Monroe-esk accent and a smile that made him melt on the spot.

"I might be, whose askin'?" Peter was never good at remembering actors to mimic but came out with a silly voice anyway.

"Only little olé me."

"I don't accept lifts off anyone you know, what sort of a man do you think I am?" he joked.

"Get in!" Heather smiled.

"Well okay then," he said, laughing out loud, then climbed into the passenger seat and shut the door.

He looked at her smiling back at him. It was like she had expected it, and he noticed a big attraction to him in her eyes. Not wanting to lead her on in any way, and thinking sensibly, he immediately went into friend mode, rather than a flirty mode. He knew the difference, and although amorous feelings were lurking around somewhere in his subconscious and begging to come out at any moment, they were going to see Marie and his kids, and that was the most important thing.

"Heather, I am so grateful to you, you cannot believe. Beautiful car by the way."

"Yeah, I like. It was a prezzie from my dad. Where are we going then?"

"It's Oyster Bay, Steamboat Landing Road, a fifty-minute drive, hope that's okay?"

"Yes, no problem, Peter," she smiled.

It was as if he had now got a chauffeur at his beck and call, It could have been worse, a lot worse, he thought. "If you go over Queensboro Bridge, then take the four-nine-five, it practically takes you there."

"Yes, that's fine. Oyster Bay? Nice neighbourhood," she said, sounding rather impressed. "You've done well for yourself, haven't you, Peter?"

"Yeah, I've done okay, I just hope she's in."

"You know, this sort of thing happens to me every day you know, helping time travellers from the past, or the future." She smiled and gurgled.

"It was lucky I bumped into you, Heather, I can tell you."

There was something remarkable about driving with the roof down, Peter thought, the sun beating down on the top of his head and the airflow cooling it immediately. The Mercedes sport suited Heather, she looked great in it. He had now warmed to her persona, she was funny, humorous, and he wondered why she was on her own, he didn't get the feeling there was someone special in her life. Although they had only just met, she never mentioned anyone and the fact that she was there with him going out of her way to help, led him to the conclusion she was single.

The four-nine-five was bumper to bumper with traffic, so they drove the scenic route down tree-lined roads meandering through the neighbourhoods, Murray Hill, Little Neck, Roslyn, Greenvale, Peter knew all the back roads to Oyster Bay, but today, however, they seemed a little different, the tree-lined streets were more overgrown than when he last came through. It would add an extra fifteen miles on their journey, but worth it not to sit in slow-moving, gas-guzzling, fume-filled traffic he thought, especially with the roof down. The sun was lower in the sky as they turned into Steamboat landing road. The journey had seemed quicker than usual as they hadn't stopped talking for a second, and with so much in common, the conversation was effortless. Heather stopped the car at the end of his driveway.

"Well, here we are," Peter said, looking over at the house apprehensively as he got out of the car, he stood by the passenger door for a moment. He didn't recognise it, he didn't recognise it at all. "Looks a whole lot different to how I remember it this morning when I left for work. Do you think they are in?" he asked Heather.

"How would I know?" She gurgled. "It might be a good idea to go and knock on the door, Peter."

"You know what? You come up with all the good ideas," he laughed. "Okay, here goes."

He looked over at the house and remembered the morning sun cascading in through the bay window earlier that day at breakfast, it seeped into every part of the kitchen and lit up everything in the room creating an ambience of brightness. He was doing the crossword, laughing with Marie and the kids; it seemed so far away now. His garden consisted of two acres of prime New York real estate, well-groomed lawns, and a huge oak tree that was at least three hundred years old and came with its own history. Many people had been hanged there in the 1800s, and some local villagers said it was still haunted. There was a swimming pool, a tennis court, but the main event was the view over the small privet hedge at the bottom of the garden. Oyster Bay Harbour was breath-taking at any time of the day. He remembered how he loved the house, it was everything he and Marie had worked for and dreamed of, and never wanted to move.

The sun was now fading over the vast expanse of Oyster Bay Harbour, he could hear the large sailing boats on running moorings out in the harbour bobbing up and down in the distance, and the familiar-sounding clatter of their halyards and burgee's in the light breeze, mingled in with the sound of seagulls squawking. A few miles away over the water was the Oyster Bay Wildlife Refuge and he and Marie would visit from time to time with the kids. The first refuge in the US was Pelican Island founded by Theodore Roosevelt in 1903. On a good day, migratory birds could be spotted like the Peregrine Falcon or the Northern Harrier. There were a hundred and twenty-six species of birds documented at the refuge, that's one of the reasons Peter and Marie loved it so much there.

It seemed a whole lot different now though, the trees that he had planted along the driveway three years previous in 1998, had all gone now, making way for a larger blacked tarmac area for cars. He thought it was a shame, as it had added a warm homely feel to the house, now it looked like a builders yard, and he wondered what possessed Marie to change it. The colour of the house had changed as well, to various shades of dark and light greens, and the porchway he had built as a project and was very proud of, had disappeared as well. There was nothing about the house now that he recognised or even liked. It seemed as though all the characters had gone to make way for functional living. Heather offered to go with him, which was sweet of her, but it was something he needed to do on his own. As he walked up to the house everything went through his mind, how would Marie take it, seeing him after all these years. Even the sound of the doorbell was different, his heart sunk when a lady in her sixties answered the door.

"Hello," she said.

"Ah! Hello, sorry to bother you, is this Marie Collins's house?" Peter said almost expecting what the answer would be because it was a silly question.

"No, I live here," she said. "This is Mira Stewart's house, and that would be me," she retorted in an Americanised Scottish accent and smiled confused by the question.

"How long have you lived here?" Peter asked.

"Almost eight years," she said. "Is there anything I can help you with?" Impatience getting the better of her, she probably thought he was a doorstep window salesman or something along those lines, Peter thought.

"Sorry, I'm Peter Collins. I'm Marie's husband."

"Why would you think she was here?" she asked, and it was a perfectly reasonable question under the circumstances.

"Yeah, we haven't been in touch for a while. I've been away."

"Oh, I see?" she said, taking a little step further back into the house.

"Oh, not prison or anything like that," he explained, putting his hands up. "God, no. You wouldn't by any chance have a forwarding address for her, would you? It would be a real help to me, please?" Peter asked as she relaxed and came around, and now had a helpful open look on her face.

"Yes, I do Peter, I forwarded the post to her for over a year. I'll go and get it for you. It will only take me a moment." She returned and gave Peter a piece of paper with the address written down. He studied it for a moment. "Westhampton Beach, just before you get to the Hampton's, a very nice area, a step up from here if you ask me and this isn't bad. You okay there?" she said, as Peter now had a confused, sad look on his face, she felt as she had somehow upset him in some way as his mood changed.

"Did you meet them?" Peter inquired.

"Yes, lovely lady Marie and her daughter Ashley, and David of course."

"David?"

"Yeah that was his name, he was some sort of a high flyer in the police, I think."

"What, were they together then?" he asked, now questioning her like she was a suspect in an investigation.

"I think so, but you can never tell, maybe he was just helping her out."

"And the boys, Tom and Jake did you see them?"

"No, I didn't," she said. "I never saw them, and she never mentioned them."

"Oh," he said. "Oh, Right." Sounding distant all of a sudden.

"Are you okay?" she asked as Peter looked a bit withdrawn.

"No, No, it's okay. And thank you so much for this," Peter said, holding the address tightly lifting his hand as if to gesture thank you. "You've been very helpful."

He slowly walked back to the car with his head down. Heather had been watching the exchange, and she could immediately tell that there was something wrong. He suddenly had a sad look to his demeanour.

"What's wrong, Peter?" she said as he approached.

"They left seven years ago, can you believe it? They now live in Westhampton Beach. We'd never thought of moving from here, it's not like Marie."

"That's close to the Hampton's," she said and placed her hand on the top of his and squeezed it gently, sympathetically.

"Can't believe it, I was only here just this morning," he said, looking out of the windscreen towards the jetty at the end of the road. "I taught Tom, Jake, and Ashley how to fish for crabs down there," he said, pointing the way. "I can still hear them laughing when Jake pushed Tom in," he laughed. "He wasn't happy at all, bless him. I wonder what they are up to at this moment. How tall must they be?"

"You miss them, don't you? It will all work out, you'll see?" Heather said positively. Peter seemed a bit 'lost in the moment' as he spoke.

"She never mentioned them."

"Mentioned who?"

"Mira Stewart, she never mentioned Tom and Jake."

"You can't read anything into that Peter surely?"

"She mentioned Marie, Ashley, and this David fella," he said, piecing the scenario together. "But not Tom and Jake. She didn't mention them."

"There are many reasons she couldn't have mentioned them."

"Name one," he challenged.

"Well, they could be at university together somewhere, couldn't they?" she concluded.

Peter thought about it for a moment, "Yeah, I suppose you are right, they could be. At university, I hadn't thought of that."

"Well let's stay positive until you know for sure, eh?"

"Yeah, your right." Stay positive, Peter. he said to himself snapping instantly out of his melancholy mood. He smiled to let her know he was fine.

Heather looked at her watch and did a few distance calculations in her head. "Peter, look, it's a bit late now to be going over there. Let's go back to my place. I'll make us some food, and we can talk if you want? I'm a good cook, you know," she said.

"I'm sure you are. Thanks that sounds wonderful Heather. I haven't eaten all day, come to think of it, that's probably why I'm hangry and a bit moody, you know, low blood sugar." Food sounded great, everything sounded great. He wouldn't think sad thoughts anymore, took a deep breath, "Great idea, we can go tomorrow if you have the time, I don't want to keep putting you out, though."

"It's no trouble Peter honestly."

"You are lovely, aren't you?" he said, and he meant it.

"I know," she said, smiling at him.

The light had given way to the semi-dark as they made their way back to Manhattan. His thoughts turned to Marie and what she must have gone through when he never came home. How must she have coped? She did cope that was obvious, and very well it looks like to now be residing near the Hampton's. He couldn't get the feeling out of his head though that he would be in for a shock in the very near future and tried not to think about it, it was there, and it would stay until he knew for sure.

He looked over at Heather, wondering about her, what was she getting out of this? A very kind-hearted human being. A very attractive, kind-hearted human being, Peter thought. He studied her like a painting in the Louvre. "Do you mind if I ask you a question, Heather?"

"Ask Away," she said, sounding open to anything he had to say.

"Is there a man in your life?" he asked.

"No, not at the moment," she replied. "In fact, not for five years."

"Why not?" he said. "You seem—?"

"I'm not a bunny boiler, you know," she interrupted, laughing.

"I was going to say. So lovely, actually."

"Ah, bless you. I have lots of friends. I have a great life, but just haven't found the right one to fill it yet. I must be too fussy."

"I suppose so."

There were lots of questions he wanted to ask but felt he shouldn't, maybe later, when the mood was right, and the moment felt right. Manhattan was busy twenty-four hours a day. There was always something going on, a party to go to, a Broadway show to see. Driving over the Queensboro Bridge and down Lexington, they were going towards Central Park. The streets seemed busier than usual. It was a warm night, with the roof still down you could see the lights on in every high-rise office with people still beavering away. The odd high-class hooker, moving in and out of the shadows to avoid the gaze of the police, more than likely to reap some wealthy custom at the same time. Sprawling cafés and bars spilling onto the sidewalks with smart-looking people in business suits enjoying early doors that had already turned into late doors. Manhattan was alive, and he loved the buzz.

"Where is it you live, Heather?" He asked.

"I have a place on Fifth Avenue."

"Wow, really?" Peter said, sounding astonished.

"Yes, really."

They stopped at a garage on East Eighty-Fifth Street. She pressed a button on a remote control device from inside the Mercedes, and the roller doors to the underground garage slowly slid open.

"Wow," Peter said again. "Nice address."

"Thank you."

Chapter 9

"Make yourself at home," she said, as they entered her opulent apartment at 1035 Fifth Avenue, Manhattan, New York.

An excellent address in anyone's language, Peter thought. "Wow, this is beautiful?" he said while glancing around in amazement.

"Glad you like it."

"This must have set you back a bit?"

"Not really, my dad left it to me in his will. He passed away eight years ago now."

"I'm sorry I didn't realise," he said sympathetically.

"No, you weren't to know. Daddy left all of our family well set up."

"What was his name?"

"Harry Lombard, he was a lovely man. I miss him a lot."

"I'm sure you do. Prime real estate this is," he said, looking around at all the tastefully chosen décor.

"Yes, I know, we have the whole building."

"Again, Wow," he said. "What did he do, your dad?"

"Insurance, Real estate, a few things."

Peter did a few quick calculations in his head, a spacious Fifth Avenue penthouse overlooking central park was worth at least ten million dollars, and they owned the whole building? She was sitting on a fortune, and yet she was unhindered by her wealth, humble and unpretentious. The furniture was exquisite. The colourful fabrics of the sofas, chairs, and wallpaper seemed like they were put together by a famous designer, probably Brad Ford, or Steven Gambrel perhaps. Expensive paintings adorned every wall, and the view of Central Park from Heather's balcony was to die for and was worth a small fortune on its own.

"This is a great place to people-watch from, don't you think?" Peter said as he looked enviously over at people jogging in the park.

"Yeah, you can see everything that goes on from up here," she said as she walked out with two glasses of Chablis, and a smile that made him weak at the knees. "Want one of these?"

"Lovely, thanks."

Their fingers touched momentarily as she passed him the wine glass, and a small spark of electricity conspired with endorphins to create a shiver down his spine.

Heather looked with him over at Central Park and said. "There are things you notice from up here, joggers, dog walkers or people just walking about, they all have a sort of routine if you study them close enough. Even from up here, you recognise them and their habits. It's really quite funny. I see this old man who walks his dogs three times a day, and is always at the same time regular as clockwork. I've never met him, but I would think about him if he wasn't there at those times, am I weird?" she asked.

"No, I'd be doing the same. I would probably want to know more. I'd have to go down there and speak to him and find out what his name was," Peter said, laughing.

"Now you are taking the—"

"No, really," Peter interrupted.

"Stop it! I am weird, I know. But that's me."

"You are funny, you know," he said playfully.

They enjoyed each other's company, that was obvious, and it felt natural to joke at the other person's expense, even though they had only just met. It was as though they had known each other for a very long time.

"Italian okay? Pasta Tagliatelle Bolognese," he said. "It's homemade, I make a whole load of it then freeze it for quickness."

Peter thought about food! Music to his ears, "That sounds terrific, Heather."

"Simple, quick, and very tasty. It has a bang to it as well," she said, smiling straight at him.

"Perfect, just what I need," he replied. *Just like you,* he was thinking, reading something else into her last statement but then quickly dismissed it.

She smiled and put her hand on his shoulder and said, "I know." She then walked over to the kitchen area to start dinner. "Put some music on if you like Peter?"

"Okay, I will," Peter said, get a bit of the boss on, he thought if she has the CD. "You like a bit of Bruce, don't you?"

"Yes, anything of his is great by me," she said.

He looked at the music centre or pod or whatever it was, and couldn't believe how small and compact things had gotten. Technology had moved on fast in fifteen years. "Where do you keep all your CD's?" he said.

"We don't do CD's anymore, just press the red button and tell it what you want, it streams immediately."

"No shit, streams, eh?" he said, looking for the button. "Okay, here goes. Bruce Springsteen, Atlantic City," and no soon as he had pressed the button and spoken, a slightly robotic-sounding woman repeated the instruction and it started to play. He turned to Heather, held his hands up in the air as if to say, how did that happen, "It seems as though I've missed out on so much," he said in amazement, as Bruce Springsteen's Atlantic City filled the room.

Dinner was lovely and seemed to last forever. They sat out on the balcony and talked well into the small hours without a break in the conversation, interested in anything and everything about each other. What they had done in their life, the experiences they had had. Tomorrow would be interesting, as Peter thought about meeting the family again. He slept in one of the many bedrooms with everything going through his mind all night, waking up every hour with positive and negative thoughts cramming his subconscious about his forthcoming reunion.

At 3:00 a.m., he woke and lay there thinking about the day that had just gone. He was probably the only person in the world to experience such an event. Twenty-one hours ago, and not even a day, he was having breakfast with his family in Oyster Bay looking forward to an afternoon's golf, and now he was sleeping in a Fifth Avenue apartment with a beautiful woman in the next room, fifteen years in his future, how could something like that happen?

He woke up early as usual but felt as though he hadn't slept much at all, but the bed was so comfy though, he was just happy for the rest. He made himself a coffee and sat out on the balcony, as the sun was coming up, very low in the sky, and there was a freshness in the air again. At seven o'clock in the morning, there was lots of activity over in the park. He could see many people of all ages jogging on the Schuman running track that went all around Jacqueline Kennedy Onassis Reservoir for one and a half miles, and he longed to get out there himself. He had run around Central Park on many a lunch hour, so he knew how it felt to get out there filling the lungs with air, and the sense of feeling fit.

While sitting there, his thoughts turned again to Marie and the kids, where they were, what were they doing? He went through his Blackberry and came across the number for Jim Watts. Surely he would be in, he thought. He gave it a try.

Jim answered. "Hi, is that Jim?" Peter said nervously.

"Yes, Jim Watts speaking, who's that?" he said.

Jim's voice sounded the same as it always had, a pleasant, friendly, welcoming voice, full of the enjoyment of life. Mellow and calm, "Hey Jim, It's Peter here. Peter Collins," he said. "Been a long-time buddy?"

"Pete! No! Is that you, really?" he said, taking a deep breath and blowing it out at hearing his voice. "Can't be?" It sounded exactly like Pete though Jim thought.

"It is mate. How are you, Jim?"

"Never mind me, how have you been? I mean, where have you been?" he said excitedly. "You disappeared on us, Pete, how long is it now?"

"It's fifteen years, Jim. It's a long story. You won't believe it when I tell you about it, but I will tell you, Jim. We'll have to catch up for a beer or two at the club," Peter said, while not wanting to get into an explanation about his situation over the phone. "I just want to re-connect right now, Jim. So I was wondering if you had Marie's new number."

"Yes I do, of course, mate, I'll text it to you. Jesus Pete, I never thought we would be speaking like this again. We all thought you were dead," Jim said bluntly and to the point then paused for a second before speaking, as though he had something important to say, "You're going to be shocked with what I'm about to tell you Pete, are you sitting down?"

"Yes," Peter said.

"There are a few things you should know, Marie has re-married, four years ago now," Peter wondered how to answer it, he instantly felt sick and listened as he carried on, "She waited ten years. He is okay though, nice fella. We went to the wedding. A nice wedding as weddings go, Marie's doing alright Pete."

"I'm glad of that, Jim, I am really, you were always a good friend to us both," Peter said magnanimously.

"She's been through a lot, your Marie, after you disappeared. She kept it all going though, after everything that happened. You probably should know as well." He stopped himself suddenly mid-sentence.

"What Jim? What's up, you can tell me?" Peter said, begging for him to carry on.

"No, not this mate,"

"Is it about Tom and Jake." he said, trying to pry the words out of him.

"Marie can tell you when you see her. It's not for me to say. I've probably said too much already."

"What a bloody mess," Peter said, suddenly sounding disillusioned.

"You can say that again, mate."

"I'll call her Jim and probably meet her somewhere first."

"I can see her now. She will be shaking like a leaf," Jim surmised. "Let me know what happens, Pete."

"Okay, Jim. I will, and I'll see you soon for a catch-up at the club. I'll call you in a few days if that's okay."

"Okay, Pete, you take care of yourself," And he rang off.

The text message came through with Marie's number almost immediately. He worked out how to save it to contacts, and then sat looking, staring at the number on the Samsung for ages wondering what she would say, and what he should say. He imagined her on the other end of the phone, probably in her kitchen making breakfast for everyone in her new house without him. He looked over at Central Park, a bit dazed and a bit sad. He realised he was four years too late. Poor Marie, he thought, what must it have been like for her? He didn't blame her in the slightest. There would now be no lovely reunion, only heartache, and despair. He was not looking forward to it now, but it was something he would have to do and try and make things right between them, there was Ashley, Tom and Jake to think of now, they hadn't seen or heard from him throughout their formative years, but now they were adults he hoped they would understand. He prayed for the news that Tom and Jake were okay.

Heather had overheard him on the phone and came out to him onto the balcony. She thought seeing Marie now would be something he would probably want to do on his own. Lending him her car so he could sort all his problems out was a way of knowing he would be coming back, she thought, and probably to her. A little bit mercenary and perhaps a bit selfish as well, but there was a connection now, that she hadn't had with someone for a very long time, and didn't want to just let it slip away. She would help him get his life back on track, and help herself to a bit of happiness along the way, and there was nothing wrong with that, there was nothing wrong with that at all.

Chapter 10

Over at Langley, Jack Graham was going through the files on Peter, and thinking about the conversation he had had with Agent Lewis. It was odd, he thought, that the NSA was looking for someone in 2016 that had not been seen or heard of since 2001. It raised many questions. Having no sightings for fifteen years was odd, considering the amount of data that flowed through the CIA and NSA databases at any one time. He read through the FBI and Police reports from the disappearance in 2001. The metadata on the small snippet of video footage sent from the NSA confirmed the date, so there was no question about it, the NSA had someone that the CIA didn't know about.

He concluded he was probably a sleeper, his background was special forces, after all, he had all the credentials, but they would know and have records of all the sleeper agents, the NSA shared all that intel with them, so they had kept it from them for some reason. Jack relayed his concerns to April Haynes, the Deputy Director and went through everything with her sitting at his console with April standing over him. He brought the photos of Peter up from 2001 and 2016, onto the screen, side by side while April watched. He used special facial recognition software to date both images. It showed there was no difference in Peter at all, they were of the same age, and how could that be?

"So, what are your thoughts, agent Graham?" April said with the two photos of Peter on screen.

"Well, could he have been cryogenically frozen for fifteen years and then revived? It's a possibility that would make him the first of a kind, I suppose."

"I've never heard of it being done before with humans, not while they were alive."

"Where is he now?"

"They don't know. The NSA has asked us to help."

"Let me make a call, and we'll look at this again."

"Okay."

April contacted Senator James Groves at the White House. He was blunt, and to the point, he gave April the order to find Peter Collins at all costs and take him out.

April summoned Jack's team to the briefing room. They all sat there logged onto their tablet computers, interfacing with the mainframe. It felt like they were back at training camp awaiting a lecture. Apart from a few brief visits and watching interviews on CNN, many of the team had never met April Haines. She was a self-confessed ball buster that had made her name in the corridors and bedrooms of power. Every so often there would be a small scandal in the press, leaked documents, and lurid claims, all masterminded by her close allies. Then the political figure in question would get sidelined, disgraced or demoted, and she would slip into the void she had calculatedly created, moving relentlessly up the ladder, and there was now only one step to go.

April pointed at the screen and said. "Hello, everyone. On-screen, is a picture of Peter Collins, he is fifty-seven years of age, although he doesn't look it. He is ex-special forces and served in Iraq back in the nineties. His military career speaks for itself, Medal of Honour, Distinguished Service Cross, this man is a war hero, but he has now gone rogue," April explained. "We believe he is currently working for the NSA as a special operative. He was last seen leaving the NSA building on Essex Street, Lower Manhattan, yesterday. We need to find him, guys, as a matter of national security. Any questions so far."

Damien Hurst, one of Jack's best analysts, was the first to ask a question. "Excuse me, Miss Haines, for being pedantic, but you said *we believe*?"

"Yes, we don't know exactly the situation yet, we have made an educated guess based on what we know."

Jade was next. "What do we know of his background?"

"When he left the army, he had a security business, quite a big one, he disappeared and then nothing for fifteen years, not seen or heard of at all. So, we need to dig into his past, who is Peter Collins, what makes him tick; because that is how we will find him. Do you agree with that, Jack?"

"Yes, we want to get eyes on his family, friends, old work colleagues, his military buddies, anyone he had close connections with," Jack summarised. "He has been in the wind now for twenty-four hours, so we need to get digging. Unfortunately, a lot of the information we need will be before everything went digital, so we will have to search archives which would now be in PDF form."

"So, can we get straight onto it, leave everything you are doing at the moment and concentrate on this," April said closing. "Keep everyone in the loop as we unfold this guy's life."

The brief meeting ended, and the team went off to their workstations to start the search. Jack knew an undercover agent from Peter's unit that had served with him in Iraq, and worked for the CIA on individual assignments, he was currently in Belize on an assignment of Jack's. He gave him a call on a secure line.

"Jerry, how are you, Jack Graham here, how is it going over there?"

"Yeah, all wrapped up here Jack."

"Everything squared away nicely?" Jack inquired.

"Yes, the UDC will be in mourning for their deputy any time soon."

"Great, you are one of the best. There is something that has come up that requires your attention and special skills."

"Sounds intriguing," Jerry said. "Tell me more."

Jerry Martin had twenty-eight kills to his name. He prided himself that all his kills were either found to be of natural courses or caused by someone close to the victim, so the finger of suspicion never pointed directly at him, taking up to six months sometimes to pull off an assignment, planning every intricate detail, and he treated it as fine art. One day soon when he retired, he would write a book about his experiences he thought and hoped it would become the hitman's manual, the go-to read for the aspiring hitman. From his balcony of the Great House Inn, he could see the lights on the San Pedro Ferry lining its way up to its final destination. A celebration was in full swing on board with firecrackers echoing, it sounded like distant gunfire to the untrained ear, he wished he was onboard celebrating with them. His job was no fun at all, and he longed for company, to correspond with another human being without an ulterior motive and to be free.

"Remember an old army buddy of yours from Iraq, Peter Collins?"

"Yes, he saved my life once, I heard he disappeared before nine-eleven though. There was no trace of him. I still keep in touch sometimes with some of the unit guys."

"Well, he is alive and well, and in New York City somewhere."

"You're having me on, aren't you?"

"No, I'm not, he is now working for the NSA, on what, we don't know, but we want you to do what you are best at," Jack said. "This comes with the highest clearance, Jerry."

"Bloody hell, Peter Collins, eh," Jerry repeated. "Okay, send me the file and everything you have, I'll be at JFK in seven hours."

"Great, I'll log you onto it," Jack said. "This one is five hundred Jerry."

Jerry gulped some air, "You must want him bad," he said, slightly pleased and shocked at the same time, $500,000 would mean he could retire sooner than he thought.

"We do," Jack said. "Anything you need Jerry, okay?"

"Wire me two-fifty for now and the rest on completion," he said confidently.

"Done, thanks, Jerry."

Jerry packed away his meagre but essential belongings into a rucksack and made his way to the airport.

Chapter 11

Peter sat riveted to his seat outside the entrance to Marie's house overlooking Westhampton Beach, with the engine still running. Well-developed oak trees slightly obscured the view of her Colonial-style house, but he could tell it was expensive. He sat there not knowing what to do, should he go up and knock on the door? It was as though super glue had seeped in under his thighs and he couldn't move an inch. Questions ran through his mind in a flash. Two days ago, he was sitting having breakfast with her and the kids having fun, a joyful time, but that was his reality, not hers, and it didn't seem possible. The internal wranglings seem to get worse, not better. She hadn't seen or heard from him for fifteen years, and here he was, staring at the front door of her house.

The ninety-minute drive in Heather's Mercedes had helped him clear his mind of any negative thoughts, but they were now back with a vengeance, nervous, overthinking, and questioning himself. His whole body trembled with anxiety and anticipation.

The military had trained him for every event known to man, physically and psychologically as well, but now found himself at a crossroads. He had called her number three times already on the way over, but chickened out at the last minute and hung up, not knowing what to say.

The house was set back at an angle with a large courtyard in front, Five-Million-dollars at least, even at 2001 prices, he thought. He could never have afforded to buy Marie this type of property, and that made him feel all the more inadequate.

There was a calmness about the whole area, though. He looked over to his right and could see and hear the North Atlantic Ocean pounding the shoreline relentlessly, never giving in for a second, permeating a sweet smell of the ocean, a fragrance of salty air that he remembered as a child on visits with his dad to New Haven.

He hadn't thought about his dad in a while, and beautiful visions of happy times started to fill his subconscious. His dad had loved Tom, Jake, and Ashley, and it was like the icing on his life's cake when they came into their lives, taking them on little trips to the park, and short excursions to the seaside for the afternoon when they were little, it had made his life fulfilled and meaningful. A very fulfilling period of time he would take with him inevitably to the next world, where we all go eventually, He just went a little too soon.

The shimmering carpet of ocean rippled in the early morning sun, he could almost make out a few small ships sailing on the horizon, although when he thought about it, they could be large tankers taking their cargo to ports all around the world.

He had second thoughts and was about to drive away, and just when he wasn't expecting it, out of the corner of his eye, he noticed the large oak door to Marie's house open. He turned and saw a young woman walking out, she wore a cream fitted trouser suit, had shoulder-length auburn hair, and looked very professional he thought, *who was she*? He switched the engine off. He had a shiver of anticipation that started at the back of his neck and travelled down to the small of his back. She looked like she was in her twenties, he thought. Turning back for a moment, she said something to someone inside the house, which he couldn't quite make out, but as he listened to the voices, and especially the tone, they sounded so familiar to him.

She turned back again with her bag now over her shoulder, her hair flicked back, and walked over to a brand new blue metallic Porsche Carrera Turbo with the roof down. The sun was bright but not hot and lit up every part of her face and hair as she went to get into the car. She then paused for a moment looking directly over at him sitting there in the Mercedes parked at the end of the driveway. It was Ashley! His heart skipped a beat, he couldn't believe it, this beautiful young woman was Ashley, now driving and all grown up, and looking like a million dollars.

She stood there watching and looking over at him sitting in his car, then walked around to the back of the Porsche to get a better look. Peter got out, as he could see that she had noticed him, and walked around to the front of the Mercedes. They stood there, both looking at each other for what seemed like ages but was only a few brief seconds, both realising with everything welling up inside, they'd found each other again, after all this time. They walked tentatively towards each other.

Ashley whispered and mouthed, "Dad, is that you? Dad, is it really you?"

She moved forward slowly at first, but as soon as she heard the words out of her dads' mouth.

"Yes, Chicken."

It all got too much, she ran towards him at pace, and they met in the middle of the driveway like two cymbals, crashing together in a crescendo at the end of a symphony.

"Dad, it's you, isn't it? It's really you?" she said as they hugged each other tightly.

"Yes chicken, oh my darling," Peter said as the tears nestled themselves in the corner of his eyes. He looked up at the sky as if to say thank you for bringing my little girl back to me.

"I knew you weren't dead, I could still feel you, Dad. I told everyone you were still alive somewhere looking down on me, I told them, I did." she said excitedly kissing his neck with her cheek firmly pressed against his chest, and the tears streaming down onto his golf jersey.

"I never stopped thinking about you for a second Chicken, I didn't," Peter said, pulling back to admire her for a moment. "Look at you, all grown up. I can't believe it," he said, then hugged her again.

Marie came to the door on hearing the commotion outside and wondering what all the noise was about. As soon as she saw who it was hugging Ashley, she put her hand over her mouth in shock. The emotion tore through her body, and she nearly lost her balance.

"No!" she said, "It can't be." Peter and Ashley started walking towards the house arm in arm, as Marie stood there mesmerised, shaking her head as if she didn't believe what she was witnessing.

"Hello, Marie," Peter said calmly, with Ashley still holding on tight.

"Peter.... How...Why?" Words flew out randomly as she came to terms with the situation. "God, Peter," she said, and wrapped her arms around both of them and squeezed tight.

"You see, Mum, I told you he was still alive and would come back to us one day, didn't I?" Ashley said, knowingly.

"You did darling," Marie said concurring. "She never gave up on you, Peter, not for a second." She pulled away to get some perspective. "I guess there is only one thing I can ask at this point, Peter, isn't there?" Peter nodded in agreement. "Well, where? Where the hell have you been all these years, all these bloody years?" she said, sobbing the words out. "Why now? Why leave it this long?" she pleaded, looking for some reason or clue to hang on to as to where he'd been.

"Marie, it's an explanation you are not going to believe," Peter said.

"Probably not, after all this time, fifteen years Peter, fifteen years I don't know what to say, I'm speechless. Shall we go inside and have a cup of tea, I might have something stronger?" Marie said, wiping the tears from her eyes.

The crying abated to a snivel as they entered the house, with Ashley still holding onto his arm. Marie walked inside with Peter and Ashley behind.

"Wow! This is nice, Marie," Peter said, glancing around, and still holding onto Ashley.

"Where are the boys? Are they working?" he asked expectantly. He didn't receive an immediate answer. "They must be twenty-five now I think, and you must be twenty-eight darling," he said, looking at Ashley. He could see from the look on Marie's face there was something wrong when she looked at Ashley right after he asked the question. His heart sunk. They both went quiet for a second as they sat at the breakfast bar in the vast open plan kitchen area.

"They didn't make it," Marie said.

"What?"

"I'll put the kettle on, they didn't make it, Peter," Marie said emotionally, walking over to the sink.

"What do you mean, they didn't make it?" The confirmation he had hoped he would never get, was real.

Ashley said, "Nine-eleven, Dad. Remember? They went on that school trip with their class? The whole class never made it, Dad. Mrs Grey, the teacher as well. We don't know what floor they were on, there were only two out of their class that survived that day, and that was because they were sick and didn't go."

"Poor Tom, poor Jake," he said, shaking his head. "I had hoped it wasn't true, It was on the front of the paper yesterday, the commemorations. I knew they had gone but was hoping they hadn't." Hearing it though was another thing. It hit him hard, and the tears of joy turned into sadness, sitting there in the kitchen, he noticed a picture of the twins, age ten, that had hung in their kitchen back in Oyster Bay. He walked over and picked it up.

"That is how we remember them," Marie said. "That was their last school photo, they look great, don't they?" She handed Peter a mug of tea.

"Yes, that's how I remember them as well." But it was two days ago for me, only two days, he said to himself, staring at the picture in his hand, remembering them as they were just two days ago in the kitchen.

"Me and mum go to the memorial a lot, don't we, Mum?" Ashley commented. "It helps a lot, their names are engraved on it with all of their classmates, it's like you can imagine they are really there, it's very comforting isn't it, Mum?"

"Yes, darling, very," Marie agreed.

"I have heard of the Memorial. I read about it yesterday, I'll have to go and see it," he said.

"I'll take you, Dad," Ashley said, holding his hand.

"Thanks, Chicken." He squeezed her hand and looked at her with a reassuring smile.

"Why don't you know all this, Dad?" Ashley asked.

"Yes, Peter, why don't you know," Marie said. "Have you been away sick or something, and we didn't know?"

They sat down around the breakfast bar, close, as a family once again, taking their time, drinking their tea. Marie and Ashley listened as Peter told his story of how he came to be here all these years later. Peter knew that it would sound far-fetched to them, and would sound like something out of a sci-fi movie. No one in their right mind would believe it, but after fifteen years, coming back with a story like that about time travel, and with Marie knowing him the way he was, and sounding so earnest in what he said, they believed every word.

"You know what Peter?" Marie interrupted.

"What?" he replied, wondering what she was going to say.

"You are wearing the same golfing jersey as when you left that day for the office," Marie said with Ashley looking at Peter's jersey as well and agreeing. "It's the one I bought you for Christmas 2000, and it was the first time you wore it, I remember," she said, smiling at him with her thoughts wandering back to that day.

"I still have fifteen-year-old boxers on as well, and they haven't even been washed yet either," he said, raising a little bit of joviality among the sadness he felt.

"Err!" They said together, laughing at his joke.

They were all caught up in the moment, it felt like old times, then Marie said, "Ashley you wouldn't be a darling would you and leave your dad and me alone for a moment so we can have a chat?"

"Yeah, of course, you guys have got a lot to catch up about, I'll be in the den," she said agreeably and released her dad's hand, she walked off to another part of the opulent ground floor.

They both sat there for a moment, staring at each other deep in thought, wanting to say something, both thinking back to when they were happy together in the kitchen at their house in Oyster Bay, with the kids creating havoc.

"Another cup of tea, Peter," she said as she got off her stool to make it. Peter nodded in agreement. "You know Peter, there is something you have to know, I mean, I need to tell you?"

"I know Marie, you don't have to explain," he said, taking the awkward conversation away, and making it easy for her.

"Yes, I think I do Peter, I have moved on with my life, I had to," she said, expecting him to be shocked and disappointed.

"I spoke to Jim this morning, he told me."

"Oh! Right," she paused. "He's a lovely man, he was so supportive to me throughout the whole thing, he is one of my favourite people. Did he tell you—"

"Only that you're-married," he interrupted.

"Oh, okay."

"And that he was a nice bloke," he added.

"Yes, he is. I'm sorry I didn't wait," Marie said with an air of regret in her voice.

"Marie, you had to move on, I would have, there is nothing to be sorry for nothing whatsoever," he said as they sat there, with emotions welling up inside like a volcano waiting to erupt at any moment. "I cannot believe what it must have been like for you, with me gone and then the boys missing, it must have been hell for you. I'm just sorry I went to work that day, maybe things would have been different."

"You know they questioned me for months. I had no explanation for them. One time they asked if I had paid a hitman," she said.

"Why would they say that?"

"They went through our bank accounts, and there was a large cash withdrawal, thirty thousand dollars. They thought it was that, you know, blood money. I had to get Jack your builder to say on oath what it was for."

"That was for the summerhouse, wasn't it?" Peter said, smiling, remembering. "Yeah, nice summer house that, never got to use it much. There is one question I have. How could you get married when you were still married to me?"

"We had to have you declared legally dead."

"Really?"

"Yeah, it wasn't very nice, but I had to move on," she said. "Don't know how that is going to pan out, now that you are alive. Sorry that sounded crap, didn't it?"

"Marie, I know what you mean."

They spoke for ages about the good times with all the kids, the fun times they all had on holidays and Christmas, it was almost like they had never been apart. Then a car pulled up on the driveway outside and came to a gravelly stop.

"Oh, I think that's David now, you'll get to meet him after all," she said excitedly.

"Great, that will be nice," he said sarcastically. "What is it, David…?" he said, trying to get his thoughts into the right place in his brain.

"Reece, David Reece, he's the Deputy Chief Commissioner of the NYPD," she said proudly, as she walked over to the door to open it for him before he got there.

Chapter 12

As he sat in Marie's opulent kitchen sipping tea gazing around the room, it felt like he was on a set in the 'houses of the rich and famous,' he thought. There were brand new gleaming appliances with marble floors and tasteful large paintings by semi-famous artists adorning most walls. As he sat there, he had the stark realisation that he didn't own anything, nothing at all, and all he had to his name were the clothes he had on and the few meagre dollars in his pocket.

In little over twenty-four hours, he had lost Marie, Tom, and Jake, and was now watching as the love of his life walked over to the front door to let in David Reece, a person he didn't know but instantly disliked. A person that in his mind, now had everything that was rightfully his, and would be spending the rest of his life with Marie and Ashley, a place that should have been for him. This man he didn't know, had stepped into his shoes, and there was nothing he could do about it.

David Reece was the Deputy Chief Commissioner of the New York City Police Department. He had been a policeman since he was eighteen years old, working his way through the ranks, until now at the age of fifty-three, was being groomed for the role of Chief Commissioner, a more political role than policing. He had been involved in many high-profile cases throughout his career, catapulting him to the top job, and that came with all the usual perks.

He walked in, all policeman-like, placing his briefcase and overnight bag by the door, and kissed Marie on the lips, not a good start, Peter thought, and he had to look away. His smart pinstripe suit was slightly too small and looked uncomfortable. He was at least seventy pounds heavier than Peter, and the buttons on his trousers were under a lot of tension, with his stomach hanging over his belt by at least five inches. Peter concluded that his portly demeanour was probably due to too many police commissioner lunches, and less actual police work, it's fair to say, Peter didn't like him at all.

"How did the trip go darling?" Marie asked, rather formally.

"You know how these events go, they start out fine, then roll on into the small hours," David said, looking over at Peter sitting at his kitchen breakfast bar.

"Darling we have a visitor I want you to meet?" she said nervously, as she pulled away from the sickly loving embrace that looked slightly stage-managed, it was like it was something that she should do, rather than wanted to do, and then walked over to do the introductions. "Peter, this is David Reece. Peter is my ex-husband," Marie commented, looking at David, presenting him as though it was a formal introduction at a dinner engagement. David had a weird look on his face looking down his nose as though Peter had invaded his space, there was no welcoming smile either.

"Peter, hi," David said as he held out his hand. "You're the one that did the disappearing act all those years ago, aren't you?"

"The very one, hi," he said.

David's overly firm handshake was a macho thing, Peter thought, a way of stamping his authority on the conversation, that he was the top dog around here. Probably it was something they were taught in the police force while training how to become a policemen type. Peter responded with a matching grip and smiled back through gritted teeth.

"You know, I ran the team investigating your disappearance," David said proudly. "What is it now? Fifteen years ago, is it?" He knew the answer but was just dam well showing off, bigging himself up.

"Yes, something like that," Peter quipped.

"Why now then. Why did you come back now? And get in touch, after all these years?" he asked, pointedly. Peter instantly felt he was an inconvenience, a problem that needed solving, and sensed a slightly hostile tone to his voice. David saw him like a dog urinating on his patch, or like something smelly, stuck to the bottom of his shoe.

"Well, David. I came as soon as I possibly could," Peter said, giving his question the same amount of credence as it deserved.

"Darling, Ashley and I were filling Peter in on Tom and Jake," Marie said, giving him a summary of the conversation so far, as a good secretary would do.

"Nasty business nine-eleven, sorry about that," David gestured, indicating a small amount of sympathy. At least he had some humanity and feelings, Peter thought.

"Peter was telling us what had happened to him as well, it's fascinating," Marie interjected, wanting to move the conversation on as quickly as possible, and escape the elephant in the room.

"Well, I'd like to hear about that?" David said, and now with his policeman's hat on. "So where have—?"

"What is it you do?" Peter interrupted before David could get the inevitable question out.

"I work for the NYPD," he replied proudly.

"A cop?"

"Well, a Deputy Chief cop actually, just a bit less cop but more paperwork," he said again verbally patting himself on the back with every boast. "Yes, I've been there man and boy, and—." Suddenly his thought process was interrupted mid-sentence.

Ashley came back into the room from the den on hearing all the chatter, making a beeline for her dad, and held onto his arm as if never wanting to let him go again. David had a look on his face that said it all. Ashley would never feel that way about him, as she did for her dad, that was inevitable, and David didn't like it. Not in his house, not on his patch.

"Met my dad then David? Told you he was still alive," she said, smiling joyously.

She had the happiest look about her, David had not seen her as happy as that for a long while. "Yes, Chicken, you did," David replied. Ashley cringed inside, Marie felt awkward.

"Jesus," Peter said under his breath.

David said, "What?" Overhearing his comment. Peter looked away.

Chicken! Chicken! Peter screamed inside, he's now calling my daughter the pet name that I have always called her. A very awkward feeling emerged in the room, they all felt it, an awkwardness had reared its head, and it was probably inevitable with the emotionally charged atmosphere. Peter willed himself to get up and make an excuse to leave, and any excuse would do, even though he had only spent a little over an hour with them after fifteen years. Five minutes with David was enough.

"Look I have to go I'm afraid, I have a hundred and one things to sort out as you can imagine," Peter said. He stood up hesitantly but didn't shake David's hand again. "Great to meet you," Peter said to David resentfully, sidling towards the door with Ashley holding onto his arm.

"Likewise," David replied, with an air of reluctance, and then said, "you know there is still an open case on you. Maybe you could pop down the station sometime soon, and we can clear it up."

"Yeah, I'll do that," Peter said, edging his way to the door.

"What, tomorrow, okay then? No time like the present," he said with persistence.

"Yes, fine, see you then," Peter said, agreeing with anything to get out of there. The awkwardness hung around like an unwanted friend, everyone felt it.

"Where are you staying?" David asked pointedly with an upward inflextion to his voice, and in a tone that only a police officer would ask a suspect involved in a crime.

Peter thought for a moment. There could be consequences revealing his friendship with Heather, he thought, so he kept it short and to the point. "With a friend," he said.

"Who's that?" David asked.

"No one you would know."

"Try me, I know a lot of people?"

"You probably do."

"So, who then? Who's the friend?" David asked again in the same manner.

The questions from him seemed to get more pointed and direct, rather than friendly.

"No one you would know," Peter repeated more firmly and sternly. The pair were at an impasse with no one backing down.

"Darling it sounds like you are interrogating him, and he's only just got here," Marie said laughing, to put an end to the deadlock and in doing so putting a halt to his line of questioning.

"That's okay Marie," Peter replied, standing his ground. "See you at the station tomorrow, then we can get all this sorted and put to bed," he said. Peter was now in control, mentally.

Ashley still had hold of his hand as they reached the front door, he turned to her. "I'll see you soon, darling, shall I?" he asked her in a normal voice, and not trying to compete for the right to call his daughter chicken, which would have sounded silly and juvenile anyway.

"Dad, why don't we go and see Tom and Jake tomorrow, at the memorial, I can meet you there if you like, we can meet at Johnson's café nearby. If you aren't doing anything that is?" she asked, fluttering her eyes.

She wanted to spend some time with her dad, and it made him feel so good inside after all the disappointment and heartache, so how could he refuse, she had a wonderful way with her that was so grown up.

"I would love that Ashley, thank you, that sounds great, I'll call you in the morning to make a plan," he said, excited but sad at the same time, glancing for a second at the picture of the twins on the kitchen table where he had been sitting. He left the house gesturing with a low wave of the hand to David, rather than say anything. He kissed and hugged Ashley, and said goodbye for now. Marie was by his side and acting like the perfect hostess showing him out. David stood, watching and studying him like he was already on trial for murder.

David had many questions he wanted to ask, but that would have to wait for the station he thought. Marie followed Peter out to the Mercedes at the end of the drive so that they could chat privately without the pressure of David bearing down on them. The sun was now high in the sky, and the heat reached seventy-five at least, the top of his head and shoulders felt hot as they walked away from the house over to his car. He had a feeling of déjà vu of happier days walking around Oyster Bay with Marie hand in hand, and the kids playing up ahead. He was now alone with Marie for a moment or two, but there would be no physical contact, no hand in hand, he knew that as prying eyes from the house would be watching.

"He's okay Peter you know, he's been good to us, me and Ashley, he's a nice man really, once you get to know him," she explained in a way, justifying her decision to move on.

"I know Marie, there are a lot of things I am going to have to get used to, I know that, and one of them is David Reece, I do realise that you know," he said looking over at the house, and Ashley still waving frantically at him, "Ashley is great isn't she, you've done her proud Marie you really have," Peter said looking and waving back at her.

"Thanks, she's turned out great that one," she replied, looking over at her as well, and smiling with pride. "At least we have accomplished something together, haven't we?" she said to Peter, who was nodding in agreement. Then out of concern for him on a personal level, she asked, "what are you doing for money, Peter?"

"I hadn't thought about it. I haven't got any if that's what you mean?" he said, laughing at the predicament in which he now found himself. "My cards are all stopped, and I guess my bank accounts would have closed down now as well. I've got a few dollars that's all, nothing much really."

Marie then produced a JP Morgan credit card and cash from her pocket and gave it to him.

"Have this card, Peter, get what you need, twenty-thousand dollars is on there if you need it, and here is a thousand dollars, that's all the cash I have on me, I'll get some more for you tomorrow," she said, passing him the cash, caring for him again, and it felt good, it felt really good. "Everything else we will have to work out as we go, what do you think?"

"That's very thoughtful of you Marie, thanks, I appreciate it," he said gratefully, looking down at the card and cash in his hand. "You were always very thoughtful, weren't you, always putting everyone before yourself." Peter paused for a second in thought, thinking of Oyster Bay, and the moment he said goodbye to her, never thinking for a moment, he would ever lose her. "It's great to see you, Marie. I never stopped thinking about you, not for a second, you know. It just feels like the rug has been pulled out from under my feet in a matter of a few days, a little more than twenty-four hours, it's a very bizarre feeling, coming to terms with all of this so quickly."

"It must be Peter, I can't imagine," she said sympathetically. "You're strong though, Peter, you always were."

"And Tom and Jake," he said, looking at the floor to hide the tears that began to percolate through the corners of his eyes again. "How do I reconcile that, losing my two boys, our two boys, we only saw them walk off to school yesterday morning. It's incredibly hard. If I could just get back there, if I could just get back there it would all be okay, wouldn't it? We would have our life back together."

"Nice thought, Peter," She said, thinking the same thing. "It was a long time ago for me now. Another world, another life."

"Yes, another world for me too, to get used to," he said, resigning himself to his reality. "Well, I suppose I had better get going. I'll see you soon, I guess?"

"Let's meet for lunch after you've been to the memorial with Ashley?" Marie said.

"Sounds like a plan."

As he drove back to Manhattan, he thought it was very thoughtful of her to make sure he was okay. He wondered if she was as happy as she made out, it didn't seem like it, was it just an act? Or was she making the best of a bad situation? David seemed okay really, he thought, straight out of a Policeman's manual, institutionalised. They were different from average working people, Policemen, they were the law, and they knew it, and they probably felt superior to everyone else in their own little way. That was, perhaps why they acted the way they did.

He suddenly had a thought, as he was not far at all from the golf club, he would call Jim Watts to see if he was around to catch up and have a few welcome beers with an old mate before heading back to Fifth Avenue.

Jim was happy he had called, and they agreed to meet in an hour.

Chapter 13

Nestled by the shore of Little Neck Bay, the Bayside Park golf and country club had flourished since 1955, taking advantage of the emerging popularity for the game. As Peter pulled into the parking lot, the trees he noticed were taller and more mature. The oak-beamed clubhouse looked more vibrant, the wood had taken a few more coats of varnish over the years turning the wood a darker shade. He had enjoyed his weekly game of golf, it was a sort of guilty pleasure, getting away from the office for five hours with his mates, and was a great way to relax and enjoy the fruits of his success. But that was long ago, everything was different now, and he longed to be back there to recapture the feeling.

He sat in the Mercedes as he waited for Jim to arrive, staring at the front of the clubhouse, the emotion of the past two hours came flooding back. Marie, Ashley, Tom, and Jake, how could it have come to this? Where was his life now going? He had no home, no business, no security. He was strong, he told himself, still only forty-two years old, even though his birth certificate would tell a different story. He would have to get back into the business, build it up again, get back into living. Ashley now was the most significant driving force, and he would do it for her, get back on the horse, what had happened, had happened, he would have to live with it and not give up.

He was looking forward to meeting with Jim though, to have a drink with him and explain why he didn't make it to golf that day fifteen years ago. He got out of the Mercedes, wiped his eyes, took a deep breath, and walked over to the clubhouse. It felt like he hadn't been here for a very long time, but the reality was, he had played here only last week. It was a weird feeling to come to terms with, and he was still wearing the club polo shirt.

In the foyer, he gazed at the names of past players' achievements on the boards for different competitions, each gaining one name every year. He was listed a few times in the late nineties and three times in 2001. He didn't feel nostalgic as it had only been a few weeks since his last win at the club's Bayside handicap trophy match, the cup he had won was in his kitchen in Oyster Bay he remembered. But not now, Marie must have given it back to the club. He walked into the bar area and was surprised that it hadn't changed at all, still the same colour walls with the same pictures of past players holding trophies, although there were a few new ones. It brought back fun memories of drinks and meals with the guys, swapping stories of the squad days in Iraq, having too many beers and leaving the car to pick up the next day. A barman recognised him and came over to serve him and say a few words.

"Peter Collins as I live and breathe, how are you?" he said excitedly, shaking Peter's hand warmly and vigorously.

"Yes, I'm okay thanks, Gary. Are you?" he replied.

Gary was thick-set, five feet nine inches tall, and with massive shoulders from playing American football in his youth. His hair was almost non-existent now, only on the sides and the back, leaving him an egg-like shiny head. A welcome face, Peter thought. It was nice to meet him. He felt like he was a human being again for a moment, and having someone who knew him made him feel less insignificant.

"Where have you been, we haven't seen you for ages?" he said inquisitively.

"I've been away, just got back yesterday. I'm meeting Jim here," Peter said, glossing over the facts and not wanting to get into a lengthy explanation.

"It's funny seeing you today," he said curiously.

"Why do you say that, Gary?" he replied, wondering about the tone of his voice.

"Two guys were in here earlier looking for you, showed me a picture of you," he elaborated. "They wore suits and ties, real government types, know what I mean. I told them I hadn't seen you for years. You had that same shirt on in the picture as well," he said nodding in the direction of the shirt he was wearing.

"What did they want, did they say?"

"They didn't show me ID, but they were definitely the government alright. They said you were a person of interest, what have you been up to?"

"Nothing at all. Government, really?" he remarked curiously. Why would someone be looking for him? he wondered. "That's interesting, Gary."

"Did they leave a number for you to call if you saw me?"

"No, I thought that was strange," Gary said. "I asked if they wanted to leave one, but they said no. Then studied the name boards on the way out for a few minutes, made a few notes, then left."

"Really? I wonder what they were after?" he said.

He thought that it was probably something to do with David, maybe they were Police, but he had done nothing wrong, he wasn't a fugitive from justice or anything like that. He ordered a bottle of Coors Light, then sat down looking at his Samsung, trying to make sense of the applications. He texts Heather to let her know he was okay and was having a few beers with Jim, miraculously she texts back, moments later, okay, with a kiss that made him smile.

There were a few four balls in the bar having lunch after playing around, and talking about their golf exploits on the course, and he wished he could get out and hit a few himself. He made a mental note to arrange golf with Jim when he arrived. He was halfway through the second bottle of Coors when he decided to call Jim to see where he was. There was no answer, and the call went straight into voicemail, same with the call twenty minutes later. He didn't want the third bottle. So, he was left disappointed that he hadn't met Jim at all. As he walked out, he asked Gary to let Jim know that he was here for an hour and a half. Peter called him again in the parking lot. It was so unlike Jim. He was always the one pushing to meet up, always there, always on good form, and always on time.

Maybe he had had a family issue, and had to sort something out, it happens occasionally, Peter thought. He would call him again tomorrow and rearrange, not a problem, he had all the time in the world.

The Manhattan streets were busy as usual as he drove the Mercedes into Heather's underground garage.

"So how did it go?" Heather asked.

"Not so good to be honest," he replied. "Tom and Jake never made it, they never came back. All their class never made it either."

"Oh, Peter, I'm so sorry."

"It's a strange feeling, but I just can't believe they are gone," Peter said. "It doesn't feel like they are gone, to me. You know what I mean."

"I can't say I do, the biggest loss anyone will ever feel is for their children. When someone gets old and dies, you feel sad, but it passes. You never get over the loss of a child, parents aren't supposed to outlive their children."

"I know Heather, but this doesn't seem real."

"How was Marie?"

"Married."

"Really?"

"Yes, to David Reece, the Deputy Chief Commissioner of the NYPD."

"I've heard of him."

"I saw Ashley as well."

"What is she like?"

"She's great, she is so intelligent and an awesome person to be around, and all grown up now."

"I would like to meet her one day."

"That would be great, you would like her, you would like her a lot."

Heather had done something special for him that evening. She had arranged for a Michelin star chef to come around and cook for them. A brilliant chef called Miguel Romano, at twelve thousand dollars a time, it was a meal with everything, a real treat. He brought the pristinely ironed tablecloths, porcelain crockery, silver cutlery, silver napkin rings, and an orchid centrepiece for the table, the attention to detail was exquisite, and it was the perfect setting with the perfect hostess. They sat out on the balcony listening to La Boheme in the background, with the stars shining brightly overhead. To start, Scampi cooked with an extract of green olives, and Piennolo tomatoes from Vesuvio. For main, a Suckling pig served with pickled vegetables and Villa Manodori Balsamic Vinegar. To finish, a Coffee Panna Cotta with fresh cream. All washed down nicely with a few bottles of vintage Tocai Friulano.

"This is just out of this world," Peter said.

"I knew you would love it," Heather said. "Miguel is a friend of mine, we've been friends for ages, haven't we Miguel? Somos amigos desde hace mucho tiempo. *No hemos sido,* Miguel?"

"*Sí, hemos sido buenos amigos por años,*" Miguel said.

"See I told you, didn't I?" Heather smirked, Miguel didn't speak a word of English.

"I see, you speak Spanish as well do you?"

"It's one of my attributes," she boasted girlishly. "One of my many attributes."

"Well, I'll look forward to seeing all of those then," he said, pushing the boundaries a little bit.

He didn't tell her that the government or Police were now looking for him, he didn't want to worry her. They spoke about anything and everything while listening to favourite music well into the small hours. It had been a very challenging day, and he wondered what challenges would throw up his way tomorrow.

Chapter 14

Wednesday, September 7, 2016

Peter stirred his cappuccino slowly in a figure of eight while glancing over the front page of the New York Times. The headlines were all about the up and coming nine-eleven commemorations, where three thousand people perished, and thousands were wounded. There were four planes, two flew into the north and south towers of the World Trade Center, one flew into the Pentagon and one targeted Washington DC, but missed its target altogether and landed in a field near Shanksville, Pennsylvania. Reading intently, he sat there, taking in all the facts again about the disaster, logging the times in his head. It read, 'It was an event that shook the foundations of society, and changed everyone's perceptions of life in the process.'

He lifted his gaze from the newspaper and looked out through Johnson's café window, over at the memorial, an iconic view surrounded by tall skyscrapers and the new One World Trade Center. He thought about Tom and Jake at rest there, both footprints of the towers surrounded by neatly groomed oak trees. It didn't seem real, it was more surreal, or that it could have happened at all, and now he was wrapped up in it, and the never-ending pain of losing close loved ones. But it was a reminder of that day for everyone, that awful day when they took Tom and Jake from them, and he couldn't get it out of his head. He wasn't there. If only he had been there to comfort them, to tell them things would be okay. He hoped they didn't suffer too much, but he couldn't be sure.

For a moment, he imagined what it must have been like on the ninetieth floor of the North Tower, like some of the victims written about in the New York Times. Stuck there, with fire all around, searing heat, and no way out apart from through an open window with a drop of a thousand feet, and the two stark choices, either stay and burn to death, or jump, which one would he choose, Peter thought? He would definitely jump, he really would, burning to death would be far too horrible.

Just as he was imagining all the horror and the devastation, he caught sight of Ashley's smiling happy face, waving frantically at him as she walked across the road towards the café. She snapped him out of it, and immediately dashed all of his gloomy thoughts, and perked up his whole being. She was wearing a white chiffon scarf and a long beige silk cardigan, a perfect outfit for a warm but breezy day, very smart and very expensive. *She looks like a millionairesses daughter,* Peter said to himself proudly. She opened the door and beamed a smile at him as she walked into the café.

"Hey Dad, you okay? Been here long?" she said excitedly.

"Hello Chicken, yes I'm good thanks. Since about nine-thirty, that's all," he replied. "You look, fabulous darling," he said, getting up to give her a hug and a kiss.

"Thanks, Dad, ready to see Tom and Jake then?" she said eagerly, anxious for him to experience it for himself.

"Yes, I have been reading about it all in the paper. I never thought something like this could have ever happened. It is almost too much to take in, the enormity of it all, it's mind-boggling."

"I was only thirteen, don't forget, but it was pretty intense I can tell you, Dad," she said. "It was doubly sad for us because you had not been found yet either. I will always remember that day as long as I live, Mum saying that things could not be worse, and then the planes hit the towers, and knowing Tom and Jake were there was one of the worst feelings ever."

"I'm sorry I wasn't there for you all, Chicken," he said sadly, as he thought about what she had just said.

"Anyway you're here now Dad, that's all that counts. Shall we go and see them?"

"Lead on," Peter said, opening the door for her.

They left the café and walked together hand in hand over to the twin Memorial pools.

He was spending time with his little girl, and they were doing something special together, and it felt good, if only Tom and Jake were here, that would have been perfect. Peter couldn't put his finger on it, but a feeling came over him. 'Sorry I wasn't there.' He wasn't there, because he was here, wasn't he? He said to himself. 'Sorry I wasn't there,' the question came back into his head again.

"There is something very soothing about hearing the running water, don't you think Chicken?" Peter said.

"Yeah, whoever came up with this idea, is a genius."

The water cascaded down the four sides of the pools and created a beautiful noise. Water had a healing and calming effect, and when the fine spray glistened in the sun, it made a mini rainbow. New York had already started its preparations to mark the event, by putting up stars and stripes bunting and commemoration signs, there were also notices that President Obama would be making a speech there at six o'clock, and his picture was on every lamppost. Ashley held his hand tight, pulling him like a child would, wanting to show their parents something interesting that they had found. Her excitement was infectious, and although it was sad, it was also very moving.

"Here they are, Dad, see?" she said. "Tom Peter Collins, Jake Jenson Collins. What do you think?" she said, smiling at him looking for a reaction as they reached the corner of the North Tower void.

Seeing their names with all the other thousands of victims engraved into the bronze parapet made it all the more real, they were part of something, a part of history. The hair pricked up on the back of his neck, he shivered and felt horripilation on his forearms as goosebumps appeared.

"When someone looks at this in a hundred years," Peter said. "Tom and Jake will still be here." And that soothed the sadness that he felt moving up through his body, right up to his tear ducts. He barely could get his words out. "Well, there they are," Peter said, rubbing his fingers slowly across Tom's name, and then Jake's, feeling them, imagining them as human beings, his little boys. He wiped his eyes with a tissue. "Even poor Mrs Grey is there, look. Unbelievable, isn't it? I'm sorry I wasn't there, Chicken," he said again, as the tears flowed down his face.

"You okay Dad?"

"Yes, I am Ashley, I am really."

"Two thousand, nine hundred, and ninety-nine people died that day, Dad, it's the worst thing I have ever seen," Ashley said, rubbing their names as well. "Mum and I come here with a picnic sometimes and have lunch. It helps us a lot even now."

"I know what you mean Chicken, all their friends are here as well, look," Peter touched their names too. "Michael and David Roth, we met their parents, your mum and me, only last week at school, oh! I meant back in 2001, I mean."

"I know Dad," she said, clinging onto him.

"They must have gone through hell, losing all their kids like that. Just like your mum," he said somberly and thoughtfully. "At least mum had you Chicken."

Ashley said, "Yeah, we had each other, it took a long time to get over it, even now it's still so clear as though it was only yesterday."

Peter pondered for a moment, thinking out loud, "I remember us sitting in the kitchen in Oyster Bay talking about it, it was going to be a trip they would enjoy and look forward to, not a trip of a lifetime but a good one. Who knew then it would turn out like this, Tom and Jake becoming a part of a memorial to the biggest disaster in history?"

"No one knew, it's now something to remember. The museum is awesome as well, Dad. Shall we go see it?"

"Yes, I would love to darling," Peter said as his mind wandered.

"Are you okay, Dad?"

"What?"

"Are you okay? You are miles away."

"Just thinking Chicken, you know about all this, Tom and Jake, just trying to make sense of it that's all." He quickly tucked the thoughts away in his head for later and stayed in the present with Ashley. "I'm okay, I am really."

"There is a photo wall as well we can see if you want, Tom and Jake are there too."

"Of course, I want to, let's go."

They walked into the museum, going down to the bedrock of the city, seven stories down. The open space was incredible, Peter thought. The powerful words emblazoned on the main wall, 'NO DAY SHALL ERASE YOU FROM THE MEMORY OF TIME.' The statement struck a chord with Peter, he thought it was one of those statements that once seen, you would remember all your life.

The picture wall was even more emotional when seen for the first time. Tom and Jake's photo with all his classmates were there in a section surrounded by thousands of other names and faces. Faces that other parents would come and see and feel the same way as he did. There were bits of twisted metal and artefacts dotted about remembering that day. Digital displays gave a blow-by-blow account of what happened, where, when, and at what time. Peter looked momentarily at some video footage of when the first plane hit the North Tower. There was a burnt-out Ambulance, a crushed fire engine, bits of safety equipment all there on that day to help the people caught up in it, but as it turned out, futile and unstoppable. The main reason why it happened and the religious reasoning behind it was lost here and not even thought about at all. 'The museum was a monument that stood as a beacon to democracy and freedom.' He read.

Ashley held onto her dad's hand as he took it all in. Then Ashley said, "I've arranged to meet mum for lunch at Gerrard's at midday. I hope you don't mind? Will you come, Dad?" she said, realising her dad's dilemma. "Please come, she wants you too?"

"Yes, that would be nice, Chicken. I'd love to come. Mum's already asked me anyway."

"You know I thought she had, she just never told me that's all, ha!"

It was great spending time with Ashley, he thought, he couldn't get enough of it, she was a refreshing bundle of energy. He had missed out on all her teenage years, but he felt happy that she was here with him. He was also glad to be meeting Marie as he had things to tell her. Things like, he still loved her, no matter what had happened, and that he would always love her, and the family was the only thing that mattered to him now.

He would make things right, be there for them when they needed him. He didn't know how he was going to do it, but would go back into business again, he thought. It was what he knew best, and he could start small this time, after all, he was going to have to do something, get back into society and re-connect with everyone.

As they came out of the museum and onto the main concourse, Peter noticed a man leaning on one of the oak trees watching them out of the corner of his eyes, at least he thought he was watching them. Then he quickly turned away once he realised that Peter had made him. What an amateur, Peter thought, under a black woollen hat was a concealed wire, Peter could see it as he touched his ear, the man was talking to someone through a concealed microphone somewhere on his body. He looked completely out of place, if only for wearing a woollen hat and a heavy scruffy grey Crombie on such a warm day. His experience in covert surveillance came back to him in an instant as he quickly scanned the concourse for an accomplice, there had to be a second person somewhere. And there he was, to his left, long-haired, scruffy, sitting on a bench, pretending to eat something out of a plastic container like a tramp. Observing him properly, he wasn't a tramp at all. It takes more than just tramps clothes to be a tramp. What about dirty fingers and ingrained filth? He had none of that, the long straggly hair hid the wire, he was pretending to listen to music. Peter carried on walking away from the museum with Ashley by his side, hand in hand, they wouldn't make a move on him at all with her there, he thought. He looked around to see if they were following but lost sight of them as they disappeared into the crowds.

Peter was now aware he was on someone's radar, first the government types asking about him at the golf club, and now this, he would have to keep his wits about him from now on, and not take anything for granted.

"You okay Dad? Is something wrong?" Ashley asked, noticing the concerned look on his face as he looked around cautiously.

"No, it's okay darling, just thought I saw someone, that's all," he replied, being a bit cagey. Was it something to do with David? He would meet with him later, find out what he was about, and make his mind up then. He put it out of his mind and enjoyed a few precious hours with his daughter. "Let's go see your Mum, shall we?" he said positively.

Chapter 15

Gerrard's was a trendy burger joint franchise, just off Liberty Street, a short walk from the nine-eleven monument. This brand of restaurant had sprung up all over America in the previous five years, serving a twist on the traditional burger with a mix of lamb or beef, but with a unique *'reggae-reggae sauce'* from the United Kingdom, and everyone was raving about it. The ambience was upmarket with low lighting and dark oak furniture, well-lit stencilled glass panels, and flowers at every alcove gave it a touch of class. Burgers were twenty-five dollars, and dearer than anywhere else, which seemed to attract even more customers as people opted for quality and uniqueness. In reality, it was the same as every other restaurant-quality burger, but with the famous *reggae sauce*. In every restaurant, there was a shop where you could buy Gerrard's merchandise to become an advertisement for the franchise, a concept stolen from the Hard Rock Cafe.

Marie was sitting at the table looking at her phone when Peter and Ashley walked in. She looked beautiful, Peter thought, and it gave him goosebumps seeing her again, a little bit older now, but just as attractive, just as classy, just as serene. The sun shone through the window onto her hair, and it enhanced the features of her face. The features he fell in love with all those years ago. His heart melted, his eyes fixated on the necklace that Marie was wearing, she wasn't wearing it yesterday, and that said volumes. He had bought it for her forty-second birthday, and I bet she was wearing it for him, he thought, he hoped, it was just like Marie, always thoughtful, always thinking of other people before herself.

"What you looking at?" Peter said as he approached the table. She turned to him immediately and smiled, in a way that she used too, it was only for a split second, but he noticed it.

"Just updating my Facebook profile," she said. She then put her phone face down on the table beside her.

"What's that?" he said.

"Hi Mum," Ashley said, as she sat beside her and kissed her on the cheek. "Social Media Dad, everyone's got one, see? That's my profile page," she said, showing him her phone. There was a picture of all the family from a holiday they had gone on in July 2000, and it was a favourite of his.

"Nice picture, Chicken," he said. "Social Media, eh! How things have changed, they're like mini-computers these phones today, aren't they? I've noticed a lot of people looking at them as they walk," he said, tapping the screen randomly.

Marie smiled at him, sympathetically, "so how was it?"

"Unbelievable," he replied. "Sad, very sad, but just as this one said." He patted Ashley's hand. "It helps immensely, such an emotionally calm place to remember them. I cannot come to terms with their names being there. I only saw them off to school the other day. It has all happened so fast, I'm still waiting for my brain to catch up, but you are both right, it helps, it helps a lot."

"I think dad's going to be okay Mum, aren't you, Dad?" she said, holding her dad's hand, looking and smiling at him.

They ordered food, ate and sat talking about old times and spending time together in each other's company, as they had done fifteen years ago. Peter felt comfortable for the first time since arriving in 2016. He had a feeling of belonging. They were a family again, almost, and cared for each other, even though now there was a complication. Ashley left the table to go to the bathroom.

"Well," Marie said.

"I know."

"It's so good to see you, Peter, it's amazing."

"But."

"But what."

"The big, but!"

"David."

"Yes."

"I can't help that."

"I know Marie, I want to say that I'm sorry," Peter said earnestly. "I'm sorry I disappeared out of your life, out of everyone's life. I couldn't help it, I had no choice in the matter. Don't forget, for me, it was only three days ago, we were sitting in our kitchen at Oyster Bay. You were making eggs, I was doing the crossword, very happy times, remember?"

"That's the last time I was happy, truly happy," Marie said. "I remember ever since then, we've had this black cloud hanging over us—me. And then you turn up."

"I know Marie, I know."

"And then you turn up, after fifteen years. How could our lives turn out any different? I kept hoping after nine-eleven, and while grieving for the twins, you might be found, and turn up one day. But that day never happened, one month turned into another month, one year turned into another, and I just lost hope, I gave up on ever seeing you again," Marie said with her eye's filling up.

"I know Marie, I will be here for you now if you need me."

"What are your plans, Peter?" Marie asked.

"Don't know yet, still finding my feet, to be honest," he replied.

"It's going to take some time."

"I'm going to go and see Jen. I think she would like that, she was a bit shocked. I think to hear my voice after so long. Also, with Lawrence passing away, I feel I should?"

"I went to the funeral, you know, very sad, you were mentioned a lot though, so it was just as sad for me. I feel a bit guilty now actually that I haven't kept in touch. I wouldn't know what to say really," Marie said.

"I'm sure you would think of something Marie?" Peter replied.

"It was when the business closed Peter, there was a court case, and things were said."

"Oh?"

"Things that can't be unsaid, you know? It's so long ago now, but it hurt at the time because I was hurting still," she said regretfully. "Give her my love, though. I shouldn't bare grudges now, especially with a seventy-five-year-old lady."

"I will, I'll tell her," he said. "I'm going to go and see your David today as well, and get that sorted."

"He's all right, David, Dad," Ashley interjected as she came back. "He takes us to lots of functions, balls, and stuff, for the Police Federation, it's quite fun some of it."

"Well, I'm afraid I can't compete with that, I'll stick at being just dad," Peter said, smiling at them both. "He was one of the investigators on my missing person case then? Wasn't he?" Directing the comment to Marie.

"It was awful Peter. It took six months to come out from under that cloud with nine-eleven and everything, and having to cope with the funerals of Tom and Jake as well," She paused, thinking. "This one helped a lot," she said, patting Ashley's hand. "This one helped with everything, if anyone was a rock, it was her."

"Arr! Thanks, Mum," Ashley said, smiling at them both while tapping something on her phone.

"Yes, I have to agree with your mum, you have turned out alright, Chicken," he said.

Peter suddenly turned his attention to the television screen that was on by the reception. It was streaming the CBS lunchtime news. A picture of Jim Watts had come up onto the screen, he couldn't believe it. What was that all about, he wondered? There was footage coming from outside of Jim's house, he remembered it as though it was yesterday. The ornate statues of Winnie the Pooh, Timon, and Pumbaa, from The Lion King, Mohammed Ali, all the guys had taken the mick out of them, but they were quality sculptures and were worth a lot of dollars, and they were all about Jim's humour, his sense of fun.

Jim's house was lit up, illuminated by the spotlights of ten camera crews at least, all trying to get an exclusive about what had happened or what was going on. Peter walked over to get a closer look. The sound was off, but the subtitled words said it all. His heart sank immediately, he couldn't believe it. *'A home invasion has taken place in a leafy New York city suburb called Whitestone. A man in his fifties and a disabled woman were both murdered. Police don't know at this moment in time what the motive was, but neighbours are helping with their inquiries. Anyone with information should contact this number, 0800 100500.'* Peter stood there nervously biting his knuckles: he was riveted to the spot as the bulletin continued, and the high-pitched noise in his ears drowned out all the ambient noise. He felt vulnerable all of a sudden like someone was watching his every move. He looked around the room nervously at all the other people seated at tables, to see if anyone had noticed him, but they were all in their own little worlds, and eating lunch, no government types here. He then looked down at his phone nervously, this was a window to the world he thought, but these people were dangerous, and his phone was trackable. They would have Jim's phone by now so they would have his number as well. He immediately switched his phone off. He felt paranoid all of a sudden. Marie and Ashley watched from the alcove.

Peter came back to the table, looking grim. "You saw who that was, didn't you, Marie?"

"It looked like Jim," she said with concern in her voice. "Was it?"

"Yeah, it was, I cannot believe it. Murdered, just like that." Peter shook his head in disbelief.

"No! Not Jim and Ruth?" Her hand was over her mouth in shock.

"What Uncle Jim? No!" Ashley said as tears immediately rolled down her face.

"Yes, murdered, Jim and Ruth, in their home, a home invasion they said."

"How awful, can't believe it," Marie said somberly, wiping her eye's.

Ashley studied the worried look on her dad's face, "You look, nervous, Dad, what's wrong?"

"I called Jim yesterday we were supposed to meet at the Golf club. I waited for over an hour before I left. Poor Jim, poor Ruth," he said, questioning himself internally.

"There's something else though isn't there?" Marie said, looking at his expression, "Something you are not telling us."

"I left five messages for him," he said.

"You will probably have to speak to the police then. Can't believe it, Jim and Ruth, though," Marie said while comforting Ashley.

"I'm going to see your David after this anyway."

"He's a good man to have on your side Peter," she said out of concern.

Peter felt she was only trying to be helpful, and he would mention it and see what he said. "Yes, well, I suppose I'd better go and see him then."

"Ah, do you have to Dad?" Ashley said, wiping her eyes.

"Yes darling, but I'll see you tomorrow, shall I?"

"Yes, we could do lunch again?"

"Sounds great Chicken," Ashley said and kissed him on the cheek.

"You okay for money still, Peter?" Marie asked.

"Yes, I'm okay, thanks for asking."

"Where are you staying at the moment?"

"Oh, just with a friend in town," Peter said.

"What's she like?" Marie said, assuming the friend was female, and a hint of jealousy had crept in.

"She's okay," Peter left it like that, and she didn't ask another question.

Marie paid the bill, and they all left the restaurant. They said their goodbyes, then Peter made the short walk over to the NYPD Headquarters, looking around all the time, and acutely aware of everyone in his vicinity.

Chapter 16

Ugly, that was the only word to describe it. Number one Police Plaza, NYPD Headquarters, built-in 1973 and designed in the Brutalist architecture style that was popular in the nineteen fifties. Peter remembered going over there in ninety-eight to get some parking fines sorted, and it hadn't changed much since then. He walked into the busy main hall, a high ceiling with dull, uninteresting strip lighting. People stood in lines going up to the front desk, that was about fifty feet wide. There seemed to be cues for everything. One had four men in handcuffs with four policemen attending, drugs Peter thought, one lad looked only about fifteen. There was a cue for what seemed to be just prostitutes, dressed up for the night's trade, but it was only two o'clock in the afternoon.

He didn't know what he was doing there. He felt drawing a line under it as David said was a good thing for everyone, and if nothing else, he could get more of an insight into what David's intentions were. After all, if the Deputy Chief Commissioner wants to see you, you probably should go, he thought, he didn't want him on his tail for the rest of his life. In light of recent events, maybe having someone like David Reece on his side was probably a good thing as well.

At the front desk, a tall, bulky black sergeant stood to orchestrate everything, a deep mellow voice and looked more like an opera singer than a policeman, but everyone knew he was in charge. His uniform was too tight for him, as his midriff bulged out over his belt. There were residues of salt from previous sweats under his arms, and he used a white handkerchief to mop the occasional sweat globule that formed on his neck and forehead in the eighty-degree heat. The whole place had an uncomfortable feeling about it, dull, lacking light, and controlled chaos.

"Next," Sargent James Rathbone said, as Peter approached. "Yes?"

"I'm here to see David Reece," Peter said.

"You mean Deputy Commissioner Reece I think, don't you?" Titles were everything to the Police, as everyone knew where they stood in the scheme of things, the pay you received, who was in charge of who. The Police by nature were institutionalised, working a system, biding their time until they could all retire on a large fat pension.

"Yes, I suppose I do," Peter replied, smiling at him.

"Who are you? Do you have an appointment?" he asked.

"I'm just plain old Peter Collins, no title," he said with a touch of sarcasm. "I don't have an appointment as such, he asked me personally to call by."

James picked up the phone, someone at the other end confirmed what Peter had said. James then asked a young policeman called Sy, to take him up to his office. Sy was a skinny young lad with not much going on in his head, he was what you would call a gofer, in the force for only six months and learning the ropes, no actual police work just running errands, making tea and general office duties. Sy was perfect for the job.

"He's on the third floor," Sy said as they entered the elevator. "You know the deputy commissioner, do you?" he asked in a schoolboy like way.

"Yes, I do sort of, he's married to my wife," Peter said, giving him information that would probably be all around the station within the hour.

Sy was more likely to be the office gossip, Peter thought and used as a kicking boy to get rumours started, "Oh," he said and didn't ask anything else, it looked like his brain couldn't cope with too many facts.

On the third floor, the deputy commissioner's office was at the other end of the open-plan office. Sy led the way down the middle passed uniformed officers interviewing suspects in cubicles on both sides. There were at least ten cubicles each side, and most had someone in them, it was a busy office, and there was a constant noise level. One Puerto Rican looking woman with tattoos on her neck and arms, saw Peter walking by and couldn't help herself.

"Hey, cutie, want my number?" She winked at him and made an obscene gesture with her left hand, while the right one he noticed was handcuffed to the table. She stuck her tongue out as if to simulate licking.

"Leave it, Shel', he's too good for you," said Sy as they walked past.

It was evident to everyone she was a regular, Peter thought, and from the track marks that dotted her arms it was more likely to be heroin than crack cocaine, or it could be both, either way, she was a mess. She got a little bit agitated by the confrontation.

"Too good, for me? Too good, like hell, no one is too good for me? You hear me? Shit. No one, you hear?" she said, shouting and creating a commotion, sounding like she had completely lost the race with alcohol and drugs. Everyone looked over at her as she ranted on.

The female officer pulled her back round to continue their interview, as she carried on. Sy had really hit on a nerve. Next to David Reece's office was an interview room. Sy left him there, while he informed the Deputy Commissioner. Peter could see through the blinds out into the central office, and where he had just walked through. He looked over at all the lowlifes and down and outs, it was incredible, the noise they all made. Peter could never see himself working in a place like that, it would drive him crazy. It was like the film, 'One flew over the Cuckoos' Nest,' a favourite of his and Marie's. David then entered the room.

"Sorry about the wait, Peter, glad you could make it." He held out his hand again with his vice-like grip, Peter was ready for it this time. "Can I get you a drink?" he asked.

"No thanks, I'm fine," he replied, anxious to get on with it.

David opened a folder on the table, placed his glasses on, and looked at him as he sat back in his chair with his hands behind his head, thinking for a moment before he spoke. He took his glasses off. "Fifteen years," he said. "Fifteen years, Peter, where have you been? And why now, why come back now?" he asked, "After all this time?"

"Look, I didn't ask for this," Peter said, irritated by the question that Marie must have already answered for him, "I woke up Tuesday morning early, went for a run, as usual, it was 2001, and as usual I went to work and somehow, I ended up here in 2016."

"Sounds a bit far-fetched don't you think? I know Marie believes you, well she would, wouldn't she?" he said, trying to get under Peter's skin. "It's the sort of thing you would see in the movies, you know, something Steven Spielberg would make."

Peter looked at him and wondered what the question was really about, "I had a wife and young children a few days ago, now I have no wife, an older daughter, and my two sons are dead. Is that possible, you tell me?" he insisted.

"You disappeared without a trace. I was part of the team investigating it."

"As you already said," Peter talked over him if nothing else to annoy him.

"We had no leads at all. Marie was under the spotlight for months, especially after nine-eleven," he said.

"I bet she was," he replied.

"That's a bit below the belt don't you think? If you must know, we met at a police dance, and I remembered her from this investigation, one and a half years earlier." There was now a big elephant in the room, and both knew the questions and the answers.

"I suppose you felt sorry for her?" Peter said, putting him on the defensive.

"She's a lovely woman," he said, smiling.

"I know. Let's leave it at that shall we?"

"I will say this, and to be absolutely clear, Marie, as far as you are concerned, is off-limits, are we clear. Ashley, I cannot do anything about," he said pointedly.

"We will see about that," Peter said, showing his annoyance.

"We will see? If there is any inappropriate contact, I will come down on you like a ton of bricks, do you follow?" David said, warning Peter off.

"Yes, I get it. You don't want me messing up your little world, is that it?"

"Precisely," he replied.

"Well rest assured, I won't be."

"Good to hear," he said, verbally drawing a line under the macho standoff.

There was a pause in the conversation for a moment, while both of them calmed down so they could get back on track. David didn't want to make it personal, and Peter didn't want to be difficult, as Marie and Ashley had been through enough, Peter thought, and if he wanted as much contact as he could, being nice was the best bet. Who knew what the future would hold for him, he thought, so he would be nice, and hope it turned out okay.

David was interested in finding out more, and now the Marie problem was out of the way, his inquisitive policeman's head appeared. "Peter, let's step back for a moment, can we?" he asked. "Can you tell me what happened, in your own words? From the beginning, paint me a picture so I can understand?" he said calmly, "You know, what happened to you?"

"Yeah! Sure," Peter replied.

The tone of David's voice changed to one of empathetic, rather than confrontational. Was he being nice, or was he up to something? He'd not committed any crime, and he wasn't guilty of anything. "Well, I was at my office, and I was going to play golf," he paused as Jim came into his thoughts, "I said goodbye to Sheila, my PA, and went down the stairs to the garage to get my car."

"Go on, don't mind me, I'll just sit here taking notes," David said, encouragingly.

"I walked over to my car, I remember, I clicked the key fob, and the headlamps flashed, someone bumped into me, I think. Then I experienced a flash of light that blinded me for a moment. When I recovered, I was in this Laboratory type place, I remember looking back through something watery, I could see the stairs and Sheila was shouting my name at the bottom, then it disappeared, and there were flashing lights everywhere that went out," he recalled. "Then I heard some commotion coming from another room. People seemed to be celebrating something, doing hi-fives."

"What did you do then?"

"There were signs all around, restricted access, only authorised personnel, which I wasn't, so I went back upstairs to speak to Sheila, but it had all gone, my company, Sheila, everything. It had all changed into an NSA facility.

And here I am, talking to you fifteen years later in 2016," Peter smiled. "In 2001 we got the notice they were taking over, the NSA that is, we would have had to move anyway," Peter said. "My business was there."

Looking down at his notes, David said. "Yes, I remember Sheila, very nice lady, very helpful I must say. She was very concerned about you."

"Yes, she would have been."

David then said. "When we went through the CCTV footage from your office and the garage, we saw you leaving the office, and then in the garage, the tape went all fuzzy with interference. The FBI checked the tape out, and it hadn't been tampered with, it was quite bizarre as I recall, reading my notes at the time here."

Peter looked at David's writing in the file and wondered what did Marie see in him. Maybe he was a nice guy after all? Peter hadn't seen much of it yet, and perhaps a fun guy to be around? Peter dismissed that one.

"While I think about it, there is something you should know, it's probably relevant," Peter said.

"Okay, I'm listening?" David lifted his gaze from writing in the file to listen.

"This home invasion on the news today?"

"Yes, what about it?"

"I was going to meet him at the golf club," Peter said. "Jim was a very good friend of mine from my Iraq days, in my unit, you know. I wanted to catch up with him."

"Nasty business, sorry about that, we are waiting on forensics at the moment, I think. But I will make a note about what you said. It might have some relevance, you never know?"

"I thought I'd ask you something as well. Someone was looking for me at the golf club, and they asked the barman, I was waiting for Jim to arrive, he said they looked like government types, was that you? Have you told someone about me, David? You know, had a conversation about me with someone, for them to come looking for me?"

"What are you saying? Why would I do that? I've only just met you."

"Well, it's strange how they were looking for me at the club, while I was waiting for Jim. And then Jim and his wife get murdered, a bit of a coincidence, don't you think?"

David thought for a moment, "Yes, I agree with you their Peter, it is a coincidence. I'll let our guys investigating it know, that could be very helpful so thanks for that," he said, writing it down in the file. "I have a friend over at the NSA, he is head of a department at the Pentagon. Don't know which department, but I'm going to give him a call, and see if he has any thoughts on this. Can I get you a drink at all? I'll only be a few minutes," he said.

"That's okay," Peter said.

Although it was upside down, Peter noticed David had written a name in his notes, Doug McClean with NSA beside it. This was probably a name he should remember he thought.

As David closed the file, He stood up, and before leaving, he beckoned Sy over. "Sy will you get Peter a drink for me?" he asked, "Look after him, I'll be a few minutes."

"Sure, what can I get you?" Sy said.

Peter refused the drink again. He was thankful though that David seemed to at least believe him enough to check it out with a friend. The NSA would know where he was now, and it could get even more complicated as it all started in the NSA building. Maybe go directly to see this Doug McClean, and see what he had to say? He felt a little jaded with all the questions though and wanted to get out, out into the sunshine rather than stuck inside David's office, listening to all the chaos and mayhem.

After fifteen minutes, Peter had had enough of waiting for David to come back, patience not being his best attribute on the best of days. He turned his phone on to call Heather to come and pick him up, then switched it straight off. He asked Sy to let David know he had left and to take it up with him again on another day. He walked out of the main entrance and over to the Parking lot. The sun was now low in the sky, it was about four-thirty in the afternoon, and he could see a slight orange reflection bouncing off the glass skyscrapers in the distance, the tallest one now being the One World Trade Center, and the familiar Twin Towers that he remembered momentarily, were now a thing of the past.

Chapter 17

Right on time and looking fabulous, roof down, sun blazing, and a smile that made Peter's heart miss a beat, the Mercedes came to a stop inches from where he was standing.

"Hi cutie, fancy a lift?" Heather said jovially, with her Marilyn Monroe voice, and with her signature underlying gurgling laugh.

"Dunno, I don't take lifts off strange women," he said, as he opened the passenger door and got in. He leaned over, kissed her on the cheek, and smiled. "You don't seem strange to me, though, darling."

"Well, that's good then. Where to?"

"I don't know, I'm all yours now for the rest of the day, and thanks for picking me up," he replied.

"Ah! That's nice, let's go somewhere nice to eat, shall we? I know somewhere."

"I knew you would; lead on, lead on," Peter said, and did a military salute as if Heather was the captain of the ship for the day.

"How did it go back there," she inquired.

"I met that David Reece," he replied, shaking his head.

"What? What did he say? He believed you. Didn't he?"

"He knows something I'm sure of it, kept asking me the same questions over and over again, he was on the team investigating my disappearance."

"He is with your ex, maybe he has a problem with you turning up like this," she said thoughtfully.

"Yeah, he does, he warned me off. Anyway, that's not it, I'm sure he knows something or someone. He has a friend at the NSA. His type is always connected."

"What do you think he knows?" she asked.

"Police are sneaky, they don't tell you zip, but expect you to tell them everything. They like holding all the cards."

"Oh, did you see the news today?" Heather asked with concern in her voice.
"Yeah, I Did."

"So, it was him then? Your friend?"

"Afraid so, it was Jim and Ruth, bloody shame, they didn't deserve that."

"How do you feel?"

"Gutted, really gutted," he said somberly and thoughtfully. "I'm trying not to think about it too much, with all the other emotions I have going around in my head, you know, with Tom and Jake and everything, it seems to be all happening at once."

"I'm here, Peter," she said, grabbing his hand. "I understand."

"That's a comfort," he said, managing a smile. "It is, thank you."

He was getting used to Heather, her ways, her empathy, her humour, her humanity, and he liked being in her company, and it felt good, it felt right. It was hard not to think about Marie as well, but she was now married to someone else. She had made her choice, and there was nothing he could do about that. So why did he feel so guilty? Having thoughts about another woman, it was only natural, and feelings didn't lie.

"Take the next right!" Peter said abruptly, with a complete change of tone to his voice, that shocked Heather. There was suddenly a concerned look that had etched itself onto his face. He leaned over and looked deep into the door mirror. He had noticed a black sedan that had been following them for a few blocks. There were two men, he couldn't quite make out their faces, but they were pursuing them and keeping a few cars back.

"What?" Heather said nervously.

"Next right, take the next right," he commanded while concentrating on the mirror.

She turned right as instructed. "Why? What's going on, Peter?" she shrieked, looking at him out of the corner of her eye's while concentrating on the road ahead. She was breathing heavier and becoming flustered.

"I think someone's following us."

"Who is?"

"I don't know. Next right, just here," Peter said, pointing his finger right. "Don't know who, but I bet it's someone at the Police station talking to someone."

"What do you mean?" she asked. "FBI, CIA, could be the NSA, it probably could be them! Put your foot on the gas then," he said, urging her to speed up. "I'm doing fifty," she insisted.

"So is he, he's right behind us now. Take the next left in 50 yards," he said, directing her with his finger again. "Wait for it, wait for it. Now!" he shouted.

"God, this is stressing me out," Heather shouted as she closed her eyes and pulled in front of an oncoming car that was forced to put the brakes on quickly. The Black Sudan missed the turning, great Peter thought, but it wouldn't be for long.

"Pull over, Heather, I'll drive," he said.

The Mercedes screeched to a stop outside a hardware store in a disabled spot, they quickly swapped seats, and Peter set off again just as they came around the corner at speed.

"Can you see him?" Peter asked weaving in and out of the traffic, bringing the Mercedes up to eighty as he came up the entry road to the FDR.

"Don't know," she replied, not knowing what she was looking for but was relieved not to be driving. "What car is it?"

"A Black Sudan, about four cars behind us," Peter said.

"Oh!" Heather said, peering behind, "yeah, I see it now."

"Okay let me take it to one-twenty, these guys are not giving up," he said, talking to himself, concentrating on the traffic ahead, while keeping an eye on the rearview and the door mirror, alternating between the two.

Peter undertook a few cars, then moved over to the outside lane, he could see them moving up on the inside.

"There is a turning off about a half a mile ahead," Heather announced, as she tapped something into her phone.

"How do you know that?" he asked while keeping an eye on the Sedan.

"Satellite Navigation," she said. "Everyone's got Google maps."

"Okay, I'll take your word for it," he said, increasing his speed to one-fifty. The Sedan kept pace and was now on the outside lane, fifty yards behind them, doing one sixty, and gaining on them fast. He could see the turning about two hundred and fifty yards ahead. Waiting until the very last moment, Peter then turned sharply right, straight in front of a brand new white *Chevrolet Traverse* on the inside lane, who wasn't very pleased at all, breaking hard and sounding his horn. Peter just managed to make the exit at speed. The turn was too tight for the Black Sedan, and it careered by on the freeway. "Yes," Peter said, looking over at them. "Now you're talking!" he shouted, feeling elated and pleased with himself, pumping the air with his fist, then he gave the Sedan a little wave. "That's a great bit of kit, Google maps, I'll have to buy one."

"You don't buy it, Peter, it's free, you just download it from the internet," she replied. "You've probably already got it on your phone," she said, as Peter pulled onto West 34th street and parked at a meter opposite a Starbucks. "That's the most excitement I've had in years," Heathers said, taking a deep breath. "Phew, exhilarating, eh!" She smiled with relief, gurgling a laugh.

"Yeah, it was pretty full-on," Peter said. "Let's get a coffee and chill for a bit."

They walked over to Starbucks and sat by the window, so Peter had eyes on Heather's Mercedes across the street, and also could see if anyone had followed them. A rest and coffee were what they both wanted at that moment, somewhere to de-stress.

"I wonder what they were after, we've done nothing wrong," Heather said.

"You don't have to do anything wrong they just have to have a reason, and it is probably something to do with me, obviously," Peter said looking about the Starbucks café and clocking everyone. "You should turn your phone off as well," he said.

"Why?" She looked at him curiously.

"Well, in 2001 they could track mobile phones back then, so they are probably ten times better at it now, don't you think? They've probably taken your plate number at the station as well, and could be tracking your car as we speak, as well as your phone," he said.

Heather suddenly had a look of paranoia about her and developed a worried look on her face. "Really? Better unplug then," she said, staring at him. She immediately took his advice and switched her phone off. "There, who needs it anyway? More trouble than it's worth."

Chapter 18

Looking across West 34th street from the Starbuck's window, he could see Macy's flagship store, Herald Square. Peter thought how busy it seemed for this time of day, with hundreds of people cramming their way through the four main glass doors at the front. The sales were on-again, that seemed to happen every month these days, rather than only at New Year and Bank holidays, as retail stores battled against the online giants. He scanned the street once again, looking for anyone or anything out of the ordinary.

"I like spending time with you, Peter," Heather said, smiling amorously.

Peter looked slightly less troubled as he came back from gazing out of the window to look at her directly.

"Me too, Heather, you've been a godsend to me. Honestly, I don't know what I would have done," Peter said.

He touched her hand and looked at her longingly for a moment. He had fallen for her as well, he couldn't hide it. The tingle that started in the back of his neck, gave him a warm, happy feeling that permeated through to his body and brain. He held her hand mildly tighter, Heather leaned slightly towards him, moving the cappuccino to one side, he met her in the middle of the table, their lips came together slowly and controlled, sensually enjoying every moment. It was a kiss they both wanted, not a snog, but a meaningful, simple, gentle kiss that meant more than anything. Heather blinked, opening her eyes slowly as she pulled away, smiling at him the whole time. He looked into her eyes again with a look that penetrated deep inside her. They realised they had crossed that invisible line, very happy, and both willing participants.

Peter was relieved that she felt the same. He was the first to speak, "Well?" he said.

"Well, Mr Collins," Heather said very amorously.

"I love spending time with you too, Heather," he said, still holding her hand and not taking his eyes off her for a second. He squeezed her hand again, smiled, and said, "Shall we get out of here?"

Heather knew he didn't mean dinner, the dinner can wait, she thought. "I would love to," she said willingly.

They walked out of Starbucks hand in hand, and into the street with a spring in their step. The sun was almost setting over Manhattan. A clear sky with flecks of orange painted like a masterpiece across the sky, promising that tomorrow would be another lovely sunny day. Almost immediately Peter noticed a face he had seen before, the man at the memorial with Ashley, only now he was smarter and wore a black suit with a black tie, but still had a wire attached to his ear, maybe he had the suit on all the time underneath his trampy exterior.

"They've found us," he said abruptly, changing the mood instantly from romantic to hostile.

"Shit, who, where?" Heather said, worryingly looking around at the sea of faces in the street.

Peter held her hand tightly and said with the precision of an assassin. "Agent to your left, three o'clock, female ginger hair sunglasses, reading a Prada magazine. Two agents, ten o'clock across the street, straggly black hair, black suits, sunglasses. Let's move," he said, grabbing her by the hand and walking swiftly across the road towards Macy's, avoiding the slow-moving traffic. All three of them saw that Peter had made them and followed hastily.

Peter and Heather entered Macy's Mall through the main entrance, squeezing by people that were trying to come out of the store. They were now running with a sort of shuffling motion, dodging left and right to avoid people laden with shopping bags as much as they could. It seemed like everyone was coming at them, going against the tide. Peter glanced back at the entrance quickly to see where they were. They had just entered Macy's through the glass doors, the men first, pushing ahead, one of them taller than the other, the one he'd seen before. He also vaguely recognised the smaller one, he'd only seen him side on, and sitting down, definitely agents, government types, and then the woman behind, she was younger, probably straight out of college or university, learning the ropes. They were now about fifty feet behind them, and these guys had a look of determination on their faces. Peter turned back and bumped into an old man who was less than pleased, almost knocking him over. Crowds of people seem to swell out of every shop into the main thoroughfare, it was definitely sales day, and soon they were at a walking pace going sideways, edging their way forward, trying to shuffle past people to get through. Peter saw one of the many escalators fifty feet ahead, he pointed it out to Heather. He looked back again and saw them looking back at him, pointing, moving forward slowly. They hadn't gained on them at all, they were in the same predicament pushing their way through the crowds.

The escalator was packed, two people to every step and no chance of getting by at all. Halfway up they both turned to look back at the same time, the agents were about five feet away from getting on the escalator, that would give him and Heather a head start when they reached the top. Peter held Heather's hand to reassure her. It didn't work, she had a look on her face that said it all, nervous, scared out of her wits, like her life was in grave danger.

They exited the escalator at the top together and went into the first shop they could see walking hastily. Derek and Danielle's were a retailer and a brand of Macy's for the older person over sixty, very expensive, and not Heather's style at all. They pushed past the racks of ladies' clothes as fast as they could, moving through to the back of the store. Peter was already looking for a way out when he saw an assistant.

"Can I help you," the assistant said, noticing that they weren't there to buy anything.

"Is there a way out of here?" Peter asked, still holding onto a very nervous Heather.

She pointed at the changing rooms. "We share these with next door if that's any help," she said. "You can get through to Derek's, our other shop."

"Brilliant!" Peter said quietly and put the thumbs up.

"Thanks," Heather said and smiled worriedly at the assistant.

He opened the changing room door allowing Heather to go through first, and then took one final glance at the front entrance. Peter saw the tall one looking around outside, probably wondering where the hell they had gone, he then closed the door. Had they given them the slip? He thought, probably not. Within seconds Peter heard talking coming from the shop through the thin changing room door, it sounded muffled, the assistant was explaining something to someone, but Peter couldn't quite hear.

The corridor to the shop next door was only about thirty feet long, with six changing cubicles on the right-hand side, each cubicle had a tall mirror, surrounded by a strip light that was off, so it was only dim ambient light they could see with, luckily there didn't seem to be anyone using them at that time. Heather went through to the other door and waited there, while Peter waited behind the first door to see if anyone entered.

"Is that them?" Heather whispered.

"Think so, ssh!" Peter whispered, with his pointed index finger over his mouth. "It will be fine."

Peter could hear someone on the outside of the door, pressing his head against it, and breathing through his nose, trying to listen to what was going on inside. Peter could sense him, feel him, he was only about an inch away with wood in between. The doorknob then started to turn very slowly clockwise, and the door opened slightly, letting in a small amount of light and creating a little audible squeak. The first thing Peter saw was a silencer protruding through the small opening, that got wider as the door opened further, followed by a Glock pistol. Then a man's head appeared, peering into the changing room corridor. Before the man could see anything at all though, Peter grabbed the Glock firmly with his left hand, and with the right hand, inflicted a karate chop with maximum force to his Adam's apple, rendering him breathless instantly. The gun went off, ricocheting around the changing room. It hit one of the large mirrors shattering it, and the glass came crashing to the floor, every bit of it, like a noisy waterfall cascading down a ravine. Heather screamed. Peter instinctively grabbed hold of the man's right arm, and twisted him around the other way, taking the gun out of his hand in one flowing movement. He then brought his foot down on the back of the man's tibia with force, the sound of breaking bone permeated the air, and it was a good break. He hit the floor face first with a thud and let out an agonising cry of pain.

Heather stood there mesmerised and stunned, with a hand over her mouth and in shock at what she had just witnessed, but it wasn't over yet, as another man entered with a gun pointing straight at her. He had a startled look to his face, like a frightened rabbit in a headlight. She shouted, "Peter!" He didn't have a chance. Peter grabbed his arm firmly, quickly twisting it around his back, put his right arm tightly around his neck, and took the gun out of his hand in one smooth flowing movement, it was like a dance, not at all like a fight. Then Peter's pointed knee jabbed into his Popliteal Fossa, putting him off balance, and straight on the floor on top of his friend, who was still groaning with a bone poking through his shin. Peter then came down from a great height and punched him in his cheek with such force, his jaw cracked immediately, stunning him, he was out cold. Blood spurted from his mouth. Both men lay there on the ground in a heap, helpless, and out for the count. There wasn't a third, she must be outside, he thought.

Peter's senses now went into overdrive, sensing everything and everyone around him, self-preservation and Heather kept totally safe was now his modus operandi. He reached into the breast pocket of the agent who was out cold, took his phone and ID card to read later, placing it in his pocket. He took the Glocks, ejected the magazines and put them in his pocket as well, then laid the Glocks on top of the agents.

"We will be seeing you then," Peter said sarcastically, giving them half a salute.

He walked calmly and quickly but with purpose through the changing room corridor towards Heather with the glass crumbling underfoot, he grabbed her by the hand and opened the other door. They entered the shop next door, which looked like the previous shop funny enough, it was the same branded shop name, but for the elderly male this time, it wasn't Peter's style either. They carried on walking through passed an assistant who smiled nervously, and out through the front door of the shop onto the walkway on the upper floor.

The setting sun came through the glass ceiling, orange in colour. In the distance, the sound of police sirens could be heard. The sound of a gun going off anywhere will always do that, Peter thought, some people had nine-one-one on speed dial for such an occasion.

Peter and Heather looked over to the outside the shop next door and could see the ginger-haired woman on her phone looking at them frantically calling someone, and probably relaying what had just taken place. The young woman looked at them nervously, she had her long ginger hair tied back and looked every part an agent, but had a timidness about her, unconfident, unsure and hesitant, she never gave chase and never showed her gun at all. Peter and Heather calmly walked by as she stood there motionless, her eyes following them communicating total acquiescence and not saying a word.

They went down the escalator and onto the main thoroughfare, going quicker this time with the crowds of shoppers so as not to bring any unwanted attention to them. He looked back for a moment to see if she'd had a change of mind to follow them. She didn't. Thinking on his feet, Peter quickly put the agent's phone and the Glock magazines into a cleaner's bin who was walking in the opposite direction brushing up some litter. Track that, Peter thought to himself.

They walked calmly back out of Macy's to Heather's car. Peter drove, Heather didn't say a word, sitting there, all quiet and in her own world, her hands shaking nervously with tears slowly oozing from her eyes but not crying, just stunned.

"You okay, Heather?" Peter asked, patting her hand.

"Just taking it all in. You know, what just happened," she said nervously. "Fuck! What did just happen? Fuck, I can't stop shaking, look at me," holding up her hands in front of her face. "Think I'm going to be sick. Fuck, where did you learn that stuff? Jesus. What just happened, Peter? Were we shot at Peter? Fuck!"

"Heather look at me, you are okay," he said, trying to reassure her.

He realised that she was probably in shock, and the first time she had ever been in a conflict situation like that when her life itself was threatened.

"Did we just get shot at?" she shouted, "Where the fuck did you learn that stuff, Jesus, Peter?"

"Oh! In the marines," he said nonchalantly.

"Fuck. Peter, you were fantastic. I wouldn't like to cross you when you were angry. Jesus, they didn't have a chance you were so fast. Brutal even," she said in admiration. "Ha, look at me. I'm still shaking. Why did they have guns? I've never been shot at before. Are they trying to kill us?" Breathing slowly now, and more controlled, more relaxed.

"It's the adrenaline kicking in, Heather," he said, patting her on the knee. "Let's take you home."

"Yes, please. Fuck, look at me, and I can't stop saying fuck! Is that normal?" she said, swearing uncontrollably.

"It's perfectly normal, Heather, it's been a shock, you are not used to danger."

"And you are obviously?" she said, taking a deep breath and breathing out like an athlete after a run. "Take me home, Peter." She grabbed his hand tightly.

Chapter 19

The Pentagon was built in 1941 during the Second World War and was the headquarters of the United States Department of Defence, located in Arlington, Virginia. It was the home of the NSA, and many other defence-related agencies, around 26,000 people were currently employed there, with an annual spend of 550 billion dollars. So, to be head of a department within the NSA was no mean feat, and took him years of hard work and dedication to get there.

David Reece had been friends with Doug McClean for some years, having met at an agency event in Manhattan in 2010, not the sort of friends that go out regularly, but just a known face to talk to, rather than making small talk to some unknown person he would never see again.

The operator answered the phone in an efficient 'Government like' manner and put him through to McClean at the NSA's office in Manhattan.

"Hey Davy boy, how's it going over there? Or should I say, Deputy Commissioner Reece, Congrats?" McClean said.

"Thanks, Doug, and no, just, David is fine, Ha!" he replied.

"What's it been, six months? Doesn't time fly? Last time I think we were both a bit worse for wear as I recall," McClean said, remembering a session that had got out of hand.

"Yeah it must be six months at least, I think you were a little worse than me as I recall. How's Marsha?" He asked.

"She's okay when I see her, I seem to spend every waking hour here at the moment. It's like I'm married to the job. Ha!" McClean joked. "How's...?" he said, forgetting her name momentarily.

"Who, Marie?"

"Yeah sorry, Marie."

"She's fine thanks," David said. "Anyway, the reason for the call is we have a person sitting in our interview room that went missing in 2001, just before nine-eleven."

"Really," McClean replied, his ears pricked up to the real reason he called out of the blue.

"Peter Collins," David said, "Ring any bells?"

"Sounds like it's a Police matter David, rather than an NSA one I think, don't you agree?" McClean said.

"Well you would think so, but he has this fantastic story about how he got here."

"Got where David?" he said, pretending to be ignorant of the fact.

"Got here, he claims that one minute he was there in 2001 at his office, and then in a flash it's 2016," he said, leaving the statement out there for a moment.

"So, what is he, on drugs or something?" McClean said, waiting for him to go on.

"We are talking about time travel, Doug," he replied, spelling it out.

"Really? Is that what this is?"

"Didn't you say you were working on something like that? You'd had a few drinks, but you were pretty jazzed about it, as I recall?" David said.

"No, definitely not, you recall wrong," he replied firmly. "Anything we do here at the NSA is classified, so you have got that wrong," McClean said. He had told him something while having a few drinks he remembered, and probably shouldn't have, but it seemed innocent at the time as Mag-Tron hadn't even happened yet and was just a theory. It was now different, and he had to either shut him down or shut him up, either way, he had to be under no illusions that this didn't happen.

"Well, you know what I think?"

"What?" McClean said.

"I think you've cracked it and it works," he said. "And Peter Collins is living proof?"

"What works David?" McClean said. "I don't know what you are talking about."

"Really?" David replied. His know all attitude began to grate with McClean who had been calm until now.

"Look, David, whatever you think you know. You don't, and as far as Peter Cummins is concerned, I think he is pulling the wool over your eyes," McClean said. "He is probably in some sort of trouble, that's why he has resurfaced after so long. Technology like that only exists in the movies, maybe you should be talking to Spielberg."

David sensed that McClean knew what he was talking about, but wasn't going to give anything away at all, and even if it were true, McClean would have to deny it existed anyway.

"It's Collins, not Cummins, Peter Collins," David said. "I can hear it now."

"You can hear what precisely, David?" McClean said.

"Man returns after fifteen years missing, no sign of ageing at all, claims time travel?" David said. "He could end up on the Letterman show, prime time."

"David, can't see where you are going with this one I'm afraid, my friend, and I have got to get on, important stuff to do, we will have to catch up soon, okay?" McClean said, shutting him down in an instant.

David heard the line go dead, and if nothing else they now knew their secret was out, and someone else knew about it, he knew he would hear from McClean again soon. So maybe Peter Collins was telling the truth, after all, he thought, and this bazaar talk of time travel was real, Peter had come from 2001.

David went back to the interview room only to find Peter had gone.

"Sy, where's he gone?" Reece asked, sounding annoyed.

96

"He said he would talk to you later, sir," Sy muttered, feeling instantly he had done something wrong.

"Why didn't you come and get me?"

"Didn't think, sir, sorry," Sy said timidly.

"Okay, Sy, carry on."

David looked at the picture of Peter in the file. He asked himself, why would he just up and leave when he had a loving wife and family? It seemed anomalous all those years ago, and now he had met Peter he felt that he could be the innocent party in all of this.

Chapter 20

McClean thought David Reece a bit presumptuous and a bit arrogant for his liking, probably something that the Police had taught him along the road to becoming Deputy Chief Commissioner. David thought he was right. It would be tough to convince someone otherwise when they were sure, or knew that they were sure. He'd hoped he would be sensible about it, but he might have to bring him into the inner circle, the circle of few, who knew about Mag-Tron. He sat in the control room, simmering down for a moment, wondering about the future of the Mag-Tron project. He summoned Edwards.

"Peter Collins has surfaced. He has already been into the NYPD in Manhattan, so why haven't we got eyes on him yet? He's making too many contacts for my liking, Edwards," McClean irked.

"We only found out an hour ago. His wife changed her name after she remarried," Edwards explained. "She now lives with Deputy Chief Commissioner Reece of the NYPD. You don't go banging on his door in a hurry without the right paperwork."

"That was sneaky of him, he didn't mention that just now when we were on the phone. So, his Marie, is Marie Collins then is it?" McClean said as the penny dropped. He felt David had lied to him when he knew all along whom Peter was.

"Yes, her name is Marie, once married to Peter Collins," Edwards said.

"Well, fuck him! There is still a level five clearance on this. We have to find Peter Collins now and bring him in before he interacts with anyone else. Edwards, literally twenty minutes ago he was in the NYPD headquarters downtown, talking to David Reece," McClean said, and out loud so everyone could hear.

"Okay," Edwards said. "I'll narrow down the trace on him."

"Also get the guys together in the boardroom in ten minutes for a briefing?" McClean said.

"Will do."

The current small team of handpicked agents had worked together many times to do with Mag-Tron issues, but this was the first mission, and to have something like this happen on the first one was terrible for the team, bad for the project, so it wasn't surprising there were tensions in the room. Edwards, Lewis, Green, and Danson sat around the boardroom table as if waiting for their heads to roll, with McClean at the head and Senator James Groves beaming in on satellite. McClean answered to Senator Groves at the White House who originally got the backing of the federal government that had funded the Mag-

Tron project from the beginning. He had a vested interest in keeping it under wraps.

"Well gentleman, Senator Groves," McClean said. "Agent Edwards, will you take us through what has happened so far, for the benefit of the senator please?"

"Yes, of course. On Monday, September 5, 2016, at 11:30 a.m. Peter Collins stepped through the Mag-Tron vortex unknowingly from 2001. He wouldn't have seen it, but nonetheless he ended up here in 2016," Edwards said. He stood up and clicked a remote control to bring the details of Peter onto the screen so the senator could see as well. The senator's face reduced to a small box at the top right-hand corner. "The vortex was online for a few seconds, so he's very unfortunate. Looking at the screen for a second, this is the missing person's report from 2001. It got buried because of nine-eleven, but as you can see, this man vanished into thin air with no explanation."

"And who let him go?" Senator Groves interjected.

"We had him in the palm of our hands," McClean said.

"It was an oversight, sir," Danson added. "Security thought he had just wandered in, asked him to go around to the security office to get a badge if he wanted to come back in, but he left the building and didn't come back. We have been working on a few scenarios, haven't we Green."

Green stood up. "Yes, there are a couple of options open to us, sir, as we can see. Number one, we send him back, but he will have knowledge of our existence, this technology, and many facts from here, and as we all know he has interacted with people for a few days. Two, we don't send him back, and he loses fifteen years of his life, he has seen the technology but probably doesn't understand it totally, he will be no threat and gets on with his life. Or three, we take him out, and all of our problems are solved."

"Take him out! Are you mad?" McClean exclaimed. "We would be in a pile of shit if that came out, and it would. The ex-wife Marie, for one thing, would be asking questions, pertinent questions. Danson what's your take on it."

"We could have him in for a chat, and see where his mind is at," Danson said. It was his idea about taking him out, so he had to think on his feet. "What type of person he is etc., etc. If he is as intelligent as he looks, then he could be useful to us, and sending him back could have benefits." Green glared at him as if to say you got me in the shit on that one. Danson capitulated with a glare back at him, signalling he was sorry.

Lewis then announced. "What we are missing is that this man has now been in 2016 for three days. Just think for a minute what he's come in contact with, technology, media, social media. Going back to 2001 with that knowledge, it would be like Biff in *back to the future* finding the almanack. He could put ten thousand dollars on Facebook stock and make a hundred million dollars guaranteed. He could corner the technology sector with the new 4G mobile phone technology, and as we all know nothing like that was available back then."

They all thought for a second what an opportunity that would be, the benefit of hindsight, and being able to live part of your life again. It was almost too irresistible to imagine.

"The power of what we have in our hands is enormous and could change history, maybe we could even stop nine-eleven from happening, but I think that would be a mistake," Danson said. "The Mag-Tron could be a power for good, but it could also be equivalent to setting off an atomic bomb. Only time would tell. The less we mess with the past, the more secure we will be here in the present."

"That being said. Peter Collins is also a father and a family man," McClean said. "And currently, a certain Deputy Chief Commissioner David Reece is standing firmly in his shoes with his wife. His child Ashley is all grown up now, and his boys perished in the nine-eleven disaster. I think I'd want to go back to get back some of what I'd lost. After all, this was our mistake, and I think we should put it right, we owe him that at least."

"What we also forget as well, he is an ex-marine, special-forces," Danson said.

"Good point," Senator Groves agreed.

"Why not use him to go back and help us track down the main terrorists in ISIS, the leaders, for instance. Just a thought, we could solve the problem before it had ever happened."

"Another good point. What do you think, Senator?" McClean asked.

"I think we can all safely say he will go along with it. He's a patriot, not a threat to National Security," Senator Groves said. "What I would be mindful of though, is this thing about changing history. Gathering intelligence to help us today is one thing, and probably a good thing, sending Peter Collins back to resume his life seems like a good thing as well, but changing history is not a good thing, because where will it end, and as someone once said, you can't change fate."

"Okay fine. Let's get Peter in here then, as soon as we can. Arrest him if we have to, but get him in," McClean said decisively. "All agreed?"

The team agreed unanimously and set about getting the CCTV footage of Peter visiting the Police station and the NYPD.

Over at the White House, Senator James Groves placed a call to April Haines, who was busy looking at the CNN footage of the house invasion at Whitestone, it was getting messy, and she didn't like it at all.

"April hi!"

"Senator."

"I've just got off a conference call with Doug McClean and his team at the NSA."

"Really, what's up?"

"This Peter Collins business, I thought we were clear on it?"

"What do you mean exactly?"

"Well he is still at large, running around meeting people, that's what I mean he needs to be stopped as we discussed."

"We have our best asset on it, Senator, a result is imminent."

"The longer this goes on, April, the more difficult it gets for both of us. I don't want to be explaining something down the line to the President. You copy?"

"Yes Senator."

"Clear the mess up April."

"Yes, sir, I'll keep you informed."

"Next time I hear from you, I'll expect a result."

"Yes, you can count on it," April said. "Just one thing?"

"What is it?"

"How did he end up here in 2016, was he a sleeper?"

"That's classified, April."

"I mean was he cryogenically frozen? It would just be nice to know if it were an experiment that went wrong?"

"I can tell you, it was an experiment, and it went wrong because people didn't do their job properly," he said. "Now we have to clear this bloody mess up. That's where you come in April, that's all I'm prepared to say on the matter."

"Oh, okay."

"A result, April, is what we need."

"Yes, and I'll get it done."

April heard the phone disconnect immediately. Her whole existence was on the line and she needed to put an end to Peter Collins. She had sorted this sort of thing before at least five times in her career. It wasn't the thing that she was most proud of, but it was part of the job.

Chapter 21

At 1035 Fifth Avenue, the ornate glass elevator went all the way up to the penthouse. As soon as the elevator door closed from the garage, Peter grabbed her waist, pressing his body up against her and pushing her against the frosted glass, he kissed her passionately. The adrenaline from the mall was still present in both of them, and an electrical storm flowed through their bodies. Heather was helpless to resist, she didn't want to resist, she closed her eyes and enjoyed the moment. After being scared and tense for such a prolonged period, she now felt chilled, even tired, calm, and open to his advances. She craved some love and affection, she hadn't experienced any for so long.

The lift buttons pressed into the small of her back, his breath on her face aroused her as she breathed it in, wanting every part of him inside her. Peter pressed the 'P' button on the panel by her right earlobe, the elevator was going straight to the top. Pleasant thoughts flashed through her mind as Peter kissed her again, his tongue venturing forward into her mouth to mingle with hers. The smell of her Chanel perfume seeped in through Peters' nostrils, turning on all the receptors. They were oblivious to anyone who might have been watching them through the stencilled glass. The elevator rose through six floors without them even realising it, when it stopped at the top, they were still embracing. The door opened on to her private corridor, with marble floors and paintings of artists Peter had never heard of but looked as though they would sell for a million dollars. They exited the elevator in a crab-like fashion, manacled together by their lips and arms, taking a few moments to get to her Penthouse door.

"Shall we?" she said, pausing for a moment to place the key in the door.

"I would love to," Peter smiled with impatient eagerness as the door opened slowly.

Milo greeted them with a few frenzied yaps trying to jump up and join in, Heather stroked him momentarily, with no attention going his way through, he went off to his basket watching their every move, eyes down and in an upset dog mode, sighing like a cat that hadn't had any cream. They were like teenagers on a first date, without a care in the world with one goal and a burning passion that couldn't be kept in check. An urge that came from deep within, unmistakable, it was like the first kiss on the playground at school, with the best-looking girl in the class, it all had to come out.

They eventually made it through to the bedroom. Peter unbuttoned her blouse, Heather unbuttoned his shirt, the rest of the clothes came off as quickly as they could. They both stood there naked admiring each other, stroking each other softly and gently. Peter, with the toned physique of an athlete, Heather with the slender, silky body of an international model. Then they laid down on the bed and looked into each other's eyes, Heather ran her fingers through his hair lovingly, Peter kissed her slowly and stroked her cheek, they wanted each other so much, and when it happened, it was such a relief.

Lying there for what seemed like minutes, was in fact hours, intently noticing every expression, every nuance of thought, every curve of their bodies, manacled together as close as they could get, and not saying a word. The act was the act, this was something else, they both felt it, and it felt great, it felt right.

"Well, Peter Collins. Well, I never!" Heather said, finally breaking the silence in her usual funny Marilyn Monroe-esk way, and the relief showed on her face. She loved him, right there right now.

"Well, Heather?" Peter replied, in a silly indistinguishable posh accent. "Are you hungry?"

"Famished."

"What do you suggest?"

The look of excitement flashed across Heather's face. "Cheeseburgers, I'm going to take you for Cheeseburgers, and not any old Cheeseburgers, the best in Manhattan."

"It's eleven-thirty at night?" Peter said, checking his watch.

"Manhattan never sleeps darling, there's a place one block from here. It serves until two in the morning. Great music as well."

"You have won me over," Peter said.

"That's good then. Didn't take much," Heather said, smiling at him, touching his nose, squeezing slightly, kissing him again. "Got to keep my hero well-fed."

As they dressed, Peter couldn't help feeling guilty, it was the first time he had made love to another woman since first meeting Marie, and it felt odd and wrong. Heather sensed it immediately.

"What's worrying you?" she asked.

"I dunno, just thinking about everything that's all," he said. "I feel like I'm in a whirlwind. You know, it doesn't seem real, like I'm living in a dream and at some point, I'm going to wake up from it."

"Hope not, that felt pretty great to me, dream or no dream," Heather said.

Vento's was a trendy burger joint on Fifth Avenue, just a short walk from Heather's apartment block. They walked hand in hand with a spring in their step, and without a care in the world, Peter put aside his feelings and enjoyed the moment. Three valets stood to attention wearing smart purple military-style uniforms and white gloves, there to take and fetch cars for guests.

Heather said hello to the doorman who knew her name as they walked into the reception, she must be a regular Peter thought. Pictures of famous 'A-list' faces, with friends and family of people who had dined there adorned most of the reception walls. Peter couldn't help but look at them momentarily to see if he recognised someone smiling back at him, one caught his eye, zooming in on a Bruce Springsteen photo, with some of the 'E' street band. "Look, Heather, my mate dines here too, see?" he joked, pointing to the picture.

"I've met him, and most of these people at some point or another," she said proudly, and she wasn't joking, she'd had an A-list circle of friends for many years.

"You've met the boss then?" he asked.

"Yes, a few times, lovely man."

"Wow! That's so rock 'n' roll. You'll have to fill me in on this one, tell me everything," Peter said excitedly.

"Miss Lombard, you look lovely tonight," the owner said, in a disjointed American-Italian accent and smiling at both of them.

"Thanks, Michael," said Heather. "This is Peter."

"Pleased to meet you Peter, sir. We find you the nicest table, sir," he said, shaking his hand vigorously, and then instructed the waiter to take them to their table.

The place was humming just like Heather had said, and the music was 'Rockin,' live and just his kind of thing, practically every table was taken. The room was lit with very dim LED lighting, as though the people there wanted to be incognito and could relax without prying eyes. He thought he recognised a few faces as he walked by, but couldn't be sure, or put a name to them, but they were famous alright. Peter noticed the attention Heather was getting as some of the men even with stunning women themselves, sat up and noticed her as they walked by. It was only a glance, a small movement of the eye, but they noticed her. The waiter seated them in a half-round alcove, big enough for four people with exotic plants draping from the ledges, but they could see the band, they were the best seats in the house. This girl had clout, Peter thought. She was a face, and on the scene, very connected, and it was his date. He couldn't help it, but he felt like a million dollars, and proud to be in her company, sitting opposite, she looked like a definite A-lister.

Heather looked composed and in her comfort zone. She wore the most stylish dress, flowing lime green patterned silk that hugged her body, with a white silk scarf, minimal jewellery, very simple but sensual and expensive, her bag was from Dolce and Gabbana, small, but no change out of a thousand dollars. He studied her for a moment, who was this girl? Where had she come from, and how could she be so perfect in every way? But the big question was, why me? Peter asked himself. The guilt reared its head again as his thoughts turned to Marie and his family, only a few days ago they were sitting in his kitchen in Oyster Bay having a family breakfast, and now here he was, with a beautiful woman called Heather, at twelve o'clock midnight, eating cheeseburgers, who would have thought it.

"Penny for your thoughts?" Heather said.

"I don't know just thinking, that's all," he said with a slightly melancholy tone to his voice.

"Thinking about what?" Heather asked.

"If you must know, I was thinking about how my life has changed out of all recognition in such a small space of time." he answered as honestly as he could. "And here I am with you."

"Life's great like that, you just have to live it for the moment, I know I do," she said.

They ate their cheeseburgers, drank a bit of wine, and sat talking about all the famous people Heather had met over the years. Peter sat there mesmerised by her charm, her beauty, her humour. Soon it was time to go, they ended the night with a nightcap on Heather's balcony at two-thirty in the morning.

Heather went off to bed, and Peter sat out on his own for a while, looking over at Central Park, wondering what tomorrow would bring. At three o'clock in the morning, the city was alive and thriving, vibrant with the noise of activity and the odd police siren going off in the distance. He would drop in and see Jen early tomorrow morning he thought, to catch up with her about Lawrence and give his condolences. It would probably upset her, but he had to do it one day anyway, it might as well be tomorrow.

He then remembered the ID in his pocket, and the altercation in Macy's that he'd had with the agent. He took it out to have a look at, and it was as he first thought, government types. The Central Intelligence Agency, his employee number 42073455-OPD. Status, Active Field Agent. His name, Brian Delaney, security clearance level five, Irish American. He now knew which agency was after him. It wouldn't be long before he saw another agent, they would never give up, they would keep coming, he needed a go-between, someone who knew people inside and could advice him. Sheila was probably his best bet. He found her number on his Blackberry and saved it into his Samsung, thinking he would speak to her tomorrow and hoped it wouldn't go to her answer service. He didn't sleep well again, there was too much thrashing around in his head, but lying next to Heather, he felt relaxed and safe for a while at least, and now very much loved.

Chapter 22

Thursday, September 8, 2016

Peter was the first to wake and left Heather sleeping. Three and a half hours of broken sleep should have left him tired, but he was surprisingly sprightly and energetic. While percolating the coffee on the stove, he looked around the apartment admiring the tasteful pieces of art she had collected over the years, it was a treasure chest, he wouldn't have a clue about what he was looking at, but it all seemed expensive. He came across some men's clothes, hanging in a closet with an old pair of trainers that were about his size. They must have been some old boyfriend's gym shoes he thought, there were shorts, socks, and a sports top as well. So, on they went, and they fitted him perfectly, as he yearned to get back into his routine of running. He eagerly slipped out the apartment, down the stairs, and out the front door nodding to the security guard that was on duty.

He took a deep breath of the Manhattan morning air as he warmed up outside the apartment block, and looked over at the Schuman running track that was beckoning him. As he started to run, he felt the weight of the past few days slowly lifting from his shoulders, and the adrenalin kicked in as his lungs deep filled with air, and in the process getting rid of all the cobwebs clogging his brain, helping him to think straighter and focus. He used to know many people who jogged on this route, but today he felt very anonymous and remarkably free of all the pressures that used to hinder him. The morning sun was rising over Manhattan, and he could smell the cherry blossom as he breathed in the scented air. Autumn had arrived, and the trees lining the route were shedding their leaves. No dogs were allowed on the track as it was designed for running or walking only, and in a counter clockwise direction. At seven o'clock in the morning, it was bustling, and it took in some of the loveliest views of the Manhattan skyline. Peter felt himself dodging slow runners all the way around, but today would be a slow jog, nothing too taxing.

Three times around the Jacqueline Kennedy Onassis reservoir was almost five miles, and he checked his watch out of habit. That was okay for thirty-five minutes, he thought. He walked over to the water fountain at the exit to the park, consciously going through his usual warm down routine. While taking some water on board, he glanced over at Heather's apartment block. There was a man with sunglasses and a newspaper under his arm sauntering back and forth, he looked odd and out of place, and Peter stood there out of sight observing him for a moment. The man touched his ear, a dead giveaway, they were onto him, he had been careless. Maybe it was because he'd taken out the two agents yesterday in the mall? How had they been able to track him, he thought, as he had kept his phone switched off all of the time. He ran back into the park and down Fifth Avenue for a few blocks under cover of trees, then crossed over and down Eighty-Seventh Street to Madison Avenue, and around to the underground garage at the back of Heather's building. He pressed the intercom, the security man answered, and he was put through to the Penthouse.

"Hello," Heather said lustrously.

"It's me, can you let me in, I've just been for a run," he said quietly, breathing heavy.

"Why use the garage? You can come in by the front door if you want?" she said.

"No, it's okay, I'm here now. Can you buzz me in?" Peter insisted.

"Okay, I'll pour the coffee," she said, and the gate began to open.

Heather opened the door to the Penthouse for him wearing a blue chiffon nightgown and looking fabulous. Peter, still a bit sweaty and blowing slightly, smiled hesitantly and kissed her on the cheek as he walked in. Milo came to greet them both, and Heather picked him up for a cuddle.

"Didn't I wear you out enough last night then?" Heather said with an alluring voice smiling at him, then she kissed Milo. "You're cute as well."

"Yes, you were great darling, but I saw these in your closet and couldn't resist, needed to get out there. When you don't do it for a few mornings you really miss it, you know, it's great to get out even for a few miles."

"I do my sweating in the gym."

"I bet you do," Peter joked and smiled at her.

"They've seen better days, I think they need a wash, phew!" she said with her fingers over her nose. "Take a shower, I'll get breakfast sorted."

Heather made breakfast of scrambled egg and ham with a hollandaise sauce. Showered and smelling a whole lot better, Heather gave him some clothes out of the closet to wear as well.

"These are fine," he said. Now sporting a checked summer shirt, and blue jeans, "whose are they? Is it an old boyfriend or something?"

"No, my brother keeps them here, he stays over sometimes when he's in town. He's about your size as well, which is perfect."

"What does he do?"

"He now runs the family business, since dad died," she said. "You know the property, rent. He lives in Texas with his family."

They sat out on the balcony in the morning sun, eating breakfast, and having coffee. Peter looked over to the front of the building, the man he had seen was still there talking to someone on the phone. His first thought was they should get out of there, but they would be safe in the apartment, for now, he didn't see any immediate danger as the security for the block was very high.

"What are you looking at," she asked curiously, as Peter had a concerned look on his face again.

"Nothing, it's okay?"

"What do you mean it's okay, not from the look on your face it's not," she said looking down at the man on the front. "Who is he?"

"I don't know, but he could be one of the crowd we saw yesterday."

"Bloody hell! I could do without another stressful day, Peter,"

"You'll be okay, I'll make sure of it. The security in this building is second to none, every lift has a key pass and a number."

"Yes I know, Daddy spent a million dollars on the system, state of the art it is and linked into a security service," she said. "I normally feel very safe up here. Are you sure they can't get in?"

"No way can they get up here, without your permission, so you are as safe here as you will ever be," Peter said reassuringly.

"Okay Then."

"Would it be okay if I used your car?"

"You don't have to ask, of course, you can Peter."

"I'm going to go and see Jen for a bit: you know reconnect, will you stay here?"

"Yes, I have things to do."

"You have a landline here, don't you?"

"Yes."

"I'll take the number, just in case."

"In case of what?"

"In case I need to call you, silly," Peter laughed. "Keep your phone off."

"Yes, I will, landline only."

She gave him the keys, and he took the elevator down to the garage.

Chapter 23

The automatic security gate rolled open slowly as Peter slipped the Mercedes into drive, and waited on the up ramp. The man who was outside the apartment earlier suddenly appeared in the bright sunshine and walked over to the middle of the exit blocking his way out. His face from the side had a sallowness about it, with pockmarks on his cheek which was probably acne from when he was a child. He wore a long black knee-length scruffy coat, open with his hands inside both pockets, very reminiscent of a gunslinger in the Wild West, a New York Yankees baseball cap covered what looked like a salt 'n' pepper hair colour, and a wire hung down from an earpiece. His movement was purposeful as though everything he did was pre-planned. He stood there for a moment staring straight ahead down the street, he then slowly turned his body around and looked menacingly at Peter sitting in the Mercedes in the shade of the garage, the gate was now fully open.

He instantly recognised the person standing before him. The image from the front page of the *Post* a few days ago came back to him in an instant. Jerry Martin, CIA assassin, once a part of his unit in Iraq in the nineties, and now here he was large as life standing in front of him, but it was, in reality, twenty years since they'd last spoken at Andrews Air Force Base, Maryland, after returning from Iraq.

Peter paused for a moment with his right foot on the brake, and checked the car was still in the drive position, ready and waiting for him to make the first move, but Jerry never moved an inch. He just stood there, his expressionless, emotionless face, with dead eyes, threatening, staring directly at him as though he was waiting for something to happen, facing him down, everything went through Peter's mind. Did Jerry recognise him? Did he even know who he was? Did he know what he was doing?

He certainly knew what he was doing all right, his right hand came out of his coat pocket and reached deep inside his coat, and in one flowing movement he pulled out a Glock Pistol with a silencer attached and aimed it straight at him sitting there.

Peter didn't wait for a second. He put the pedal to the floor, the Mercedes wheels squealed and smoked as Jerry fired from twenty feet away, the bullet pierced the windshield shattering it instantly, and hit Peter in the right ear, taking part of his ear lobe away with it as it glanced off the side of his head. Another shot rang out a second later, but by that time Peter had hit Jerry head-on, and at speed, catapulting him upward, Peter heard him roll precariously over the roof and land in a heap behind with a thud. The Mercedes sped out into the street and jerked to the right coming to a dead stop as Peter applied the brake. Peter took evasive action and put his fist straight through the windshield to clear his line of sight. '*Jesus they are trying to kill me,*' he shouted. He looked back and saw Jerry in a heap, and not moving. His second thought was for Heather, this place would be swarming with agents in a short while. He pulled the car over to the side of the road, switched his phone on and called her landline number.

She picked up the phone, "Heather!" he said, breathless and anxious.

"Hi Peter, that was quick darling."

"Heather, listen to me carefully. Get dressed now and get out of there, they are coming for us," he said firmly, like an order he would have given to his unit coming under fire, so she knew he wasn't joking, unambiguous, and to the point.

"God, Peter, are you okay?" she asked, with tension in her voice and panic welling up.

"Never mind me, just get out of there fast, I'll meet you outside the front in two minutes. Grab the essentials, and don't delay darling," he said.

The glass went everywhere in the Mercedes, and the knuckles of his right hand were now bleeding as well as his ear, he brushed the glass off the passenger seat into the well of the car as best he could, with the adrenaline now at full dosage he didn't feel any pain at all. He drove quickly around to the front of the apartment block on Fifth Avenue and waited patiently for Heather at the front entrance with the Mercedes still in the drive position, he tapped the steering wheel nervously and looked into his rear-view mirror as traffic sped past, and looking for anything or anyone out of the ordinary. The doorman must have thought something was not quite right, driving up with a busted windshield and a big hole where his fist had gone through, but he never commented at all, just smiled and waved back at him.

Jerry wouldn't be moving very far any time soon, Peter thought. He must be really fucked up, and good riddance, so he was safe for a moment or two. Jerry might have had a chance to call it in, but it was doubtful. Jerry Martin, the Medal of Honor winner that he didn't deserve, what was he doing here? Peter speculated. Was he still a mercenary? A paid assassin? And after the Angola thing, was still on the payroll of the Government? Either way, he's in the hospital with at least two broken legs and a headache.

The large glass door bellowed open and hit the stops before it smashed, as Heather appeared in a panic with a small bag under her arm, she ran out of the building and straight into the Mercedes, the doorman tried to help but wasn't quick enough to open the door for her, so he just waved at them. Peter put his foot down hard as the car lept into action and sped away down Fifth Avenue.

"No, Milo?" Peter asked while negotiating the morning traffic through the hole in the windshield.

"The dog sitter will look after him, he'll be fine," she said nervously sitting very uncomfortably on bits of glass digging into the back of her thighs. She could see the blood as it dripped continuously from Peter's earlobe onto his shoulder. "You're bleeding Peter from your ear, do you know? Oh, and your hand? What—"

"Don't worry, it's a scratch, the bastard shot at me, and look at your windshield, they are trying to bloody kill me again, I don't know why, but I don't want you involved Heather," he said out of concern for her safety.

"Well it looks like I am involved, doesn't it?" she said stubbornly, dabbing his hand and then his ear with a tissue she had found in her bag. "They could be after me now as well have you thought of that?"

"Have you a safe place to go," Peter asked anxiously.

"Yes, my mum lives in Queens, she would love to meet you. We can go there."

"Good, I'm ditching the car," he said abruptly, as he turned down Seventy-Eighth Street.

"Where?"

"Just here." He brought the car to a standstill, five blocks away from Heather's apartment. The car was too much of an eyesore with the windshield shattered. If stopped by police, they would be arrested for driving a car like that, then he would have to explain everything. The CIA would then find them, this was the best way Peter thought. They exited the car and just walked away, leaving it in a no parking zone, Eighty Thousand dollars' worth of car just sitting there unlocked. It would be towed away within the hour, or stolen, Heather thought. They walked into the crowds that were gathered on the corner, ditching both their phones into a bin as they rushed away to become anonymous to the world.

After walking a few blocks, they were now on Third Avenue and could relax, Birch Coffee House was a welcome place to sit down and rest for a while, drink a cappuccino and think about what to do. Peter went off to the bathroom to clean up his appearance and wash his wounds. The coffee shop was practically empty apart from an old lady in the corner reading a paper, and having a coffee, it reminded Heather of Luigi's steeped in family history that would be passed down through generations.

After five minutes Peter arrived back at the table, looking purposeful.

"I've got a plan," he said.

"We are going to have to get that ear looked at Peter, it looks angry, it could get infected and your hand, was that the windshield?" she said, touching it.

"Owh!" He snatched her hand away quickly, "Yes, the glass is quite sharp. It's just a scratch, nothing to fret over," he smiled at Heather's concern.

"You should take care of yourself a bit more," she said, stroking his arm.

"You sound like my mother, it's okay, really it is Heather, but I can't go to the hospital," he said. "They would be able to find us there. We have got to get ahead of this. They have too many cards in their favour."

"What do you suggest?" she asked calmly.

"We need to get some wheels first and get you over to your mum's in Queens, that's the plan, then I'll be happy," he said. "We will need to pick up two phones as well on the way."

"What will you do Peter? Don't go and get yourself killed," she said anxiously.

"There is someone I need to find, she will be able to help, she has connections."

"She?" Heather said abruptly.

"My old P.A. Sheila, she had connections in the White House and government," he said. "Sheila's okay and smart as a button and knows everybody."

"She sounds like superwoman."

"She is, she was, should I say. A good person, believe me, she meant a lot to me back then, and practically ran my business for me," Peter said. "She used to work for the government, I'm sure she could help us."

"How old?" she asked curiously.

"What now?" He thought for a moment, "Sixty, sixty-five perhaps."

Heather smiled, "Oh! That's okay then."

"That's okay then, silly." He smiled at her comment, "There was never anything romantically between us. Sheila's one of the most trustworthy people I know. She worked for Al Gore as well for two years you know."

"I've met him many times," Heather commented.

"Oh! We do move in different circles, don't we?" Peter joked.

"No, my dad knew him very well, he'd come to our house sometimes for dinner, and they would talk privately for hours at a time."

"I bet Sheila would have known your dad. I'll ask her when I see her," he said. "Right, we have things to do, drink up."

They left the café and carried on walking down Third Street. Renting a car was easy if you had an ID, so Heather had to do it while Peter sorted the phones out in cash again, two brand new Samsung smartphones, something new for Peter to get his head around. A Buick was less conspicuous than the Mercedes Heather thought, and she could pay cash as well, so no card payment would be recorded.

In forty-five minutes, they were in Jackson Heights. Olive Lombard lived in a quaint white panelled house on Eighty-Fifth Street overlooking Gorman Park, and it was the most prominent house in the street. She had lived in Queens all her life, and fifty years in that house, never wanting to move, even though they had the money to live anywhere in the country. All her friends were there so *why move elsewhere and be lonely'* she would say, and she had a point. Olive now in her late seventies would always be out at some function or another, socialising and hosting regular coffee mornings at the house. When she opened the door, Peter could see a lot of Heather in her, it was a remarkable likeness and thirty years between them. Olive was immaculately dressed with hair and makeup professionally done as though she could be going somewhere special at the drop of a hat, something she must have passed onto Heather, he thought. Heather introduced Peter to her, Olive liked him instantly, and they hit it off straight the way. Olive probably believed that Peter was of the same age as Heather, so he was a perfect match for her daughter who up to now had never settled down or found Mr Right.

Heather set about washing Peter's ear with some antiseptic solution and applied a neat dressing that made it look less suspicious. Olive gave him a T-shirt and a brown leather jacket that belonged to her late husband. They made up some story 'on the hoof' about a dog that had bit his ear in the park, utterly unconvincing, but Olive went along with it knowing there was more to the story than just a dog. Anyone connected with him would be at risk from now on he thought, so he would have to be extra vigilant, extra careful. He paired the new phones up putting in each number on a speed dial so that they could keep in contact should they need to, and told her not to call anyone she knew that way she would stay off the grid.

Chapter 24

Peter had left some important papers on his desk, Sheila noticed, he would need them later to go through at home before a ten o'clock meeting in the morning with his lawyers. If she was quick, she could catch him before he drove off to play golf. She grabbed the papers from his desk and dashed down the stairs as fast as her high heels would allow, going down slightly sideways and keeping her legs together. As she reached the bottom of the stairs, she stood for a moment looking around, it was all quiet, and Peter wasn't there.

"Peter?" she shouted nervously scanning the garage left and right. "Peter, where are you?" she said again curiously as if he was hiding like a child would, and pop up at the last minute to catch her out. Her voice echoed all around the stale dimly lit garage that had a slight smell of spent gasoline. Then she heard something that sounded like Peter's voice far off in the distance somewhere, it was ethereal in nature, then it stopped. She walked hesitantly and slowly over to check on his car, all she could hear were her stilettos clicking on the concrete floor and some faint murmurings from the offices upstairs. She tried the door to his new Mercedes, it was unlocked, his pride and joy, but no Peter anywhere. What had just happened? She went over it in her mind, questioning it. He had gone down the stairs only a minute before she had noticed the papers. She saw him go through the office door, so he definitely would have ended up in the garage as there is nowhere else to go, there was no toilet down here either as that was in the main reception area. She had noticed someone come up from the garage though, just after Peter had gone down, but that couldn't be anything, could it? So, she dismissed it. Is it possible Peter could have been picked up? But Peter would have said something? She would have known his schedule. She went back up to the office and called his cell phone. The call went straight to voicemail. Her next call was to the police.

That was the last memory Sheila had of Peter in 2001, that day fifteen years ago until she answered an unknown caller on her mobile and instantly recognised his voice, it was a bolt out of the blue, she was overjoyed to hear his voice, his dulcet tones, and that he was still alive after all these years of not knowing. She used to think about him a lot and where he could be, a mystery that needed solving, it was always there in her subconscious. The heartache she had gone through with the business and Marie, all came flooding back in an instant. They arranged to meet at a Starbucks near the Yankee Stadium within the hour as it was only a few minutes from where she worked.

Sheila left the office for an early lunch and walked the few blocks with a smile on her face that wouldn't go away. She felt excited, like a schoolgirl going on her first date, curious to hear the story, the mystery, she could hardly contain herself.

The Starbucks on 161st Street, the Bronx, was very busy at that time of day. Peter got there with time to spare and bought the coffees. He was sitting there drinking his Cappuccino and playing with his new Samsung when Sheila walked in. Five feet ten inches tall, she was wearing a white tailored trouser suit, and looking fabulous just as he remembered. The September sun lit up her neatly groomed short auburn hair, minimal makeup and looked like a film star ready for her first take. Many people turned around thinking she was someone famous, a regular occurrence as Peter recalled. She had aged a bit in fifteen years, but she had always been a fit, good looking, confidently strong woman, and had kept herself in great shape, so even at sixty-five she looked amazing and a lot younger than she was. The emotional reunion in the middle of the floor got most people's attention.

"Hello, Sheila," Peter said, greeting her standing up with a big hug and a long kiss on the cheek for his long-lost friend.

"Hello, you," she said, pushing him jokingly with her fist. "Let me have a look at you. Don't mind me," she said, wiping her eyes. She looked him up and down, noting the damage to his ear and hand. "You haven't aged a bit, Peter, you look amazing."

He was only a few days older since the last time he'd met her, he thought, "I took the liberty of getting you a flat white."

"Very thoughtful thanks."

"How have you been Sheila? It is so good to see you. You haven't changed much either, you look fabulous," he said, and he meant it.

She took a tissue out of her matching leather handbag and sat down at the table. "You're being kind now, I know. Look at me, blubbering away. I'm older, Peter, that is obvious, and it takes longer now to get me into this state I can tell you. It's great you called though, you know I would always have been there for you, Peter. It's bizarre, I think about you every day, where you are, what you might be doing, who you are with," she said, wiping her eyes to avoid the mascara running. It was apparent to anyone watching they had a lot of love for each other, the sort of love a mother and son would have.

"I'm sorry I called you under these circumstances, Sheila, but thanks for coming, I didn't know who else to call."

"Well, thank God you called me then and saved me from this fifteen-year mystery," she said, holding his hand. She moved slightly closer and looked at him directly. "So, what happened to you, Peter? After you called, I recalled the moment to myself when you disappeared. It was horrible, you know eerie, we were all left in a sort of limbo."

"I'm still trying to find an explanation myself. When I left you to go and play golf, I walked through the garage to my car, and something happened to me. My whole world changed from 2001 to 2016 in an instant."

"Sounds almost Sci-Fi," she smiled.

"I cannot explain it any better than that, but two days ago I was having coffee with you in our office, and now I'm here talking to you in 2016, fifteen years later."

"The Police were all over it, in the Papers and everything, appeals went out for information," she said. "Then all hell broke loose with nine-eleven."

They looked at each other for a moment, both thinking the same thing.

"Tom and Jake, they were—"

"Yes I know, you poor thing, they were so young as well, so tragic."

"Still cannot believe it even now," he said reminiscing. "Anyway the government is behind it somehow, someone knows what happened. Only now the CIA is trying to kill me, for what? I don't know. Earlier today an ex-marine, which I had fought alongside in Iraq I might add, tried to kill me. Jerry Martin, he shot at me with a silenced Glock, took half my soddin' ear lobe away. And yesterday, I had a run-in with two agents in Macy's. I took this ID from one of them," he said, handing it to her. "I was hoping you still had connections and could find out why they are after me? then I can deal with it, hand myself into the right people, I'm a sitting duck out here, it's only a matter of time before they find me."

"It looks like you've been in the wars, Glocks are standard issue for the CIA that's for sure," she said touching his ear tenderly.

"Owh! That's tender," he flinched.

"Oh sorry," she said, pulling her hand away. Then she studied the ID for a moment. "Brian Delaney, I know him, he's good."

"Really," Peter looked surprised.

"He's up there with the top few you can rely on to get the job done, that's all I know," she said. "Lucky for you he didn't have back up."

"He did."

"Really?"

"There were three of them, two men that I took out, and one girl, she looked scared out of her wits."

"You didn't kill them?"

"No."

"Good," Sheila said, studying the card.

"Just put them out of action," Peter elaborated. "They must be in the hospital I would have thought, one having his leg plastered, the other would be having his jaw wired," he smiled.

"Thank God, you are okay though," Sheila said.

"Remember Jim?"

"Yes, I heard."

"What you wouldn't have heard is that I had arranged to meet him at The Bayside Golf club yesterday, you know, our old golf club where I was going that day," he said, looking around and keeping his voice down to a whisper. "And another thing, people were looking for me before I got there, 'Government types.' The barman said. They showed him a picture of me."

"Really? That's odd, did they show their ID."

"No, they didn't."

She looked at Peter. "It could be the CIA, I hear about most operations, not all, this sounds like covert, undercover, you know a need to know operation. We have these factions within the intelligence service that sort out problems. There are some high-profile ones we hear about, and when it's in the public interest, we then can tell the media it was the CIA working on their behalf to make them feel safer. If it's not, and it is covert, you will never hear about it, but people will be dealt with, the job will get done. I'm not saying this is one of those, but a house invasion by an unknown person or persons and the way they were shot as well, leads me to think it was professionals."

"Poor Jim and Ruth, though, what did they ever do to anyone?" Peter said somberly.

"I know it's deplorable."

"So, you went back to what you know best then?"

"Since Edwards and Collins finished, I have been doing some work for the CIA here in New York City," she said. "I'm almost retired now, so I do a bit of temporary work. You get to hear what's going on, the big thing at the moment is drug cartel's operating here in New York City. Last week there was open warfare on the streets of Manhattan as two cartel's shot it out, five civilians got caught up in the crossfire."

"Do you think you could find out why they are after me?"

"I would have thought your name would have popped up somewhere, I haven't personally seen anything, Peter."

Sheila had friends in every area of government that she could use for information purposes. She was the *go-to girl* for information of any kind. "I will have to do some digging around for you and try to find out what's going on. I will have to let you know later."

"That's good of you Sheila really," he said, feeling relieved. "These people are dangerous. I would tread carefully, don't go rattling any hornet's nest. I suppose you can tell I'm a bit paranoid about the whole thing," Peter said.

"Yes, I know Peter, it's nice that you worry," she said, stroking his chin. "I know who to ask and who I can trust, believe me, Peter, I've been doing it long enough. Are you sure you're okay? It looks like it needs attention?" His ear was now throbbing badly and looked angry.

"Yeah, I'll live. I've had a lot worse. Anyway, what happened to the company with me gone, I know we went out of business, but when was that? I spoke to Marie briefly about it at lunch yesterday, but it wasn't the right time to bring everything up?"

"Lawrence died of course in 2004, so we finished the business in 2005, very sad for everyone concerned."

"His heart finally gave out, did it?" Peter asked. "I spoke to Jen on the phone but didn't have time to ask her, I think she was too upset with hearing my voice after all this time. She sounded so frail as well."

"It wasn't his heart at all, in fact, he was back at work taking on your role for three years quite seriously and doing great. No, he went on his usual hunting trip up into the Rockies with his pals, you know, Buster, Dave and the guys, and Buster killed him with an arrow by accident. Though he was a deer, Lawrence was in between Buster and the deer, a classic hunting accident that has happened many times before no doubt. You survive all that he went through with his heart only for some dumb-ass mistake to finish you off. There is no justice in this world."

"Oh dear, poor Larry," he said, imagining the scenario. "He loved his hunting, I could never imagine doing it myself, but that's me, I guess. And what happened to the company, was it dreadful?"

"Yes, I ran it, quite well I think for a while, we were making good profits then there was a big bust-up with Marie and Jennifer, so they both wanted their money out then, can't blame them. They didn't get a fraction of what it was worth though, the lawyers had a field day. All water under the bridge now though, eh Peter. We need to get you sorted now, don't we?"

"Yeah, that would be great if you could find out something at least I would know which way to go."

"Okey-doke, well I'd better get to it then, I'll make a few calls from the office, then I'll be home later. I'll give you a call in a bit, say four o'clock is that okay?"

"I'll switch my phone on then and call you. I don't like anyone tracking me."

"Yes, good thinking, I'll be in touch at four."

She kissed him on the cheek again and left to get on with things in a very business-like manner. Peter looked around the café, scanning every face, no one seemed to alarm him, he was safe for a while.

He drove over to the shopping mall in Queens to have a look around, and maybe buy some clothes. He couldn't even think let alone buy clothes, so he sat in a coffee shop reading the Post for a while, and thinking about what he could do to get himself out of this situation.

Chapter 25

McClean sat at his console in the Mag-Tron control room. He had just got to hear about a shooting that had taken place in Manhattan nearby Fifth Avenue earlier that day. No one was killed, but a male Caucasian was en-route to St. Luke's hospital with broken bones and concussion.

"What do we know about the shooter Edwards?" McClean asked, looking at the mapped area where it took place.

"He is a freelancer, works mainly for the CIA, by the name of Jerry Martin, ex-marine, basically a gun for hire, our guys are checking it out."

"What are they doing? Carrying out this sort of thing in public, it's crazy," McClean said, the irritation etched into his expression as he scratched the side of his unshaven face. "Can we find out who he was shooting at? Have we got anyone on the ground?"

Edwards had anticipated McClean's thought process after working with him for so long, "yes, we have. We have accessed the CCTV footage from a camera at number 1 East Eighty-Fifth Street, which overlooks the underground garage for 1035 Fifth Avenue. We should have footage coming up shortly,"

"Good Man," McClean said.

When the footage came up on the monitors, it showed a side view of Jerry shooting at the Mercedes, and then the Mercedes striking him. Frame by frame showed his legs breaking from the impact and then rolling over the top of the car as it came out of the garage at speed. A glimpse of the driver could also be seen smashing the shattered windscreen outward as he stopped the car right in front of the camera.

"Ouch! I bet that hurt," McClean grimaced. "Well, I guess we've found Peter Collins then, he's a busy boy our Peter, isn't he? Where is he going, I wonder?"

"He is standing still about five blocks away on the corner of East Seventy-Eighth and Park Avenue not moving."

"Standing still?"

"For the last ten minutes at least, he's dumped his phone, probably a burner anyway. He could be anywhere now."

"That's useful. Not. Have we a trace on the Merc?" McClean said, sounding irked and looking at the screen with Edwards.

"Yes, sir, it's registered to the Lombard foundation."

"What's that?"

"You know, Harry Lombard, big financier, committed suicide eight years back."

"So, we can assume this is not his car then, can we?" McClean quipped.

"We are working on that."

"So he has help, and is working with someone, where is he now?"

"We have two teams trying to locate him as we speak to bring him in. He has just been a little elusive, it's challenging to track someone with no ID, no credit cards, and now no phone."

"I get it, Edwards," McClean concurred. "But that's the second time an attempt has been made on his life. Why are we getting everything second-hand? We have to get ahead of this, or we will have a corpse to deal with."

"There is something else that is in play here, sir, another chess piece on the board. They wouldn't have known who he was if we hadn't told them, and asked them for help," Edwards said, thinking now that it was a mistake to let his mate Jack in on it. "It's obvious they want him dead, there is another agenda."

"They, being the CIA?"

"Yes, sir. The order must have come from high up," Edwards speculated.

"Yeah, and I know who would have given it."

"April?"

"Yeah. April can be a bitch when she wants to be, steps on everyone's toes to make herself look a little better and get further up the ladder, one day she might be President."

McClean made the call to April Haines, the current Deputy Director of the CIA. She had served as Deputy Counsel for the NSA, which is where McClean had met her three years earlier. She knew how both agencies functioned. It seemed like both agencies worked together to the outside world, but they were very much entirely separate entities, hardly sharing anything for the common good. He didn't expect to get anything out of her, but he thought it was worth rattling her cage.

"April, how are you? Doug McClean."

"Yes, good thanks, Doug, long time," she said efficiently.

One thing that April hated was small talk, so you'd better get to the point real quick, or she would cut you off at the knees. A real ball buster for male staff, which is why she rose to the heights she did so quickly. Many times, when interviewed on TV, April would come across as a stylish orator, knowing her stuff, sharp as a button, and quite pleasant, most women envied her. She wore very plain but classy clothes, and her whole persona was stage-managed to get the best effect, all the media lapped it up like ice cream on a hot day. The Director of the CIA, John Owen Yellen, relied on her judgment implicitly and he, in turn, reported to the incumbent president, Barack Obama directly.

"Yeah, it is. Have you anything to do with the shooting today just off Fifth Avenue?" he asked bluntly.

"Well don't beat around the bush there Doug, just get straight to the point why don't you?"

"Well, were you?" McClean challenged.

"Well, what?"

"Were you involved? Was it you, the CIA?" McClean pressed. "It's a simple question, April." He imagined her sitting in her ivory tower with all that power at her fingertips, she was power-hungry, power crazy.

"Doug, I'm not going to be bullied by you or anyone," she retorted. "We work to different agenda's here, you of all people would know that more than anyone, wouldn't you?"

"But Peter Collins is not a threat April. He's a family man and a national hero from the Gulf war. You cannot go around just shooting people at will. We are handling it April, and if you don't like it, speak to Groves, he has given his backing to our plan," McClean said. He knew she knew something, he sensed it in her reply.

"Maybe you can answer me this then?" she asked.

"What?"

"He is a sleeper, isn't he?"

"No!"

"Then how did he get here? Where has he come from?"

"That's classified April, sorry."

"I'm sorry too."

"I can see I'm going to have to go over your head on this one then."

"Be my guest. We bang to a different drum here at the CIA Doug, you know that different budgets etcetera, etcetera," she said glibly. "Goodbye, Doug."

The phone went silent, April ended the call abruptly. McClean didn't trust her for a second. Someone had made decisions about Peter, and if it wasn't her, it was someone higher up. He would have to make Senator Groves aware of the situation and the current impasse.

Chapter 26

April Haines slammed the phone down, she felt like she'd been ambushed. She always avoided direct questions from anyone and liked to know about everything beforehand. Senator Groves had introduced her as a candidate for Deputy Director, and the President signed off on her appointment, she never took sides in an argument and was always the one who came out best. 'Politics is like warfare,' April used to say, keep your head above water long enough for all the other sons of bitches to drown because of their incompetence. She never got angry or flustered in a heated discussion and always ended on an appropriate point, a winning strategy that had taken her to the top, a formidable woman. She walked into the CIA Control Centre at Langley and tore a strip off the first person she saw sitting in front of his console. That person happened to be Agent Jack Graham.

"Agent Graham, why is it that I'm not kept informed," she asked pointedly.

"Sorry, I don't understand ma'am," With a look of bewilderment and dread on his face. A silence fell over the office as everyone stopped to look and listen.

"I just got off the phone to Doug McClean over at the NSA. So why is it that I'm standing there naked, with my dick in my hand?" she said metaphorically speaking. The right corner of Jack's mouth began to quiver and turn upward just a nanometre, creating a tiny half-smile as he tried desperately to hold it in. "Eh, why is that Graham, can you tell me?"

Breathing heavily through his nostrils and felt the eyes of the office behind him drilling into the back of his head, he said. "Again, ma'am I don't kn—!"

"For God's sake Graham, and everyone else for that matter," she shrieked. Raising her voice while standing up slightly taller and looking around the office at the six agents who turned quickly back to tapping at their keyboards, "I need to be kept informed."

"There have been two, I repeat two bungled attempts on Peter Collins's life and why don't I know about it, why am I being told this second-hand by a has-been at the NSA."

"Oh, sorry ma'am, I thought you would only want to know if we got a result," he said apologetically.

"Who is this, Peter Collins? How does he survive not one but two attempts on his life by the CIA?" she asked. "I thought we had our top men on this?"

"He is military trained, special forces, he fought in the gulf war with the Marines, so he's no pushover. He took two of our agents out at a shop in Macy's store yesterday and one of our top agents earlier today. He has put them all in the hospital, maybe we have underestimated him, he could have killed them I suppose, but didn't, he let them live."

"We were supposed to take him out along with the people he has come in contact with, this should have been contained days ago, and instead he is still out there interacting with everyone. The worst thing for us is that if this gets out, it will make us look inept, weak, unprofessional, do you hear me?"

"Yes, I do loud and clear. He has been staying with a Heather Lombard on Fifth Avenue. Our agent confirmed it, albeit before he got hospitalised. Her family has property all over Manhattan, a very wealthy family, we have people on the ground, checking these addresses out."

April stood over Agent Graham and said. "He has ditched all trackable communications as well I suppose?"

"We have no up-to-date comms, but we have a lead. Only two hours ago someone here at the CIA was asking a few questions that led us to believe that she had been in contact with him, we are checking that out as well behind the scenes."

"Okay then, I'll be in my office. Remember to keep me informed in future, okay?"

"Will do ma'am."

He sat there for a moment taking in a deep breath and smirking to himself while looking at his screen, everyone in the room was listening to Agent Graham as they stared at their screens.

"I had my suspicions about her," he said quietly. "A dick? She was probably once called Andy," he sniggered, and a muted laughter filled the room, and everyone had a smile on their face at April's expense.

Chapter 27

As Peter sat killing time at the Queens shopping mall while having a coffee, he felt vulnerable all of a sudden being out in the open, he nervously looked around, but no one paid him any attention at all, it was all in his mind. The time was 3:45 by his watch and 3:47 by the clock on the café wall, when waiting for something, it would always seem longer, and he hated waiting for anything. People were chatting at tables talking about things that mattered to them, at this time of day most people looked older, retired possibly, he thought. The sun beamed in through the skylight of the mall, and the atmosphere was calming with Matt Monroe playing in the background on the sound system, almost cutting through the noise of people chatting and laughing, with the occasional phone going off. But he felt anything but calm, he felt tense and looked at the time again, barely a minute had gone by, since he last looked.

An old man went by on a motorised floor polisher with a smart janitor's uniform on, and a constant smile on his face, saying hello to anyone and everyone. He smiled at Peter, and it was impossible not to smile back, instantly changing his mood. He was happy in his work and satisfied with his lot, no stress, just a ride around the mall for a few hours and for God's sake don't bump into anyone, pick up your paycheck at the end of the day and go home to the wife, a lovely life with no pressure. 3:55 arrived, not long now, he thought, He took the Samsung out and placed it on the table, ready to switch it on for Sheila's call.

People watching was a thing he and Marie loved doing on days out, asking each other questions like, 'what's life like for that person or the other person? Where do they live? What do they do for work? Are they married, divorced, kids, no kids' and so on? He missed those times, those days. He missed them a lot. He missed Marie, and her lovely ways, her humour, Ashley with her vitality, her laughter, her joy of life, and he missed Tom and Jake most of all, they were always with him in his thoughts as he thought of a hundred and one other important things, it was all crammed in there seeping through the edges of his thought process at every moment of the day and night.

At 3:58 he switched the Samsung on, a little impatience entered his thought process as the phone took its time booting up. He hadn't had any calls apart from Heather who'd left him a message to let him know she was okay and missed him. She never said 'love you,' that was probably too soon in reality.

Every minute ticked heavily and slowly over to the next, he tried not to look at the time, but every twenty or thirty seconds he couldn't help it, it was there nagging him, prodding him. After five minutes it was 4:03, and Sheila hadn't called, and that was unlike her, it bothered him because she was meticulously punctual, and if she said four o'clock, she would have called unless something had happened. So he called her number breaking a golden rule he had recently thought of, the call went straight to voicemail. 'If someone had her phone, they would now have his number, and that meant danger.' He said to himself. He switched the phone off and walked to the Phone shop in the mall to buy a new one, leaving a recently brewed coffee on the table.

He chose the same Samsung 'Pay as you go' as he had gotten used to the workings of it, but he purposely bought it on a different network, AT&T. The young girl in the shop set it up for him. She asked him if he had his old phone to transfer all the numbers and data over. This operation took less than ten seconds as there were only a few numbers on the phone anyway. She could have asked 'why are you buying a new phone when the Samsung you have is perfectly okay and brand new?' But she didn't, she was happy to have the commission she would get selling him a new one. He now had three phones weighing down his pockets, but he would dump the old Samsung later to his advantage.

As 4:30 ticked over, another cappuccino drank with the dregs now cold. Peter switched the phone on again, there was still no message or a call from Sheila, and now he was worried, very worried, he called her again, it went to voicemail once more. He deleted all the contacts from the phone and switched it straight off again. He sat there for a moment feeling apprehensive looking around still, then as he usually does, he took control of his fear and emotions and made his way to the exit. As he got back to the Buick, he noticed a black Lincoln Continental come through into the underground garage and park up. There were two agent types inside, and he watched them from a vantage point slumped down inside. Were they there for him? Quite possibly, he thought. Both agents exited the Lincoln looking around and surveying the garage. Dark sunglasses, black suits, black tie, they were not there to buy anything, that was obvious, they walked upstairs to the mall. Peter then left the garage in an orderly fashion.

Sheila lived in Utopia, Queens, a middle-class neighbourhood about ten minutes away from where Heather's mum lived. He parked the Buick on the leafy Sixty-Fifth Avenue about ten houses away from Sheila's, and sat in the car surveying the street, slightly nervous, and still apprehensive. After a few minutes, Peter stepped carefully out of the Buick, crossed the road and walked down towards the house, quickly surveying all the cars in the street on both sides. He took his Samsung out and put it in front of him pretending to read something on it, he'd seen people walk with their phone out in front of them, oblivious to their surroundings and perfectly normal behaviour nowadays. It was strange seeing them do this, he thought, but that gave him an excuse to walk slow.

The branches of the trees overhung the road on both sides, and the bronzed leaves were now under the gravitational force of the earth, falling to the ground, gathering in random heaps by the cars and curbstones, flicking up in the gentle breeze, fall had started a few weeks ago. As he got closer to her house, he ducked down quickly behind a large red Toyota Land Cruiser, as if to tie his shoelace, and peered through the side window and windshield down the street. There was a car parked about four houses past Sheila's with two guys in the front seats, he saw one of them light up a cigarette. Agent types, CIA, they had to be, he thought. Staking the house, Sheila's house, what were they doing there?

He retreated to the end of the street where there was a public footpath that went all the way down the back of the houses. At the entrance to the path, there were discarded needles scattered aimlessly about, graffiti slogans daubed on the brick walls, and dog excrement dotted about, it was probably a meeting place for drug addicts to gather later in the evening, Peter thought. Any public footpath in Queens was chancy, but at that time of the day though, it was clear. He walked down to the back of Sheila's house. There was a double wrought iron metal gate to the left about ten feet tall backed with rusty sheet metal so that you couldn't see through it, then a five-foot brick wall next to it and a wooden fence on top going the width of the garden. He jumped on top of the wall using the gate to step up, gaining enough height to peer over the fence carefully. He could see the light on in the house and the flickering of a television that was on in the front room, but he couldn't see any real movement at all.

It was a large red brick house with white painted architrave, and there were mature overgrown trees dotted around the lawn area, the grass had grown two feet tall and looked like it hadn't been cut all summer. Sheila had lived there on and off all of her life, and had lived alone there for the last twenty years since her mother died. She kept the house as a base in New York and bought another home in the Florida Keys by the sea, which she would eventually move to when she finally retired.

He climbed over the metal gate and jumped down onto the long grass which cushioned his feet, he walked in a 'stoop-like' fashion up to the back door, continually watching for movement of any kind surveying the windows. Peering through the large window into the lounge area, he could see the television was on with no one watching it. He tried the back door, and luckily it opened, so he entered quietly, the door let out a high-pitched squeak, not a good start.

Peter listened for any movement in the house over the faint sound of the television. He walked through the ground floor as he would have done in Iraq looking for insurgents, clearing every room, every nook, and cranny. When he got to the front window, he peered out and could see the car still there with two agents observing the house. Taking the stairs up to the top floor, he called out, "Sheila," he whispered, "Are you there?" No one answered, but an eerie silence ensued. The smell of the same perfume that he had smelt on Sheila earlier at Starbucks invaded his nostrils. She was close, he thought.

He walked carefully into the main bedroom, opening the door slowly and as wide as it would go, no one was there, but the room was spotless like a hotel's room with the bed pristinely made, same with the other two bedrooms. Just along the landing, he could see the bathroom door and a light on through the glass panel at the top. He went up to it, knocked quietly, and whispered Sheila's name, no answer. There was a sound of dripping water as he opened it slowly and gently. He could now see the constant trickle that had gathered into a puddle underneath the antique cast iron bath and around the ornate feet. A white shower curtain was drawn around the outside and almost touched the floor, and a flicker of candlelight shone through the curtain. A very romantic setting on any other day, but today it felt ominously tragic. He went over to it tentatively and pulled the curtain back slightly so he could see around and into the bath. His dark thoughts had been justified. He took in a quick deep breath at the shock, and let it out slowly and controlled. Lying there in the overfilled bath was Sheila with a bullet hole through the socket of her left eye and another to the chest, her head was half in the water cocked to one side and slightly back as if she had fallen asleep. She still had on her white trouser suit and the bathwater had turned to a bright shade of crimson. He turned the water tap off.

Peter instantly felt sadness, tears welled up into the corners of his eyes as he stood there, feeling helpless, looking at her innocent face semi-submerged. 'It was my fault, my fault you are lying there dead,' he told himself. There was no way to get around it. 'If he hadn't met her earlier today, she would still be alive.' His sadness gave way to anger and revenge that came up from deep inside, the last time he felt that way was in Iraq when a dear friend had been shot at close range by three Taliban rebels. He was going to have to think straight, there was a car outside with agents that were waiting for him, if he showed his hand now, they would have him, and probably Heather too, so there was nothing gained in alerting them to his presence.

Peter looked objectively at the way Sheila was lying there in the bath for a moment, thinking about her and noticed her right arm was outside the tub, her index finger seemed slightly raised to the other fingers of her delicately manicured hand, it was as though she was pointing at something. Peter always knew how resourceful and quick-thinking she was, and just maybe she would have left him something to find. He pulled back the shower curtain and looked around the floor, first under the large woven mat that covered the oak flooring, as he picked it up the water came up with it, dispersing it further over the floor like a mini tsunami. Then noticing a set of pine draws by the back wall, he looked through the top drawer, everything was neatly folded as it should be. Then he pulled open the second draw, the same could be said, all neat and in place. The third one, however, had some towels that had been disturbed and put back haphazardly and looked slightly out of place, and sure enough under the first green towel was a hand-written note from Sheila, he couldn't believe it, it was like she was speaking to him from the other side. He looked over at her with pride and love, he smiled at her and said thank you. The note read:-

"Peter, they are at the door, I messed up. The CIA has a contract out on you and everyone you have met, be careful. Jerry Martin is at MS St Luke's, seek out Doug McClean NSA he can help you. Love always S."

He re-read the note and noticed the handwriting was almost perfect as he remembered, not rushed at all. Sheila knew precisely how much time she had Peter thought, then folded it in quarters and put it away in his back pocket next to his wallet. His military brain now went into overdrive. He took his new Samsung out, switched it on and called Heather.

"Who's that?" Heather said as she had not recognised the number.

"It's me."

"Thank God. I wondered when you would call. New phone, eh?"

Peter then said, "Yes I needed to," he paused, "Heather, Sheila's dead, the bastards killed her."

"Oh my God. Why? Who?"

"It's the CIA. They are onto me. They have killed her because of me, Heather."

"Jesus, Peter, what are we going to do?" she said, sounding as though she was at her wit's end.

"We need to take action."

"What do you have in mind?"

"First, you and your mum get out of that house just in case."

"In case of what!" she said, raising her voice.

"In case they are tracking your phone as well."

"Oh, God."

"Take this number down quickly and text me where you are from another phone, ditch the phone you are on, we'll get you a new one? Don't delay Heather, they will try and get to me any way they can."

"Okay, Peter I'll talk to mum straight the way," she said panicking inside, Peter could hear it in her voice.

"I'll be making my way over in your direction shortly as soon as I leave here."

"Where are you now?"

"I'm in Sheila's house, the agents are outside," he said quietly.

"What! Peter, get out of there for God's sake."

"I'm leaving now."

"Okay, I'll text you."

The phone went dead.

He took one final look at Sheila, said a little prayer to her, kissed her forehead and then backtracked out of the house, making sure he didn't disturb anything. He took meticulous care to wipe away any fingerprints he might have left behind. Thinking ahead, he didn't want to be accused of her murder, if it was ever made public. As he thought about the agents in the mall earlier, the only way they would know where he was, was through the phone, that was his only contact with the outside world. He took his old Samsung out and switched it on, placing it on the kitchen drainer and wiping it clean on his way out. He closed the back door and walked down the garden through the long grass, climbed over the metal gate onto the wall, walked along the footpath to the end, and then walked around to the Buick calmly as if he was casually going to work.

As he got into the driver's side, he saw the agents running up Sheila's driveway in a hurry. He quickly called Heather, it went to voicemail, she'd turned her phone off, he turned his off too, thank God, he said to himself. He turned over the ignition and eased the Buick into the drive position, then as controlled as he could, drove past Sheila's house looking straight ahead and not at the agents that were now coming out of the house. He stopped at the end of the road to see if they would follow, they didn't, one of them stood outside the car looking about while on his phone to someone, probably in a control room somewhere, he could see him in his rear-view mirror. He made his way back to Heather purposely doing things by the book, keeping to the speed limits, not bringing any attention to himself. As he drove into Heather's mum's street, he switched his phone on again momentarily, there was a text message from Heather to say they were okay, and at Aunt Jill's house about twenty-five doors down on the same road. He noted it was a different number Heather had texted from, he was pleased about that.

He stopped outside her Aunties house gathering his thoughts about what to say to her mum, what questions would she ask, but he didn't need to, Heather had sorted everything, and her mum was nicely tucked up in bed by the time he got there. Aunty Jill wasn't as accommodating, she had a few questions for him and wanted to know everything. Heather handled it very well, and they could stay there as long as they liked, it was a family-owned house anyway, and she probably had no choice in the matter as the Lombard family seemed to own property all over New York.

Later that night around ten o'clock, he made an excuse and went out on his own in the Buick. Heather didn't say anything she knew there was something important he had to do. She followed him out to the car in her nightgown while her Aunty Jill watched her favourite program, a re-run of Friend's. She kissed him on the cheek as he got into the Buick.

"Be careful, darling?" she said with a feeling deep in her gut that she might not be seeing him again.

"I will Heather really," touching her hand. "Keep your phone off, I'll be back soon as you like. I need to do this, you know."

"I know you have." Tears came flooding down her face uncontrollably, probably because of all the stress she was going through. "See ya!"

Driving off with Heather in bits wasn't easy, but he had to do it, there was a lot at stake.

'MS St Luke's,' the same hospital where all his kids were born. What would he get from there? He didn't know, but he would see Jerry 'the snake' and hope he had an answer to some questions that had been nagging him. Like why would he now be a target and a security risk worth taking out? He didn't know anything for God's sake. Why did they kill Sheila, Jim, and Ruth? Innocent people, what had they ever done to deserve that? None of it made any sense at all.

Chapter 28

At CIA Headquarters, Langley, Jack Graham's team had located Peter at the Queens Mall, agents on the ground had entered, but Peter had already gone. Jack had spoken with the head of security and was now connecting remotely to the Mall's computer system in the security office when the agent walked in. All data from the Mall then uploaded to the CIA Mainframe as Jack's team got to work.

"Thank you for your cooperation, sir, it is much appreciated," the agent said.

The head of the mall's security said, "Anything to help national security."

"Jack, right, I'm in," he said, sitting down in front of a consul of many screens and put his phone on speaker. "I have twelve screens in front of me, Jack. What do you want me to do?"

"Nothing, just sit there and observe," Jack said. "I'm resetting all the monitor screens for thirty minutes ago. Look at the main atrium screen, see if you can spot Peter Collins."

The head of security and his assistant stood at the back of the room in awe, observing what was going on. The mouse cursor flicked around the main computer screen turning the footage on and off on the small screen then zooming in on various people as Jack sifted through video footage on their computer.

The agent then spotted Peter on the Atrium screen, "I've got him at the coffee shop looking at his phone."

Jack zoomed into the screen. "Right that's him, let's fast forward it and see where he goes."

They observe Peter leaving his table in slow motion for the phone shop. Ten minutes later, he comes out and goes back to his table in the coffee shop, orders himself another coffee then sits down. Minutes later, he gets up and leaves.

"What is it you want me to do?" The agent said.

"What is it you think I want you to do?" Jack said pointedly.

"Go to the phone shop and get his new number?" he asked.

"Well done you are on the same page and back in the room, thank God."

The Agent thanked the Head of Security for his help and made his way to the phone shop. The young girl gave the number to the agent but purposely got a few digits wrong, she liked the look of Peter and didn't want him to get in any trouble. So, when checking the phone, it would come up as not activated yet. On the screen at Langley, Jack ran through the rest of the footage. Peter was in the underground garage at the mall, got into a car and drove off, the camera angle wasn't quite right, but he noted the make was a Buick and the colour Grey, there were also a couple of the plate numbers that were just visible.

As Peter's phone switched on again, a warning signal popped up on an agent's console at Langley, then they notified the agents that were staking out Sheila's house in Utopia.

Chapter 29

Peter parked the Buick on West 112th Street at a designated parking spot and paid the correct fee. At the end of the road was the overpowering 'Cathedral Church of Saint John the Divine,' lit up against the night sky, standing tall, August and majestic on Amsterdam Avenue. It was built on Morningside Heights in 1892, the most elevated part of New York. Over the years, skyscrapers grew up all around and somehow made it more prominent. It was the fifth largest Christian cathedral church in the world. He remembered his children being baptised there ten years previous, then he thought about it again, it was twenty-five years ago in reality. He marked a little cross on his chest, remembering Tom and Jake as he walked over the crossing with the large five arches in front of him. He turned left along Amsterdam Avenue towards the hospital. St Luke's was only a block away on the corner of West 113th Street. He turned right at the lights and stood for a moment on the opposite side of the road, observing the comings and goings in the Ambulance bay. After ten minutes, three ambulances had come and gone depositing patients on trolleys, and there were now two ambulances in the bay. That would be his way in, he thought.

He walked in the entrance to the bay, passing in-between the ambulances, and had only got twenty feet inside when a security guard noticed him and made his way over. He was West Indian and looked like he worked out, and probably was around a foot taller than Peter, not someone to mess around with, Peter thought.

"You're in the wrong place, sir, where are you supposed to be going?" he asked, looking directly at him and pointing with his two-way radio in his right hand. The bay was his domain, it was his area to control and look after, and he did it with pride.

"Err! Sorry, it's my first time here. I'm here to see a patient of mine, I'm Doctor Jones," Peter said, he was even convinced himself saying the first thing that came into his head.

The security guard stood down and relaxed his stance as he mentioned the Doctor word. He was now closer to 'God' in his eyes.

"You look like you need a doctor yourself," he said jovially.

"What do you mean?"

"Your ear," he said, pointing at it with his two-way.

Peter had forgotten entirely about the throbbing, adrenaline had taken over, the blood had seeped through and now looked like he had a red earlobe, at least it wasn't bleeding, just dried haemoglobin that had semi flowed through the plaster that Heather had put on for him. He had more important things to think about though other than himself.

He brushed it aside and said, "Oh, that's nothing, just a scratch, the ear probably needs re-dressing," again, a compelling performance he thought.

The now over friendly security guard put his left arm around Peter's shoulders and with his two-way radio in his right hand said, "You will need to go to reception on the first floor then, you can take the elevator," as he pointed towards it situated at the back of the busy Ambulance bay. "You take care now, doctor."

Peter waved at his new friend as the doors opened. Now in the Elevator, he relaxed a bit, it was surprisingly easy he thought. He looked at his ear in the mirrored button panel, must get that looked at soon he said to himself.

He was now in the right place but looked more like a patient than a doctor. He stepped out of the elevator on the first floor as instructed, at eleven o'clock at night the reception was unusually busy due to a pile-up on the FDR, and it was no trouble to slip past and into the main hospital. He saw a changing room on the left, in there he found a white coat hanging up and a stethoscope, now he even looked like a doctor. He walked down corridors with nurses and doctors walking passed, smiling and gesturing as though he was one of them. He roamed about for a while passing patients on the wards smiling and getting used to his new role, he plucked up the courage to ask someone for directions. That someone was Anne Walsh, an English nurse over here in the states for a year's training, brown curly hair with a few freckles, piercingly blue eyes, a natural look that Peter found quite attractive.

"Sorry to bother you, nurse," he said. "I'm a bit lost."

"That's okay, we are only here to help, Doctor..." she replied in perfect English.

"Oh, call me Jones, Doctor Jones. I'm looking for a patient of mine, Jerry Martin, you wouldn't be able to find out where he is for me, would you? I can't walk around here all night."

"I'll have a look for you no problem, Doctor Jones, you have a cute face," she said, he'd heard that before somewhere but never got tired of hearing it.

"That's nice of you, thanks."

She turned to a computer screen and typed in Jerry's name. It came up straight. "He's on the top floor, that's the sixth floor, ward eighteen, room three. It's a private room, expensive. He must be either important or famous?" She smiled.

"No, he isn't famous, I can tell you, infamous perhaps, ha! Been in the paper, that sort of thing!" Peter smiled.

"Oh well," she said, shrugging her shoulders.

"Thanks ever so much you've been a great help."

As he left her smiling face behind, he walked to the stairs at the end of the ward to go upward and glanced back momentarily, she was still standing there smiling at him, so he gave her a little wave and mouthed, 'thank you again,' she waved back enthusiastically, lovely woman he thought.

Now on the sixth floor and outside the door of ward eighteen, he peered through the oval glass. Most of the lights were off, or down very low as patients slept. There was a reading light on at the end of the ward, possibly a nurse's station, he thought, more likely to be a nurse there as well writing up her notes. He walked onto the ward and straight into room three unchallenged and closed the door behind him quietly. Jerry was asleep, the low light on his bedside table lit up his face, lots of bruising, a few cuts around the eyes, but it was Jerry all right. With casts on both legs and bandages on the top of his head and arms, he looked a mess Peter thought, but alive which was the main thing. There were no machines for life support, just the monitoring of his heartbeat through a finger clip.

He stood at the end of the bed observing him for a moment, remembering when they were in Iraq on a mission to clear out several houses in Baghdad. Jerry had gotten trigger happy when entering one of the insurgent's houses and shot the whole family, children, everyone, even a baby, and they stuck a medal of honour on him for bravery. It was one of the events that were never spoken about again and never repeated, to have done so would have been foolish as the classification for such an act was a war crime, and he would have been tarnished along with his troop forever. Peter always felt the guilt from that day as it happened on his watch, he was in charge, and it came flooding back in an instant with Jerry lying there.

He walked around the bed to Jerry's side and stood over him next to the heart monitor that was keeping an eye on him. Jerry immediately stirred and opened his eyes, he must have sensed someone was there. When he saw Peter, the monitor started to beep faster. Jerry was about to say something, so Peter quickly put his left hand firmly over his mouth and leaned into him. Jerry looked at Peter with trepidation and apprehension written all over his face. His eyes tiger-like, wide open as if he had seen a ghost, Peter pressed down hard, he didn't want him to make a sound. Jerry thought at that moment, his whole life was about to flash in front of him. He grabbed at Peter's arm pathetically, but he had no strength at all, the morphine had relaxed him. The heart monitor beeped at one-fifty but not enough for an alarm to sound, but it meant he was under extreme stress.

"Hey, Jerry?" Peter whispered, leaning over him and looking directly into his eyes, he was about two inches away, in his face, and he could feel his frightened breath as he gasped for air, nowhere to run, not now. "Remember me buddy, the one you tried to kill earlier today? How are the legs? Now I'm going to count to three and release my hand from your mouth, I don't want to hear a fucking sound, have you got that? Nod if you agree, Jerry?"

Jerry nodded agreement almost immediately. Peter relaxed his hand slowly. Jerry lay there looking shocked open-mouthed and wondered what Peter had in store for him.

"Hey! Pete, what's up?" Jerry said, catching his breath with a muted croak in his voice.

"What's up? What's up? I might ask you that, fucking what's up, you fucking little shit, you shot at me, Jerry. Look at my fucking ear, that's what's fucking up!" Peter said with force but muted.

"Pete, sorry, I didn't want to do it, mate, they made me."

"Mate? You're no fucking mate, are you? Who are they anyway? You work for the CIA, don't you?"

"That's it! I don't know."

"You don't know who you work for? What do you mean you don't know?"

"I get a call. They give me the job, I do the job, I get paid," Jerry explained, trying to justify his actions.

"That's even worse Jerry, you knew it was me, and you went ahead and shot at me anyway, the one person who saved your life in Iraq, did you forget that? I had a dear friend who was murdered today as well, was that your lot?"

"Don't know who you mean Pete, what lot are you on about," he said, still being evasive and that made Peter even angrier.

"Okay, let's see if this jogs your memory." Peter put his right hand this time firmly over Jerry's mouth, then took a swipe at his left cast with his clenched fist, bringing it down hard almost breaking it, a little puff of white plaster came up from the impact into the air. Jerry let out a muffled scream as Peter pressed his hand down firmer over his mouth, blocking his airways momentarily. His heart rate was now at one-seventy. "Well, do you fucking want more? I can rearrange these fuckers again for you, do you want that Jerry? Well, do you want me to do that?" Peter said again, looking over him.

His head was shaking left to right in a 'no' motion, "Please stop, stop Pete, please," he said, still muted by Peter's hand and sounding like a ventriloquist's dummy. Sweat streamed down Jerry's face as he reeled in agony, his body contorted as he tried to wrestle with the pain internally.

"You'd better start talking you bastard, because this is going to get very bad for you very quickly if you don't."

"I'll tell you what I know, Pete. I'll tell you," he said, trying to control the agony.

"Right, okay, I'm listening," Peter took his hand away, taking a moment to calm the situation, and looked at him awaiting the confession.

"Yes, thanks Pete," Jerry said with the relief evident on his face. "Remember the unit, our unit, remember?"

"Yes of course I do, what's that got to do with it, that was eight…no twenty-three years ago now, for you. You'd better start making sense," Peter's impatience now getting the better of him. "Shush!" he said, turning towards the door, putting his hand back over Jerry's mouth, not hard this time, just enough to keep him quiet. Peter heard footsteps coming up the ward, getting louder and louder as they got closer, then stopped momentarily almost at the door to Jerry's room, and then went away getting quieter and quieter. "Okay, let's hear it?"

"Five of us after Iraq were recruited by the CIA for undercover ops. I couldn't have made it on the outside like you did Pete, so we worked for the CIA and went all over the world. One day we would be in Sydney, Australia, then London, England. Then back to the states."

"Doing what exactly?"

"What do you think?" he said. "Taking People out, of course."

"Who? Taking who out?"

"Politicians, High profile people."

"So why kill Sheila Vine?"

"That wasn't me, but she knew too much, asked the wrong questions to the wrong people, they wanted her gone."

"And Jim Watts and his wife, Ruth? What had they done?"

"The same, that wasn't me either."

"Yes, but why?"

"Because you met with them Peter," Jerry said as he finally got to the point.

"What me? It's all about me?"

"It's all about containment."

"Containment?"

"Yes, Containment. I don't know what it is you've done, but this goes right to the top. There is a contract out on you and everyone who you have come in contact with."

"What, Marie, Ashley?" he asked, hoping for a different answer.

"Everyone, Pete," he said, nodding his head. "Deputy Commissioner Reece as well, everyone has been mobilised."

"Jesus, what the fuck?"

"Where did you go Pete you disappeared way back, we all thought you were undercover somewhere."

"No, it's a long story, not for now. I must warn them. Who is responsible for this?"

"Well, I can't," he hesitated. "If I tell you, I'm a dead man."

"You're a dead man already Jerry, you died in Iraq. You should have died in Iraq with you know what? You bastard."

"I know, Pete, I've lived that day over and over, it never goes away. Why did I do it?" Jerry lay there thinking about that moment for a few seconds as a few tears crept into his eyes. Peter almost felt sorry for him.

"So, do something good in your life. Tell me?" Peter pleaded. "How can I save them, who is it that's running this show, who is in charge of all this?"

"Jack Graham is the one who contacts me, and I do freelance for him, he works for April Haines, she is the Deputy Director of the CIA, and Senator Groves, they are the ones behind it all. The NSA wants you alive, I don't know why they must be the good guys in all this, but I can't remember his name. The CIA wants you gone, you know too much, about what? I don't know, it's as simple as that, and the CIA never fails Pete."

"God, what a mess."

"Pete, if I can give you any advice at all, it is, go underground, get yourself lost, don't do anything twice and certainly don't use the same phone more than once. They have eyes everywhere now and can tap into any system."

Peter suddenly remembered the note from Sheila, it was in his pocket, he pulled it out and reread it.

"Doug," Peter said.

Just then, a nurse came into the room to check on Jerry. Peter turned around looking a bit startled.

"What's going on here? You cannot be in here, who are you?" she snarled.

He put the note back in his pocket. This interrogation had come to an abrupt end. He couldn't risk getting caught, so he left as quickly as he could, he didn't feel comfortable calling himself a Doctor either.

"Oh, I'm just an old friend, just catching up with my buddy Jerry here, isn't that right Jerry?" he said, looking at him for a nod.

"Yes, he's an old friend from way back," Jerry confirmed, sticking his thumbs up to the nurse. "We served in Iraq together."

"Well buddies or no buddies, you still can't be in here, you will have to go before I call security, this is not allowed at all, it's out of hours."

"Okay I'm going, I'll see you soon then Jerry," he said, patting his chest. "Doug McClean is that him?" Peter asked.

"Yes, that's him," Jerry confirmed, with Peter making his way out of the door.

He put the thumbs up. "See you later then, Jerry."

"See ya' and good luck, Pete," the door shut behind him.

"Has the doctor been in here?" The nurse asked, noticing the white coat and stethoscope on the bed.

"Yeah! He's just gone," Jerry said, bringing a wry smile to his face. "I need some more morphine nurse, can I have some now, my leg is killing me."

Chapter 30

Peter jogged down the twelve flights of stairs and left St Luke's through a public entrance en-route back to the Buick. He was aware of everyone walking on both sides of Amsterdam Avenue up or down who looked the slightest bit odd or didn't belong. Luckily there was no one like that going either way. The tree-lined avenue looked majestic at night, especially with Saint John's up ahead, he crossed at the lights then a short walk down West 112th Street, and got back to the Buick very much alive, at least for now he thought.

He sat in the Buick with the engine off thinking about his options, and what Jerry had said, '*the CIA never Fails.*' Well, they had failed up to now, he thought. But he didn't want to have these guys on his tail for the rest of his life, and what about Marie and Ashley, they were in danger now. The NSA and Doug McClean seemed like it was the right way to go and corroborated by two people. It wasn't great being the hunted, he needed to turn this around.

As he looked through the windshield, he focused for a moment on The Cathedral Church of Saint John the Divine at the end of the road, it was illuminated beautifully against the dark, clear sky, he'd seen it many times before. A very imposing postcard-like picture, Peter thought. It was a beautiful moment for everyone at the baptism of Tom and Jake when the water dripped over their heads, he remembered. He held Tom while Marie held Jake. The look of pride on Marie's face he will never forget. The twins, both dressed in small white trouser suits, white shirt, white bow tie, a waistcoat and tiny white shoes that Tom insisted on kicking off every time they put them on, his mum fussing around making sure everything was just right. The whole congregation looked on with smiling happy faces, his mum, Marie's mum, brother, aunts, uncles, they were all there for this joyous event he could see them all sitting there. As he studied the ornate façade of the Cathedral, he heard echoes of the past.

"Christ claims you as his own. Receive the sign of the cross. I baptise you in the name of the Father, and of the Son, and of the Holy Spirit. Amen," Reverend Davidson said.

It was like it was only yesterday, and so vivid in his mind. Jake suddenly did a large bulky diaper that went all over his brand new white trousers, over Marie's arm and onto the floor, the smell was incredible. The vicar laughed out loud, he had seen it all before, but probably not quite as bad. Where it all came from they didn't know to this day, Jake must have secretly eaten a three-course meal beforehand, but Peter always enjoyed regaling the story at every birthday the twins had ever since. Jake, at ten years old had grown tired of hearing it though, but it was still a funny story nonetheless, and memories like that stick with you throughout your life.

He started the Buick and headed back to Eighty-Fifth Street in Queens and Auntie Jill's house, he couldn't stop thinking about everyone, his fault, the danger, the CIA. While going over the two Kennedy bridges cutting through Randall's Island, he came to a decision he would give himself up. There was no other way to prevent the inevitable happening, he was at the end, had gone as far as he could, nowhere else to go.

Heather was waiting for him sitting on the porch with candlelight and a cup of Brazilian roast as he pulled up. She was reading a newspaper as she looked up and waved at him. Peter walked up the driveway and was met with a welcoming hug and a kiss on the lips. A spark of adrenaline mixed with endorphins entered his brain, and he felt alive again, she had brought him back from the brink with a single kiss. Life, after all, was worth living for a moment like that. He noticed the Daily Gazette open on the chair, today's edition, Heather was reading about the house invasion in Whitestone yesterday.

"Nasty business eh, poor Jim, poor Ruth?" Peter commented.

"Surely they will be able to find who did it?"

"Yes, they should, but it could be something else."

"What do you mean something else?"

"You know, not just a random house invasion by persons unknown, that's what I'm saying. It could be something to do with this whole mess I seem to have brought onto everyone, like some unwanted baggage."

"It's not your fault Peter," Heather said, taking him by the hand.

"I know, but I just cannot help feeling responsible."

Her aunt had gone to bed, and the house was still and calm. It was a lovely warm starry night, so they sat in the garden for a while enjoying a nightcap on a swing seat, Heather had made supper, just some cheese and biscuits but Peter wasn't fussed, he was hungry after all he'd been through, and they went down a treat. They sat there thinking not talking, quietly enjoying each other's company. A little bit shell-shocked but happy they were together to share it.

"So how did you get on?" Heather asked, breaking the thoughtful silence.

"I saw him, Heather, I bloody saw him."

"Who?"

"The man who shot me."

"Where?"

"At the hospital, St Luke's."

"Who is he?"

"His name is Jerry Martin, he used to be in my unit in Iraq. I saved his life for God's sake."

"And he shot you, Jesus' whatever for?" she asked.

"Because he was being paid to do it."

"Paid? By whom?"

"The CIA."

"Like those men outside of Sheila's, they were CIA, weren't they?"

"Yes," Peter thought for a moment.

"Peter!" Heather said. "What are we going to do?"

The seriousness of the situation had got to him, the CIA had a contract out on everyone, anyone could be the next target. He felt like a dead man walking, still alive at the moment, but he couldn't sit around and do nothing, waiting for something to happen.

"Your phone?" he asked suddenly.

"It's off, been off since you said," she replied.

"Good girl, we will get you a new one," he said, holding and patting the back of her hand nervously. "They cannot track us unless we give them something to track. I need a phone number for the NSA, and I need to speak to a man called Doug McClean who works there. How can I find that out without using the phone? Is there a phone book of numbers or something?" Peter asked.

"Aunty Jill has got a laptop somewhere, we could search for it on the internet," she said. "Why do you need his number?"

"Doug McClean is someone who can help us," Peter said. "Sheila mentioned it in a note."

"A note, you never said?"

"Yeah, there is something I didn't tell you because I didn't want you to worry."

"What, Peter? You don't have to keep shielding me from all this stuff, I'm a big girl, you know."

Peter took the note out of his pocket and let her read it, it probably wasn't a good idea, but it felt like he was doing the right thing.

"I know you are Heather."

She read the note.

"Oh my God!" she said, putting her hand over her mouth tightly to stop whatever noise was about to come out. "That means everyone?"

"Yeah, afraid so."

"How was she killed?"

"I found her lying in the bath, shot in the head."

"All of us could end up like that then?"

"It's not going to happen Heather."

"How can you tell?"

"Because I'm not going to let it. I must find this Doug McClean in the note, he must be able to help us and make all this go away. Jerry confirmed it, Doug McClean's the man."

"He shot you, didn't he? Now he's giving you advice?"

"Yes, but he was only doing his job, I suppose. I saved his life in Iraq."

"You have some fucking nice friends I must say, Peter."

"I suppose."

"But oh my God, poor Sheila, you poor thing I bet you feel awful?" she said sympathetically.

"Yes, she was a good friend, she didn't deserve this at all, she was about to retire, you know," he said. "By coming here, I've seemed to have messed things up for just about everyone and put everyone in danger."

"Peter, whatever you think, you couldn't have stopped this happening, I cannot imagine what it must be like, losing fifteen years of your life, finding out everything and everyone has changed all around you. To also find that you have lost a part of your family as well must be tough. You are a strong man Peter, I can tell, and you will come through this." She kissed him lovingly.

Listening to Heather made a lot of sense, "I love you, Heather," he said with his hand cradling the side of her face.

Words that she had longed to hear. "I love you too Peter, more than you will ever know," she said, holding onto him, she had a feeling she would be letting him go soon. "Why did I have to fall for a man who's a time traveller and wanted by the CIA? Why couldn't you be bloody normal like everyone else?"

They both broke into laughter, kissed, and pushed each other playfully. That's what was lovely about Heather he thought, her humour, always a joyful person to be around, she had a very endearing nature about her. They sat arm in arm looking at the stars for a while, wondering about what lay ahead for them, not saying anything, they both felt that something was going to happen soon and the anticipation was deafening.

Chapter 31

Peter woke up at first light as the early morning sun seeped through a crack in the poppy patterned curtains onto his face. Waking up with an anxious feeling was never a good way to start the day, Sheila and Jim had been on his mind all night as he tried to put things together in his mind, and finally drifted off to sleep around three o'clock. Looking over at Heather sleeping, she had lived a relatively secure life so far with not many ups and downs in her life and lived with relative stability. But as she lay there next to him, he had to admit to himself he had now put her directly in the firing line, and she could be next if he didn't do something. Heather stirred.

"Hey, did you get any sleep at all?" she asked, stretching her arms in the air, yawning and wiping her eyes.

"I've had enough, it seems as though I don't need much to function properly at the moment. Do you want coffee?" he asked.

Peter stood up and looked out of the window onto the back garden and the swing seat where they had been talking with Heather until the small hours, he smiled, remembering the kiss.

"Yes, that would be great."

"We need to get going as soon as we can," Peter said anxiously.

"I know. I'll be ready in five."

Peter walked around the bed and leaned over her, he kissed her gently on the lips, stroked her face, and smiled. "I do love you, you know."

She smiled back and grabbed his hand. "I know, me too Peter." They both felt it, it was real, and it felt great, but nervous energy filled the room, and an apprehensiveness made them both edgy as today could be decisive one way or the other.

Auntie Jill had already put the coffee pot on so all he had to do was pour. She was watching the CBS Breakfast News, he could hear it coming from the living room as he poured two cups, added the milk, and then went in to join her.

"Hi there, anything interesting?" he asked, perching himself on a chair by her sofa.

She was wearing a fancy dressing gown emblazoned with poppies, not dissimilar to the curtains in the bedroom where he had slept, he wondered if she had done it on purpose and it was a conscious choice, or whether she just liked poppies. She was in her sixties but still a good-looking woman and kept herself in shape, it must run in the family Peter thought. Pictures of her newly departed husband were strategically placed around the room mixed in with pictures of her grown-up children with their respective families.

"Have you lived here long, Jill?" Peter asked, purposely making small talk.

She finally spoke. "I have lived in this street all my life and in this house for about twenty years. Where do you live?" she said bluntly and with a disapproving tone to her voice.

"Oyster Bay, you know near the harbour."

"Pretty swanky, eh! What are you doing in Queens then?"

"It's a long story, let's just say I'm sorting stuff out."

"Sorting what stuff out?" she pressed.

"This and that, just stuff, you know."

"Oh, okay, I understand you don't want to tell me, that's fine."

"No, it's not that."

"So, tell me, why are you in trouble and have the CIA after you then?"

"Oh, you overheard?"

"Only bits, I wasn't prying or anything, just trying to get to sleep, it was hard not to listen. The CIA! I wouldn't have thought you would want to mess with those people? That sounds serious."

"No, you're right."

"Heather's a good soul, naive in the ways of the world, and I would hate to think she'd get hurt in all of this."

"It's complicated Jill, lots of misunderstandings that need sorting out."

Heather came into the room brushing her hair and ready to go, she wore black fitted trousers, a white silk patterned top, almost see-through, and a lime green scarf. She looked fabulous, Peter thought, where did she get all those clothes? Because he never saw her with any luggage.

She said, "What needs sorting out? Hi Auntie Jill, we are up early, aren't we?"

"She overheard us talking last night. I said it was a misunderstanding," Peter said, explaining the interrogation.

"Always up for the seven o'clock news, Heather, you have to start the day right. The CIA Heather?" she tutted. "I hope you aren't into something way over your head, my girl?"

"So, you've been bending Peter's ear then Auntie Jill, have you? And no, it's not over my head. We are going to see someone today hopefully who can help him out."

"No, I only asked. I wasn't bending anything, was I Peter?"

"No, not at all she was fine," Peter said, handing Heather her coffee and giving her a strained look.

"Thanks. We have to get going Auntie Jill, are we okay to stay here again tonight?" she asked. They both stood up.

"Yes, of course, you are always welcome, you know that. I enjoy the company. And don't worry, I'll look after Olive, I'll make her a coffee about nine."

"You're a treasure."

The bulletin on the CBS news channel turned to a house that was on fire in Westhampton Beach. The caption read, an explosion at Westhampton Beach. Peter looked closer, he recognised the house.

"No, please, don't tell me this, not now," directing the comment to the television.

"What is it, Peter?" Heather asked.

"What's up?" Auntie Jill asked, looking at Peter who seemed in a state of distress.

There were Ambulances and Fire Engines in front of the house, half of it was still standing and intact, the other half where Peter had met Marie and Ashley only yesterday, was utterly demolished.

Auntie Jill turned the sound up as they listened to the broadcast. `*Overnight in this usually quiet neighbourhood overlooking Westhampton Beach, an explosion could be seen and heard more than a mile away. A suspected gas leak could have been responsible, one of the first responders said to us. As you can see from the footage, the house has all but been destroyed. We have been told that there were four people in the house at the time of the explosion, and they have been taken to the Nassau County Burns Center in Hampstead. One of the people that were in the house at the time of the explosion is said to be David Reece, the current Deputy Chief Commissioner of the NYPD. The Westhampton Fire department of Suffolk County is currently looking into the causes of the blast and will report soon. We will have more for you later as this develops and more information becomes available, but today there is a Westhampton Beach Community in shock.* `*

"Oh, Peter!" Heather said, putting her arm around him for comfort.

"I've got to get over there, Heather, to the hospital, I need to see them," Peter said, wiping the tears away and breathing heavy. He blew his nose.

"It's only about half an hour's drive from here," Heather said. "Let's go." She put her coffee down on the table in front of the television.

"Who is it? Who are they, Heather?" Auntie Jill asked quietly out of concern.

Peter was out of the door. Heather looked at Auntie Jill and said, "It's Peter's ex-wife and child."

"Oh! My God! Oh, dear! The poor thing, let me know if there is anything at all I can do Heather please?"

"Will do, and thanks for everything Auntie Jill, I appreciate it," Heather said as she rushed out to the Buick with the porch door slamming against its frame. Peter was already in the Buick with the engine started.

Heather switched on her phone to use Google maps and get the best route ahead of the traffic. It directed them onto the Grand Central Parkway. Peter put his foot down as they sped off.

"Peter, don't go so fast we don't want to get caught, that could be the worst thing at this moment," Heather said.

"Yes, I know, sorry you're right. Jesus Heather, these guys don't give up, do they? Jerry was right, they want to kill everyone, and it's me they are after."

"We don't know the full story yet, Peter. It could have been an accident like they said."

"What, first Jim and Ruth, then Sheila, then this. And what about my ear? They want me dead. I don't know what to say, Heather. Thinking about it, I'd better drop you off back at your Auntie Jill's, and you'd better stay away from me for a while because you could get hurt in all of this, and I don't want that for you."

"I'm not going anywhere Peter, just get that straight, we are in this together."

"You wouldn't have a problem if you hadn't met me, I didn't want this for you, or us."

"I know it just seems right that I am here now, that's all."

Over at Langley, Agent Sara Jerome, one of Jack Graham's team, had a warning light come upon one of her screens. "We have a hit, Jack," she said. "It's one of the phones used to call the subject a day ago, it's just come back online. We don't know who, it's probably a burner, but it's on the Grand Central travelling east."

"If it is Peter Collins, where is he going?" Jack said. "Travelling east, eh? Come on, people, let's get some answers fast."

Agent Hurst said. "The explosion that happened last night at Westhampton Beach involved David Reece, you know? The Deputy Chief Commissioner of the NYPD. He lives with the subject's wife and only child, they were involved as well. They were transferred to the Nassau County hospital in Hampstead, that's in the direction they are currently travelling unless they turn off somewhere else of cause."

"What do you think, Jerome?" Jack said. "Could it be him?"

"Yes, could be, it seems favourite, it's still on the Grand Central."

"Let's get a team down there to check it out. It's fair to say if it were my family, I would want to be there."

After thirty-six minutes, Peter and Heather turned into the tree-lined Carman Avenue, and on the right-hand side was the nineteen-story Nassau University Medical Center building. Once called the Meadow bank hospital, the NCMC was now the premier level one trauma centre and with a state-of-the-art burn's unit. The hospital now boasted twelve hundred beds and had become Nassau's tallest building and a familiar long island landmark. They found a parking spot almost immediately and made their way to the reception. Heather saw the worried look on Peter's face.

She grabbed his arm as they walked, and said. "Peter, no matter what happens I'm here with you, I'm here for you all the way."

"That helps enormously, Heather," he said. They stopped at the reception area. The woman behind the desk seemed disinterested in her work, she was texting on her phone to someone, Peter had to cough to get her attention.

"I'm here to see Marie Collins and Ashley Collins. Sorry, Marie's married name is now Reece," Peter said. The anxiousness he was going through had etched into his face, it was the agony of a father, a look of desperation.

"And who are you?" she asked in a 'matter of fact' way with not an ounce of empathy.

"I'm Peter Collins, Ashley's father, there was an explosion last night, they were brought here they said. CBS News that is."

"Oh, I see," she said, as the realisation on her face gave away too much information, she quickly sat up and overly compensated for her nonchalant attitude. "Let me make a call, and I'll get someone out to see you."

Peter could tell it wasn't going to be good news, and already, his heart sank. They took a seat with their back to the wall on the left of the waiting area. He kept an eye on the front door acutely aware of everyone around him. The reception was very open and modern, making use of tall green shrubs and flowers to give a relaxed, professional feel to the place rather than a stark medical one. There were enough seats for around fifty people at a time, currently, only ten people sat awaiting their turn. There were two security guards by the front desk armed with guns, CS gas canisters, and a baton. The security system seemed to be more than adequate Peter thought. He noted where all the cameras were, and there were only a few blind spots as he could see, but the cameras looked more advanced than the ones he used in his company.

"Hope they don't take too long," Heather whispered, breaking the silence.

"They should be out soon, she seemed to know who we were."

A few moments later, Peter noticed two men come into the reception area and sit at the back by the entrance. Peter didn't look at them but could see them from their reflection in the top of a chromed waste bin. They were agents, dressed in suits rather like in the mall yesterday, he thought. They didn't speak to each other and had a stern look about them, they didn't come up to the reception to check-in either. He never said anything to Heather, but they were CIA all right, and they were there for him.

The doctor came through from the primary treatment area to talk to them. "Mr Collins?" he said.

"Yes, that's me," Peter said as the two men stirred and moved in their seats. They now had their target, Peter sensed them move out of the corner of his eye.

"I'm Dr Vance, will you come with me please."

They both got up and walked over in the direction of the treatment centre, passing the front of the reception. Peter glanced at the smoked glass on the front of the reception desk and saw the reflection of the agents looking over in their direction. One of them was now on the phone, they were safe while they were in here, Peter thought. There wasn't any way they could get at them in this type of public place. A few feet along the corridor, Dr Vance turned into an assessment room.

"Let's go in here shall we," he said. "Take a seat please, can I get you both a drink?"

Peter said. "No thanks, we need to know if they are okay?"

"Well, what do you know so far?" he asked.

"Not a lot, apart from the explosion we heard about on the CBS news an hour ago, what can you tell us, doctor?" Peter said anxiously.

"It's not good news. I'm afraid," Dr Vance said solemnly, but to the point.

"They are not dead, are they?" Peter asked, preparing himself for the worst news.

Dr Vance took his time and slowly laid it out. "Four people were admitted last night Mr Collins, David Reece died at the scene, Christopher Allen, unfortunately, was DOA. Marie Collins Reece," he paused for a moment. "She's going to be okay, she is currently in surgery, and will lose an arm, possibly a leg as well. Ashley Collins was in a critical condition with internal bleeding, but for the moment she is stable." Peter breathed out slowly, more out of relief than anything else. "Her right leg may need amputating, but we are assessing it at this time, she is talkative and in good spirits. I'm sorry I cannot give you any better news, but it's good news for Marie and Ashley as it didn't seem the case when they first arrived here."

Heather held Peter's hand as he spoke. "Is Marie going to be okay?" Peter asked.

"Can't say, at this stage, I'm afraid, we won't know until she is out of surgery and can make an assessment."

"And Ashley, what are her chances?" Peter asked and squeezed Heather's hand.

"We expect her to make a full recovery. I wouldn't say it if that were not the case."

"Can I see her?"

"Yes, of course you can," Dr Vance said. "I'll go and see if she is okay with that, and I'll come and get you."

"Okay with that? What do you mean?"

"It's hospital policy. I'm afraid I need Ashley's permission, that's all."

"That's fine," Peter said.

"I'll be right back."

Peter smiled tentatively at Heather and patted her on the hand, "They are very lucky."

"Thank God."

After five minutes, Dr Vance came back into the room.

"She's okay with that, Peter."

"I knew she would be," Peter smiled.

"I must warn you though, she looks a bit of a mess, lots of bruising and cuts to her face and hands, all superficial though and they will heal. She may end up with some scarring to her face, but overall she's a very lucky girl indeed."

"Thank you, doctor," Peter said earnestly, as he got up to leave the room.

"Do you want me to come?" Heather asked. "Because I don't mind."

"Yes, please come. I want you to Heather. I want you to meet my wonderful little girl."

They walked to a private room a little way down the corridor. Peter noticed the security cameras covered every part of it, facing each direction, he wondered if they were being watched and whether the CIA could tap into the hospital's CCTV system. At the door, he glanced at Heather and smiled a cognitive smile and walked in behind Dr Vance. Ashley looked up and smiled as soon as she saw her dad.

"Look who's come to see you, Ashley," Dr Vance said. "I'll leave you now, she's doing great."

"Dad," Ashley said with tears tracking down her face.

"Hello, Chicken, been in the wars, eh?" he said, crying through the smiles.

"A little bit, Dad."

"I'm so happy you're going to be okay Chicken," he said. "The doctor said you are doing great."

"What about mum, though, Dad? She's not doing so great, is she," she said, with the tears now streaming over the plasters on her face, creating blood-red tears that dripped from her face onto the brilliant white hospital pillows.

"No chicken, but she is strong, she will pull through, you'll see."

"I know Dad, but what if she doesn't," she said. "Don't know what I'm going to do."

"Darling we will get over this together, you and me."

Through the tears, Ashley noticed Heather standing back and smiling sympathetically at her.

"Who's this?" she said.

"Oh, this is Heather, my friend," Peter said.

"Hello, Ashley. I am so pleased to meet you. Your dad has told me so much about you. I think you are very brave," Heather said, touching her hand.

"You're very pretty," Ashley said.

"Why thank you, Ashley."

"I wish you both could have met Christopher. He was so lovely. You would have loved him, Dad," Ashley said sadly.

They chatted for what seemed like hours but was only twenty minutes. It was as though they were catching up for all the fifteen years of no contact.

Then Peter's Marine brain kicked into gear. "Chicken what can you tell me about what happened?"

"What, the explosion?"

"Yes, darling the explosion, what happened?"

"We were having dinner, Chinese, it was very nice."

"Where were you?"

"In the kitchen at the table. I remember I got up to go to the bathroom, David had already gone to the fridge for a beer for Christopher, and that's when it happened. I felt a big force slamming into my back, and I hit the wall. Then all I can remember is I was in an ambulance with pain in my leg and back looking up, and here I am."

"Was there anything unusual?" he asked. "You know, a smell of gas?"

"No, no gas, tar maybe."

"What about almonds did you smell, almonds?"

She paused and thought for a moment. "Almonds yes, a bit weird but yes almonds."

"Okay Chicken, you look tired, we are going to go now, and I'll stop by later, let you get some rest, I think you need it."

"What about the almonds, Dad?"

"It's nothing Chicken."

"What do you mean nothing?"

"Sometimes explosions do smell of almonds, that's all," he said. "We will go now and let you get some rest darling."

"Oh, okay, Dad. Love you," Ashley said, as he leaned over and kissed her bloodied face. "Pleased to meet you, Heather, will you come back to see me as well?"

"Yes, I will if your dad lets me," she laughed.

"Of course, see you later, Chicken, love you loads."

As they left the room, they both waved at Ashley, and walked towards the reception, after a few feet, Peter stopped and looked around up and down the corridor. Then he looked at Heather.

"What is it, Peter?" she said curiously.

"It's C-4 that's what it is."

"What is?"

"The smell of almonds, it's military-grade C-4 explosive."

"How do you know?"

"We used it in Iraq. So, a deliberate act, not an accident at all, the CIA I bet, almost certain," he said, still looking up and down the corridor nervously, "I don't think we should go this way either, Heather."

"Why not?"

"I just don't. Have you got your phone?"

She took her phone out and looked at the screen, then said, "Oh shit, sorry."

Peter took the phone, switched it off and put it in his pocket, "No problem, this will come in handy later, let's go the other way."

At the end of the corridor was a café to the left, it seemed busy enough, and more importantly, it had an exit out to the parking lot. Peter went to the door and looked out at the front of the hospital, he noted the distance between them and the parking lot, it was about two hundred and fifty feet and seemed too far, they could get picked off in the open very easily. He thought it was better to stay where people were, so they took their time and didn't rush. They got a coffee and waited for the right moment. Heather didn't say much because she knew what was going on, and she felt guilty about the phone, how could she be so stupid, she thought. Peter was on the game though, and on high alert, she'd seen him in action, and she knew the signs.

Peter noticed one of the agents from the reception area come into the café, get a coffee, and sit behind them and pretend to read a local newspaper, the Nassau County News. It was now or never, Peter had to make his move and went to the restrooms at the back of the café.

"Won't be a sec," he said to Heather as he got up.

He went into the gents, turned a tap on, and pretended to wash his hands. Almost immediately, Peter sensed someone on the outside of the door. The door opened slowly as the sound of the flowing water echoed around the restroom.

First through the door was the end of a silencer followed by the Glock and a hand gripping it tightly. Peter put his full weight behind his right foot and slammed the door on the forearm pinning it to the wall and hitting the agents face on the side in the process. The gun went off, and a silenced bullet ricocheted off the wall and embedded itself into the sidewall of a toilet cubicle with a loud thud. Peter grabbed the Glock and the agent's hand together with a vice-like grip, so the angle of the barrel was pointing away from him, and he couldn't get shot.

Peter then pulled the agent into the restroom. Using his right leg, he tripped the agent up, so he lost his balance and hit the floor on his back, then Peter came down on him with a right-handed blow to the gut, still gripping the gun with his left hand and pointing it away from him while twisting his arm. The agent kicked Peter in the face in a standard defensive move when on your back. Then he tried to get up with a gymnastic flip which Peter anticipated perfectly, and as the agent almost got to his feet and upright, Peter punched him firmly and squarely in the face with a haymaker, straight to the nose, stunning him, and then another punch as he went back down onto the floor. Peter then kicked him in the face with the bottom of his right heel rendering him unconscious.

He peeled the Agent's hand from the Glock, took it apart like a seasoned professional in a few seconds, and threw the bits into the toilet of the first cubicle. He then dragged the agent into the next cubicle, tucking him up neatly by the toilet bowl and closed the door. Peter looked into the bathroom mirror on his way out, no significant damage apart from a graze on the chin from the kick. He re-joined Heather.

"You okay?" she said.

"Piece of cake. Let's go." Peter grabbed Heather's hand.

They took the coffee and walked out of the café with a small crowd of people over to the Buick. As they exited the parking lot, he could see the other agent in his rear-view mirror looking around for his partner and talking into his phone. At the first set of traffic lights on Carman Avenue with the traffic going slow, Peter saw a grey Ford Pick-Up coming up slowly in the opposite direction. He quickly opened his window, switched Heather's phone on, and threw it into the back of the truck as it went by.

"There," Peter said. "Have fun with that."

"Good idea," Heather said.

"I know, I'm full of them today, let's go find this Doug McClean."

Chapter 32

The LaGuardia Shopping complex was about forty minutes from the NCMC, they had initially planned to use a payphone there, so Peter stuck to the plan. They could have a coffee and something to eat there while they tried to get a message to Doug McClean.

The sun was over the Manhattan skyline in the distance as they travelled down the Grand Central Parkway, and then the extremely uninteresting Astoria Boulevard. There was one notable difference to the Manhattan skyline Peter noticed, and it immediately brought back memories of Tom and Jake, popping into his subconscious to say a quick hello to him again. Overhead three or four planes circled in the sky awaiting their approach to LaGuardia airport less than a mile away. Peter had an air of positivity about him that things would be okay and turn out for the best. He was looking forward to meeting with Doug McClean.

There was a warmth in the air, but the air conditioning in the Buick wasn't the best, and it was clunking as if it were on its last legs, so the windows had to come down a bit to let a breeze of fresh air in to cool them down.

"A little different to your Mercedes isn't it," Peter said.

Heather did miss her car, it was her baby, and it was probably in a compound somewhere by now, she thought. Probably the tow pound by Lincoln tunnel, or if she was really unlucky, it could be at College Point in Queens, where cars seemed to get damaged quite a bit, it had a terrible reputation and many lawsuits against it, so she would be lucky if she got it back with no damage to the bodywork. She was very pragmatic about the whole thing though and said. "It's only a car that gets you from A to B, nothing to fret about."

"It's special to you, and we will get it back for you after this is all over, I promise. It can't be easy for you," he said, touching her hand affectionately. "It's all my fault."

"You have been looking stressed Peter if you don't mind me mentioning it."

"I'm just trying to do the right thing by everyone that's all. Everyone I have come in contact with on a personal basis has either been killed or blown up, and I don't want anyone else to get hurt needlessly."

"My dad committed suicide!" she said abruptly.

"Really?"

"Yes, really. I wouldn't lie about something like that, would I?"

"No, you wouldn't, sorry, I didn't mean it the way it sounded, I was just taken back a bit that's all."

"He was stressed, trying to keep everyone happy. But he couldn't handle it all in the end, it all got too much for him."

"Oh, I see. I am far from committing suicide, Heather. I was taught to handle stress in the army on the front line, your whole training is about handling stress, working under pressure, and stressful situations."

"I know Peter. I just wanted to share that with you if anything happens, you are the first person I have told since it happened," she said openly. "I think about it every day and wish it was different. Was there something we could have done for him? I don't know. We were all wrapped up in our own little lives, selfishly thinking about ourselves and didn't see the signs, none of us did. We thought he had everything under control. He had enough advisors and managers looking after stuff. But it was too much for him eventually. It must have worn him down, you know, trying to keep everything together. He had all these people around him. But the sad thing for me was why did he feel so alone that he had to do that?"

"How did he...?"

"The Port Authority found him on the side of the east river. They thought he had jumped from either the Brooklyn Bridge or the Manhattan Bridge, could have been either I suppose."

"Thank you for sharing that with me, Heather. I'm sorry for your loss, it must still hurt after all this time."

"Yes it does, every day."

"You are so lovely, you know that?"

"Yes, I know." She smiled and squeezed his hand.

He parked the Buick in the underground garage, and then they both walked up to the shopping complex. There weren't many people around for a Friday, it was still only ten-thirty, and he felt like he had been up for hours. His jaw was aching from the kick he had taken from the agent, but apart from that, everything was fine. Peter looked around surveying everyone and everything to get a sense of his surroundings should anything happen. He noted where the exits were, and the escape routes should it be necessary, the security cameras and the direction they were pointing.

They both sat in the coffee shop sipping cappuccinos and having a bite to eat, Peter had the BLT while Heather had a chocolate chip cookie, not ideal, but she needed a sugar fix. Making a call from anywhere had its risks, as they could leave themselves vulnerable to whoever was listening, but Peter felt that today, it was a risk worth taking.

He left Heather at the table and walked over to the payphones on the other side of the mall. Heather was still in view as Peter looked over. Out of a bank of six phones, only two were in working order, the others had been vandalised and smashed. Payphones were practically obsolete these days, he thought, which was probably why phone companies would not rush to fix them, soon there would be none left at all, then people would miss them. Peter picked up the phone with his index finger and thumb, wiping it first with a serviette he got from the coffee shop. He held it with the serviette like it was diseased or he might catch something from it, he then fed a few dollars into the slot and dialled the number.

The NSA switchboard was located at the former AT&T Long Lines Building, at thirty-three Thomas Street. It was five hundred and fifty feet tall and built in the heart of Manhattan. It was the NSA's mass surveillance hub, and known as one of the most secure buildings in the world, monitoring millions of calls, and billions of pieces of internet data on a daily basis. The building was famous for being another example of the Brutalist architectural style, with no windows in its flat concrete slab façade. Not a healthy place to work, with no sunlight penetration, at night it became a giant shadow blending into the darkness, minding its own business, beavering away while everyone else slept.

He spoke to the operator who tried to locate Doug McClean for him. She put him on hold for a few minutes, and he listened to the frustrating piped music. With the tension Peter felt, it seemed like an hour. He looked over at Heather and smiled, he shrugged his shoulders at her as if to say he'd been put on hold. After a few more minutes he put the phone down, shook his head, took the excess dollar from the tray, and then walked back over to Heather looking dejected.

"What's up?" Heather whispered as Peter approached.

"Don't know. I got through, but the woman looked for him, then came back to me and said that there was no one working there by that name, shut me down."

"That's strange," Heather said.

"They kept me on the bloody line for ages, and then came back with that, what a bloody cheek. Typical government shite."

"What shall we do next then do you think?" Heather asked, looking at Peter for an answer, questioning him with a look, pursed lips, and a big question mark in her eyes.

"Well, maybe it would be best to go to the police. We have to do something I suppose. We cannot sit around here doing nothing and waiting for something to happen, we are sitting ducks out here."

"If that's what you think let's get on with it then."

"Well they have me on file at least, even with David Reece not there, they should be able to help us and offer us some protection."

"Yeah, sounds like we need a bit of that," Heather said, agreeing to the task in hand.

They finished their coffee and walked through the complex back to the exit, which would take them back to the car park.

Heather looked up, and noticed a large insect buzzing away in her peripheral vision in the sunlight, coming at her on the right-hand side, she had to look again because it was a funny-looking insect. At first, it seemed like a bee, but now as she looked closer at it, it looked more like a small mechanical bee, just hovering overhead, it's wings were like a hummingbird and very quiet, the size of a half-dollar coin, it was probably a toy she thought, she had seen things like that on TV. Peter noticed it as well. He had never seen anything like it before, it was definitely man-made, Peter thought, and as they walked, it kept pace with them like it was looking at them, following them.

Peter glanced around the mall, there didn't seem to be anyone paying much attention to them at all, they were ignoring them and going about their business. But then he noticed that the security cameras on the walls were now trained on them, not only one camera but all of them, following them as they walked. It felt a little disconcerting and worrying, then Peter grabbed Heather's hand and went for the exit, quickening their pace. Peter sensed something was happening, and the bee was still hovering above them, buzzing away, which made them both feel even more uneasy. At the end of the complex, they could see the door to the car park and the way out.

Just then, two suited men walked through the door and stopped blocking their exit about fifty feet in front of them, agent types! Dark suits, white shirt, black tie, sunglasses, shiny black shoes. Peter turned around and could see four more agents walking towards them from the opposite direction, it was like they had appeared from nowhere. They were now trapped between them as the men walked at pace towards them closing them down, giving Peter no choice and no way out, six agents were a little too many. Heather held Peter's hand tightly.

"What's happening, Peter, who are they? What do they want?" Heather said nervously.

"I don't know, but we are going to find out soon enough." Peter looked at the men walking towards them, he made a quick assessment. They all had guns, that was obvious, he could see the straps and a slight bulge under the right shoulders of their coats, but they weren't drawn, and they didn't have their hands on them, and they didn't look threatening at all, just official and efficient. Peter and Heather stood still, hand in hand as they approached walking calmly, the bee thing was still hovering above buzzing away, one of the men took his sunglasses off as he approached so they could see the whites of his eyes and his friendly expression.

"Peter Collins?" he asked, sounding very official and decisive, but friendly.

"Yes, that's me," Peter replied.

"Agent Gerome, NSA, we are here to bring you in," he said calmly, shaking Peter's hand.

"Oh, right."

"Sorry for all the cloak and dagger stuff, but we had to do it right, so no one gets hurt, you understand?"

"Is that with you?" Peter said, pointing at the bee-like thing still hovering above them.

"Yes, it is state-of-the-art tech. Very useful, it's a B760 drone to be precise," Agent Gerome said. "With an emphasis on the 'b,' sorry about the pun."

"What's a drone?"

"I've heard of them," Heather said.

"We send them in first to assess the situation, it saves unnecessary things happening that we don't know about beforehand, in many cases, it saves lives as well."

"Where are you taking us, Agent Gerome?" Peter asked.

"That's classified. I'm afraid Peter, let's just say, it's somewhere safe, and it is for your protection. From what I've heard I think you could do with a bit of 'safe' for now?"

"Yeah, you're right there," Peter said.

"Follow us to the garage, and we will get you out of here."

They all walked out of the mall together calmly. People in the mall had noticed what was going on and had stopped what they were doing, some were filming it on their phones. At the garage, there were three large black Mercedes GLS four by four with blackened windows, standard issue for government security, all parked close together and in a line. Peter and Heather were shown into the back of the middle car, and all the other agents filed in the car's front and rear. Peter smiled an apprehensive smile at Heather, who drew a deep breath as if to relax.

"I think the phone call got through after all," Peter said.

"What do you think will happen, Peter?"

"I don't know, but I think we are safe for now, though. They don't want to harm us. I get the feeling they want to help."

The three cars sped off together fast, close, and controlled out of the LaGuardia shopping complex.

Chapter 33

The Mercedes Benz cavalcade turned down Essex Street at pace, Peter instantly recognised where they were going. He nudged Heather and pointed over at Seward Park.

"Yeah, that's where we first met," she said, squeezing his hand and smiling.

He looked at her, thoughtfully, kissing her on the cheek, and said, "Lucky for me. It will all be okay, you know, I've got a good feeling about everything."

It looked like they had fortified the old building from the front. There was a four-inch-thick silver steel door, twenty feet wide, that was already open as the cars approached. Through the side windows of the Mercedes, he could see the whole front façade of the building, all mirrored black glass and a very modern look to it, with the familiar revolving door in the centre, where he had come through only five days ago having had the pleasure of meeting the lovely Errol. It had changed out of all proportion though from when he last worked there. The offices of Edwards and Collins were somewhere inside he thought, but they were a million light-years away now.

They entered the underground garage and went down the ramp with the door then rolling shut slowly behind them. A very slick operation by any stretch of the imagination, it was as if the president or a superstar had arrived, Heather thought. Another large steel door rolled slowly to the left in front of them to let them into the lower parking area, all three Mercedes went through and parked side by side in unison, choreographed to perfection. They got out and were escorted over to the elevator. Peter noticed the wall-mounted CCTV cameras followed their every move, like when they were in the mall. For some reason, it felt like it was the same person behind the camera, even though he couldn't be sure. The garage looked so very different now to when he last drove his new Mercedes in that morning, the structure was the same, but it didn't look like a garage anymore, it was more akin to an underground sophisticated bomb shelter with armed security everywhere. They entered the large elevator, and Heather smiled and held Peter's hand again for comfort. The agent in charge spoke into his microphone, giving a running commentary of their status, they were all doing their job calmly and professionally.

On the top floor, the elevator doors opened, and the six agents exited first, their shift executed successfully, the agent in charge nodded to another agent who then took over.

"Hello, Peter, Heather, I'm agent Edwards," he said, shaking both of their hands.

"I remember this place," Peter said as he looked around.

"Yes, you probably recognise it from a few days ago, we have it all on video," Edwards laughed.

Heather looked around apprehensively and said, "What is it? Where are we?"

"The start of everything," Peter said.

"What do you mean?"

"This is where my whole world changed."

"Changed?"

"To 2016," he shrugged his shoulders. "Well, I ended up here."

"All will be explained Peter, I promise you that," Edwards said.

Heather held Peter's hand tightly. Without saying it, she felt like there was something final about it all, with them both being there. She prepared herself mentally for a shock, a situation she would have no control over, no say in, and it felt like it was going to be sad, very sad.

They walked past the glass-walled room that Peter had seen the agents celebrating in once before. Today there were no celebrations though just people with their heads down studying screens intently. It looked like there was an intense operation going on with a group huddled around a large screen, they all had headphones on, and one person seemed to be directing events, Peter caught a glimpse of the screen, it looked like somewhere in the middle east, he thought.

"Where's that taking place, agent Edwards?" Peter asked, pointing over at the group.

"Just Edwards is fine, Peter."

"Okay."

"That's Afghanistan. A Taliban stronghold on the outskirts of Kabul," he said.

"It looks like Iraq, those places all look the same. I've been there, Jesus, it looks so clear, so defined," Peter said.

"Satellite technology is so good nowadays, you can see a pimple on someone's nose."

"Really?"

"As long as they are looking up, Ha!"

"Yes, your right there," Peter laughed.

Edwards showed them into a room, the sign on the door said Tactical Briefing. "If you could wait in here, we will gather the troops," Edwards said politely.

There was a long oak table with tall beige leather directors' chairs either side, and everything looked and smelled brand new. The room was fitted with Hi-tech conference calling equipment in the middle of the table, and whiteboards for communicating around the globe. Peter recalled he had those in his boardroom back in 2001, but these were so much more sophisticated. As they looked around the room, large monitors were showing live scenes from around the world in High-Definition, with each screen having a time clock ticking away in their time zone. The monitor on Afghanistan was on, and it looked like something was about to happen as people were scattering everywhere in a mad panic, women, children, children with rifles, and soldiers. Heather wondered what she was looking at on the screens.

"So, what are you thinking, Heather? You seem a bit…"

Heather laughed at the question. "I don't know what to think, it's all a bit out of my league. It looks impressive, whatever they are doing though. For some reason '*Clear and present danger*' popped into my head," she'd seen all the Harrison Ford movies many times. "It's funny how fiction becomes a reality in an instant."

Peter smiled, "Yes, a good one, great film. I've seen that a few times myself. In reality, the NSA touches every part of our world, they have missions going on all the time, to keep us safe."

"Well we're not very safe are we, and especially you," Heather raised the tone of her voice. "You are being hunted by the CIA for Christ's sake."

"You are as safe as you will ever be, now you are here," McClean said as he walked into the room with Edwards shuffling in behind. "Peter, we finally meet. Doug McClean." He smiled and held out his hand.

Peter shook it and said. "Yes, good to meet you, Agent McClean."

"And this must be the lovely Heather."

She held her hand out as well, he took it gentlemanly-like and kissed it, Heather said. "Err, sorry for my little hissy fit there," Heather smiled.

"Hey, not a problem, stressful times eh, for you both?" McClean smiled. "And not stressful anymore, eh?"

Doug McClean had a calmness about him, an air of authority. He was in charge, and his friendly likeable demeanour made them both feel less apprehensive. Heather still felt like a bombshell was about to land though, and couldn't put it out of her mind.

"It's a bit of a relief to be fair, it felt like things were closing in on us, options were becoming a bit desperate."

"We had trouble finding you Peter, you kept well under the radar, we were very impressed," McClean said while opening a folder on the table marked Peter Collins in a big red marker pen. "It was lucky you called today and came in when you did, as I doubt you would have lasted another day, we learned the CIA had their best men on it, here in New York."

"Yeah, I literally bumped into one of them yesterday," Peter said with a wry smile. "Jerry was from my unit in Iraq back in ninety-five. Well, you know that of course. I don't know how he got mixed up in all of this, I saw him at the St Luke's hospital when I visited him last night, it was most revealing."

"You managed to get in and speak to him?" Peter nodded, "I'm impressed again. That place is crawling with CIA agents. Why was it revealing?" McClean asked.

"Do you know an April Haines? She's CIA, her and this Groves fella, think he said he was a senator or something, they are behind it. They are the ones trying to kill me and everyone that I know."

"Yes, I know April."

"They have practically killed everyone, David Reece, Sheila Vine, Jim Watts and his wife Ruth, the only ones left are my daughter Ashley and Marie, and they are in a bad way at Nassau County, it's touch and go whether Marie will survive at all."

"We have an agent there now, don't we Edwards?"

"Yes, two to be exact."

"So, no more harm will come to them. Ashley and Marie will be okay, the CIA is standing down on this one now, I can assure you of that. You were the prize, and now we have you," McClean said, shrugging his shoulders.

"But how can you be sure?"

"This comes from the top Peter," Edwards said.

"You mentioned Senator Groves just then?" McClean said, glancing at Edwards shaking his head as if to say something, but he kept quiet, it was obvious something was wrong, but he never let on. "Let's say that we have our agenda, and they have theirs, sometimes we meet somewhere in the middle, but it seems on this occasion other forces were in play. You are the key to all this, Peter. I don't know why they wanted you dead. That was not the brief we had with them."

"Well, that's a relief," he said, holding Heather's hand.

McClean noticed the fondness they had for each other and said, "So, Peter, how are you finding it here in 2016?"

"It's been tough to be perfectly honest, I never thought things could turn out the way they have, with friends dying and family getting attacked it's all happened so fast, and if it wasn't for Heather here, I think I would have topped myself by now. All I want from now on is to be left alone to get on with my life here in 2016, our life." He looked at Heather and patted her hand. "You know without fear and without that knock on the door one day. I suppose I'm still grieving for Tom and Jake as well, it's still so recent, I know for you it happened fifteen years ago. But for me, it was only a few days ago, and I need time to get everything in order. I'm sure you understand. You look like a man that would understand that."

McClean looked at Peter with a sympathetic look in his eyes and said. "All this was our mistake, Peter, it was a sequence of events that couldn't have been avoided or predicted. Who would have thought you would have come through our vortex just as we were sending someone through on a mission."

Peter looked and sounded confused. "Vortex? A mission? To where?"

"We sent one of our agents back to 2001, and that's where you came through by accident at precisely the same time. That agent will be coming back in four days hopefully."

Peter had a look on his face that said a thousand words. A realisation of what he had thought all along, that there was a way back. Heather had a feeling in her gut as to what was about to happen, the bombshell. Sadness invaded every part of her being all of a sudden as they spoke, it sounded all muffled in her head as reason went out of the window.

"So, you can go both ways? Back and forth just like that?" He twisted his index finger right then left.

"Yes, just like that," McClean confirmed flippantly as though this sort of thing happened every day.

"And that man I bumped into is an agent?"

"Yes, that's Jed Ryman, he will be coming back on the thirteenth of September."

"What is he doing there?"

"Just gathering some intel for us, to help us out here in 2016."

Edwards became official all of a sudden. "Yes, you are here now, Peter, because we want to send you back."

"What! Really? I hadn't...I," he hesitated. "Back to 2001?"

Heather looked the saddest he'd seen her. She was right, it wasn't going to be a happy event for her after all.

"We feel you have to go back, Peter, call it a karma thing. Keeping things right, and in order," McClean said.

Heather, in agreement and unselfishly said, "you have to go back, Peter. It's what you want."

"Yes, but," he said, looking at her, holding her hand.

"I'll be okay, Peter. You must go back."

"Well, I want to, I just thought until now that that could never happen, and it wasn't an option. Yes, I do want to go back," Peter said firmly. "When would I—?"

"In about twenty minutes," McClean said abruptly.

"Wow, okay, really? That soon, eh?" Peter said, McClean nodded.

As he looked at Heather, he suddenly felt torn and almost hesitant, he didn't want to go so soon and wanted a little more time with her, to get to know her a bit better. How could he leave Ashley? She would miss him, and he would be out of her life again when she needed him the most. How could he be so cruel? Marie, how could he go with her in surgery?

"Peter. You need to go. I'm a big girl, and I'll be okay. I'll still be here if it doesn't work out," Heather said.

"I'm not just thinking about us, what about Ashley, and Marie is still in surgery?"

"Peter, think about time itself," McClean said. "About the concept of time."

"What do you mean?"

"About time. Think about 2001? All of this here in 2016 hasn't happened yet for you," McClean said.

The penny dropped as he spoke. It suddenly became clear as day, he could go back and save Tom and Jake. Ashley and Marie would be okay, and he could meet Heather here in fifteen years, which would be now. He had the best of both worlds and could live the fifteen years he had lost to arrive back at this exact point in time. Only now he would have the benefit of hindsight and twenty-twenty vision.

"Okay, let's do this. What day and date will it be, you know in 2001?"

"Sunday, September 9," Edwards said.

"We want you to do us a favour when you get back as well," McClean said.

"Oh! There's a catch then?"

"No not a catch at all. Call it a favour."

"What is it you want me to do?"

"We want you to take some documents back for us and give them to someone."

Sensing there was a problem he said. "Someone? Who?"

McClean said plainly, "Me! When you go back, I want you to find me, and give me these documents."

McClean handed over to him a zipped up black leather document case that contained papers within five files. He opened the case and peeked inside, then zipped it up again. "Okay, that's no problem, a piece of cake?" Peter replied, relieved that the task seemed so easy.

"I wouldn't say that," McClean answered.

Peter looked at McClean and Edwards curiously, their faces didn't tell the full story.

"Wouldn't say what? Why? What's the problem? Seems fairly straightforward to me." Peter looked at them a bit bemused.

"Because I won't believe you,"

"Why not."

"I remember what I was like back then."

"Like what?"

"Ambitious, driven, sceptical even. I won't believe you because I know what I was like, I didn't believe in sci-fi movies, the paranormal or anything remotely like that. I didn't believe in God or Jesus either. Still don't."

"That's okay, many of us don't either, but still go to church and speak to him when we're in trouble," Peter said.

"Yes, but I never did any of that either. I won't believe you, Peter."

"What's in the files?" Peter asked, pointing to the case.

"The whereabouts of Osama bin Laden and a network of Al-Qaida operatives."

"Wow! Important stuff then?"

"To give me the heads up in the fight against terror, I needed it back then even if I didn't admit it to myself," McClean said.

"Why wouldn't you believe me if I had proof with me. You did work for the NSA back then, didn't you?"

"Yes, but it was everything by the book back then. If I saw you with classified documents, I would probably kick your ass and arrest you as a suspected terrorist."

Peter smiled and said. "Really? Well, how am I supposed to do it then, to make you believe? Don't think you would be able to kick my ass by the way. I didn't want you to 'big' yourself up or anything," a hint of sarcasm crept in, Peter smiled. They all sniggered at the thought.

"Yeah, you are probably right on that point. I'll give you a bit of information, very personal to me that only I would know, and hope that works, he would believe you then. Jesus, I would believe you, and I'm him." McClean smiled.

"Tell me what it is, and I'll tell him…I mean you, sorry? If you know what I mean."

McClean took Peter to one side out of earshot of everyone in the room and whispered something in his ear. Peter looked surprised by what he heard and raised his eyebrows in surprise.

He sat down next to Heather and said. "Well okay, then."

"We can get everything ready if you want to say your goodbyes, there is a recreation area just down the hall. We will come and get you when it's time," McClean said and shook Peter's hand firmly. Edwards did the same.

McClean said. "You know Peter when you go back you will be the only man on earth that has seen the future."

"Yes, the thought did cross my mind."

"The information you have gained here you cannot use."

"There is one thing I am going to do," he said. "I'm going to try and save my family, save Tom and Jake if I can."

"I don't know whether it's possible, no one does. I don't remember you at all coming to me with these papers back then in 2001, so I know that it hasn't happened yet, but as someone once said, 'you can't change fate'."

"Only time will tell, eh?"

"Exactly," McClean said.

McClean and Edwards left the room to get the process started and get the Mag-Tron fired up. Peter and Heather sat in the recreation area and had a coffee. The sun came through the Atrium glass roof about thirty feet up, and it felt like they were in a giant greenhouse with well-groomed trees and plants dotted around in a circular pattern, and with gravel paths going towards the centre like the spokes of a wheel. It looked and smelled like spring, as the scent of the flowering plants hit their nostrils. They didn't say anything, they were both deep in thought, was this going to be the last time they were together? Peter held her hands across the table and looked into her eyes and smiled lovingly.

He then said, "I love you, Heather. I'll never forget you."

"I Love you too, Peter," she said.

"There is so much I think I should be saying to you, so many things I want to share with you, but there isn't time."

"We happened for a reason I am sure of that, but don't feel bad about going back. I'm a big girl, you know."

"I know you are. I just feel we have something here, and I don't want to lose it."

"I'll still be here in fifteen years, maybe we have all the time in the world."

"It's weird, isn't it? Getting your head around this time thing," Peter said.

"It is. It's a little confusing."

"That fifteen years for you is now!" Peter said, looking at his watch. "Come to think about it, I could meet you in half an hour, thirty minutes from now, that's twelve o'clock-noon at Luigi's, what do you think?"

She thought about it for a moment and said, "Luigi's, well yes, I suppose so. It is weird, isn't it, I cannot get my head around it. Why do I feel I am saying goodbye forever, though?"

"It's the perception of time that is altered. Our brains struggle with that concept."

"They sure do," Heather said smiling, her eyes glazed and small tears nestled in the corners. "We had better go, do you think?"

"It will be fine, you see. I will meet you in thirty minutes, okay?"

"Okay, I'm okay, really. I am Peter."

She wasn't, she was far from okay. Just as they got up from the table, Edwards appeared with the thumbs up.

Chapter 34

They walked back through to the control centre and waited outside the lab with agent Edwards. The Mag-Tron was starting up, and a muffled low whirring noise emanated from the room. The control room with its see-through glass walls looked like mission control at Cape Canaveral on launch day. At every desk, there were two agents with white coats and microphone headsets on, working away at their computers. Each was looking after a different aspect of the vortex. As he thought about the impending few steps he would take to get back home to 2001, a couple of things bothered him. It was a step into the unknown, a leap of faith. Like jumping out of an aeroplane, and that moment just before the parachute opens, the anxiety of will it open or not. What if he got back and things were different? What if he ended up in another dimension and a different place entirely? He couldn't come back here, he would be stuck wherever he was. But what if everyone was there and it was exactly as when he left, and nothing had changed? He could save Tom and Jake avoiding all the heartache that Marie and Ashley went through, and change history in the process, what if he could do that? There was no choice, he had to go, take a chance, he had nothing to lose and everything to gain.

"Won't be long now, she's kicking into gear," Edwards remarked, looking at a clock ticking its way to eleven-thirty.

"Yeah, something is revving up in there. What do you call it?"

"It's called the Mag-Tron, the inventor named it."

"How does it do it? You know, to send someone through time?"

Edwards reached for a quick answer and said. "Electromagnetic power is needed and lots of it, through Laser Technology it's like we open a door into 2001, and you simply walk through it. There is nothing for you to do apart from walking a few paces."

"Doesn't seem feasible, does it?" Peter gestured to Heather with a shrug of his shoulders.

"Don't ask me. I can barely use a microwave," she smiled.

"Wonder what it will be like?" Peter said, thinking about what he would find on the other side.

"It will be like going home," Edwards said.

Peter's mind instantly flashed back to the good times, the happy times with all the family around the breakfast table in Oyster Bay having fun, that morning before he came here, with Tom, Jake, Ashley, and Marie, lots of laughter, joyfulness, happiness, and togetherness. The family, he longed to see them again. He wanted to go. He needed to go. His family needed him.

McClean opened the lab door and stepped out with his headset on, Peter could see the Mag-Tron briefly with its lasers flashing in a circular motion around a shiny silver frame. It seemed to be speeding up, and the noise got slightly louder, the energy in the room was immense and the atmosphere electrified, and there was a hum, a purring, a musical note like feedback from a microphone at a concert. The door shut behind him and the noise dampened.

"Ready then Peter?" McClean said.

"Ready as I'll ever be."

"You'll be needing that," McClean said, giving him the case.

Peter put it under his arm and hugged Heather for a moment like he didn't want to let her go. He kissed her gently. He kept it quick as he didn't want to be inappropriate in front of McClean and Edwards.

"Go and be with your family Peter," Heather said, touching his face gently with the palm of her hand.

"Remember Luigi's at twelve o'clock-noon," Peter said, pointing his finger as if she was a naughty schoolgirl.

"I'll be there," Heather said, smiling through her tears.

"Where are we, Edwards?" McClean asked.

"We are about two minutes out," he said.

Peter went into the lab with Edwards where the Mag-Tron was revving up to full power. Heather had a last glimpse of Peter before the door shut behind them. Edwards explained to him to stay at a particular mark on the floor then when told to walk forward through the eye of the vortex. Edwards then left the room leaving Peter standing in front of the Mag-Tron, with one minute to go. It felt like it was almost at full power with a high-pitched vibration like the sound of a hundred hummingbirds.

"Well, I guess this is it," Peter shouted.

"You'll be fine, just walk through when we tell you," Edwards said to Peter over the loudspeaker.

Heather watched on the monitor outside with McClean. Edwards went into the control room. Peter smiled and gave a little wave to the camera. Heather saw it and waved back at the monitor. A circular wall of shimmering water appeared in the middle of the Mag-Tron vortex. 2011, 2010, 2009. The clock ticked back in years as it went into overdrive. 2005, 2004, 2003. Peter took a deep breath. Heather stood with McClean, he held her hand for comfort as she looked on nervously, 2002, 2001. Edwards said now! Then Peter walked forward through the vortex and disappeared in front of their eyes.

Heather whispered. "Goodbye, my love, my life."

"You'll be okay," McClean said sympathetically. "You'll be fine, you see."

"Hope so."

"He's a good man Peter, I can tell you will be seeing him again soon," McClean said.

Heather looked like she had lost the love of her life. The Mag-Tron lasers went out, everything slowed down, and everyone in the control room congratulated themselves again on a good job done.

Chapter 35

Sunday, September 9, 2001

He was back in the garage. It felt a little eerie, cold, and most of all, deafeningly quiet, he could hear his breath as he inhaled and exhaled through his nose. His heart was still beating fast, and the adrenaline made him feel like he could run a marathon. He looked around, getting his bearings. His car was still there, on its own but with a Police notice on the windscreen that read, *'DO NOT TOUCH – SUBJECT TO A POLICE INVESTIGATION!'* Someone was investigating his disappearance then, it was probably David Reece.

"Hey! I'm back," he shouted excitedly and punched the air.

It echoed around the garage. 2016 suddenly seemed a lifetime away, at least he had that to look forward to now, it was in the future. He felt elated knowing he would be seeing Marie and the kids again soon, with their excited little faces, it made him glow inside. He had missed them all so much. He clicked his key fob, it worked! The lights on his Mercedes flashed as the doors locked. He then ran up the stairs to his office, noticing things were pleasantly back to normal just as he remembered, his brand-new Edwards and Collins sign was back, with the reception back to how it was.

The main office was open with a few people working in one of the side offices, which was usual for a Sunday. It felt great to be back in his place of work again, he'd missed it a lot. He now had his life back, a family, an income, his credit cards would more than likely work, he had money, property, a business, and it meant so much, he felt like a whole human being again. He remembered the last time he was there five days ago, it was a different office entirely with Errol breathing down his neck, as though he was a nobody that had just wandered in off the street. He walked over to his office, pausing for a moment to look at some notes on Sheila's desk and recent scribblings of hers, he smiled and had a warm feeling inside. It was a comforting thought knowing that she was very much alive and that he would be seeing her soon as well. He then walked into his office and sat in his favourite green antique leather chair, very comfortable he thought, and sunk himself into it, sitting back he looked over a quiet Manhattan, and took in a deep breath again. "I'm back!"

He put the black leather case that McClean had given him on his desk. From his left trouser pocket, he took out his Blackberry and laid it on the table, in the other pocket was the Samsung phone. He looked at it for a moment with its elegant black glass façade and realised that the mobile technology in it hadn't been invented yet, let alone thought of, and he was potentially holding the future of mobile phone technology in the palm of his hands.

He switched on the Blackberry pressed speed dial number one, Marie's name came up straight the way, 'Wow! It works again,' he said to himself as it sparked into action connecting to the network. He pressed the call.

At the house in Oyster Bay, Marie looked at her phone, buzzing in her hand and started to shake nervously, she put her hand over her mouth, not knowing what to do. She couldn't believe it, Peter's name was flashing up as if he had returned from the dead, so she answered it breathlessly and anxiously.

"Hello, who is this?" Marie said sternly.

"Hi, Marie, it's me," Peter replied.

"Me who? Is this some sort of sick joke?" she barked.

Raising his voice, he replied, "Marie darling, it's me, Peter. I'm back!"

Tears of relief and joy instantly oozed from her eyes, she said, "My God, Peter, is it really you? Are you okay? Oh my God!"

"Mum, are you okay?" Ashley said, noticing her mum's distress and her hands were shaking.

"It's your dad, he's okay, he's alive," he said, Ashley grabbed the phone off her.

"Dad?" Ashley shouted with excitement.

"Yes, Chicken, I'm here at the office, I'm okay," he said, smiling and sitting back in his chair. "I'll be home soon, Chicken, can't wait to see you all."

"I knew you were okay Dad, I just knew it, I said to mum, didn't I Mum?"

"Put your mum back on please, Chicken, I'll be home in a bit to give you all a hug."

"Hi, you have an excited daughter, I think, Peter," Marie said, wiping the tears of joy away with the back of her hand.

"How about you?" he said mischievously.

The anger and frustration got the better of her, and then she said, "Where the bloody hell have you been Peter? We've been worried sick, five days Peter for God's sake. Five days. I've been going out of my mind," she sobbed. "God, I can't believe it, you're okay though. I've missed you."

"I've missed you too, Marie. I know what you must have been going through darling," he said sympathetically.

"I've filled out a missing person's report at the police headquarters as well, the police have been at your office."

"I know you have Marie," he said, he was going to say 'with David Reece' but stopped himself.

"How do you know that?"

"Why wouldn't you? I was missing darling. There was a police notice on my car. Now I'm back though, and we can sort everything out."

"So, what have you been doing for five day's Peter? I don't understand. What have you been doing all this time?" she asked suspiciously.

"There is an explanation Marie, you won't believe it, I can tell you that because it is unbelievable, but it's an explanation all the same," Peter said. "I'm on my way home, darling. I'll see you in a short while, is Tom and Jake there?"

"Yes, they are upstairs playing on their Gameboys, I'll shout them. Tom! Jake!" she said, gaining her composure.

"What is it, Mum?" Tom replied.

"Your Dad's on the phone come down and talk to him."

They both raced downstairs as fast as they could. Marie put the phone onto loudspeaker as they gathered around.

"Hey, Dad you are okay then? Ash said you would be?" Tom shouted.

Peter couldn't help smiling happy tears as he heard Tom's excited voice. "Yes, Tom, I am okay, hey it's great to hear both your voices. Missed you both loads too."

"Me too, Dad," Tom said.

Jake wasn't far behind and grabbed the phone. "You coming home soon, Dad?" he asked.

"Yes, I am on my way. I'll be there in fifty minutes."

"Cool."

"Love you, Dad," Ashley shouted.

"Love you too. I've missed you all. See you soon."

"Bye darling, hurry up and get here then," Marie said.

"I will." He pressed end.

He felt great, thrilled to be back, and he couldn't stop smiling to himself, 2016 was long gone. Looking at the Samsung phone laying there on the table, he picked it up caressing it in his hand momentarily, remembering what it did. He switched it on, all the bright colours of the applications came onto the screen as clear as anything, far better than his new Blackberry. He pressed contacts, and there was Heather's name staring back at him, urging him to call, so he pressed call on the screen. There was no service and a continuous tone, it could not connect, he knew that it wouldn't. He smiled at it, remembering her and wondering what she would be doing at that very moment. Probably walking over to Luigi's, he thought, but then when he thought about it, it wouldn't have happened yet, he was back in 2001, and she would be Twenty-Seven years old. He switched it off, wrapped it in a white cloth serviette, and hid it under papers in the safe in his office, he then locked the safe.

As he drove back to Oyster Bay, he couldn't stop thinking about Tom and Jake. He would keep them safe no matter what, they were not going to end up as a footnote in history on a monument, he thought.

The streets of Manhattan were quieter on a Sunday, not the usual mad rush to nowhere. In the distance he could see the ever-familiar Twin Towers pointing upward, strong and powerful, uncompromising and steadfast, they looked like they almost touched the sky. How could they possibly not be there in a few days from now? It was inconceivable. The car seemed to drive itself, it was effortless. He looked at his manual dials on the dashboard, then he remembered Heather's Mercedes with its touchscreen, rather like the mobile phone, he would get one of those as soon as they came out, he thought, after all, he could afford it now.

He made a plan in his head to call the school first thing tomorrow and make them change their scheduled visit and not go to the World Trade Center until later on Tuesday. He would suggest an alternative and had the exact one in mind. Then go and see the young Doug McClean, that will be a fascinating encounter he thought, he was looking forward to that.

Chapter 36

Marie was ecstatic as she saw Peter get out of his Mercedes on the driveway, she ran out of the house and jumped into his arms holding him tight and kissing him, a bit different to their last meeting Peter thought, all the kids followed suit.

"Hey look at this," Peter said in a group hug. "It's great to be back home guys."

"We all missed you, Peter," Marie gushed.

He was back in the bosom of his family, and it felt great, everything else seemed to fade into the distant past, or the future, depending on which way you looked at it.

"I've got a great idea, kids," Peter said excitedly.

"What, Dad?" Jake said.

"Let's go out for that meal I promised the other day,"

"What Beano's?" Tom asked.

"Yeah, what do you think?"

"Sounds great, Dad," Ashley said, holding his hand tightly as they walked up to the front door. Peter smiled as he looked at the house, it was back to normal, his trees were back, and the ghastly green paint had gone.

"Great, Dad," Tom said excitedly.

"You know what I'm going to do?"

"What, Dad?" Jake said.

"Spoil you all rotten, that's what." Peter laughed.

After play fighting with the kids for an hour, Peter and Marie sat at the kitchen table over a cup of tea, listening to the kids being kids with all their boundless energy.

"Are you going to tell me then?" she said inquisitively.

"It was the NSA Marie, I stumbled on one of their operations, and they couldn't let me get back until now."

"What operation?"

"They are taking over our building, you know."

"Yes, but what's that got to do with it?"

"I stumbled on this secret mission by accident, it was going on in our building."

"So you were in your office building all the time?"

"Yes, I mean, no, no I wasn't but…it's hard to explain, I said you wouldn't understand."

"So explain then, Peter," Marie said pointedly.

170

"I walked through something and into a different dimension, I don't know how, but that's why I went off the grid and couldn't contact you, they couldn't let me back even if they wanted to."

"Through something?"

"Yes, it was a part of the NSA mission."

"Really?"

"It sounds far-fetched, I know, but I walked through it by accident."

"By accident?"

Peter was not getting through to Marie at all, she wasn't buying it. "Marie, you keep repeating what I have said, it's as though you don't believe me."

"Is there a woman involved Peter?"

"Jesus, why would you say that?"

"Because you look guilty."

She was right, it was written all over his face, "I met a girl called Heather, who helped me find my way back to you and Ashley. There, are you satisfied?"

"So this girl called Heather helped you find Ashley and me?"

"There you go repeating it again. Marie, believe me, there is nothing to do with another woman in this at all. It was an NSA mission, Doug McClean was in charge, I stumbled upon it, and went through by mistake."

"Okay, let's drop it," Marie said stubbornly.

"Drop it? Marie, if I could have called you I would have," he held her hand. "I saw things I didn't want to see and had to fight for my life for God's sake. The CIA had a contract out on me. Doug McClean saved us, and I came back."

"Really?" She pulled her hand away abruptly. "So this Doug fella saved you both then?"

"Yes, I was lucky to get back at all, look at my ear. That's a bullet wound Marie, it took half my sodding earlobe away," Peter implored, pointing at the scar, "Why would I lie about it?"

"I can't tell you what we were going through here, it was an absolute nightmare. Just imagine Peter for one second, Police searching our home, they went through everything, Tom, Jake, and Ash were distraught, their dad missing presumed kidnapped or dead, how could I explain that? I had to explain thirty thousand dollars I took out of my bank account to pay that builder for the summerhouse. I'm sure they think I paid a hitman to have you done over or something."

"Yes, I know Marie."

"I haven't had a wink of sleep. The stress has been horrendous. I don't understand why you couldn't have called me to let me know you were okay, or a message, anything," Marie said with her eye's moistening.

"I don't know how it happened Marie. I don't understand the technology. Even though I was here, I wasn't. I was in a different dimension in the future."

"The future? There you go again, Peter. Dimension, future? It just doesn't make sense, and now you mention this woman, what's her name?"

"Heather."

"And you expect me to believe you. You probably had a fling with her for a few days and then started to think about your family, then came back. That sounds just as plausible, probably more plausible than being on a mission in a different dimension in the future. I bet she's pretty as well?"

"Well?"

"There you go I can tell from your expression she is pretty, probably beautiful?"

"She…" he stopped himself.

"What?"

"What do you mean Marie? Why are you acting like this? Aren't you happy for me to be back?"

"Pretty or beautiful?"

"Heather helped me, that's all. There was nothing in it."

"Well?"

"Well, what?"

"Is she?"

"If you must know, beautiful."

"Okay great that's sorted, I believe you. Are we going out then?" she said, smiling through gritted teeth and changing the subject.

"I can tell by your face, you don't—"

"I believe you okay," she interrupted, looking irritated and ill at ease. "You didn't mention Tom and Jake that was all."

"What about me, Dad?" Tom shouted.

"Nothing Son, it's just your mum and me chatting that's all." He looked back at Marie. "You don't want to hear about that Marie, really you don't," he said under his breath quietly so only she could hear.

"I might if you try?"

"Look, Marie, all will become clear."

"I'll look forward to that then."

The cold sub-zero temperature hung around in the atmosphere for a while but thawed a bit before they reached the restaurant.

Chapter 37

The town of Oyster Bay was located in Nassau County, and was once an English settlement bought from the Indians under the reign of Oliver Cromwell. Now with a population of 300,000, it was one of the most picturesque towns in New York, overlooking Oyster Bay Harbour. Beano's Steakhouse & Marina Café was a favourite haunt amongst families offering the best in seafood and steak in the area, and all sourced locally, and always fresh, daily. It also catered for the yachting fraternity at the marina, offering '*On Board Your Yacht Meals*' at any time of the day. As usual for an early Sunday evening, the parking lot had room only for one car out, then one car in, with cars parked on verges lining the streets on the run-up to the restaurant. Alfresco dining was the most favourite part of the restaurant and to see the sunset over the harbour.

Peter had called Lawrence and Jen earlier that evening, and because Lawrence had been feeling a lot better, they joined them for dinner. He also called Sheila to let her know he would be in first thing tomorrow. She was thrilled to hear his voice, just as much as he was to hear hers. Visions of her lying in a bloody bath came back to haunt him, so vivid in his memory of the last few days.

At Beano's they sat at a big circular wooden table outside, with a white tablecloth set for dinner with crystal wine glasses and cloth napkins. Fifty feet away from the restaurant veranda you could have a paddle in Oyster bay if you wanted to, with the soothing sound of the small waves turning over, and the clattering of the yacht's burgees and sails from the marina, the setting was perfect. Peter always enjoyed having the seven-ounce Filet Mignon with Herb Fingerling Potatoes, and Jumbo Asparagus with Stilton Sauce, he would never venture from it, and they made it to his liking especially for him. Marie was all for the fish, fresh Salmon, Cod or locally line-caught Sea Bass or Seabream. The kids had the usual array of Pizza and burgers and left most of it because they had been snacking on crisps and sweets as usual. Lawrence and Jenifer had pasta with scallops and prawns.

Peter felt so happy to be among them again, enjoying a family meal, and he would never take it for granted again. He looked over at the kids, all smiley and having fun, and Marie with a slightly sour look on her face, but she would get over that, and he thought how much he loved them all.

After the meal, there was a play area the kids could go off and let off some steam, leaving the adults to talk about serious stuff over a Brandy for the men, and Tom Collins for the ladies. It was always very amusing to Tom that he had had a drink named after him, and that it was his mum's favourite tipple.

Lawrence was happy that Peter had come back, as he wasn't fit enough to get back in the saddle yet, as far as the business was concerned.

"It's good to see you are okay, Pete," Lawrence said.

"It's been an experience, I can tell you. You don't know what it's like, you know, to lose everything dear to you. Or think you have," Peter said looking back.

"You'd better not tell people where you have been Pete, you know, government, NSA, mission's etcetera," he said, looking around to see if anyone was listening. "They might think you are a nutter, and have you locked up, you know what I mean?"

"Yeah don't worry about that one Larry, I know it sounds ridiculous, they would probably deny it anyway," Peter replied. "I've got to go and see this NSA chap tomorrow, and give him some papers he gave me."

"You are seeing him about the papers he gave you?"

"Yes, I know how it sounds, it's hard to explain."

"You be careful, Pete," he said. "Getting messed up in that world is not healthy."

"Did he tell you he met a girl, Larry?" Marie interjected sarcastically.

Peter gave Marie a quick stare, "Heather was just someone who helped me get through it," Peter explained.

"I'm sure she did. Ha!" The Tom Collins had started to kick in!

"She helped me get back here to you guys. Don't listen to her Larry, there was nothing in it at all," Peter said, shaking his head at Marie. "Imagine if it happened to you? Your credit cards don't work, nothing works. I cannot tell you how alone you feel, I'm just glad I didn't have to stay there. There was this special agent Doug McClean from the NSA, he ran the operation. He sent me back here. There is going to be a lot more serious things happening over the next few days though."

"What Pete. What's going to happen?"

"That's all I can say about that really," Peter backtracked. "Do me a favour anyway, Larry."

"What's that, Pete?"

"No more hunting trips with Buster and Dave eh."

"Why ever not?"

"You'll live longer, believe me," Peter said, Lawrence, laughed.

"I'm not letting you go anyway," Jen added.

"You, letting me go? What are you talking about woman?" Lawrence said, shaking his head at her. "This is what fifty years of marriage gets you, a woman who thinks she owns you."

"You know what I mean, Mr," she said sternly. "With your heart, you know."

"Oh right, as long as you aren't telling me what to do."

They all laughed at the exchange. It was great to be back, Peter thought. It was apparent Marie didn't believe a word he had said earlier, it didn't matter too much in the scheme of things. It was a short but pleasant ride back home, Tom and Jake fell asleep in the car, Ashley wide awake and Marie sitting there not saying much. She would come around soon, she would understand everything in a few days.

Chapter 38

Monday, September 10, 2001.

As Peter approached Manhattan on the four-nine-five, he looked over at the familiar skyline that had been there for as long as he could remember, and wondered if it would be the same tomorrow in less than twenty-four hours. He felt anxious for Tom and Jake, if all else failed he would not let them go at all, how important can a field trip be? There was no way he would let it happen, he thought, even if he sounded like a madman for a few hours, and Marie would then believe him eventually. It was inconceivable that someone could attack the World Trade Center at all, but for it to collapse as well? It must have happened, he thought. He had after all, read it in the New York Times.

At the office, they couldn't believe their eyes as Peter walked through the door alive and well. Everyone was so pleased to see he was okay, as a rumour had circulated around the office last Wednesday, that he had been kidnapped or even worse murdered, and the Police presence on Thursday and Friday had been very disconcerting for the whole office.

He was especially happy to see Sheila, who was already standing there, waiting to give him a hug as he walked over.

"Oh my God, you're okay?" she said as Peter approached.

"Yes, I'm fine. It's terrific to see you, Sheila, it really is," Peter said and took a moment to give her an extra special hug, remembering the last time he had seen her. "How's everything here?" Peter asked.

"Thanks for calling me last night to put my mind at rest, I wasn't looking forward to this week at all," she said. "We have not had much time to do anything here, really. The Police have been swarming over this place since last Thursday looking for clues and taking fingerprints from everyone. They made a bit of a mess going through your things."

"Let me guess, David Reece?" Peter said.

"You know him, do you? He was in charge," she said. "A nice man, very concerned for your well-being though, I must say."

"I bet he was," he said with a hint of jealousy.

"Why do you say it like that? Do you know him?" she asked, wondering about his comment.

"No reason, I just know his sort, that's all."

"His sort?" Sheila smiled at him wondering why he should say it like that, sounding paranoid, it was very unlike him, "Anyway, they took away a few things, and left us an inventory they said they would be in touch. I'll call them and let them know you are okay and found. I'm sure they will want to talk to you at some point. Coffee' brewed, do you want some?"

"Yes please, I've missed that."

"And when you get a moment, you can fill me in on what happened?"

"Of course, I will," he said.

He took the coffee into his office, then uncharacteristically closed the door behind him. Sheila thought it was a bit unusual locking her out like that, having just got back, but these were strange times, so she never said anything.

He dialled the number for Theodore Roosevelt Elementary. His company had done some security for the Ambassador of the Bahamas overseas a few months ago. She was currently in town and staying at the Empire State Building, and wanted to meet him for drinks, *so he could use her* he thought to divert the school trip away from the World Trade Center tomorrow. She would definitely go for it, he thought, so at least they would be a few miles away.

He got through to Irene Grey, their course teacher. He had met her a few times before at parent's evenings, and he had formed an opinion of her that he liked her a lot. A woman in her late fifties, an ardent smoker as was a lot of the teaching profession of her age. Never married but put her whole being into the children and their development. She had worked her way up to being head of the English department and was respected in her field. She had also written books on the teaching of English in schools with multi-faith and multi-race pupils. She wore a pleated dress and white blouse with a Scottish theme, and polished black flat shoes with a tassel on the front near the laces.

"Irene Grey speaking," she shouted as the faculty lounge was a bit noisy from all the other teachers vying for the coffee pot, and a quick cigarette before lessons started.

"Hi there Mrs Grey, this is Peter Collins here, you teach my two boys in class two A, the twins Tom and Jake," he said.

"Yes, I remember, a great pair you have their Peter, they are thick as thieves," she said laughing. "Always do their homework on time though, so no complaints there, you are doing a good job with them. Anyway, how can I help?"

"This trip you are going on tomorrow to the World Trade Center, I wondered if the children would like to see a real-life Ambassador, Nicole Avante? She is in town and staying at the Empire State building and wants to meet some local schoolchildren. I thought about our school. Then you could go on to the World Trade Center later on in the morning. Think it would be great for the kids, what do you think?"

"That sounds great Peter, but I'm not going tomorrow."

"Really?" he gasped.

"Yes, Miss Wilson is going with them instead, she's never been on a field trip so it will be informative for her as well as the children."

"Are you sure?" Peter said.

"Yes, I'm sure why wouldn't I be?" Mrs Grey replied curiously.

"Oh, no reason, I just thought you were..." he paused. "Is Miss Wilson there?" Peter said, now a little bit disconcerted that something was wrong and not going the way it should. Could he pull this off he wondered? Her name was definitely on the memorial, he had seen it with his own eyes.

"I'll get her for you."

Miss Wilson was twenty-one and not long out of university, a gorgeous petite woman with short spiky blond hair and bags of energy and humour. Peter went through his plan for the class to meet with the Ambassador, and she thought it was a great idea.

"So, I'll set it up for ten o'clock tomorrow. There will be refreshments for them there. The ambassador is looking forward to meeting them all," Peter said, even though he hadn't spoken to the ambassador yet, but he knew what she was like, anything for a bit of publicity. He would get a few pictures for her to take back to the Bahamas, she would go for it in a flash. The most important thing was that they wouldn't be anywhere near the World Trade Center, and that was the main focus.

"That's brilliant, Peter. Thank you, so much, and very kind of you. The children will love it. I look forward to seeing you there," Miss Wilson said, gushing down the phone. The call ended. "He sounds like a dish," she said to Mrs Grey rolling her eyes.

"He's one of the parents, you know?"

"I know, he can still be a dish though. He has blood running through his veins, doesn't he? And he's a man," she said shamelessly with Mrs Grey shaking her head in the background.

Peter came off the phone and felt elated, he had been able to sort it out, and save his boys and the school from what would be an ordeal that no one would ever have wanted to go through.

He sat in his office looking out of the window and deep in thought. It hadn't happened yet, the Twin Towers were still there, standing tall and mighty like two obelisks painted against the Manhattan skyline. He felt a significant weight on his shoulders, and there was no way he thought that anyone would ever believe him, with what he knew. His friends and family had accepted what he'd said because they knew him, apart from 'Marie and the Heather issue' he thought, but anyone in authority would question his sanity. He could save thousands of lives, and all those endless stories of tragedy and loss would be gone, all the heartache and misery, he now had the knowledge, and the three thousand names that he had seen at the World Trade Center Memorial, they could all be saved.

Then he remembered what McClean had said to him and told him not to do. Changing something like that was not possible, he couldn't change world events, it was too big. 'The information you have gained here you cannot use! You can't change fate!' McClean said, but this event would change the world forever, and he had the knowledge, stopping it was another thing.

Chapter 39

The NSA Special Operations Division was at the corner of Greenwich Street and Warren Street. A very modern space-age looking building for its time, shrouded entirely by smoked glass that was home to the SCS, *'the Special Collection Service,'* codename F6, a program that was described as the United States, *"Mission Impossible Force."* A secretive joint CIA-NSA clandestine SIGINT organisation, responsible for close surveillance and eavesdropping in far off difficult to get places. The SCS was involved in operations from the Cold War to the fight against terrorism, and undercover operatives were based in US Embassies worldwide gathering Intel.

Peter walked in through a large revolving door in the middle of the glass frontage to the building, something of a recurring theme he thought. It was a perfect greenhouse effect as the sun shone in, creating its own microclimate inside, and was kept at a specified humidity at twenty-one degrees all year round, so you could stand around in a suit and feel comfortable.

At the reception, there were four uniformed women, all with a very concerned look on their faces, as though something serious was about to happen. The leather briefcase that McClean had given him was tucked under his arm, but as he walked up to the front desk, he realised that he hadn't read what was in it, and he was about to give it to the young McClean, maybe he should have read it? Perhaps it was about the World Trade Center? A warning of the impending disaster about to happen in less than twenty-four hours. *These documents could get him in deep water,* he thought.

He became very nervous all of a sudden and hugged the bag tightly as though he had something in it other than the papers. It caught the attention of a thickset Security Guard who instantly honed in on Peter with a hand on his revolver just in case, as Peter's anxiousness was apparent to anyone.

"Excuse me, sir, why are you here today?" He said calmly as not to create a stir.

"I'm here to see Agent Doug McClean," Peter said.

"What's in the bag?" he said bluntly and to the point.

"Just papers for Agent McClean." Peter held them tighter.

"Can I see?"

"Yeah sure," Peter said, complying with the request and opened it for him.

The guard looked in the bag, and the lining, checking for anything out of the ordinary and then zipped it back up and handed it back to Peter.

"Okay, sir, thank you for complying with that request. Everything is in order. We are on high alert today."

"Why is that?" Peter asked.

"We get this all the time, sir, the threat level is at the highest today. It's red, and that means severe."

"What is going on?"

"We don't know yet, but it's red when there is a real threat to human life."

"Aren't you scared of a bomb or something?"

"No, I get on with it. If it happens, it happens, that's life."

"Great philosophy that."

"Enjoy the rest of your day, Sir the receptionist will see you now."

"Yeah, thanks."

He felt like there was a burden he needed to get off his chest, and wanted to tell him there and then what the threat was, he knew what was going to happen and he was the only person in the whole world who did, and he felt like he had a superpower. Peter was sweating as he walked up to the desk, it was like someone had turned the heat up all of a sudden, and he had to wipe his brow and the back of his head. The receptionist looked him up and down momentarily, then she sifted through some paperwork on her desk in front of him.

"Hi, I'm here to see Doug McClean," Peter announced.

She was a big lady. Her uniform looked about three sizes too small for her. She was probably on a diet Peter concluded and was refusing to give in to get a correctly fitted one, opting to lose weight and stay in the one she had on. She didn't make eye contact with him just shuffled through papers on her desk, Peter felt she was a little ignorant.

"Do you have an appointment?" she snapped, with her nose in the air.

Instantly irritated by the woman's attitude, he snapped back, "No, I don't need one, I have some important papers to hand to him personally."

"As I said, if you haven't got an appointment, you ain't getting in," She said, looking at him directly and now smiling in a cheesy way. Peter felt like slapping her smiley, ignorant face.

He felt like it, but didn't, "And as I said I don't need an appointment. I know you are on red alert, but I have some vital documents here to hand over to Agent McClean, and only Agent McClean, it is a matter of national security so would you kindly get him on the phone and get him down here or shall I take this higher?" Peter said, looking directly at the woman with an equally cheesy smile on his face leaving the woman open-mouthed and no option, he had won this mini-battle of wills.

"Okay, I'll have a go, sir," She said reluctantly, then picked up the phone and dialled a number. Peter could see her talking to someone describing him in detail to whoever was on the other end. "You're in luck, he will see you in waiting area number two, it's the one with the water fountain," she said, pointing her finger to the right.

After a long ten-minute wait running his fingers through the water cascading down the fountain, in walked the young Doug McClean, more hair but overall not much had changed. His hair was darker, his eyes were more youthful, his movement a little quicker, but overall, he seemed more or less precisely like that seriously driven nice person he saw only yesterday.

"Doug McClean, how may I help," he said politely offering his hand, it even sounded like him.

"Ah, Doug good to see you," Peter said, shaking his hand firmly.

"Have we met?" McClean asked, noticing Peter's familiarity.

"Not in this life we haven't," McClean looked at him curiously trying to work him out. "I have some important information for you," Peter said, getting straight down to business, he unzipped the bag, took out the five files and handed them to him. McClean Junior looked at them for a moment, he noticed his signature on one of the documents that were unfamiliar to him, he'd never set eyes on them before.

"What is this? Is this some sort of a joke?" he said sternly. "How would you get hold of something like this?"

"I don't know what's in them exactly, I've not read them, all I know is they are to do with the whereabouts of Osama Bin Laden, who you are actively looking for, and Al Qaeda operatives, these papers are to help you locate them," Peter said explaining what he had been told to say.

"Again, how would you get hold of something like this?" He looked at Peter open-mouthed looking for an answer to a simple question.

"I was given them and told to bring them to you personally," he replied. "No one else, just you."

"By who exactly?" McClean asked again.

"That's classified," Peter said sternly. "I've done my job and delivered them to you. That's done so, I'm out of here."

McClean didn't say anything as he thumbed through the papers. Then he said, "These are all classified documents here, are you an agent?" he asked.

"No," Peter said, shaking his head.

"Then what are you?"

"Just a messenger with papers that will help you, simple as that."

Junior McClean wasn't getting the answers he wanted from Peter, "I could have you locked up for having stuff like this in your possession."

"Yes, I know you could, but you won't will you," Peter said smiling, pushing his buttons.

McClean moved close to Peter and took up an aggressive stance looking directly at him. Peter took a step backwards. "Listen to me, you son of a bitch. I want answers. You have documents requiring the highest-level security clearance, and what's more with my signature all over them, but I have never seen these before, what's going on, who are you?"

Peter smiled at his impetuousness. "The person who gave me these told me you would be like this, everything by the book, he knew you very well indeed."

McClean suddenly grabbed Peter by the throat, "You'd better tell me or…?"

"Or what? You will have me locked up?"

"Something like that," McClean said, as Peter smiled at his attempt at anger, "You are not going to tell me, are you?"

"I will if you back up a bit and stop this silly attempt at rage. Mr McClean, I wouldn't like to break your arm." McClean could see Peter's muscles tensing up, rippling underneath his shirt, and thought he would give him the benefit of the doubt, so he let go of his grip and walked around the glass-walled room, thinking of what to do with Peter.

"You want to know who?" Peter asked.

"Yes."

"Sure?"

"Very sure."

"You did."

"What?"

"You gave me these."

"You are not making any sense."

Peter looked at him directly with a serious tone to his voice, "Mr McClean, you gave me these papers yesterday."

The young McClean laughed at the ridiculousness of what Peter was saying, "I gave you these, yesterday, did I?" he repeated. "I was here yesterday, you were not. You better start making sense because I am losing it with you."

"You gave me this yesterday in 2016."

"What, Ha!"

"You gave me these papers yesterday to bring back to you to help you in your search for Osama Bin Laden. That's all I know," Peter explained. McClean looked at the papers and then looked at Peter. Peter could see it in his face, struggling with it internally. The whole concept of time travel was alien to him, as to most people, it was something everyone knew about, had heard fictional stories about but was impossible to comprehend. "You told me something very personal to you, that only you would know about, and that I should tell you if needed."

"It's needed, believe me." McClean turned his head, and Peter whispered something in his ear, McClean looked surprised at first, then his demeanour changed to one of a friend, not foe. "Oh, I see," he said.

"It is hard to believe, I know. Time travel hasn't been invented yet. But I do know it will be in 2010. I accidentally went through a vortex, a portal, whatever it was, I spent five days in 2016, nearly got my head blown off by the CIA, you saved me and sent me back here to where I belong. Back to my family. And so, I came here as you told me to, to give you these."

McClean thought there wasn't any way this man before him would know something so personal about him, without his story being truthful, even though it was unbelievable. He looked at Peter again wrestling with what he had just said to him. "So how did I look?" he said calmly, thoughtfully, intrigued and eagerly wanting to know more.

"Not a lot of difference as I can see. A little older, a little greyer, probably a bit wiser," Peter smiled. "I'm only joking."

"Not all bad, then?" McClean said, smiling, relaxed, and calm.

"No, not bad at all. Now I have done my bit for the cause, I'd better go, I think," Peter said. "But before I do, there is probably something you would want to know, it may be contained in the papers, a major incident…"

"We know, we are at red alert, severe at present, that's why you see all the activity around here," he said.

Peter sat down with McClean and went through what he had seen and what was going to happen to the World Trade Center, how both of the towers would come crashing down and at what time, McClean didn't seem shocked he just listened, it was like he already knew something big was going to happen. Peter spoke of the memorial he had seen in 2016 and the number of people on it that would perish.

"Life as we know it will change tomorrow," Peter said.

"But if you've seen it with your own eyes, and you know it happened, I won't be able to stop it, or anything for that matter, surely that is fate, isn't it? It will happen," McClean said wrestling with it internally, "Otherwise this conversation wouldn't have happened, would it?"

"You can't change fate! That's one of your sayings," Peter said, he took out his wallet and gave McClean his card. "Call me if you need to." Peter left feeling happy he had done something, anything. Whether it would make a difference or not was anyone's guess. *Can you change history with things that haven't happened yet? Only time would tell,* he thought. He was in a privileged position now, the bearer of hindsight, and he knew it.

He walked back out through the revolving door with McClean watching him go, shaking his head. Peter wondered what McClean could do to stop it from happening. When he thought about it, *were we just observers? And things happened because everything was pre-set, like in a movie, and we were in a real one that had already been made. It was like contemplating infinity*, he thought, *you get to the end, and there has got to be something on the other side, surely, even if it's nothing.* As he went back to the Mercedes, he thought about all these things, He had done his bit, and the rest was now in the lap of the Gods.

Chapter 40

McClean sat in his office pondering, mulling over and questioning his whole existence, the explosive papers Peter had delivered to him were laid out on the table. His office, and being a relative junior agent, was a sparse soulless place. No pictures on the dull, uninteresting walls, trestle tables for desks that could be dismantled at a moment's notice, and plastic chairs with no comfort to the seat at all, and made his backside ache if he sat in them for more than half an hour. He had a cigarette in his hand, black coffee and a 'do not disturb' sign on his door, he rolled his sleeves up and got to work.

As he read through the papers, he realised the enormity of what was before him: a mountain of hurt and heartache, an event that he would never see again in his lifetime, and it hadn't happened yet. There was nothing in his entire life that had prepared him for what he was about to see. He had butterflies in his stomach. His hands nervously shook as his fingers moved over every line. He checked the time, it was 15:33, seventeen hours, and thirteen minutes until the first plane flies into the North Tower. Sweat dripped down the back of his neck into the small of his back, with a handkerchief he wiped the back of his head and worried brow.

He read report after report, but the transcript from CNN.com said it all. Dated September 16, 2003, two years after nine-eleven, and signed by himself, Doug McClean in 2016. It was a strange feeling seeing his own handwriting. A bizarre warmness, it felt like he had a friend lurking somewhere in his future, someone he could look forward to meeting one day, but there was only one way he wrote his name, the small c and big C he had always done it that way, so there was no doubt it was his signature. McClean read it with trepidation.

September 11, 2001 – Nineteen men hijack four commercial airlines loaded with fuel for cross-country flights, to carry out a terrorist attack on the United States orchestrated by Al Qaeda leader Osama bin Laden.

-- 8:46 a.m. EDT – American Airlines Flight 11 travelling from Boston to Los Angeles strikes the North Tower of the World Trade Center in New York City. The plane is piloted by plot leader Mohamed Atta.

-- 9:03 a.m. EDT – United Airlines Flight 175 travelling from Boston to Los Angeles strikes the South Tower of the World Trade Center in New York City. The plane is piloted by hijacker Marwan al Shehhi.

-- 9:37 a.m. EDT – American Airlines Flight 77 travelling from Dulles, Virginia, to Los Angeles strikes the Pentagon Building in Washington. The plane is piloted by hijacker Hani Hanjour.

-- 10:03 a.m. EDT – United Airlines Flight 93 travelling from Newark, New Jersey, to San Francisco crashes in a field in Shanksville, Pennsylvania. The plane is piloted by hijacker Ziad Jarrah.

McClean went over all the documents carefully, methodically, and then sat back in his chair wondering what to do. Should he bury them? Burn them? Pretend he never saw them? How could he be believed? He had in his hand's information from the future. It was a question he couldn't answer. *His career in the NSA might be on the line if he brought it to the attention of his superiors,* he thought. They would probably think he was mad or unstable to consider them as genuine, and they would probably want him to take a psych review.

As he sat staring out of the window over Greenwich Street, at the Starbucks across the road, for some reason he started focusing on the people going in and out, and walking by, strangers to him, what were they doing? He counted around sixty and wondered about everything that was possibly going on in their lives, some were probably going to a cinema somewhere, or a party or just a family meal or to meet relatives or a friend. Then he imagined what three thousand people would be like, he turned back to the documents splayed out in front of him.

McClean began to think about his own life, his wife Racheal and his two girls Emily and Ella barely in first grade, he relived the events of the recent lovely holiday in Florida they had just been on, and he wanted to be back there. Sandy beaches, ice cream, playing ball with them in the sea. Cocoa beach was a paradise with the sun beaming down on them. *Two weeks was not enough*, he thought, back to the dilemma.

On his PDA was a missed call from his dad Jack. He called him back, wanting to hear his reassuring soothing voice. Whenever he had an issue to deal with, he would always call his dad for an unbiased opinion. Jack McClean was a professor of psychology and toured around universities in the US giving lectures to undergrad students, and he took his mum Doreen with him everywhere. They had a wonderfully balanced life, living in top hotels for six months of the year all expenses paid, then relaxing for six months doing whatever they fancied, with no pressure from the outside world. He had a particular knack of knowing what the problem was within a nanosecond, an inflextion in the voice, the timbre in a cough, or a sniff in the wrong place, he was like a human lie detector.

"Hey, Dad, how have you been?" McClean said.

"Hi Douglas, yes all is well here Son, how's the high flier at the NSA?"

"Great, Dad."

"Really?" Two words were all it took.

"Yes, everything is great."

"It's just you don't sound great, Son." He had already spotted there was a problem, "Do you need money?"

"No nothing like that, God forbid."

"What is it, Douglas, talk to me?"

"We are on high alert for this Al-Qaeda thing. You must have heard, it's all over the press?" he said. "How's Mum?"

"Yes, I've heard. Your mum's your mum, she loves you, she's fine, but, how are you? Tell me what the problem is, I'll try and help as much as I can, I can do no more than that for my son?"

"I dunno, Dad." He let out a big breath, shook his head and then just came out with it, "Dad?" He paused and suddenly tears forced their way through from the back of his eyes, his face reddened, he sniffed, "If you had a piece of information that could save countless lives, that you knew it was true, but that information came from somewhere so ridiculous you would be ridiculed if it came out. What would you do?"

Jack thought for a moment, "This ridiculous place, Son, where is it?"

"You won't believe it. It's the future, 2016 to be exact," Junior McClean said waiting for a sceptical response that never came.

"Tricky to explain that one Son, you know me, I don't believe in clairvoyants or ghosts, I'm an atheist who thinks God was a spaceman. Rational, logical thinking is what I believe in, but I also believe in the spirit of man, and Son, I believe in you. This information? What makes you think it's good information and reliable?"

He was amazed there was no scepticism, but real meaning to what he said. McClean looked at his signature on the document in front of him, giving the whereabouts of Osama Bin Laden and signed by himself. "The way this came into my possession, I know it's good information and from a reliable source."

"I remember 'Back to the Future' was one of your favourite films. Do you remember?"

"Yes, I remember that."

"You must have watched it a hundred times."

"I know, still a great film though, eh Dad?"

"Yes, it is a great film. But it's a film."

"Not reality."

"Yes, not reality, exactly, and you will have to convince someone otherwise," Jack said. "This information, is it strong? Watertight?"

"Completely watertight."

"Well, there you have the answer, Son. Present it to someone higher up and let them make the decision. That's how you get on at the NSA, you have to be a team player Douglas, one day it will be your time to shine, let someone else deal with this, and don't be too hard on yourself." His dad was good at reading people, so grounded, and in the present, he never dwelled on anything. "I never thought I would hear of time travel in my lifetime?"

"Yeah, me neither."

"You are in a privileged position if it is true. You know that."

"Yes, I do."

"I'm presuming a terrorist attack?"

"Yes."

"A big one?"

"Huge."

"New York?"

"Yes?"

"They have been trying to bomb the Twin Towers for years, many, many threats. Only as soon as a few weeks ago there was something in the news about it. Osama Bin Laden is supposed to be behind most of it, he probably had something to do with the bombing in 1993, and that Ramzi Ahmed Yousef was probably the fall guy. Whoever you tell will need to know how you came about the information, otherwise, they could think you are an insider, and involved in it in some way."

"I've thought about that as well."

"Seems to me you know what to do Douglas, don't you?"

"Thanks, Dad, you have been a great help again, we will have to catch up when you are next in town?"

"Yes, your mum and I would love that Son. Good luck and let me know how it goes."

There was something about his dad that brought calmness to any situation. He had always been there for him and his brother throughout their lives, teaching, guiding, advising. Whenever they fell, he'd pick them up, and he valued his opinion more than anyone.

McClean poured himself another coffee in his dull unloved junior office and called a trusted friend and ally, David Edwards worked in the same building, and he came straight over. McClean wanted to ask his opinion as a sort of mental back up before leaping into the unknown with Willy. Edwards was quick off the mark entering his office within three minutes of taking the call and left the 'do not disturb' sign on the door.

"What's up, Doug? It sounded serious," he said as he sat down opposite McClean.

"I want you to take a look at these papers Edwards, and give me your assessment," McClean explained.

Edwards scanned over a few pages he could see a signed document dated 2016, then looked up at McClean open-mouthed. "What am I looking at here exactly, Doug?"

"It's an event that's going to change the world as we know it, in little over sixteen hours."

"How? How is this possible? Or Plausible," Edwards asked.

"I don't know, a person I know brought these documents back with him from 2016. I don't know how or why I cannot answer that. I do know that in the future we will be able to do a lot of things we never thought possible, or even dreamed we could do," McClean pointed to his signature, "This is me."

"Fucking wow, I mean if this is true, this is dynamite." Edwards loosened his collar and tie, the sweat of the afternoon heat was visible on his brow as he tried to focus.

"Yes, but it's what to do about it I'm worried about," McClean said wrestling with his dilemma.

"I think you will have to send it upstairs and let them make the decision," Edwards said reassuringly. "I mean fuck, three thousand people Doug, and we have a chance to stop it. Jesus, I cannot see how this could happen anyway, it's too far-fetched. I mean the fucking World Trade Center for God's sake," he said fuck a lot.

"Yeah, it's blown my mind as well," McClean said. "Okay Willy's in the building, isn't he?"

Edwards nodded his head, "Saw him earlier, they have been having meetings about Al-Qaeda all week, maybe they already know what's happening."

"They don't know about this I can assure you."

William Balding Black Jr was Deputy Director of the NSA, at the age of sixty-five most people would be thinking about retirement, but Willy, as he was affectionately known, was a career man, he had retired once but came back a month later following a messy divorce, and took up his current position in 2000. Over his distinguished career, he had overseen some significant developments in information technology and had been the head of many prominent departments within government.

McClean entered his office with a feeling of trepidation, and worried that he was doing the right thing. The militarily decorated office had an air of age about it from its previous inhabitants, a fustiness of spent cigar smoke from meetings that had gone on long into the early hours, and now ingrained in the fabric of the curtains, and had turned the oak wood to a darker shade, it invaded his nostrils immediately. Pictures of Willy's family were placed strategically on the oak and leather inlaid desk, to give the appearance of a family man, no photos of his ex wife, just children and his grandchildren. There was the obligatory stars and stripes flag as well behind him. He had a pleasant demeanour about him as McClean approached.

"Ah! McClean good to see you again." Willy held out his hand.

"Thank you for seeing me, sir, at such short notice, yes good to see you again," McClean said hesitantly.

"It sounded serious, this had better be good, I'm due at the club for drinks at four o'clock," he said getting straight to the point.

"It is as serious as it gets, sir, I don't know where to start though," McClean paused.

"Why not start at the beginning, I find that's always a good place," he said calmly.

McClean began to unzip the folder. "These papers and documents came into my possession earlier today, and although on the surface it seems ridiculous to consider them because of the source and where they came from, it is something that I feel I have to make known because the consequences are so catastrophic," he said, holding his nerve.

"Let's have a look at them then," Willy said eagerly.

McClean laid them out in front of him. He took his time sifting through them one by one for what seemed like ages. McClean sat in the chair opposite, not saying a word until Willy spoke. Willy didn't talk, but after he finished each report, he looked up to McClean over his reading glasses perched on the end of his nose as if he was about to say something, then dived into another one, this sequence of events took exactly forty-five minutes by the clock directly behind Willy. McClean knew how to handle the top brass, give them the information, then they could present it as their own, it was how it was done in the NSA, and every government department was the same.

"Well, I don't know what to say, McClean," Willy said. "Your signature, I notice, is all over it, can you explain that?"

"I must have signed them, sir."

"But can you explain how you signed this one in 2016?" Willy pointed at the CNN.com report. "Or is that a misprint or something?"

"No, sir, these papers have come back from the future via a courier that I apparently sent back," he explained. "In the future, I can only imagine that there is technology around that we don't understand yet, as it's too far advanced for us to even think about, and discoveries we haven't made yet."

"I see where you are coming from McClean, but we really couldn't take this seriously. It would be like presenting a sci-fi movie as real, wouldn't it, and expect people to believe it as true."

McClean went to a document that he had signed in 2006, about an Al-Qaeda cell here in New York, it had been stamped with the NSA's official stamp and countersigned by the Deputy Director of the NSA, John C. Inglis, who would become Willy's successor. He pointed to it, so he could be sure he understood the significance. McClean knew he would pay attention to that one, his successor, the person that would eventually take his job.

"Oh, isn't that something, well look at that," he said flippantly and smiled. "You're right, and it is unexplainable."

Willy looked stunned for a second, and as McClean studied his face, he realised he didn't know how to handle the information he had before him. He was as stumped about how to handle it as he was.

"Surely we have to bring this to the president's attention, something like this, don't you think?" McClean said.

"Now hold on a minute McClean, you can never give information of any kind, and particularly in this form to a president. It has to be vetted and re-written."

"Why's that, sir?" he asked.

"Because that's how it's done, McClean. You don't give a president anything he has to make a decision about. We make the decisions in government and then advice the president. You see where I'm coming from McClean?"

"Oh yes sorry," McClean thought for a moment. "I see, so the President will never be taken to task for decisions that are made."

"Exactly. I'll keep these and advice you shortly what we will be doing about it."

"What does that mean exactly, sir?"

"What it means is, according to these papers, we don't have a lot of time, do we, McClean. If we are going to do something about it, I need to present it to the joint chiefs, and I'll advice you shortly McClean. In the meantime, keep this all under wraps, under your hat. And not a dickybird to anyone, you hear me?"

"Yeah, fine, sir."

They shook hands, and he left Willy with the papers and documents, it was out of his hands now, and it felt great like the weight had lifted from his shoulders. He didn't have to worry about it anymore, and he could rest easy. McClean looked at his watch, fifteen hours and ten minutes.

Chapter 41

Peter studied Marie standing at the Aga, preparing the evening meal, singing to herself. She was happy that he was back, he could tell, and the trauma of the previous five days was now a distant memory. She had also forgotten about the Heather thing as well, at least it looked like she had, or she had put it to one side in her mind to bring it out sometime in the future. Either way, it felt good to be back home.

He watched the kids playing and talking about really serious stuff, the Power Rangers, Pokémon cards. It made him smile at the innocence, they had not a care in the world. Jake had a swapped card from school he didn't want, and Tom could have it if he gave him another one that he didn't want to give. It was amazing, the power of persuasion young people had over one another even at that age. Ashley sat calmly reading her new book, Seabiscuit: An American Legend. It was a typical family evening that he had thought would not have been possible only a few days ago. The calmness, the pleasant atmosphere, no tension, this was how family life was supposed to be like, spending time with each other. He had missed that.

But it was anything but typical, the thought of what was going to happen tomorrow filled him with dread, and it came flooding back like a collapsed dam. For a moment he took a step back and suddenly he was in a different world, he was on the outside looking in, it was like they were in a fishbowl, with him peering in through the glass, observing there every move, listening to what everyone said, a weird feeling came over him as he looked at all of them. Would this be the scene tomorrow? He doubted it, he doubted it very much.

For a while that evening, he had been making a fuss over Tom and Jake, probably overly so, and doing things that he wouldn't normally do with them, like play on their Gameboys. He couldn't help it, the thought of them perishing tomorrow morning made him feel sick, and he wanted them to stay close, be safe, be secure. Daddy was there for you.

He thought about the school trip to the Empire State Building in the morning and then the World Trade Center later on, which wouldn't happen anyway. He was comfortable with the plan he had hatched, and happy that he'd managed to sort it out, and that they wouldn't be there when the towers collapsed, so he felt quite confident.

There was, however, a nagging doubt. A doubt about fate. *'You can't change fate.'* What if he saved them from the towers and they died anyway because of something else? Maybe it was their time, and all he did was change the way they would die and nothing else. Ashley noticed her dad was thinking about

191

something serious, and he wasn't in the room, his mind was elsewhere from the look on his face, so she went over to comfort him.

"Hi, Dad, what are you thinking about?" she asked.

He paused a beat, "about you Chicken, Tom, Jake, your mum, all of you really, I was thinking about how much I love you. All of you. That's all," he said. Marie smiled, looking over at Peter.

"Ah, Dad we are all okay now, aren't we, Mum," she said as she snuggled up to the side of him, holding onto him as if never wanting to let him go again…

Then Peter said, "I realised how much I missed you guys when I was away, even after only one day, it was horrible. I thought for a while that I'd never get back here like this. It makes you realise how important family is."

As much as he tried not to, he thought about Tom and Jake all night and what they must have gone through. Re-living the moment at Luigi's café when he realised what might have happened to them on the school trip. But it hadn't happened yet. *Could he change the outcome? Could he do it?*

Chapter 42

The statue of George Washington stood tall and proud in front of the Federal Hall on Wall Street in Lower Manhattan, with the New York Stock exchange just across the street. Federal Hall, apart from being a major tourist attraction, was the recognised birthplace of American democracy, it was where Congress met in 1789, and the bill of rights was passed. It was also a meeting place for high-ranking government officials and was the perfect venue for an urgent meeting of the Joint Chiefs of Staff to take place.

The Chairman, General Joseph F. Dunford and Vice Chairman, General Paul J. Selva were on a video link from the Gold room at the Pentagon, this was the usual place they met. William B. Black Jr (Willy) walked in with his personal assistant and the documents. General Mark A. Milley and General Robert B. Neller were also there, and Admiral John M. Richardson was on speakerphone. A stenographer was on hand to take the minutes of the meeting. Willy started the session.

"Thank you for all coming at such short notice gentlemen, but I'm afraid this couldn't wait. There are grave things ahead to consider. You have before you copies of correspondence given to me a short time ago, and although on the surface it seems bizarre and out of our comprehension. It is now twelve minutes past nine and in eleven hours and thirty-four minutes, a plane will be hurtling into the North Tower of the World Trade Center, that is at precisely eight-forty six tomorrow morning. Gentlemen I have looked over these documents, and I believe them to be true, can I take your views on this matter?"

The Chairman 'General Dunford' spoke first out of protocol. "Gentlemen I have also looked at these documents, and like you, William said, they seem fine, but no one could, or would ever put their backing to them or endorse them. What would people and more importantly, the press say if we acted on papers that had supposedly come from the future? If indeed that is what they are, we would be laughing stock. They would probably say that someone like Darth Vader is now in charge of the security of this country, gentlemen it is laughable, but like Willy, I feel this has credence, and as much as my whole being wants to act on it, I can't. We are currently on high alert with the prospect of an immediate terrorist threat, something gentlemen is going to happen. Yes, this could be it, what this would give us is a mandate to go straight into Afghanistan no questions asked or needed. That is where I'm coming from."

Vice-Chairman Selva spoke only to back up the comments from General Dunford.

Most were nodding their heads in agreement. Willy was astounded, rage pumped up through his body and pounded his brain, he was the only one shaking his head, he couldn't understand them, they had obviously spoken to each other before the meeting and made a decision.

General Malley of the United States army concurred. "I happen to agree wholeheartedly with General Dunford's assessment. I, too, have been over these pages, and I can only see an opportunity here. We should embrace it. Stand down some of the security measures at Logan, Dulles, and Newark where these terrorists are going to board the flights. What we don't want is some enthusiastic security guard detaining any one of them, this, in my view, has to go ahead unchallenged. This will be a good thing in the long run and will help us in the fight against terrorism. Granted three thousand people will die, but we are looking at the end game gentlemen. You know where I stand."

General Malley was a warmonger and a combatant that was obvious to everyone. His answer to any situation was war, and he'd had a hand in most conflicts over the past ten years.

Willy made a plea. "Gentlemen are we saying it's okay to let three thousand people perish at the World Trade Center because I'm not at all comfortable with that scenario. We have got to stop this. You can still have your war on Afghanistan," he said.

Dunford took the lead. "William, we as the joint chiefs are here to recommend and advice and I think I speak for everyone that this has to go ahead, we cannot stop it."

"I disagr—"

Dunford interrupted, "For the simple reason is if these papers are true, it has already happened, so what are we here debating it for?"

"We can stop it, we can change the future."

Admiral John M. Richardson on Speakerphone added a view. "I think we are talking about fate aren't we," he said. "Fate is something you cannot mess with it could end in the destruction of the earth as we know it."

"That's a bit far-fetched isn't it John," said Willy.

"I don't think it is at all. Just imagine, for a second, you could go back and stop all the wars, all the conflicts. Where would we be now, we would be weak, we would have no identity, no common bond, or anything of that nature. We are where we are today in history because of conflict, because of wars that have been fought in the past. You cannot right every wrong in this world because that is what shapes our world and yes people die. By stopping this attack because of something or someone had the benefit of hindsight could set off catastrophic events."

"I agree totally," said Dunford. "I think we should take a vote on letting this go through and standing down security at the airports involved."

Willy put his hands up in defeat. The vote was unanimous.

Chapter 43

Tuesday, September 11, 2001

The day started like most glorious late summer days in New York City. The sun slowly rose over the Hudson as it always did, there was an apparent calmness and a freshness in the air again. The sky looked crystal clear, with a few wispy clouds infused with an orange hew, as though lovingly painted as flecks on a canvas behind the backdrop of the Manhattan skyline. People went about their daily routines, of jogging, exercise, coffee, breakfast meetings, all wrapped up in their little worlds, oblivious to anything that was about to happen over the next two hours.

From his Mercedes, Peter caught a glimpse of the Twin Towers from a distance, standing there like pillars of economic strength, pointing upward, iconic symbols of New York that everyone in the world recognised from postcards and billboards. It was hard for him to imagine them not being there, he wondered if Doug McClean had managed to stop the attack, he hoped, only time would tell. In his mind, though, he planned for the worst-case scenario.

It was pretty much free-flowing traffic going over the Williamsburg Bridge, slowing occasionally. The Manhattan skyline was blocked out momentarily as trains passed by in the centre of the bridge. When it came back in to view through the crisscrossed RSJ's, he noted the time, seven forty-three, in little more than an hour the world was going to change, and he was helpless to do anything about it now. He had done all he could, and that was that. It still seemed so far-fetched that it could happen at all, but he couldn't be sure, not entirely sure. The memorial with Tom and Jake's names on it came thundering back into his mind, and he couldn't get the image out of his head.

Just on a whim, and because he was thinking about them, he rang Tom on his emergency phone which was only to be used in emergencies, and not taken into class. He wanted to check all was going ahead as planned, putting his mind at rest, as they had left for school at seven o'clock, *which was a bit early,* he thought.

"Hi Tom, are you and Jake okay?"

"Yes, we are fine, Dad, it's going to be a great day, thanks to you," Tom said excitedly.

"Think you all will enjoy meeting the Ambassador, she's a very nice lady Tom, I'll try and get over there myself to say hello. And then afterwards you will be going to the World Trade Center, it's going to be great fun."

"Yeah, we are on our way to the World Trade Center first though, I think. Having a great time Dad, Jake says hi," Tom said.

On hearing those words, Peter put his foot down hard on the brakes, and the Mercedes skidded three feet, bringing it to an abrupt stop. The hair pricked up on the back of his neck, a shiver went down his back, and he felt like the sound of ten klaxons had gone off in his head all at once. The sound of car horns going off behind him though brought him back to reality.

"Tom, what did you say? The World Trade Center? You are going there first?" Peter confirmed anxiously.

He could hear their bus sounding its horn through the phone and the laughter of the kids playing games with each other.

"Yeah, it's going to be great, Dad," Tom said, sounding like he was having the time of his life with his classmates.

"Tom, listen to me very carefully, something is very wrong here, is Miss Wilson there?"

"No, it's Mrs Grey, Dad, what's wrong?" Tom said, noticing the stress in his dad's voice, and that made him a bit agitated.

"Will you give the phone to Mrs Grey please, Tom? Hurry Tom!"

Tom did what his dad said. He walked as fast as he could down the bus to the front, holding the phone in his hand, a few of his classmates pushed and jeered at him as he passed, Mrs Grey was currently buried in conversation with another teacher about timetables for the school, Tom tapped her on the shoulder.

"Excuse me, Mrs Grey," Tom said nervously.

"Yes, hello, Tom, what is it?" she snapped, slightly annoyed by the interruption.

"It's my dad, he is on the phone. He would like to speak to you," Tom said, giving her the phone. The bus suddenly stopped and jerked to one side, the driver sounded the horn, distracting her for a moment.

Putting the phone to her ear, she said. "Oh, hello, Mr Collins. Mrs Grey speaking, how can I help again?"

"Hi Mrs Grey, where is Miss Wilson? I thought you said yesterday that she was making the trip?" Peter asked frantically.

"She phoned in sick today, these twenty-year old's you know always do, get a little cold, and that's it, you don't' see them for weeks on end, why what's the problem?"

"I arranged with Miss Wilson to meet the Ambassador to the Bahamas you see, at the Empire state building at ten o'clock?" he said. "But Tom said you are on the way to the World Trade Center what—"

"Yes, I know," she interrupted and then said firmly. "We are doing both Mr Collins, I originally arranged this, so I know we have enough time, the kids will love it, it will be a great experience for them."

"But you can't...trade..." Peter's phone signal started to break up. "Mrs Grey," Peter shouted.

"Your phone's a bit crackly Mr Collins. I didn't get that," she said. "What did you say?"

"Mrs Grey are...there? You can't...trade...tre...attac—"

"Mr Collins, I didn't get that, what did you say?"

196

Mrs Grey looked at Tom and shrugged her shoulders.

"Can you hear me, Mrs Grey?" Peter shouted from inside the car.

"Oh, you've come back now, what did you say, Mr Collins?"

"I said, you can't go…o…the w…cent…!" The phone signal died completely and went to a continuous tone.

Mrs Grey turned to Tom again, putting her hands up. "Your dad's gone, Tom. The signal went funny. He's okay though so don't worry," she said, handing the phone back to him. Irene Grey went back to her in-depth conversation with her colleague, and Tom went back to his seat next to Jake putting the phone in his bag.

Peter sat in his car, banging his Blackberry frustratingly on the dashboard. "Just when you bloody need it, it doesn't bloody work," he said out loud to himself, still stationary in the middle of the road with cars and buses sounding their horns trying to squeeze by him, some were making rude gestures at him as they passed, wondering what the hell he was doing. Peter looked at the time on his dashboard, it was 7:52. He immediately went into survival mode, he put the Mercedes into drive and pushed through the traffic as best he could, cutting across cars, much to the annoyance of other drivers, who shouted abuse out of their windows at him. He headed directly for the World Trade Center instead of the office, passing Essex Street on the left. He pressed speed dial number one on his phone, Marie answered.

Marie was going about her clean up chores when she saw the phone lighting up, she answered. "Hi darling, how are you?"

"Marie, they are going to the World Trade Center first," Peter said vehemently.

"Are they Peter? What's wrong with that?" she said, noticing the anxiousness in his voice.

"Because they are coming down," he shouted.

"What's coming down?"

"The Twin Towers, The World Trade Center, they are going to be attacked, and they will come down, you know, collapse!" he said, "They will be attacked in about an hour."

"Collapse Peter, are you sure? You are worrying me now. How do you know?"

"Planes will be hitting the towers, I've seen it, it happened, believe me."

"But how could—?"

Peter interrupted her scepticism, "Try and get hold of Tom on your phone, I just spoke to them, but the signal died. Try Marie, call them please, for Tom and Jake's sake, do it now Marie if you get hold of them, tell them not to go at all, and stay clear of it," he said. "If you get hold of them, call me immediately."

Peter clicked the phone off as he manoeuvred the Mercedes towards the World Trade Center, going slowly through the traffic crawling along Delancey Street, *too slowly by far,* he thought, as Tom and Jake would probably be there by now. He cut through a few streets to get onto Lafayette, then turned right onto Leonard Street, after a few blocks and still going slow, he was on West Broadway

197

with the Towers now straight ahead, the immenseness of the towers as he looked, overpowered everything in their midst. There seemed to be a constant flow of people walking towards them like migrating lemmings. Just as many people that travelled there on foot also arrived there through the underground system of trains and tunnels.

There were a hundred and ten floors in both the north and south towers, with a total of ten million square feet of office space. Fifty thousand workers inhabited the towers, this coupled with 200,000 visitors each day, it was a mini-city on its own, with its own shopping centre and even had its own Police Force controlled by the OCC, '*the Operational Control Center.*'

His Mercedes couldn't go any faster, the traffic had backed up, and he started to panic and thought about abandoning the car in favour of running. Luckily an opening occurred on Greenwich Street, and a right turn onto Fulton Street allowed him to get around the back of the North Tower, he pulled his car up as close as he could to the entrance and got out, he looked at his watch, it was now 8:21, it had taken far too long.

As he got out of his car, he looked up at the North Tower with the sun bearing down, it was about sixty-eight degrees with clear skies. A traffic warden spotted him pull his car up in a zone that was designated 'No Parking, unloading only!' She had stopped writing a ticket out for the vehicle she was dealing with at the time and quickly walked over to Peter.

"Hey, sir, no, no, no, not there please," she shouted, pointing at the sign. "You can read, can't you, sir? The sign says 'No Parking at any time. Do you see?"

"Sorry, I'll only be five minutes, I'm just picking up my sons," he said, locking his car and walking away while talking to her.

"Sir, sir, where are you going? I need this moving, and now!" she said louder and with more force as he walked away.

"As I said I'll be five minutes promise," Peter shouted back apologetically but kept walking.

"In three minutes, this will be towed," she shouted, sounding flabbergasted at Peter's attitude.

Just then a rather portly Policeman overheard the angry exchange and came over to lend a hand.

"Sir, move your dam car," he said loudly and sternly. But Peter had walked about fifty feet away from the car already, and he wasn't stopping for anyone. He started to quicken his pace into a jog. It left the warden standing by Peter's car, shaking her head and writing down the details of the offending vehicle. The policeman gave chase as fast as his overly large frame would allow, with his intercom stuck to his ear talking to control. He was quickly out of breath after thirty feet of running and had to stop, exercise was not his forte, he could hardly get his words out, and control could not understand him.

Peter disappeared around the corner out of sight on his way to the entrance to the North Tower.

Chapter 44

As he rushed through one of the many automatic doors into the main lobby of the North Tower, his heart sank. There was a sea of people trying to get to their place of work, all aiming for one of the thirty-four elevators to take them skyward. He had been here before many times but not at this time of day, and not with hundreds of people swarming like locusts over a well-grown field of corn. From inside the lobby, the tall Gothic-style plate glass windows let in the sunlight, it was supposed to create a feeling of open space, but today it felt cramped and closed in. As he looked around the lobby, there were as many people coming up from the underground stairs as there were coming in through the outer doors, and it was at least thirty deep queuing for the elevators.

He looked at his Blackberry for a second and noticed there was a small signal, so he stopped and called Tom as people pushed into him trying to get past.

"Tom, are you there?" The phone went to voicemail, he shouted over the cacophony, "Tom, get out of the building if you can hear this." In his panic, he texted Tom and Jake a message.

He then went with the flow of people as he jostled his way towards an information desk at the far side of the Lobby. At first glance, it looked like there was no one there until he got up close, and there was a man in a security uniform sitting low down on a small seat behind the counter, out of sight of everyone, eating a sandwich as if he didn't want anyone to notice he was there.

"Excuse me," Peter said, peering over, "can you help me please, I'm looking for my sons."

The man got up slowly looking at Peter as though he had taken him away from something quite important. Now upright he was at least a foot taller than Peter, and more the size of a basketball player or a linebacker. He was finishing off his sandwich, probably his breakfast Peter thought, and he had stopped him from enjoying it. Peter noticed his name badge read Errol. It couldn't be, he thought? He looked vaguely familiar, a younger version perhaps. If it was him, it was one of life's coincidences.

"Hi, sorry to disturb you, Errol, I'm looking for my sons, they are in this building somewhere."

He swallowed the current mouthful so he could at least answer, "Are they lost, sir?"

"No, they are on a school trip here."

Errol placed his half-eaten sandwich back in his neatly packed lunch box. His wife must have packed it for him, Peter thought, as he didn't look neat by any means. There were a few sweat patches by his armpits and a strong smell of musky body odour from not washing but spraying over the sweat, which had made it much worse and got right inside Peter's nostrils. He tried to only breathe through his mouth. He asked himself a question: was he wasting time talking to Errol? And would this man be able to give him the information he needed? He wondered. Time was ticking away, it was now 8:28 when he glanced at his watch.

"What's the name, sir?" he asked, too slowly and too calmly for Peter's liking, as he then wiped the sandwich residue from his lips with a neatly ironed handkerchief.

"Tom Collins and Jake Collins."

"Not their names, what school, sir, the name of the school?" he enunciated as if Peter was incapable of understanding.

"Theodore Roosevelt Elementary, just need to know where they are, that's all," Peter said with the tension showing on his face, "could you hurry?"

"Give me a minute, sir, I'll be as quick as I can," Errol said as he picked up an intercom from underneath the counter and pressed a button slowly.

Control answered, "Hi Control, I have a gentleman here who is looking for his sons who are on a school trip," Errol paused, listened for an answer for what seemed like minutes but was in fact seconds, Peter tapped his fingernails on the desk anxiously. He looked at his watch again, it was 8:31. Then Errol said, "Theodore Roosevelt Elementary is what he said." He listened again for an agonising moment longer and then looked at Peter and said, "What time were they supposed to meet here, sir, control said?"

"I dunno 8:30," Peter said, shaking his head and wondering how many Theodore Roosevelt Elementary schools could there be coming to the World Trade Center on the eleventh of September.

"Hi, control, he said 8:30," Errol said, then listening to an answer again, as though he had all the time in the world.

"Is this going to take much longer?" Peter said.

Errol wasn't looking at him but listening to Control. "Aha, aha, okay, okay." Then he put the intercom down and said nothing for a split second while he gathered his thoughts, it almost looked like he had forgotten momentarily what the person in the control room had said.

"Well, did you get something? Anything?" Peter asked, looking at him with a blank expression, pleading with him.

"Yes, yes, my friend, no problem. They are scheduled to meet at the Skydive Cafe Restaurant, at 8:45 on the forty-fourth floor, so, in about thirteen minutes time, sir, so you are in luck. Glad to be of help. So, if you—"

"Great thanks," Peter interrupted not listening to him then ran towards the elevators where Errol was about to point. Peter knew where the Skydive Café Restaurant was and the express elevator to take him up there directly.

When he finally got into the elevator, his watch clicked over with a mighty thud to 8:37, he had nine minutes to find the twins, he wished he had more time and was feeling the stress about the whole situation. Events were slipping through his fingers, time was running out. A woman looked at Peter in the elevator, and half smiled, she was holding some large notebooks close to her chest and stood in the corner staring at him. It made Peter feel a bit self-conscious. She was studying him while carefully, analysing the anxious look on his face, he was sweating profusely and continually looking at his watch agitated by something. She was trying to read him and find out what he was doing that was so important that he got himself into a state like that.

The packed, sweaty express elevator finally stopped at the forty-fourth floor, and the doors opened, Peter had to push his way out by a few people before the doors closed. He was the only person to get out on that floor, leaving all the people left in the elevator to travel upward, and possibly to their deaths he thought.

Peter's thought process was now so fast it made everything seem much slower than it was actually happening, rather like when a car crash occurs, he looked around frantically for any clue as to where Tom and Jake might be. There seemed to be lots of children on trips with their teachers shepherding them into groups, and going in each direction along the corridor, he was now in the right place he thought. Then out of the corner of his eye, he thought he spotted Tom's red rucksack as it disappeared around a corner to his left, he followed and caught up to him, it looked like Tom from the back, he thought.

"Hey, Tom," Peter said, grabbing his shoulder and turning him around.

"*Qu'est-ce qui ne va pas, monsieur,*" said the startled child.

"Oh! So sorry, very sorry. I thought you were my son, sorry," Peter held his hands up. It wasn't Tom, much to the annoyance of the child's teacher who rattled off something in French.

"*Qu'est-ce que vous voulez exactement,* idiot?" The teacher said, patting the child's back consoling him and giving Peter a stern look as they walked away.

Peter didn't have to be French to know what he was saying, "Very sorry," he said again looking somewhat dejected. He then quickly headed for the Skydive where Errol had told him to go. It was just after 8:43. Peter entered The Skydive Café Restaurant and looked around anxiously at all the other kids that had assembled on their school trips. It looked like Theodore Roosevelt School either hadn't got there yet or had planned to meet somewhere else he thought. Kids were queueing for drinks in the restaurant while teachers huddled together to chat about anything other than the school curriculum.

The sun shone brightly through the thick crystal plate glass between the concrete Gothic pillars, they were only on the forty-fourth floor, but you could see right out across the Hudson River glistening and shimmering as the sun hit the blue water. Long barges meandered by, full to the brim with aggregates on their way up to WestPoint, Cargo ships going in the opposite direction, out passed Ellis Island and the trusted Statue of Liberty to the North Atlantic, taking goods to ports all around the world.

Peter looked around frantically wondering what to do, his face riddled with the agony, the turmoil, the regret, the futility, tears began to emanate and ooze from his eye's as his futile mission seemed to be buffering up against solid rock, with the clock slowly but surely ticking its way to the inevitable 8:46. He wiped his eyes and made his way into the Café to ask someone a question. He happened upon a teacher deep in conversation with two other teachers, he tapped him on the shoulder. The man turned around and he could see Peter was upset about something.

"Excuse me, sorry to bother you," Peter said. "But do you know Theodore Roosevelt Elementary? They are supposed to be here."

"Are you okay?" the man said sympathetically.

"No, not really I'm looking for my sons, my twin boys," Peter said. "They are supposed to be here with Theodore Roosevelt Elementary?" he repeated.

"I know Theodore Roosevelt, I do, I almost taught there myself, but I wouldn't know if they were here or not, sorry," the teacher said. "This is the meeting place for every school, so they will be here at some point unless they have been and gone already, and are on the way to the top, that's where we always go for the stunning views."

"Not to worry I'll keep looking," Peter said dejectedly, then looked the teacher in the eye and said, "Do yourself and your school a favour and get out of here while you can, there will be something happening soon, so do as I say don't delay."

Peter walked away with the man looking at him open-mouthed as though he was a terrorist or something and then turned back to his colleagues. One of them asked him what Peter had said because he looked worried, and he told him.

"He said we should get out before something happens, what a nutter, he did look a bit stressed, he was probably on drugs," the man concluded.

It was 8:45. Peter went back out into the main hallway to see if Tom and Jake were coming down to the restaurant, they were nowhere to be seen. There were kids still coming out of every elevator with not a care in the world, laughing, joking to each other and playing tricks, each class with their agendas, following behind their teacher. He could hear the sound of children laughing in the Café as they played tricks on each other behind their teacher's back. He looked over at them playing, and he imagined for a moment Tom and Jake were there playing with them, being happy boys, with their whole life ahead of them. Peter had blanked out all the external noise and was standing there in his own world, the tension, the stress, the strain, the pressure, everything came down to this moment, he looked at his watch.

Chapter 45

At 8:46, a loud bang was heard above, the building juddered and swayed noticeably, there was a sonic boom that came down the elevator shafts and stairs, that hurt the ears, the floor shook like a massive tremor had struck after an earthquake, making the floor feel unsteady underfoot. The fire alarms sounded almost immediately, the concrete columns vibrated, and the lights flickered. People stopped what they were doing and where they were going, and just stood looking at each other in astonishment, looking upward at the ceiling most of them as if something was about to crash through at any moment, and wondering what had just happened. The kids in the café restaurant weren't laughing anymore, they now had worried looks on their little faces, along with their teachers who were trying to reassure them with the same worried look. As he looked out of the windows, there were masses of small pieces of paper everywhere, billowing around like the Ticker-Tape Parade on Saint Patrick's Day, and cascading downward.

The teacher Peter had been talking to a moment ago looked over at him standing in the hallway and made eye contact, his eyes burned into the back of Peters' eye sockets with an intense, angry stare, as if to say 'how did you know?' Peter looked back at the man with a resigned look on his face as if to say 'it was inevitable, I told you so.' Everyone radiated towards the windows to have a look at what was going on, one man shouted, 'there's fire coming down from everywhere!'

What really got everyone's attention were the large pieces of burning debris that had started to fall past the windows on its inevitable journey to the ground. A woman let out a hysterical scream, as she caught a glimpse of a burning body falling past the window. That wouldn't be the last scream she screamed this day, Peter thought. People looked upward out of the windows apprehensively.

Agent McClean hadn't been able to stop it, he probably tried, but it was too much of a task, it was all too difficult. The day would now all have to play out as Peter had seen and read about before. The towers would collapse, and it would be the worst day in the history of America.

His priority was to get Tom and Jake out now, but what could he do? Where could they be? He tried Tom's phone number again in desperation, his hand shaking as he nervously tapped in the number once more. The screen on his Blackberry showed no answer, and then those inevitable flashing beeps at the top left-hand side that meant 'no service, no connection, you aren't getting through, the frustration, the anger, it felt futile, but he had to do it. He didn't know where they were or what they were doing, he thought about going up a few floors to see if they were there, had they got his message? There was no way of knowing. A man asked him a question that brought him out of his insular existence and back to reality.

"Hey, buddy that sounded like something bad eh, what do you think? Is it an explosion? A bomb, perhaps?" The nervously, excited man asked.

As if he was reciting the front page of the New York Times, Peter said. "That bang you heard was American Airways flight number eleven, a Boeing 767 with Eighty-Seven people on board crashing into the ninetieth floors above us while we stand here. In around fifteen minutes another plane will fly into the South Tower. Three thousand people will die today. You'd better get out as quickly as you can and save yourself."

"Jesus Christ, what are you some sort of fucking clairvoyant?" he said disparagingly.

The television was on in the Skydive Café restaurant, and it suddenly clicked over to the CBS news channel that was showing the North Tower and where the plane hit, this only served to bring more panic to people watching it inside. Then over the P.A. system came a worried voice message. "We advise people not to be alarmed and to remain where you are until instructed further."

Peter stood there for a moment just watching as the man realised what he had said had actually happened, he looked at him and said. "Thanks, Pal, appreciate it," then went off in a hurry in the direction of the elevators.

Peter shouted over to him, "You'd better use the stairs, the elevators are out," The man waved his arm at him in acknowledgement as he quickly walked away.

People had already started rushing for the elevators, ignoring the instructions, trying to get out. Panic had set in very quickly. He could see their faces etched with torment as they tried to call loved ones on their mobile phones to let them know they were okay for now. But they wouldn't be able to use them for hours now, as everyone was trying to make calls at the same time all over the world jamming the most sophisticated networks, only landlines were available.

Peter walked over to the windows where it was about five deep as people were necking, and trying to get a good look outside. When he got his turn, he looked down over at the rooftops of the nearby buildings. There were fire pits and burning debris on them like the fallout from an erupted volcano. Those buildings would soon be alight. He looked at his phone, and he miraculously had some signal, so he called Marie, she answered straight the way like she had been expecting his call.

"Marie, it's me. Have you heard anything?" Peter said, sounding stressed as if in a war zone and got straight to the point.

"Peter it's on the news, the North Tower," she said panicky. "It's been hit, Looks like a plane!"

"Yes, I know, have you spoken to Tom and Jake, Marie?"

"No, I can't reach them, Peter," she said, "I've been trying since you last called. What are we going to do, I want my boy's back Peter?"

"I can't find them, Marie, I've looked everywhere they could have gone."

"They were going to the World Trade Center, you said?"

"Yes, I have been looking for them there."

"What! You've been there?"

"No Marie, I am here now on the Forty-Fourth floor at the Skydive Cafe," he said. "They were supposed to all meet here. I asked security so their school should have been here."

"Peter I'm watching the news the North Tower is burning, what the fuck are you doing there for God's sake?"

"I'm looking for our kids, Marie."

"Get out, Peter, get out of there please," she cried.

"I will, Marie, I'm just going to look a bit further, I have time, I'll call you soon."

"What do you mean you have the time?"

"I have about an hour. I'll be okay."

"What do you mean, you have an hour? What the fuck, Peter?"

"Marie, I'm okay. I'll be okay. Believe me."

"I do. Just get out of there please, save yourself darling for me. I love…"

Marie broke down sobbing on the phone inconsolable, Peter said. "I'm leaving now, I'll be home soon, love you too, Marie."

He ended the call and stood there devastated, he couldn't find them, he was in turmoil inside. Could he go higher? Upward to the other floors above? But it was nine o'clock and how long would it take him to get down forty-four floors? Possibly two minutes a floor? That was eighty-eight minutes. He had already run out of time, and there was nothing else he could do apart from getting out of there to safety if he could. He imagined the memorial with his name etched into it forever beside Tom and Jake's. A fitting end to all this horror, he thought, as he would be with them in solidarity, father, and sons together. But he fought through the morbid thoughts, the negativity, and the sadness, and started thinking about Marie and Ashley. He needed to live for them.

More debris fell past the windows from above, and the lights flickered as if they were about to go out. Peter had no choice, it was the hardest decision he had ever made, to leave his lovely innocent boys there to the trauma of the towers collapsing and becoming a part of history. He wiped the tears of regret away from his eyes and began to make the arduous journey down to the lobby. He walked over to the stairwell with everyone else, deflated, dejected and defeated.

Chapter 46

At the house on Steamboat landing road, Marie's phone clicked off as Peter ended the call abruptly. She tried to call Tom and Jake, again and again, it went to voicemail. She sat at the kitchen table where only a few hours ago the family was eating breakfast happy at the prospect of a lovely day for them. Her phone was the only form of communication with Peter and the twins, not knowing what to do she felt like she was in limbo, time suspended until further notice. She felt helpless.

The house phone then rang it was her brother David. "Hi Ree, are you watching the news?" he said with a concerned tone.

"Yes," she sobbed.

"Are you okay? You sound—"

She interrupted and said, "David. They're at the World Trade Center on a school trip,"

"Who's there?"

"Tom and Jake they're on a school trip with all their class. Peter's there now looking for them, but he hasn't found them yet."

"No! Not there?"

"Yes, Peter's in the North Tower on the forty-fourth floor as we speak looking for them, I don't know what to do David. I'm going out of my mind. Can't get hold of Tom and Jake, it's a living nightmare!"

"Oh God Ree, how awful. I'll come over right away."

"Okay," she said.

As Marie was watching the television, a large passenger jet flew into the South Tower, and a massive fireball billowed out. On the CNN news feed, the reporter didn't realise what had happened and said, *'Well it looks like there has been an explosion of some kind, maybe because the fuselage is within the North Tower. Oh, hang on a second we have reports of another plane crashing into the South Tower. Oh my! This has possibly turned into a terrorist incident in a second.'*

"Oh, Ree! Did you see that?"

Marie screamed as it happened, "It's got to be terrorists? They said, terrorists. Those poor people. Oh my God, those poor people."

"I'm coming over Ree, will be there in twenty," David said.

"Okay. Hurry David."

Ten minutes later Ashley arrived back from school having been given the day off due to the North Tower attack, everyone at the school was preoccupied with the school trip that had gone there, and they hadn't been able to reach them yet. Marie sat looking at the coverage.

"Mum! Mum! Did you see what's going on in Manhattan oh my God?"

"Yes, darling I've heard from your dad, he's there searching for Tom and Jake now."

"Mum, it looks so bad!" she cried, "I hope they make it, Mum. It looks so bad."

"If they are there your dad will find them, I'm glad your home."

"Hope so, Mum, hope so."

"Whatever happens we will get through this I promise, we will get through this."

They sat huddled up together on the kitchen chairs comforting each other, there was nothing else they could do, it was happening before their very eyes. They couldn't go over there and help look, the whole world was over there, they probably wouldn't be able to get anywhere near, there was no point. Marie tried Tom's phone again. There was no connection.

Chapter 47

It was very slow, going down the North Tower stairwell number one, single file step by step, while first responder firefighters came up the other side with breathing equipment, hoses, and anything else they felt they needed to put a fire out in a skyscraper thirteen hundred feet tall. It was very packed and very claustrophobic with only the emergency lighting to see the way. Women and children were crying out of fear as they slowly went down. Every so often, the walls creaked as though something catastrophic was going to happen and cave in at any moment, leaving everyone trapped. The stairs and stair rail vibrated occasionally and with every vibration came the anxiousness to get out of there. Smoke had entered the stairwell, and it became hard to see and breathe. The crying gave way to coughing, and people suddenly stopped walking down.

"Keep going, and we will all get out safely," Peter shouted. "Come on, don't stop, keep moving." Slowly but surely the line started moving again with other people voicing words of encouragement to help everyone through, and down to safety.

As they reached the forty-third floor, everyone in the stairwell heard a muffled but loud explosion outside. It came from the South Tower. It was the United Airlines flight 175 right on cue at three minutes past nine, Peter thought as he looked at his watch. Not many people knew there were planes involved at all at that point, it just sounded like explosions to them from inside the stairwell. The noxious fumes smelt of burning wire and metal and seemed to get more intense, and the coughing increased.

"Oh my God, we are not going to make it, we are all going to die," a woman screamed.

"Keep going right on down madam, you'll be fine, it's not far," a brave young firefighter said as he went up the stairs to meet the danger that lied ahead, and without any fear at all noticeable in his voice. He had a job to do and was proud to do it. Those few words made all the difference to that woman Peter thought. She was five steps down in front of him, and she didn't scream again. Floor number thirty, then twenty, and after around thirty minutes of going down, they finally reached the lobby. Peter let out a big sigh as he cleared his lungs of the smoke. It was much quicker than Peter had anticipated. He looked around to see if he could see Tom and Jake. It was pandemonium with people running in every direction. Outside the streets were strewn with papers and debris that was still falling out of the sky. He looked at his watch for a moment, he had about thirty minutes to get far enough away from the towers before they collapsed.

A Port Authority Policeman was shouting instructions to people not to just run out of the building as debris was continually falling, his orders fell on deaf ears as everyone ignored him and ran out. One woman screamed as she almost stood on a severed woman's leg complete with a stiletto attached as she ran over the road to safety.

Peter rushed out of the main doors and around to where his Mercedes was illegally parked, he kept close to the building, paper and small bits of debris rained down on him as he walked. It hadn't been towed at all like the warden had said it would be, but there was now a large concrete block that had crushed the roof and hood, and it was stuck in there like it wanted a lift home with him, his car was going nowhere. As he turned and headed for Fulton street, he heard two dull thuds simultaneously just behind him, he glanced back and saw the crushed, mangled bodies of a man and a woman right beside his car missing it by a few feet. He came over all cold. He had read about it before and seen a short video on YouTube with Heather, but now he was in it and living it. They must have jumped together. Peter thought, a last act of togetherness to get through a difficult moment. A choice given to only a few people, jump to your death or burn to death.

To Peter, it felt like a war zone in Iraq, he ran as fast as he could over the road and away from the towers with more thuds and screams happening all around as he ran. The streets were packed with people on the sidewalks, so he had to run on the road dodging all the debris that had collected on the ground.

He said a little prayer for Tom and Jake hoping they managed to get out, he wondered where they were at that very moment, probably frightened, he wished he could give them a big hug and tell them it would be okay, but it won't be okay. He had failed, fate was the winner. It had happened before, and now it was happening again.

Both towers were ablaze at the top with thick fuel-filled smoke spewing out of the plane size holes and rising hundreds of feet into the air. It seemed to be burning more ferociously minute-by-minute. Lots of people were looking up huddled together in groups for comfort as Peter ran past, they were standing only two hundred feet away behind a police cordon with phones glued to their ears, trying to call loved ones or friends they knew to share the experience. The constant noise of fire engines and emergency vehicles sounding their sirens could be heard above everything else. Screams rang out from the crowds as more people jumped to their deaths rather than being burnt alive. Their dull thuds as they hit the ground would live in the minds of the people who witnessed it for many years to come.

A lot of people were walking away from the scene, but many more innocent, brave firefighters were running towards the towers, eager to get there and save lives, oblivious to the danger they faced and the towers collapsing.

At the corner of Greenwich Street and Warren Street, Peter stopped running and stood with a crowd of onlookers gazing in awe at the towers billowing smoke from the top. Women were crying, men were crying, all in a collective sorrow for the thousands of people stuck in the towers.

"Hey man, never seen anything like it, we are under attack here in New York City, who would have thought that?" The man said in a pinstriped business suit, briefcase still in hand and sucking hard on a cigarette.

"My sons are in the towers somewhere," Peter said sadly. "They are only ten years old. Couldn't do anything about it."

"Hey man, so sorry."

"Yeah, thanks," Peter said, showing no outward physical emotion but broken up inside.

The man insisted on talking to him as a friend or colleague would, out of nervousness.

"They should be able to put that fire out, there must be a working sprinkler system."

"They won't be able to, it's too high, and the heat is too intense," Peter said.

"It will probably burn itself out?"

Peter knew different and said, "They will collapse,"

"No!" the man said, wondering what the hell Peter was talking about.

"They are man-made, nothing can survive that intense heat. After the metal melts, there is nothing to stop it. The towers will both collapse." The man didn't say anything else. Peter had stifled the conversation, nothing else to say but watch.

At 9:59 the South Tower collapsed with clouds of dust and debris scattering over half a mile. From where he stood, Peter could see people running away from the towers screaming as they were engulfed by a massive dust cloud that looked like a white monster trying to eat anything it could find, and billowing up in the air as it got bigger.

He remembered reading an eyewitness account in the New York Times. It was about two men and a woman who survived the collapse of the South Tower. They said that one minute they were in the stairwell almost at the lobby, then the next minute they were looking directly at the sky with the sunlight streaming down on them and all of them unhurt, either it was a miracle, or they were just very lucky. Peter thought the latter was the more accurate statement.

At 10:28, the North Tower collapsed, producing even more dust and debris, and it seemed to reach further afield this time. The crowd of people watching with him were all quiet now, a calmness and sadness came over everyone because nothing worse could happen, as the worst had indeed already happened. Peter was covered in white dust and stared at the Manhattan skyline without the towers, numb from the neck down, his plan in tatters. Why didn't he just not let them go on the trip at all? Why did he have to be clever and change the school plans placing them in harm's way? It all seemed so easy to sort out, but he hadn't considered the variables, and Miss Wilson being off sick was one of them, the one that sealed Tom and Jake's fate. He had one chance to put this right, and he blew it, and there would not be another. They could have all been at home watching the tragic event on T.V. not involved at all. Now he would have to endure years of heartache and pain grieving for Tom and Jake, his little boy's, the 'terrible twos.' Life sucks, Peter thought.

What would Marie think of him now he wondered, how would life go on without the boys in their lives he thought, those beautiful boys. There was no rehearsal for this, the heartache, the agony, the tears that hadn't been shed yet, the funerals, the beautiful cards of condolence and commiseration, he had it all to come, and he wasn't looking forward to it at all.

Slowly everyone started to saunter away as there was nothing else to see, it was like a huge crowd walking away from a rock concert at a large stadium. No more encores, the show was over, all going home to their loved ones, all with the same thing on their mind, what they had just witnessed. With the evacuation of lower Manhattan, there were thousands of people walking together side by side as comrades over the Brooklyn Bridge, with the smoke, dust, and rubble behind them in the distance. Emergency vehicles could still be heard making their way towards the ruins, it would be a search and rescue operation now if anyone possibly could have survived the collapse, which was doubtful. Peter glanced back at the dust cloud and the skyline without the towers. He had left Tom and Jake there, and it felt dreadful.

Peter tried his phone again, but it was out of charge, he longed to get home and see Marie and Ashley to comfort them. After Brooklyn Bridge, every bank of landlines he came across had queues, so he kept walking.

Chapter 48

At the end of Steamboat landing road, Peter got out of a grey damaged Chrysler Four by Four truck and thanked the man kindly for giving him a lift. He had gone out of his way to help him get back home, and he appreciated it, Peter gave him his card and said if he needed anything he was to call. There was a lot of helping each other out that day, with people going out of their way to help out their fellow man. A catastrophic event seemed to bring people together for a while at least, if only too briefly.

The long, arduous, painful walk up the driveway seemed to take ages. Peter walked it with trepidation, what would he say? How would he explain? The sun was lower in the sky and remnants of the dust cloud from seven hours ago still hung relentlessly over Manhattan in the distance, it was a stark reminder that the day had been one of the worst days in the history of New York City and the United States. There was a light sprinkling of dust and small bits of debris everywhere from the towers on the ground that crunched underfoot, the rooftop to his house, the leaves on the trees down the driveway, the porch as well, everything was covered in it, carried by the wind and distributed for miles around like a sand storm from the Sahara. It was 3:30 in the afternoon and all the streets were empty. Everyone was at home with their families glued to the World Trade Center News coverage, it was covered on every channel, each station looking at the situation from a different angle trying to outmanoeuvre the other, vying for the best clips, the best content. Celebrities made interviews and comments about how upset they were as if ordinary people weren't upset enough, some made racist remarks out of anger and prejudice.

As he reached the house, Peter listened for a moment outside to the muted conversations and news bulletins that were going on inside. He then opened the front door to a house full of people, all rallying around to support Marie who sat in the middle of the sofa distraught, there wasn't a spare seat in the house. The next-door neighbours from both sides, the brother in law, his brother, Marie's brother David, and all the children. They all meant well, but this was a time he wanted to be with Marie and Ashley alone. Smiles of relief could be seen on everyone as they all got up to greet him.

"Oh, thank God you're okay, Peter," Marie said with tears streaming down her face. "We thought we'd lost you again when you didn't answer your phone. I thought you were still in the North Tower."

"Hi, darling," he said. "Hardly anyone could get through, my phone completely died, I did try to call you back. Have you heard from the boys yet?"

"No, not yet, I've tried a hundred times Peter they are not picking up, what are we going to do?" Marie said, clinging onto him.

"Hi, Dad," Ashley said, joining in for a hug as well.

"Hello, Chicken, how are you holding up."

"You didn't see them then?" Marie asked.

Everyone stopped talking to listen to Peter.

"No, I didn't, there was too much confusion, too many people, it was horrendous Marie. They were supposed to meet on the Forty-Fourth floor at the Sky Lobby, but I couldn't see them, they weren't there where they should have been. Then the plane hit, and everyone just got out as best they could," Peter paused for a moment to get the words out, welling up inside. "I don't think our boys are coming home darling," Peter said as he dropped his head in failure, and with those words, Marie had to be taken to sit down as she lost her balance and almost fainted.

There was an air of collective sorrow as Peter's words sunk in, most people in the room shed tears. Mick and Jenny Roth were there as well, as their sons had been on the same school trip and they only lived around the corner in the next street. They had come around for company rather than stay at home staring at four walls, a worried look was permanently etched onto their faces. They were in the same situation as Peter and Marie, he wanted to tell them that all four names were on the memorial he saw in 2016, Tom, Jake, Michael, David, and that they wouldn't be coming home.

Peter semi-smiled at them out of sympathy, then said, "You never know they may all be okay somewhere, that's probably the reason why they weren't where they should have been in the sky lobby, let's keep all our fingers crossed and hope for the best," he said optimistically. It didn't help at all, it was false hope, and Peter knew it, he wanted to tell them the truth and put them out of their misery.

A very tired Dan Rather, the anchor man on CBS news, came on the television with yet another report update. *'September 11, 2001. You will remember this day as long as you live. On a day where the worst disaster in living memory happened here in New York City, we can only pray for the missing, the trapped, and the bereaved. The Towers of the World Trade Center lie in ruins, where hundreds of emergency personnel are now sifting through the debris for survivors. We will remember this day. There is currently no information as to how many people were actually in the towers when they collapsed, but we do know, it is not hundreds, it is thousands, and our heart goes out to each and every one of them all on this day. Let's now go over live to Melanie at the Pentagon for an update.'* At the Pentagon, it was the same commiserating story.

Someone suggested firing up the barbecue so everyone could be fed. Ashley played games with the other kids, they were a lot smaller than her and didn't understand what was going on and why everyone was upset and crying, it just looked like a big party to them. They laughed and joked with each other with not a care in the world. They were all there for each other, spending time together on this sad day and giving support. The beers came out, and the men chatted around the barbecue about the effects this would have on the United States and what might it mean for the country as a whole, would it spark a war? Peter hadn't got an opinion on it at all because he knew what was going to happen, he had seen it, he had read about it. He had even seen it on video.

"What do you think, Peter?" David, his brother-in-law, asked, "Will we go to war do you think?"

"Bush will want a war, presidents always want to go to war for a cause, and he will have the backing of the people for this one, you can bet on that," Peter said.

He saw Ashley sitting on the wall on her own looking down the driveway, she turned and noticed he was looking at her, she waved and smiled at him as though she was waiting for something to happen or someone to arrive, a sixth sense, hope but not false hope.

The conversation around the barbeque was still on the prospect of war, and Peter just paid lip service to it. Then out of nowhere two small figures covered in white dust appeared at the end of the driveway, they looked like mannequins you would see in Central Park, covered in white paint with a bowl in front to get your loose change. Ashley stood up. Peter looked over at them. They moved slowly up the driveway towards the house, bags over their little arms, their little faces covered in dust with streaks of skin visible from the tears that had been cried.

"Oh my God, Tom, Jake," Ashley screamed as she ran down the driveway to meet them. "You are okay, aren't you?"

"We're okay sis," Tom said rather sullen and dejected as Ashley hugged them both.

"Okay, Ash?" Jake said in the same vein looking tired and hungry.

Peter couldn't believe it and ran down to meet them. Everyone heard Ashley scream Tom and Jake's names and came out to see what was going on. Ashley and Peter were in the middle of the driveway hugging a very dusty-white Tom and Jake. Marie came alive with happiness and joy as she joined the family reunion. Everyone else stood there, watching the five of them and enjoying the moment. It was a scene of love and family reunion in stark contrast to the devastation and loss felt by so many in Manhattan.

"Oh! Tom, Jake, you are okay, thank God, we are blessed," Marie said. "Peter, they are okay, can you believe it?" Marie said, smiling and crying happy tears.

"Boys, welcome home we've all missed you. I thought we'd lost you for a while," Peter said, also relieved with tears of joy streaming down his face as well. Peter couldn't quite believe what he was witnessing. This wasn't the script, this wasn't the way it was meant to turn out. The agony of seeing their names on the memorial, it all seemed to drift away, a memory erased. He hugged them both with all his heart.

"How did you know, Dad?" Tom asked, suddenly and pointedly.

"How did I know? What do you mean, Tom?" Peter answered.

"The text you sent us, Dad, how did you know?" Tom repeated, everyone wondered what Tom was saying. He then reached into his rucksack, took his emergency phone out, and clicked onto the messages from his dad.

They all could see as Ashley read it out.

'TOM, JAKE WE ALL LOVE YOU SO VERY MUCH. IF YOU GET THIS MESSAGE AT LEAST YOUKNOWITRIED. GET OUT OF THE WTC TOWERS NOW!!! PLANES WILL HIT IN 15 MINS AND COLLAPSE AT 10.03. GET OUT, GET OUT NOW AND SAVE YOURSELF PLEASE DAD XXX.'

There was a collective silence as everyone cautiously looked at each other, and then at Peter, how did he know? Questioning him mentally without asking him a question, a moment of epiphany and not understanding, but it had happened, and everyone apart from Mick and Jenny was ecstatic about the news. Peter, visibly emotionally relieved.

Ashley looked at her dad, hugged him and cried, "Dad, what can we all say, you are something else, and we love you so very much."

"It just goes to show that the future is not set, Chicken, and things can change," Peter said. "I'm glad, and so thankful you are both okay and that you got that text in time. You were able to save yourself, I am so proud of you, you should be very proud of yourselves."

"We saw that text in the lobby, Dad, and we just looked at each other, didn't we Jake?" Jake nodded. "We told Mrs Grey, we needed the toilet, then we just ran off and hid in a café down the street, a nice man gave us a cup of tea, it wasn't far enough away as it happened because the clouds of dust eventually came into the shop and we couldn't breathe very well. We stayed there for ages, hours, in fact, then we just walked away with everyone else didn't we Jake." Jake nodded again.

"I think a shower and something to eat for you two then," Marie said, stroking Tom's head.

"Sounds great, Mum," Jake said excitedly.

"Me too, I'm starving," Tom said.

They all walked back inside to celebrate the homecoming. Mick and Jenny Roth walked off slowly back to their house together. It wasn't going to be a celebration for them. Peter felt sad for them that he'd not managed to save their boys or anyone else from the school trip. At least they were a family again, and he was thankful for that. The nightmare that started at Luigi's for him seven days ago was now over.

Chapter 49

Friday, September 9, 2016.

Peter sat in Johnson's café, stirring his cappuccino in a figure of eight while waiting for Ashley. He had been waiting for this day for a very long time, and now it had arrived he felt quite apprehensive about it. He also had a feeling like it was Christmas day when he was a young lad, having woken up very early, wide awake and not a hint of tiredness, very excited, and looking forward to opening his presents, he could hardly contain himself.

The New York Times had an article on the front cover about nine-eleven, a feeling of *déjà vécu* came over him when déjà vu became a reality. It had been fifteen years, but it suddenly felt like it was only yesterday. He was sitting in the exact same seat he had sat in fifteen years ago, with the same paper, same coffee, and as he looked around the same people were sitting in the same places, and the barista and his assistant were laughing as they had done. He smiled to himself, he had arrived back to this day, his fifteen-year journey was over. His reflection in the window, however, looked a little older, a mass of grey flecks had attached themselves to his dark brown locks, but all in all, he looked good for his fifty-seven years. Ashley said it made him look more distinguished, but now he felt the reflection looked correct, it looked right, he was the right age for the year. He had weathered the years very well and was in great shape and super fit, and still running ten miles a day chopped in with a few marathons and senior triathlons throughout the year with his ex-military buddies.

Life was good, and it had treated him well, and now he was almost a billionaire, courtesy of a few nifty social media investments early on in the noughties. Nowadays, though, he was more of a philanthropist than a businessman, giving his time to charitable work and the rehabilitation of military personnel coming back from wars around the globe.

His marriage to Marie, however, hadn't stood the test of time, they had grown apart and gone their separate ways as the kids grew up and left home, but they were and always would be good friends. She and David Reece, the new Police Commissioner, had tied the knot a few years ago. He seemed to always be on the scene after he had disappeared for those five days back in 2001.

Tom and Jake had made a name for themselves in the mobile phone sector at the tender age of twenty-six with a new type of smartphone, and they were now taking on the likes of Apple and Samsung for a share of the market. Ashley became a Vet, something she'd always wanted to do, the love of animals and rescuing them from impossible situations seemed to be her calling in life. Larry never went on that fateful trip, and Sheila never worked for the CIA again and was still a part of his trusted team. And as he thought about his life and how it had turned out, he felt lucky and blessed, and the one thing that he didn't regret was going through the vortex as that brought him here to this time and place.

The preparations at the Memorial had started for the up and coming Nine-Eleven commemorations, the familiar stars and stripes bunting and pictures of President Obama were on every lamppost, and he was due to make a speech on the day at six o'clock. It all felt too familiar like he was retreading the day again, like in Groundhog Day.

Just then he caught sight of Ashley crossing the road to the café. Peter had to smile to himself as she was wearing the exact outfit she had worn fifteen years ago.

"Hi, Dad, you okay?" she asked. "What are you smiling at?"

"You darling. I was thinking to myself how lovely you look."

"Ah, Dad, you are so nice to me."

"You deserve everything in life, Chicken. Shall we go see them then?" he said.

"Yes, let's do it, I don't know what it is, but I love coming here and remembering them."

"I know Chicken. I feel the same, and I feel we have to come and remember."

They walked over to the memorial where the school names were. The sun was up above, and it was a beautiful clear day, not a cloud in the sky and a very comfortable seventy degrees. The spray from the water cascading down made mini rainbows as the sun shone through, and there was a calming feeling from the noise it made. Peter ran his fingers over the names of the class of 2001 as he had done before, but not Tom and Jake's, they weren't there now, and he said a little thank you to someone up there for that.

"Do you ever wonder what life would have been like, Dad, if Tom and Jake had never come home that day?" Ashley asked.

"I've asked myself that very same question every day for the past fifteen years, and thank God they did."

"Lucky for us you came back when you did as well."

"I found a way back with the help of a great man, and I shall never forget him, I owe him a debt of gratitude."

"Who was that?"

"Doug McClean, he works for the NSA."

"You should look him up, Dad, you know, to keep in touch."

"Somehow, I feel we will be meeting soon."

"What are you doing the rest of the day, Dad?" Ashley asked.

Suddenly looking a bit preoccupied and smiling to himself, Peter said, "Oh look, it's 11.30?"

"Yes, I know, Dad." She looked at him. "You're up to something, aren't you?"

"What do you mean?"

"I can tell. It's written all over your face."

"Do you fancy dinner tomorrow night?" Peter asked. "Saturday night? Bring what's his name?"

"I see changing the subject, eh? It's Christopher, Dad, remember?" she said, rolling her eyes.

"Yes, I remember Christopher, not Chris, eh?" he said, smiling at his own little joke.

"That will be fun, Dad, thank you. I'll tell Christopher and give you a call tomorrow."

"There's a new place just off Park Avenue that's nice, does Mediterranean food you'll like it I think."

"If you like it, Dad, that's fine with me."

"I'll be bringing a friend hopefully."

"Really! Tell me more? I told you, you were up to something? I knew it."

"No, I won't say anything now because I don't want to jinx it."

"Jinx it? What do you mean? Who is she? What's her name?" Ashley begged.

"I'll tell you later, Chicken, I will honestly," Peter said with a wry smile and a glint in his eye.

"Oh, I can't wait now. I'll look forward to that. You've gone all coy and shy, haven't you?" she said, poking him in his side playfully. "Never seen you like this before, Dad."

"Ha! Don't do that I'm ticklish," he laughed.

"Okay, love you, Dad." She put her arms around him. "See you tomorrow. Whoever she may be? She is a very lucky woman."

"Love you too, Chicken, thanks, can I drop you somewhere?" Peter asked and kissed her on the cheek.

"No, it's okay. I'm meeting Christopher for lunch close by here."

"Okay, love you."

They parted and walked off in different directions out of the memorial. Peter looked at the time, he had twenty-five minutes to get to Luigi's, he didn't want to be late, especially after fifteen years. He called Gerard to bring the car around which he did almost immediately. It was unusual for that time of day as it didn't seem too congested for once. He had butterflies in his stomach as he looked out of the Bentley window. He hadn't felt like that since he first met Marie, Peter recalled, he'd kept all those feelings locked up inside for so long until this day and this moment, and it had been at the forefront of his mind for fifteen years.

His driver Gerard noticed him smiling to himself and then said, "Meeting someone are we, sir?"

"Yes, an old friend Gerard, an old friend."

"That's nice, have you known her long?"

"I haven't seen her for fifteen years."

"Has she been away? Never heard you mention her before?"

"No Gerard, it's a long, fascinating story. I'll let you in on it sometime."

"Oh, okay, I'll hold you to that."

"I'm sure you will?" Peter smiled.

He arrived at Luigi's with ten minutes to spare and sat outside in the shade under a large umbrella as he had done many times before, and ordered himself a cappuccino. It's just this day seemed different, all these years he had waited, all these years he had hoped to meet her.

There was a couple on the next table giggling to themselves at something they saw on their phone. He remembered after a few drinks one night, a few years ago, he had sent Heather a friend request which she had never taken up, probably thinking he was a stalker, she wouldn't have known who he was anyway. As he sat stirring his cappuccino in a figure of eight looking over at the junction of Delancey and Allen Street and the people crossing the road, he thought that maybe this was a part of the story that wouldn't come true, and they would never meet again after all.

He started to doubt himself and became very sombre all of a sudden. She had said she would meet him here and he confirmed it with her before he went through the vortex. But what if that event was erased from time and he had never gone through, he wondered? What if it never happened, after all, Tom and Jake survived, and that wasn't in the script? One piece of a massive jigsaw missing! The more he thought about it, the more pessimistic he became. He remembered he had given her a burner phone, as her phone was compromised by the CIA. Over the years and changing his phones, the number got erased so he couldn't call her, he had to wait and eight minutes was a long time when waiting.

Twelve o'clock arrived, and he looked over at all the people crossing the road, a few had blond hair, but it wasn't her she wasn't there. Two minutes past twelve and still no sign. She only would have had to walk two blocks from Essex Street, and that would take five minutes tops, he thought. Four minutes past twelve and still no sign. She wasn't the sort of person that would have been late for anything. Lots of people were filing across the road, and he didn't recognise anyone. That was that then, he thought, it didn't happen, and there would be no meeting, no reunion, no happiness and no joy. Fifteen years of waiting for nothing, it suddenly turned into a very bleak day. At fifteen minutes past twelve, he thought that was it. She isn't coming.

Then he saw a blond-haired woman come into view and walk across the road junction when the lights turned red, and the green walk sign came on. His heart missed a beat as she looked over and waved at him sitting there. As she reached the pavement on his side of the road, she walked towards him smiling, her blond hair flowing in the light breeze and glistening in the midday sun. He rose from his chair, excited, and walked a few paces to meet her halfway. Her arms went around his, and they stood there on the pavement hugging like long lost friends. He kissed her gently on the lips and smiled.

"How have you been, Heather?"

"Better now, Peter. I felt pretty low about half an hour ago, though."

"I cannot tell you how much I have been looking forward to this moment. I've waited fifteen years for this. You haven't changed a bit from how I remember you, you really haven't. It's amazing."

"I shouldn't think so, I would have aged about thirty minutes since I watched you go back through that thing."

"I love you, Heather."

"I love you too, Peter."

The End